BREAKING FREE

How do you survive when you're trapped between two sides, each wanting what you've fought so hard to build, but for widly different reasons?

Cheryl F Taylor

Sequel to the award winning Gone to Ground

Copyright 2023 Cheryl F Taylor
FIRST EDITION September 2023

ISBN: 978-0-9982122-5-8

Printed in the United States

Published by:
CT Communications
9535 E. Marilyn Ln.
Dewey, AZ 86327
cfaytay@gmail.com
cherylftaylor.com

No portion of this book was created utilizing Generative AI. All characters are fictional and any resemblance to actual people, living or dead, is a coincidence. The canyon named in the setting is also fictional, although the names of actual towns and geographical features are used. The descriptions of the actual locations may have been modified to fit the book.

To Mom

And to Greg Peterson who showed me all the sights to be seen on the trails around Seligman. For those wondering, yes, there is a sailboat back there somewhere.

And to Eric Rogers, Action Automotive, who has, for the last ten years, asked me where his book was every time I came in for an oil change.

Other Books By Cheryl F Taylor

Post-Apocalypse/Post-Pandemic
Gone to Ground
Breaking Free

Cozy Mysteries
Up North Michigan Mysteries
Up North Murder (1)

Rock Shop Cozy Mysteries
Stone's Gems & Murder
Murder on the Wind

Acknowledgements & Author's Note

Pandemic: 1) a disease prevalent throughout an entire country, continent, or the whole world. 2) Universal or widespread

I believe there have been four pandemics declared during my lifetime and a few other pandemic scares. Unlike the H5N1 pandemic described in *Gone to Ground* and *Breaking Free*, pandemics don't have to have a high mortality rate—they just have to be widespread and have a fairly high morbidity or rate of contagion.

When *Gone to Ground* was being written, we had a pandemic scare of bird flu, or the H5N1 influenza, which is what I ended up deciding to label my imaginary pandemic in the future. It was a little disquieting to go through that pandemic while writing a book that features a pandemic, but it did give me more information.

Breaking Free was started in approximately 2016. For one reason or another, it kept getting delayed. I finally really worked on it in earnest in late 2019, then bang, 2020 hit. It felt wrong to be writing about a pandemic during a pandemic. The story had to come out, though, and in the spring of 2023, I was ready to finish it. It still feels a bit ghoulish to write about an imaginary pandemic so soon after a real one, but I desperately wanted to go back to the ranch lands in northern Arizona, and revisit Hideaway, O'Reilly, Maggie, the kids and, of course, Houdini.

Thank you to everyone who has been asking for a sequel for the last ten years, especially Eric Rogers, owner of Action Automotive in Prescott, Arizona. Here it is, and I hope I did it justice! Thank you to Linda Schwandt, Schwandt Editorial Services for editing, and to Dr. Caere Dunn for reading the manuscript, giving me corrections and suggestions.

Huge thank you to Greg Peterson for hauling me all over the area around Seligman and east of Wikieup. Because of this, I had some great mental images of the area, not to mention the photo for the cover of the book.

Thanks to Mom for reading, giving me corrections and telling me she liked it and to keep going, and to the encouragement of so many others.

Note:

The towns described in the book exist, though maybe not quite as described (it is set in the future, after all). The ranch land where most of the action takes place, also exists, and is much as described. However, the actual ranch names, camp names and specific geological features are fictional. While it is rough land, broken by several deep canyons, the Adobe Canyon described in the book is fictional.

Unfortunately, the challenges that ranchers face from some recreational land users is not fictional, and should you decide to explore this area of Arizona, remember that we all share this land, and should do our best to care for it. Please pack out what you pack in, stay on roads, leave the waters the way you find them, do not harass the cattle (they have a right to be there, too) and please, please, please if you open a gate, close it behind you. Also, remember that not all this land is public, in spite of how empty it seems, and respect signs forbidding trespass.

1

The man squatted on the edge of the cliff, overlooking Interstate 40 as it dropped off, continuing the long trip down from the Colorado Plateau and heading west toward Kingman, Arizona. He nodded, fingering the rifle resting across his knees. All was in order. If his information was correct, the semis should be along very soon. He glanced toward the highway sixty feet below, where five or six large granite boulders rested. It had taken several hours of hard labor for him and his group, removing the barrier fencing and moving the rocks into place right where a large truck barreling around the curve in the divided highway wouldn't be able to avoid them. He looked to his right, where three piles of boulders waited, levers in place, ready to be dropped onto the asphalt far below. Across the two lanes of westbound pavement rose a second steep bank, with an additional pile of boulders perched on the brink

"Granger," came a voice from over his left shoulder. The man, Granger, turned to look at the speaker, a tall woman with short black hair named Linda.

"What's the report?" Granger asked as he turned back to look at the highway below.

"We just got the signal from Duncan's team. The supply trucks just passed Anvil Rock Road west of Seligman and are headed this way. There are only two trucks, one a tanker. No outriders, according to the signal."

Ethan Granger smiled grimly to himself, feeling the deep scar on the left side of his face tighten in response. In a previous life, he'd been an upstanding citizen, a business owner and someone who'd never consider doing what he now had set in motion. But

1

the influenza and the reorganization of the country changed all that. Now he was considered an outlaw, a ghost, and he and his fellow band of ghosts would do whatever it took to ensure their group had the food and supplies they needed to survive in this new world, no matter who tried to stop them.

Gripping his rifle, Granger rose to his feet, shaded his dark blue eyes and looked back toward the east, half expecting to see the two fully loaded semis barreling around the blind curve, heading in his direction. The potholed pavement remained empty, but if the lookout was correct, it wouldn't be for long. He turned, raised his hand to his mouth, and produced a piercing whistle that drew the rest of his group from farther back in the junipers where they'd been resting after the exertions of moving the boulders to the edge of the cliff. Four men appeared on the other side of the highway, emerging from the brush in the median.

"Okay, everyone. Get to your positions. Wait until I signal before dropping the boulders on to the road. Timing is everything." Stopping briefly, head cocked, Granger could hear the low rumble of the diesel engines, whispering through the pine and juniper-covered mountains and valleys, moving in his direction. His body tensed in anticipation as he readied himself to give the signal.

2

Maggie Langton stood in the doorway, looking at the black and white rooster on the front stoop of the stone house built under an overhang in the cliff wall of Adobe Canyon. She debated her next move. Below the house, in the open area between it and the barn, several hens were scratching in the dirt and sparse bunch grass, eagerly snapping up whatever they seemed to find there. She remembered going to grocery stores, back when there were grocery stores, and willingly paying extra for eggs from vegetarian, free range hens. No one had told her that those same chickens had never asked to become vegetarians and didn't follow the rules while they were wandering around outside. A picture crossed her mind from a month or so before, shortly after the visit from Captain Seth Rickards and his team of Enforcers. One of the hens had unearthed a nest of newborn mice. A feeding frenzy ensued that would have put a school of sharks to shame. Needless to say, that was one litter of mice that wouldn't be moving into Maggie's house anytime soon, and she might have been inclined to feel some warmth toward the patriarch of the mouse eradication crew if it wasn't that he seemed bent on her eradication as well.

The most irritating thing to Maggie was that Houdini, so named because they'd yet to find a way to keep the feathered alarm clock cooped up, was totally ignoring her. The two of them had held a running feud since the day he'd arrived at Hideaway, stuffed into a container on the back of a horse, a few months earlier. He *had* to know she was behind him, yet he acted as though she didn't exist. She gripped her broom more tightly, sure that his complete disinterest in her presence would turn into a shin-bruising attack the moment she stepped out onto the patio.

Maggie looked around the home pasture, as they'd come to call the meadow surrounding Hideaway Camp, the remote ranch camp located at the bottom of Adobe Canyon, back in the ranch land north of Prescott, Arizona . . . or what used to be Prescott, Arizona. None of the kids were in sight. She frowned. That wasn't normal, although maybe Alysa, Christina, Mark, Nick and Ryan were simply in the barn working on some chore that O'Reilly had given them. However, the kids had developed something close to an obsession with the cave network at the far end of the meadow where they had hidden from the Enforcers when they descended upon the ranch camp, determined to capture fugitive deputy, Jim O'Reilly.

Maggie frowned momentarily, and she glanced quickly at the tree at the northern end of the valley, then back at the rooster. He hadn't budged, but Maggie wasn't fooled. She was sure he knew her every movement.

She gritted her teeth. The kids knew better than to go into the caves by themselves. Heck, as far as she was concerned, she never wanted to go into those caves again. However, instead of being afraid of that dark maze of tunnels, the children all seemed to feel safer there than in the house. In fact, for several weeks following the invasion by the authorities, Nick and Ryan had adamantly refused to sleep anywhere but in the small, hidden cave which she and O'Reilly had provisioned for a siege.

Maggie could see O'Reilly over in the garden, walking up and down the bright green rows of carefully tended produce, bending over occasionally to examine something that she couldn't see. He still wore a sling but once again had pulled his arm loose. The bullet wound in his shoulder had nearly healed, but it still ached at times. That injury had impressed on Maggie her lack of skills for living out in the wilderness like the pioneers of a century and a half before, as if she hadn't already realized it during her months at Hideaway.

Maggie opened her mouth to call out. That blasted rooster might have it in for her, but he darned sure wouldn't stand up to O'Reilly, injured shoulder or not. Just as she took in a breath to shout, Houdini turned his attention back to her, tilted his head, a yellow eye meeting her green ones. He shifted slightly and then shook himself, the hackle feathers on his neck standing out for a moment, then laying flat. He aggressively scratched the dirt several times, then stopped and stared at her, tipping his head from one side to the other.

A movement from behind Maggie startled her, causing her to jump, and two-year-old Lindy brushed past her legs, toddling out onto the patio and making a beeline for Houdini. To Maggie's annoyance, the rooster didn't stir as the little girl ran over and picked him up like a stuffed animal.

"Dini, Dini, Dini! My Dini!" Lindy chanted as she gripped the rooster around the middle, pinning his wings to his sides. Instead of struggling to get away from the little girl, Houdini, guardian of the barnyard and scourge of mouse nests and Maggie's shins alike, hung his head over Lindy's shoulder, eyes half closed.

"Really, you animated feather duster?" Maggie muttered, disgusted by the rooster's behavior. Lindy had become the chicken whisperer, which Maggie figured was appropriate, considering that O'Reilly had brought both her and the chickens back to Hideaway at the same time. Still, it was revolting how Houdini, whom Maggie was convinced had the blood of pterodactyls running through his veins, was a floppy rag doll in the toddler's grasp.

On the other hand . . . Maggie looked at the rooster, firmly gripped in the little girl's chubby arms, and she started to take a step out the door. Houdini's head, which was resting on Lindy's left shoulder, rose a few inches, his golden-yellow eyes opened, and he stared at Maggie in challenge, making her squirm. She swore that if his beak had been capable of it, he would have had a smile of derision on his face at her hesitation.

"One of these days, you escapee from a pillow stuffing factory, one of these days you're going to push it too far," Maggie grumbled as she finished the first step. When Houdini made no attempt to escape from Lindy's grip, Maggie decided that she was safe and headed toward the garden, calling for the little girl to follow.

O'Reilly had squatted down and was closely examining a row of bean plants, apparently unaware of Maggie's approach.

She paused for a second at the edge of the garden, studying his movement, the stiffness still not totally banished from his muscles. It had been a little over a month and a half since he'd been shot when Rickards and his team of Enforcers raided the camp in an attempt to capture O'Reilly and take him back to the Laughlin Authorized Population Zone. Maggie was still amazed that, in the end, Rickards had let her go, although, to be fair, he did expect O'Reilly to die from his injuries. As far as Maggie knew, he may have expected her to die as well, trying to survive in the wilderness without O'Reilly.

An image of those last moments in the caves flashed through her mind, causing an internal shiver in spite of the warm early September weather. Rickards wasn't the only one who thought that Maggie's future would be bleak without O'Reilly's knowledge and support. When Maggie and her son, Mark, had run away from Prescott, heading out into the ranch lands of Arizona to avoid the government's concentration of the population remaining after the deadly influenza pandemic, they had none of the skills and precious few of the materials needed to survive.

Unfortunately, as Maggie realized later, they also had the same overabundance of cocky confidence that many of her generation possessed. Confidence that eventually things would right themselves, and they'd be able to move back into their homes. Confidence that the government would get things under control, and everything would soon go back to much as it had been before the influenza, despite her husband Mike, Mark's father, being dead. The confidence that, regardless of her lack of knowledge, she'd manage to grow food and figure out how to prepare it, or even worse, kill something in order to eat. Food came from the grocery store, even if it was a natural one.

Maggie's confidence had taken many sharp blows during those first few weeks, shaking it to its roots, as she and her son had gotten settled in Hideaway. Then O'Reilly, ex cowboy, ex Enforcer and current fugitive, had shown up and given her an ultimatum . . . work with him, or leave. Maggie made the only decision she saw possible, and as she realized now, that decision had probably saved her and Mark's lives.

O'Reilly had all the skills she lacked, and in short order, food started to populate the shelves of the previously bare pantry.

The hard rock in the center of her chest that made itself known whenever she thought about the coming winter had eased, and she began to look at the future with, if not excitement, at least complacency, knowing that starvation wasn't likely to rear its ugly head anytime soon.

That was before she learned that James O'Reilly was on the run and that he knew things that pretty much guaranteed he'd be chased and killed if at all possible. He had information that shook Maggie's core belief in the foundation of the country and its leadership and finally made her realize that things would never be "normal" ever again.

In that last showdown with Captain Seth Rickards of the Laughlin Enforcers, deep in the caves that pocked the walls of Adobe Canyon, the final minuscule shreds of hope that Maggie held deep inside – hopes that it was all a colossal mistake and that the country, after all, would hold together and the government would protect its people – those hopes were destroyed once and for all.

Maggie mentally shook herself, trying to dispel the ghosts left by those moments in the caverns, and stepped into the garden. O'Reilly looked up, sun glinting off his dark mahogany red hair, brown eyes serious.

"Hey, Maggie. These beans are ready to be picked, and those chiles and bell peppers look like they're ready as well. There are also quite a few cucumbers that need to come off before they get too much larger."

Maggie looked over the garden, which had expanded exponentially under O'Reilly's influence. Maggie and Mark had planted some vegetables when they first arrived at Hideaway. However, when O'Reilly appeared on the scene, he'd quickly informed them that they had planted too little and the wrong things. Even though it was late in the summer to start plants, he was able to encourage more out of the garden than Maggie had ever thought possible.

"So, I take it I'm going to be learning canning skills?" Maggie said. She'd been dreading her first foray into food preservation ever since she'd heard horror stories of the dangers of inappropriately canned food.

"Some we'll can, but I think we should dry as much as we can, and a lot can be pickled. The monsoons are pretty much over, and

7

we can use the sun to dehydrate a lot of these vegetables. We'll be able to store more that way." He looked at Maggie from the corner of his eye. "Besides, there's less risk of botulism in dried food."

Maggie opened her mouth to protest, then snapped it shut so quickly that her tongue would have been in danger of being severed if it had been in the vicinity of her teeth. She turned to study the row of beans, trying to pretend she hadn't heard O'Reilly's jab. He already knew that her experience in preserving food was limited, and he had selected the safest method of keeping them fed for the winter. She turned and stared at him with narrowed green eyes but couldn't think of a suitable rejoinder.

O'Reilly continued to give her a bland look for a few seconds longer, then tilted his head to study the canyon's black, grey and red streaked walls, squinting at the bright blue sky.

"I think we can make a good solar dehydrator using some of the materials I brought back from Wikieup before the Enforcers came. A canyon isn't the best spot for getting enough sun for a solar dehydrator, but the wider areas should work. It dried the jerky at least."

Maggie examined the garden even more closely, chewing her lip. The plot seemed huge to her. The idea of picking all of the vegetables in that space, and then having to dry or can them, was daunting, to say the least. She briefly thought of those people living in the APZs. They would be eating this winter. She turned to O'Reilly and started to open her mouth, but he was already talking.

"We're making progress toward putting up enough food for the winter, and we can still harvest some supplies from other ranches and camps that haven't been eradicated yet, but we should be looking into some of the other supplies available naturally." He looked at her with a smile. "And no, you can't move to an APZ."

"I wasn't going to say that!" Maggie protested, although she knew that O'Reilly had read her mind as he frequently did. Instead of answering, O'Reilly just smiled, making Maggie's clenched fists itch to wipe the expression off his face. Maggie deliberately turned her back and squatted to examine some green beans.

"I was thinking about something else as well," came the deep, gravelly voice from behind her shoulder.

Curious, Maggie turned back to look up at O'Reilly and was surprised to see that the smile had disappeared. She rose slowly to her feet, groaning internally at the popping in her knees. This pioneer lifestyle was not for the weak of spirit or body, that was for sure.

"Are you planning on letting me in on those thoughts?" Maggie asked. She felt the clench in her abdomen and focused on her breathing. So far, most of O'Reilly's "thoughts" had usually involved danger, either to himself or to her and the kids.

"I'm thinking we might want to consider moving camp." He noticed the panicked look on Maggie's face and hurried on. "Not immediately. Maybe not until next spring, but best to do it before the garden would have to be planted."

Maggie's eyes were wide, and she felt as though the air had been knocked out of her. "What? Why?" She stammered. "We are safe here. Why would we leave, and where would we go?"

"I've been thinking of this for a while," O'Reilly said in a soft voice. "Rickards knows where we are now."

"But he let me go. He doesn't even know if you lived. Dammit, we're safe!" Maggie felt a wave of panic begin to wash over her at the thought of leaving this little canyon far from the APZs. Her throat tightened and squeezed her voice into a harsh croak.

"Listen to me for a moment."

"No, I . . ." Maggie's attention was captured by a yank on her shirt hem, causing her to jump. She looked back and saw Lindy, grubby fist wound into Maggie's shirt, a scared look on her face. Maggie groaned, turned and picked up the little girl.

"It's okay, Lindy. It's okay." Maggie whispered into the toddler's ear, and Lindy snuggled into the crook of Maggie's neck. Maggie hid her face in the little girl's hair as she fought to control her emotions. She hadn't been farther than a few miles outside the home pasture since she and Mark moved to Hideaway. Even though Maggie knew it was irrational, she had the fear that as soon as they left that remote canyon, Enforcers with guns would swarm over them, hauling them off to the APZs or worse.

"We're safer now than we were before. Rickards is no longer looking for me. He might not actively steer people away from this area, but I doubt he's going to turn us in, either. Still, there are some other remote camps, over to the east, where we'd have easier access to water, wood, and even more importantly, which are set up to run on solar power."

Maggie looked up to see him studying her. He gave her a crooked smile, one mahogany eyebrow rising. "You could have a refrigerator, electric lights and some of the other modern conveniences again." The wheedling note in his voice brought a smile to Maggie's lips, and he laughed.

That moment of ease was fleeting, however, and a cloud settled back into O'Reilly's eyes, his face taking on its familiar stern cast. "There's another thing."

Maggie felt her heart plummet back to the bottom of her feet at his tone. She shook her head. This adrenaline roller coaster couldn't be good for her, she thought, as she took a deep breath, held it for a moment, then blew it slowly out through pursed lips.

"Okay?" Maggie drew out that one word. "And that would be?"

"It's time for you to start practicing with the rifle again."

If O'Reilly had suddenly turned green, sprouted three heads and announced that he was an alien from the Horsehead Nebula looking for a select few humans to populate a planet on its outermost edge, Maggie couldn't have been more surprised. Still, she had to concede to herself she should have known it was coming at some point. She shivered as though the warm fall day had suddenly turned brutally cold. Maggie looked at O'Reilly in silence, unwilling to trust her voice.

"You know it's well past time," O'Reilly continued as he stared at her. "If someone shows up here, I want someone other than a few kids to back me up."

"Dammit, O'Reilly, I saved your life in those caves, and I did it without a gun, I might add," Maggie exploded. In her arms, Lindy whimpered. Maggie hushed her, bouncing the toddler on her hip, then squared her shoulders, determined not to allow O'Reilly to provoke another outburst. A rustle of movement caught her eye, and she glanced toward the end of the garden. Houdini was perched on a rock, staring at Maggie. Malevolence glittered in the golden eyes, and she was positive he was watching her, determined to swoop in to protect the little girl if he deemed it necessary.

Maggie looked over at O'Reilly and saw that he had noticed the rooster's focus of attention as well. His lips twitched as though a laugh lurked behind them, and he was trying hard to keep it suppressed. More than likely, Maggie thought as her eyes narrowed in suspicion, because he valued his life.

"We only have one rifle now," Maggie stated, her frustration still evident in her voice, and Lindy wriggled in her arms. Maggie loosened her grip and continued, "Besides, we don't have enough ammunition stockpiled. You said so yourself."

Getting his expression under control, O'Reilly answered, "It's true, we don't have as much ammo as I'd like. That's why you'll also be learning to use the bow and, if I can figure out how to make one out of that damaged rifle, a crossbow," he said, referring to the gun which had been caught in the cave-in. "Still, the rifle will be our best bet if we're attacked."

Maggie's eyes narrowed even more at O'Reilly's statement, as though she could direct a beam of high-intensity energy straight through his forehead, and she opened her mouth as she prepared to argue the point. "I . . ."

O'Reilly continued on as though he was unaware of Maggie's laser stare. "Besides, it's not as though you haven't carried a gun before. Hell, you're the one who brought it with you to the canyon. You obviously realized its necessity back then."

Maggie's stormy expression didn't lighten. "I brought it because I didn't know what Mark and I were getting into when we escaped from being sent to the Phoenix Authorized Population Zone," she stated. "I knew eventually we would have to kill for food. But I've never used it. I haven't even touched a gun since Rickards left. When you were shot, I . . ." Maggie's voice trailed off, her eyes clouded, as she relived those long moments in the caves when she wasn't sure if O'Reilly would live or die. When she wasn't sure if *she* would live or die.

She remembered the rapid staccato report of the guns, the roar of the cave-in and the thick, cloying smell of rock dust that filled the air. She could see the look in Enforcer Captain Seth Rickards' eyes as he considered O'Reilly's and her fates. She relived the sinking feeling in her chest at the sight of O'Reilly lying on the ground in front of her, blood seeping through the dust, glinting in the glow cast by the flashlights.

When Captain Rickards allowed Maggie to live and left the caverns alone, Maggie found herself faced with trying to save O'Reilly's life without adequate medical knowledge or supplies. The operation that followed taxed Maggie's strength to the limit, although she reluctantly admitted later that it probably had a more dramatic effect on O'Reilly. Certainly, the scars left across his shoulder attested to the pain he'd endured as Maggie dug the slug from under his collarbone. While Maggie had not been enamored with guns prior to the confrontation, she now felt an overwhelming desire to be elsewhere when they came out. However, now O'Reilly wasn't just requiring her to be in the same room as the weapon; she was expected to learn to shoot it, to carry it with her and use it if necessary.

She knew it was an essential tool. She knew she needed to overcome her aversion, but God, she didn't want to touch the smooth, burled wood of the stock or feel the cold steel of the trigger against her finger. She never again wanted to see flesh torn by the entry of a bullet, at least not human flesh.

She also didn't want to admit her weakness to O'Reilly, to let him see that here was one more survival skill for which she just wasn't prepared.

She looked up to see O'Reilly studying her face as if trying to read the various expressions which flitted across its surface.

"It's time, Maggie. You know it is." O'Reilly's naturally soft, gravelly voice softened even more, and his dark brown eyes looked deep into her green ones, causing Maggie to squirm on the inside. "You were sloppy and ignorant when you came out here. There are things in this land that can kill you. You knew that, or you wouldn't have brought the gun with you in the first place, but still you'd go out unarmed. No more. You can't be the only one on the place who doesn't know how to protect herself if needed. Mark's learning. The girls are learning," O'Reilly said, referring to Christina Craigson and Alysa Thalman, the two fourteen-year-old girls who escaped from the APZ after O'Reilly and made their way to Wikieup, where O'Reilly found them. "Hell, if Houdini could hold a gun, I'd bet even he'd be carrying."

A burst of choked laughter blew out of Maggie at the idea of Houdini, arrogant rooster and her archnemesis, strutting through the chicken coop armed. The thought of what her life would be like as Houdini's designated arch enemy if he should find a rooster sized gun was frightening. He usually won all of their confrontations handily with his spurs and wings alone. Give him a gun and Maggie would never see another egg.

Still, Maggie knew that O'Reilly was right. She had gotten careless, relying on O'Reilly for many of the tasks with which she was uncomfortable, and hunting, or anything weapon related, fell into that category.

Following the previous year, after the H5N1 bird flu blasted the population of the planet, wiping out the majority of the citizens of the industrialized nations, the government was faced with the dilemma of how to make sure that all the people left alive were adequately cared for. The solution; concentrate what was left of the citizens into localized areas called Authorized Population Zones. The people were told that it was a temporary solution—just until lines of supply could be reestablished, and they could move back to their own homes.

Maggie, hearing disturbing reports from contacts already ensconced in the APZs, instead decided to take Mark, her son, and head into the empty rangeland of Northwestern Arizona, aiming for a small ranch camp she knew about. At that time she helped herself to a number of items left at abandoned homes in her neighborhood on the outskirts of Prescott. Among those items was the gun in question. Maggie realized the need to be armed when heading off into the wilderness, but she'd been grateful that she'd never needed to use the weapon.

Maggie chewed the inside of her cheek as she studied the ground at her feet. Finally, she looked up again, meeting O'Reilly's eyes and boosted Lindy higher on her hip.

"Fine," she said, "In a few weeks after you've healed. But if I shoot you in the butt, you've no one but yourself to blame, and don't expect me to remove the bullet this time, either." Spinning on her heel, she stomped off into the house.

3

Captain Seth Rickards of the Laughlin Enforcers sat at his desk, staring at the bottle of antacid resting in a place of honor right in the middle of the blotter. He grimaced as the burning pain in his guts began to subside. Even though he knew it was temporary, the respite from the discomfort was welcome.

Ever since returning to the Laughlin Authorized Population Zone, or APZ, from that small ranch camp in the northwestern Arizona wilderness, Rickards had been aware of a growing sense of disillusionment. At that last showdown in the caves, where Rickards had confronted a wounded James O'Reilly and the woman he had partnered with, Maggie Langton, O'Reilly had posed a question that haunted Rickards.

"What was 'Phase One'?"

While O'Reilly had been stationed in the Nursery, the converted hotel where APZ officials housed the many children displaced and orphaned by the influenza pandemic, he had accidentally intercepted a number of documents that were mistakenly included in a standard census report. After reading this report, O'Reilly had suddenly bolted from the APZ, disappearing into the now empty western wilderness of the United States. It was only through luck, and the later disappearance of a young girl also connected with O'Reilly, that Rickards tracked the man down at all. When O'Reilly posed his question, Rickards wasn't sure what he meant. When Maggie asked if Rickards would look into the situation, Rickards wasn't sure how to respond.

However, when Rickards returned to Nevada and the Laughlin APZ several days later, he found his mind haunted by the question, by the look in O'Reilly's eyes as he lay bleeding on the floor of the cave, and the matter-of-fact tone in Maggie's voice as she questioned his intent. He hadn't been able to resist looking through the file he'd confiscated from O'Reilly's station, and what he found shook his world to its bedrock.

"Phase One: Reduction of Population."

Ever since reading those five words, Rickards had been questioning their meaning and his own belief in the importance and purpose of his job as captain in the Enforcers.

Was there an innocent explanation? Maybe Phase One wasn't a human-caused attempt at genocide, as the headline made it appear. Perhaps it referred to an initial natural event that then put into motion further phases initiated by man—a triggering event.

The influenza pandemic could certainly qualify as a "natural event," couldn't it? An uncomfortable, heavy feeling sat in the pit of Rickards' stomach, however. A feeling that said while the influenza was possibly natural and couldn't be blamed on human interference, maybe the utter failure of the government's response could. He remembered his wife telling him that she couldn't understand why the portion of the population usually lightly affected by viruses such as influenza was getting the sickest—was dying the quickest. She couldn't figure out why those people who were vaccinated were succumbing as though they'd never seen the sharp end of the needle.

As this conundrum churned in his mind, he found himself doubting his purpose as an Enforcer in the APZ, as well as the APZs themselves. Was he truly here to protect and guide the people assigned to his care, or was he an instrument of Central Control, put here because he was a good little drone and followed orders without question? Was concentrating the population really the only way to ensure that everyone was cared for?

Rickards ground his teeth in frustration, and his stare shifted to the stack of reports sitting on the left side of his desk. As if that ethical dilemma weren't enough to turn his brain into sludge, now there was this, a report on a rumor circulating through the Laughlin APZ regarding a group of residents determined to bring down the APZs and allow the people to return to the lives they lived before the influenza pandemic eradicated the majority of the Earth's population. From discussions with the commanders of the various APZs, similar rumors were rife in those other groups as well.

The problem was, in Rickards' opinion, that those former lives no longer existed.

Despite Rickards' misgivings about the way the government handled this disaster, especially in light of the reports to which he'd accidentally gained access, he had to admit the authorities appeared to be correct in some respects. There *were* too few people left to maintain the normal flow of goods and services. In addition, even fewer who had any idea how to support themselves or their families without access to the modern conveniences of grocery stores, reliable electricity, clean water, gasoline or any of the other services to which the modern industrialized nations' citizens had become accustomed.

Rickards thought about the few thousand people under his care. How many of them, he wondered, would actually be able to grow enough food to last them for a year? How many would be able to supply their own basic needs? Back when the country was first founded, so many years ago, nearly every family living outside of a town or city practiced subsistence agriculture, were able to grow their own food, make their own clothes and were able to trade with neighbors for the few things they couldn't grow or make themselves.

These days, however, as with any progressive population, people had become specialized. For many, if not most, the only thing they knew about their food was how to pick it up from the shelves in the grocery store or how to order at the restaurant. Sure, there were those who had the necessary skills to survive, but they were far outnumbered by those who expected—no, demanded— that their needs be met and had no interest in developing the independent living skills that would be needed by anyone trying to survive far outside of the sheltering arms and government assistance of the APZ.

Some were trying. Rickards grimaced at the thought of the "ghosts," those people who had managed to evade the reorganization and concentration of the country's remaining population. Of course, even the majority of those rebels still lived off the government, albeit illegally, by stealing supplies bound for the larger populated areas. Most of the bands he'd seen reports on had been pirates, living off the supply trains, not pioneers, trying to actually support themselves through their own sweat and labor. They were outlaws in the eyes of the government, whether pioneer or pirate.

Rickards recalled a story he'd heard. It was back around the time of one of the previous "end of the world" scares, if he remembered right. The Mayan one, or one of the others. Who knew? There'd been so many recently. A few men had met in the local hardware store and began discussing all the chaos going on around the world. One man was talking about how he had a garden and was growing his own food, trying to become as self-sufficient as possible. Another man said that it was too much work to maintain a garden and raise livestock, and he preferred to just go to the store to get what he needed. When the first man protested that if the world went to hell and the grocery stores were no longer stocked, where would he be, the second man looked him in the eye and said seriously, "I don't need to grow my own food. I have guns, and I've stockpiled plenty of ammo." Rickards was told by the person who'd overheard this conversation that it was very clear from the look in the second man's face that he didn't mean he would supply all his needs through hunting, either. It said that he would take what he needed, and anyone who got in his way be damned.

What would happen if the rumor was true? And what would happen if this group of subversive APZ residents was allowed to progress unchecked? Would Rickards and his force be faced with trying to police a group of people who, because they lacked skills, instead resorted to killing others to get what they needed? How could the authorities ensure everyone was provided for if the citizens were spread all over hell and beyond?

Rickards brought his hands down on the dark mahogany desk with a crash, causing the bottle of antacid to jump into the air. A sudden flurry of noise from outside his door indicated that at least one of his subordinates heard the noise but was probably too intimidated to come in to determine its cause. *Good*, he thought. The last thing he wanted was some solicitous toady, *probably that damned Knox*, coming in and oozing concern. He knew he was being unfair to Deputy Knox, his assistant, but at that moment, he really didn't care. What he wanted was to be left alone.

No, what he really wanted was things back the way they were, with him patrolling the streets and casinos of Laughlin, making sure tourists weren't mugged, or muggers themselves, and that the bars weren't over serving. He wanted this pandemic to have never occurred, and he wanted his wife alive again.

Instead of subsiding, the commotion in the outer office increased and finally penetrated Rickards' preoccupation. Frowning, he rose from the desk and was headed across the tan Berber carpet toward the office door when Deputy Knox entered in a rush.

"Sir, there is a group of people here to see you. They're sort of insistent." Knox's pale blue eyes were wide, and the prominent Adam's apple bobbed nervously as he swallowed.

Rickards took a deep breath, and instead of snapping the deputy's head off, which was his first inclination, he nodded abruptly.

"What do they want?"

"Well, sir, the man who seems to be in charge said that a group of them were planning on leaving the APZ and returning to their homes. He insisted that they be issued supplies and allowed access to vehicles."

Rickards felt his stomach shift lower. So the rumors were real. The question, of course, was how insistent was this group going to be and how amenable to persuasion. He'd heard from several other APZ commanders about violence erupting, resulting in equally aggressive measures to control the unrest. So far, he'd been lucky in that department.

"Fine, Knox. Show them in."

"Uh . . . There are quite a few of them, sir. Too many to fit in your office. Maybe the conference room instead?"

"That will do. Tell them I'll be there in a moment." Rickards turned back to his desk, looking for the bottle of antacid. He had a feeling he was going to need it.

Rickards squared his shoulders and pushed open the large, dark walnut door of one of the hotel's several conference rooms. He stepped inside, only to stop short, a frown creasing the landscape between his eyes. Knox hadn't been kidding when he said there were a few too many for Rickards' office—close to twenty too many.

Every head turned at Rickards' arrival. The cluster of people was mainly men, although a few women were scattered among the faces that looked back at Rickards. Everyone froze for a moment, then one man, apparently the leader of the group, stepped forward. Rickards released the door, which was stopped from swinging closed by Knox, who had been following close behind.

Rickards felt a momentary jolt of gratitude. At least he wasn't going into this confrontation without backup, even if the backup was a tall, skinny geek, long on yessirs and nosirs and short on initiative.

"Captain Rickards?" the man said, offering his hand.

Rickards nodded at the man and put out his own palm. "I am, and you are?"

The man's grip was firm, the skin smooth. Rickards studied the face in front of him—clean shaven, haircut neat, which was not that common these days. With barbers in short supply, most people bore hairstyles that screamed "amateur" at one extreme and "wild child from Borneo" at the other, with nothing much in the middle. However, this man's light brown hair looked as though he'd risen from the stylist's chair moments before. Rickards' hazel eyes narrowed slightly. The man's clothes were also neat. Nothing fancy, just jeans, a black T-shirt and older red running shoes. He had an air of command. Rickards wouldn't mind having someone like him in the Enforcers, although some people like this had trouble following orders. He thought about Deputy Harlan, the resident pain in Rickards' butt. No, come to think of it, he didn't really care to have many more subordinates like him.

"I'm Rickards. Your name?" Rickards repeated as he met the man's gaze and held it. The man didn't look away, to Rickards' surprise.

"Nick Ludeman, from Henderson." There was a moment of silence as each man waited for the other to speak.

Finally, Rickards nodded sharply, dropped Ludeman's hand, moved toward the long table and pulled out a chair.

"What can I do for you, Mr. Ludeman?" Rickards said as he took a seat, gesturing toward the others to make themselves comfortable.

Ludeman pulled out a chair on the opposite side of the table and sat while the other members of the group found seats as well or stood along the dark paneled walls.

"Well, Captain Rickards, there's a group of us who have been talking, and we'd like to know exactly when we're going to be allowed to leave the APZ and return to our homes. The pandemic is over, isn't it?" A murmur spread through the group, and a number of heads nodded in agreement. Rickards cast his gaze around the room and noted facial expressions ranging from angry and upset to hopeful and eager.

Rickards' eyes narrowed. Ludeman was well-spoken, phrasing his requests politely. Had Knox exaggerated the group's demands earlier? Were they open to reason? Something about the man made Rickards doubt it. If he had to bet, he would have staked everything he owned, or used to own, that Ludeman was a politician, saying what he felt he needed to say to get what he wanted.

"I understand that it's been a tough time and that you are missing your homes, but at this time we just aren't able to provide services to everyone if you leave the APZs. There just aren't enough people left," Rickards said, watching closely for any reaction.

The murmuring among the others of the group grew, and Rickards could see fewer hopeful expressions and more angry and impatient ones. Ludeman pushed his chair back and fixed Rickards with a pale gray stare. "I don't know that legally you're entitled to keep us here." His voice dropped in timbre, the congenial notes disappeared, and a commanding tone came to the forefront.

"You do realize that martial law was declared during the pandemic?" Rickards stood and looked around the group. "And we are still under martial law. That most certainly gives me the legal right to determine the best way to proceed, as well as to insist that all citizens comply."

It was as if a match had been struck and thrown into a pool of gasoline. The murmur became a roar, with people all talking at once. A large, heavy-set man, well over the 250-pound mark, pounded on a table.

"We want . . ."

"You can't keep us here against . . ."

". . . not right, just not right!"

Rickards looked over at Knox and gestured for him to get reinforcements, then pivoted back to the mob. Ludeman had stood and turned to face the group, calling for calm. Gradually the roar decreased to a murmur, and Rickards began to relax. He looked at the door and saw Knox with several other deputies from the main office. He gave them a slight head shake and a "wait" signal. Things might be calming right now, but there was no guarantee they would stay that way.

Ludeman turned back to Rickards and gave him another one of his direct stares.

This guy could be bad news, Rickards thought. During the influenza pandemic, people had been demoralized by the decimation of the population, and they'd looked for anyone to come along and take charge. The declaration of martial law had been accepted much more smoothly than anyone had a right to expect, with most people willingly moving into the APZs as they had found it nearly impossible to get supplies or medical services in other locations. Even those people who had escaped the concentration were relatively few in number and generally disorganized. A few true survivalists still existed who had cultivated the skills in food harvesting and gathering, agriculture and hunting that would allow them to live for a protracted time off the land. Rickards doubted that Ludeman was one of these.

Rickards sat once again and gestured for Ludeman to do the same. The man lowered himself slowly into the chair, his eyes never leaving Rickards' face.

"Captain Rickards," Ludeman said, his voice maintaining the calm tone of command. "The pandemic has ended months ago, if not longer. Martial law was extreme but understandable at the time. However, the crisis is now over. Those who don't feel comfortable returning to their towns, knowing that obtaining supplies might be a bit more difficult, are welcome to stay within the APZs. Residents who are willing to embrace the challenges of this new lifestyle *must* be allowed to return to their homes."

The murmuring in the room began to increase in volume once again, and Rickards looked at several of the closer faces. Ludeman had a strong hold over his people. Stronger than Rickards' control, it seemed. It didn't matter if what Ludeman said made sense upon closer analysis or not. These men and women believed in him.

Rickards pushed himself straighter and met Ludeman's eyes. His next words, however, were aimed at those gathering around.

"How many of you here have ever planted a garden?" Rickards' voice was a deep, soft rumble. He heard the low murmur of people repeating his words to others who hadn't been able to hear him at the back of the room.

He looked away from Ludeman's face and cast his gaze around the chamber. A few hands went up. Some people nodded, smug smiles on their faces. His next words put a dent in some of those smiles.

"And how many of you have used your gardens to provide *all* your fruits and vegetables for the year?" His voice was a little louder this time.

Hands went down, and faces that had previously sported smiles now wore frowns as they looked at each other and then back at Rickards.

"Just because they haven't done it before . . ." Ludeman protested.

Rickards could see that he'd found a tiny crack in the man's confidence.

"How many of you know how to preserve food without the use of freezers or refrigeration because there's no guarantee that you will have electricity when you get home?" His voice rose even higher. It was clear from the gathering that no one had trouble hearing him this time.

He carefully didn't mention that their homes might not even be there. Most had agreed to concentration on the assurances from law enforcement that their homes would be protected from looters. They knew some places had been destroyed, presumably by ghosts, or in the name of public health when a virus reservoir was located. However, they no idea that the government had targeted all the buildings outside the APZs and that they'd planned on making the concentration permanent, at least for now.

Rickards could see all eyes fixed on him. The muttering had quieted. The room held a tension, almost as though all the people were holding their collective breaths.

"How many of you have butchered out an animal? Pulled out the entrails and preserved the meat?"

Silence.

"And how many of you have shot and killed another person, whether or not that person is threatening you."

Rickards' final words ended on a roar as he pushed himself up from his chair and cast his eyes across the faces of his listeners.

In front of him, Ludeman pushed himself slowly to his feet, his face set in stony anger.

"You do not have the right to keep us here," he growled.

"I not only have the right and the responsibility, as specified by the government of the United States, but I also have the duty as a public safety officer to keep those committed to my care alive. I can't do that if people spread out too thinly." Rickards' voice was cold and hard, making it obvious to the listeners that there was no room for argument. Then his voice began to drop. He adopted a note of persuasion, gesturing to the gathered people.

"Right now, you would be returning to communities that may have no working utilities. That means no electricity. No clean water. No gas. You wouldn't be able to get supplies, and even if you know how to grow your own food, it's September now, and winter is knocking on the door."

Rickards could see that he had everyone's attention. They were listening, and he noticed several of the men who had been the angriest begin to nod in agreement.

"I suggest we discuss this again in the spring," Rickards said, ruthlessly subduing an internal clench of guilt. He knew the government was no more likely to sanction the dissolution of the APZs in the spring than it was now, but at least it bought him some time. "In the meantime you can start to learn the skills you will need to survive."

Ludeman's face hadn't thawed at Rickards' words. "You have supplies here. It may not be convenient, but we can come to the APZ to pick up food and other things that we need. It is rightfully ours after all." His voice was steel, and it was clear he wasn't willing to hear anything that didn't agree with his own beliefs.

24

Rickards met the man's stare with one as stony. "The refineries are still down, which means that gasoline and diesel are in short supply. The stores that are available are reserved for the APZs. We cannot waste these resources since we don't know when we'll have the ability to reopen the refineries. So, while there is food and other supplies for you here if you stay, you would not have access to it if you chose to leave."

Once again, Rickards quelled a feeling of nausea. Everything he said was true. What he didn't address was that if anyone left the APZ, they would be immediately labeled as a subversive—a ghost—and even if food and supplies were available, and the person was able to find a way to get back and forth to the APZ, they wouldn't be allowed to pick up rations.

Ludeman opened his mouth to offer a rebuttal, but a large man with an exuberant red beard put a meaty hand on his shoulder.

"Nick, he's right. We ain't got what we need right now if what he's telling us about our towns is right. I've had a garden for years, but I ain't never had to use it for all my food year round. Sure, I'm a good hunter, but I've never had to cut it up, and I've always had a freezer to put the meat in. Maybe we should take the next few months to learn how to do that stuff."

The bearded man looked up at Rickards. "Are there people here that can teach us to live like pioneers since that's what it sounds like we're going to have to do, least for a while?"

Rickards looked at the man, then around the conference room. "I don't know, off-hand. I recommend you start asking around. Find out what everyone's skill level is, then start sharing information."

Maybe, just maybe, he thought, *next spring will bring a thaw to the government's position on the APZs,* knowing that it was unlikely. He also knew that most of those still alive who had extensive knowledge of survival skills hadn't let themselves be concentrated into the APZs in the first place. The phrase, *Phase One,* floated into his mind, but he willed it away.

He could see the simmering anger on Ludeman's face, and Rickards gave him a hard stare, daring him to bring up another argument. To his surprise, Ludeman turned away and started walking among the gathered people, talking quietly to them and gesturing them out of the conference room. The deputies who had been standing at the door, prepared to intervene if things got out of hand, stepped back to allow the group to leave.

Just before he walked out the door, Ludeman stopped, turned and looked back at Rickards. "We'll be talking again, Captain Rickards." The tone of his voice, while not overtly aggressive, made it clear that the topic of people leaving the APZ was not being dismissed—just being put on the back burner.

A very smart man, Rickards thought. *A very smart man, and one who will be trouble.*

4

The small convoy of UTVs wove its way up a steep hill and through a thick copse of shaggy bark junipers, piñon and white pines, eventually pulling into a flat gravel parking area next to a large, tan, steel, pole barn. Scattered around the spot were four older motorhomes and fifth wheels. A tiny, weather-beaten cabin was nestled back among the trees.

Ethan Granger pulled his extended bed Ranger to a stop next to a 32-foot motorhome and pulled himself from the seat, tired to the bone. He stood next to the dull green vehicle for a moment, looking around the compound—the name his group had given the remote property buried back on the edge of the Juniper Mountains southwest of Seligman.

A red quad pulling a small trailer parked next to him, and a blond man stood and swung his leg over the saddle. He walked over to Granger and clapped him on the shoulder.

"*Woo Hoo*, that was something, wasn't it," the man laughed, inviting Granger to join in the joke.

Granger looked at the man, feeling something close to disgust. "Yeah, Lucas. That was something. That was a damned disaster."

Kyle Lucas, Granger's right-hand man, appeared oblivious to his anger. "The way that truck went up. Holy sh . . ." His arms gesticulated wildly, mimicking a huge explosion. The man's eyes held a manic light that irritated Granger more than usual.

"Quit it, Lucas," Granger snapped, cutting him off. He noticed the pale blue eyes shift suddenly to icy, making Granger shiver in the warm September weather. He quickly softened his tone. "I'm sorry, Kyle. We just needed those supplies, and that truck going up like that ruined everything."

Granger noticed the thawing in Kyle Lucas's eyes and knew that the crisis had passed—for now. He had a feeling, however, that there was going to be a confrontation in the future that wouldn't end as peacefully. He ground his teeth in frustration. What strange twist of fate had put him in this position? He just wanted to be back in his home, see his daughters, and work at his shop—not be a leader of a rogue band of plague survivors.

Prior to the pandemic, and the dramatic restructuring of the planet's population, Ethan Granger had a peaceful, prosperous life in Mesa, Arizona, one of the cities in the vast interconnected Metro Phoenix area. He owned and operated *The Grange*, a small army surplus and gun store which catered to survivalists and preppers, both dyed in the wool and dabblers. He was divorced, but his ex lived nearby with his nine- and ten-year-old daughters, and he spent as much time with them as he was able.

Life was good. He enjoyed his business and enjoyed interacting with the various characters who came to the store. While he tended more toward the prepper side of the fence, he found he also had many sympathies with those who came in, espousing the more extreme survivalist mentality. Kyle Lucas was one of those, and when the pandemic hit, wiping out a large share of the Metro Phoenix area, including his entire family, Lucas had talked Ethan into heading off into the wilds of northern Arizona with him.

Lucas told Granger he had built a hidden bunker on the national forest lands, stocking it with everything needed to ride out the apocalypse. Actually, if Lucas were to be believed, which Granger was not entirely sure, the wide expanses of public lands were riddled with hidden bunkers built by like-minded individuals. With nothing left, and the looming reorganization of the population, including the creation of the APZs, Granger supplied himself from the little left on his own shelves. During the panic prior to the peak of the pandemic, store shelves everywhere had been left bare as people grabbed everything imaginable, whether they needed it or not. However, Granger had made sure he kept a supply of necessary goods in the back storeroom and brought it out a little at a time, raising the prices as the pandemic continued and the supplies dwindled. Now he loaded what he could into a backpack, shouldered the straps, and left, locking the door behind him.

It turned out that Lucas had told the truth about their destination. He had turned an abandoned mine off Route 66 into a shelter, outfitting it with freeze dried food, ammunition, clothing, and everything else he thought he might need when the apocalypse came.

What he hadn't done, unfortunately for Granger, was hide the mine portal well enough from prying eyes. When Lucas and Granger, as well as two boys they'd picked up on the journey, arrived at the shelter southeast of Peach Springs, it was obvious that someone had been there before them. Lucas had created a false door, designed to look like traditional mine gobbing, or piled stones, over a branch of the main drive. Someone hadn't fallen for the subterfuge and had managed to work out the hidden latch and open the door.

From the state of the shelter, it was clear that the vandals hadn't been anyone interested in survival. Granger figured it had probably been done prior to the worst of the pandemic, although certainly after Lucas's last visit to the shelter a year and a half ago, before the government instated travel restrictions.

It looked as though a pack of undomesticated five year olds had run amok. Much of the stored food had been scattered around the room, destroyed or eaten. The walls were covered with fluorescent spray paint, and the clothing was torn and soiled. The room smelled like an abandoned, overflowing outhouse. Naturally, the weapons and ammunition which Lucas insisted had been stockpiled, many of which he had bought from Granger's store, were missing.

Kyle Lucas went into a rage, throwing items around the room and generally destroying everything that hadn't been smashed by the vandals as Granger shooed the two boys out of the mine. For the first time, Granger felt a qualm about working with Lucas. What did he actually know about the man?

Granger watched as the anger drained out of Lucas, leaving as quickly as it came. "We'll be fine, Granger. There will be other convoys."

"We needed that gas, Kyle." Granger looked around the compound. Seven other quads and side-by-side UTVs had pulled in and parked near Granger and Lucas's vehicles.

During the journey to Peach Springs, Lucas, Granger and two boys they'd picked up along the way had traded the horses they'd liberated from a ranch they'd passed for the small, mobile vehicles, siphoning gasoline from abandoned cars and trucks as needed and carrying extra five-gallon containers with them.

Later on, as they picked up new members of their group, they also picked up more vehicles. At the same time, they started finding their traditional sources of fuel drying up. Northern Arizona, at least the remote portion of northern Arizona that Granger and his group occupied, had always been sparsely populated. However, it seemed that others were out there, gathering up abandoned supplies and gasoline and torching empty homes.

"We got plenty for now, Granger. You worry too much. We'll head off toward Ash Fork and check some of the more remote places. Guarantee we'll find plenty of gas," Lucas scoffed. Once again, Granger could feel the push back from Lucas and wondered how much longer he would be a benefit to the group instead of the liability he was becoming.

Linda, the dark-haired woman, walked up and put a hand on Lucas's arm, and he turned back to look at her, a grin on his face. "Wasn't that something, Linda?"

"Yeah, something," she said, although the twist of her lips indicated that her "something" was very different than Lucas's "something."

In Granger's opinion, the plan had been perfect. They had blocked westbound Interstate 40 in a steep, narrow, winding area where fallen rocks were common. The piles of boulders they'd had prepared on the cliffs that rose from the sides of the highway would have been used to keep the trucks from reversing or otherwise escaping the trap. What they hadn't planned on were apparently inexperienced drivers going way too fast on the dangerous road. The first semi in the convoy stopped in a squeal of brakes, smoke boiling out from under the tires, and came to rest across both lanes of the rough, potholed pavement. The second, a tanker carrying a full load of gasoline, had been following too closely. The driver lost control, ramming the truck into the first semi, turning them both into a tangled mass of metal. A shower of sparks ignited the spilled gasoline from the tanker and erupted into a fire which quickly spread. The resulting explosion rocked the surrounding mountains. Flaming debris rained down.

Granger's crew quickly found themselves at the ignition point of a violent wildfire as clumps of grama and bunch grass burst into flame which spread rapidly to the loose strips of bark on the shaggy bark junipers perched on the cliffs above. Everyone ran for their quads and UTVs. Thick knobbed tires tore up additional clumps of grass as the group tore out of the area and headed back to the mountains southwest of Seligman and safety from the flames.

Even now, if Granger looked toward the northwest, he could see the billowing clouds of smoke, the Arizona winds carrying it off to the northeast and away from their compound. Granger shook his head, face twisted in anger and frustration. Over the past few decades, forest fires across the West had become more violent and deadly, requiring hundreds of hotshots and firefighters to keep them under control. This would be the first forest fire since the pandemic, or at least the first that he knew about. News from other states, as well as other parts of this state, had been sparse to non-existent.

No firefighters would be rushing to extinguish the flames this time. No hotshots, no slurry tankers. Nothing would stop this fire except nature in the form of a late monsoon storm or the Grand Canyon. The towering pillar of smoke continued to drift away from the Seligman compound. As long as the wind didn't change direction, they should be safe.

Granger turned away and looked around the current home of his group of eighteen. Many of the others were also watching the smoke in the distance, but several had moved off to work on other projects.

Three women were busying themselves in the small garden they had planted upon their arrival. Granger felt his stomach sink. The tiny plants didn't look as though they would be providing much nourishment any time in the near future. A few small tomatoes and cucumbers had been harvested, as had some lettuce. The carrots he'd seen would make a rabbit laugh, or cry, and he had yet to see a potato. They still had cans of vegetables that they'd looted from empty homes in the area, but these weren't going to last through the winter.

"Hey, Ethan, me and Andy are going rabbit hunting if that's okay." A voice pulled Granger's attention away from the garden. Daniel, one of the kids whom he and Lucas had picked up on the journey to Peach Springs, was standing a few feet away, a bizarre contraption in his hands and his younger brother by his side.

"Yeah, that's fine," Granger said, his mood lightening at the sight of the weapon Daniel was holding. Because of the finite supply of ammunition, Granger had been pushing the members of his group to learn how to use the various bows and crossbows they had found. The number of hunting arrows was limited, but it was easier to replace a broken arrow than it was to replace the bullets, although the arrows they had made so far were poor substitutes for the hunting arrows they had found with the bows.

Daniel had decided to try and build his own hunting crossbow using an old .22 he'd found in the ruins of a burned house near Peach Springs. A metal cabinet had protected the weapon from the flames, but some components had been damaged in the heat, making it unreliable, in Granger's opinion.

Daniel had strapped two thin pieces of PVC pipe to the barrel to create a channel for the bolt to sit in and mounted a small fiberglass bow to the front. The trigger mechanism had been the most challenging part of the project, and more than once a member of the group had nearly found himself on the receiving end of a blunt arrow.

Daniel had been messing with this creation for several weeks and, to Granger's surprise, had finally gotten a homemade bolt to launch at a reasonable speed, although the accuracy left something to be desired. Daniel must have thought he'd ironed out some of the bugs if he believed he was ready to hunt with it.

"Thanks, Ethan," Daniel said, then turned to his younger brother. "Come on, Andy, I'll let you take a few shots." The two boys took off running down the road, feet crunching on the gravel surface, then dodged off the track and into the white pine and juniper forest. They disappeared in a matter of seconds.

Ethan smiled, a warm feeling driving out some of the frustration and anger from the day. The longing for his daughters was a constant presence in his life, a gnawing pain that was sometimes overwhelming. Over the past several months, however, he'd come to see the boys almost as his sons and that went a little way toward filling a hole in his heart. Neither boy was much of a talker, but from the little Granger had been able to glean from their discussions, he had an idea of what they'd been through after the pandemic roared its way through the Phoenix Metro area—and some of their life before as well—and their resilience impressed him daily.

From what Granger had picked up over the past months, Daniel and Andy had been raised by a single mother on the south side of Phoenix, among the gangs and drugs and dilapidation. The boys' father, a member of the largest of the area's gangs, had been killed in a drive-by when Andy was only six months old. In spite of that heritage, the boys' mother had worked hard to make sure both her sons had stayed out of the gang and drug culture. Although there was only a four-year age difference, Daniel had accepted responsibility as the man of the house and had worked hard to ensure that his younger brother never became involved in the various illegal activities their father had embraced so readily.

When the pandemic hit, stealing their mother from them, the south side was reduced to a desolate wasteland, and Daniel found himself trying to protect Andy from an entirely new set of challenges. Daniel made the decision to get his brother out of town and to a healthier environment. The problem was that neither Daniel nor Andy had been beyond the city limits before in their lives other than one visit to relatives on the Navajo reservation in the four corners area of New Mexico. The closest they'd ever been to camping had occurred the few times the boys found themselves living under a bridge for a several days when it wasn't safe to go home.

Granger could still remember the first night that he and Lucas spent in the foothills of the Bradshaw Mountains north of the Phoenix Metro area. In an attempt to halt the spread of the disease, the government had closed the highways and put restrictions on all travel between populated communities. Lucas, not to be stopped by a few simple roadblocks, and much more familiar with the empty desert around Phoenix than were the scattered remnants of the law enforcement agencies, easily led Granger out north and west of the city limits, stopping by an abandoned ranch to pick up several horses and saddles, making their escape easier and quicker than it otherwise would have been.

That night they camped northwest of Black Canyon City, making a small campfire and talking about the plan for the next few days. Lucas maintained they should go north into the heart of the Bradshaws, then head west from there, up past Prescott, and even further north toward Ash Fork, eventually reaching the Seligman and Peach Springs area where Lucas had built and provisioned his "fall back shelter" as he called it.

Gradually, tired from the day's exertions, talk died off, and the two men sat, staring into the campfire, each lost in his own thoughts. As Granger sat, thinking about his daughters, trying to picture their faces, he became aware that Lucas no longer had a distant look in his eyes. Instead, his focus had sharpened, and he was slowly reaching for the rifle he'd laid at his side.

Startled, Granger began to turn to look over his shoulder, starting to rise. Lucas temporarily shifted his attention to Granger's face and frowned, shaking his head slightly, but

Granger was unable to restrain himself. After the brightness of the flames, the area outside of the circle was ebony dark. Granger could hear Lucas picking up the gun and shifting in his seat.

"Who are you? Show yourselves," Lucas growled, even though Granger still couldn't see anyone. For all he knew, a pack of javelina was surveying the scene—checking to see if any food was to be had from the careless humans. He started to turn back to tell Lucas just that, when out of the corner of his eye he saw two boys move hesitantly forward into the light, the larger one pushing the smaller one behind him as they moved.

The older boy—no, Granger thought, a young man about fifteen or sixteen—looked warily at Lucas and the rifle, shifting his weight from one foot to the other. His dark eyes sparkled in the firelight, and a frown creased his forehead. From around his shoulder a younger boy, probably around twelve in Granger's estimation, peered, seemingly torn between fear and hope.

"I'll ask you again, who are you?" repeated Lucas, rifle aimed straight at the older of the two.

"For cripes sake, Lucas, they're kids," Granger protested, but Lucas ignored him.

"Daniel Espitia," the older of the two boys said. "This is my brother, Andy."

"What are you doing sneaking up on people like that? I coulda shot you."

Daniel looked from Lucas to Granger to Lucas again, as if trying to decide who to talk to and what exactly to say. Finally, he took a deep breath, shifted his focus back to Granger, and spoke in an unexpectedly deep, soft voice tinged with distrust and anger.

"We, my brother and me, we were trying to get out of the city. It's too dangerous there now. No food. People dying and being left in the streets to rot 'cause no one's takin' care of things. We was headin' for the res, up by the four corners. Our mother's people live on some sheep camps up there. Been there once, years ago. Thought it would be a safe place to go, but we got lost. Ran up on some guys on UTVs back down toward the valley. They pulled guns on us . . ." Daniel looked at Lucas with a scowl. ". . . stole our food and clothes. We got nothin' now." The boy rubbed a grubby hand across an equally dirty face, brushing dark hair out of his eyes.

Granger looked back at Lucas, then stood, reaching out with his right hand toward the boys. "Well, *we'll* help you. Come on, sit down and get warm. Do you want some food?" Granger gestured toward the pot sitting next to the fire, ignoring Lucas's dark look from beyond.

"My name is Ethan Granger, and this is Kyle Lucas. We're heading north too and wouldn't mind some company."

Daniel and Andy Espitia became part of their small group at that moment. Lucas frequently complained about becoming a nursemaid to two kids, but Granger overrode his arguments, forming a pattern for things to come.

With one last look toward the spot where the boys had disappeared, Granger turned back to his UTV and reached for the rifle he'd secured to the frame behind the seats. He pulled it loose and slung it over his shoulder. When he and Lucas and the boys had first come north, Granger hadn't worried about carrying a weapon with him, while Lucas made sure that he always had, at a minimum, a handgun and a knife. It hadn't taken long, however, before Granger had learned the virtue of always being prepared.

Following the discovery that Lucas's bolt hole had been vandalized, he, Granger and their two young companions had wandered the area, breaking into houses that they came across and taking what supplies they needed. Often they would stay a few days in some of the more remote locations, but they always moved on eventually.

Most of the places they walked into were empty, but occasionally they'd come across a lone person, or maybe a group of two or three. For the most part, these were people who had run when the call for concentration had come through, thinking that they were perfectly capable of providing for their own needs. That particular chunk of Arizona had long been a draw for people desirous of living off the land, or at least off the grid. Most had drastically overestimated their abilities and had soon found themselves wandering the land, looking for empty homes and hoping to find enough supplies to keep going another day. The majority of the time these people were thrilled to find others who were also trying to survive, and soon Granger found himself the leader of a small band of men and women.

Because it *was* Granger whom everyone they met saw as the leader, and not Lucas, even though the blue-eyed man was the one who originally convinced Ethan to go with him into the wilderness. Granger wondered about that sometimes, but then he watched Kyle Lucas and realized that the man's innate dislike of other people and his antisocial tendencies tended to leak out. Many of the members of the group avoided Lucas and were nervous around him. Even the women who seemed attracted to him—women like Linda—seemed wary around him, almost afraid at times. Still, Granger and Lucas had always communicated well, and Granger still felt as though he owed Lucas something for bringing him along on the trip.

Granger breathed in deeply, inhaling the air scented by white and piñon pines, junipers, heat and dust, then headed for the steel building. The sound of metal striking metal was emerging and he figured that Tony was working on the windmill again. When the group had moved to this small compound nestled in the hills, the well was operated on a solar powered pump. The ready supply of water was one of the things that attracted the group to this property since wells in this area were scarce. Unfortunately, shortly after their arrival a bolt of lightning during a monsoonal thunderstorm fried the system and nothing they'd done had been able to get it running again.

Tony, the resident tinkerer, had hauled up some solar panels from other homes in the area but hadn't been able to get the well operating. His next move had been to rescue an old windmill and drag it up to the compound. He'd been working for several weeks to try and get it fitted into its new home. In the meantime, members of the group were hauling water from a different windmill located in a valley several miles away.

A 3,000-gallon resin storage tank which had been located next to the well was dragged over to the large pole barn, and the down spout from the roof of the barn had been diverted into it so that any passing rainstorms would channel water into its depths. Unfortunately, since the ground had not been well prepared for the weight, the resin container had quickly developed a leak.

They needed the water, of course, but Granger cringed at the need to use their small supply of gasoline for the mundane task of running the UTVs back and forth to the windmill in the valley and he was uncomfortable having his people exposed to possible surveillance. Still, it needed to be done. It was much too late to replant a garden elsewhere.

He stopped then turned to look at the towering column of smoke again and suddenly felt very tired.

5

"You want to do what?" Maggie asked incredulously. She stood looking at Alysa and Christina.

Surprisingly, it was Alysa who spoke up. "The prickly pear fruit and pads are near the end of the season, and they need to be picked. The juniper berries need to be gathered too. We're late. The rains were good this summer, so there should be a lot of them."

Maggie frowned as she studied the two fourteen-year-old girls standing in front of her. She'd heard of prickly pear jelly and syrup but had always thought of it as a gag gift. One of those things you sent to your relatives when you visited Arizona, but you didn't actually eat it as part of your normal diet.

"They're good for you, and they're delicious," Alysa continued, pushing her heavy black hair out of her eyes. "A lot of vitamins and minerals is what my mother always told me. And the pads make a great salad. They sort of taste like bell peppers." Alysa's mother had been raised in the four corners, on the Navajo reservation, even though she'd moved away as a young woman. According to Alysa's stories, the family had lived on several ranches across the Southwest, and the young woman certainly knew more about living off the land than Maggie, or possibly even O'Reilly.

The girls looked at Maggie, excitement clear on their faces, and Maggie knew she was going to be doing battle with a cactus in the near future.

The next morning found Maggie, Alysa and Christina winding their way along the switchbacks, up out of the canyon to the north of the meadow where the camp was located. Each of their three horses carried roomy, thick leather saddlebags to carry their harvest back, and in a fit of optimism, Maggie had also decided to bring a pack horse with two large panniers. Snugly ensconced in a leather scabbard was the .30-06 hunting rifle that O'Reilly had insisted she carry.

She'd argued once again that there was no need for the extra burden, but O'Reilly was adamant, pointing out that while they were unlikely to run into any humans out there, mountain lions, the recently reintroduced wolves, and other wild animals might look upon the trespassers unkindly, or hungrily, depending on their luck hunting recently. Maggie had managed to put off her shooting lessons for nearly three weeks, but she knew the time was fast approaching when O'Reilly was going to insist on her using the rifle. Requiring her to carry it today was just the first step, she figured.

Living out on a ranch camp had always meant that fresh supplies were a weary distance away. In these days especially, with the production of goods temporarily derailed by the pandemic and the APZs controlling of most of the supplies that were left, taking advantage of what the land provided was even more essential. O'Reilly, maven of food production, had been in favor of the mission when Maggie mentioned Alysa's suggestion. As O'Reilly had pointed out earlier, their garden was doing well and it promised to provide a bounty of vegetables to be preserved, but the prickly pear fruit and nopales, or pads, could prove to be a welcomed addition to their diet this winter.

If she could figure out how to prepare them.

For that matter, if she was able to harvest them without making herself into a pincushion. Alysa had assured her that she knew how to pick the fruit without danger of lethal blood loss in spite of the fact that they had no tongs, but Maggie could still imagine herself covered with the fine stickers that sprouted from the multitude of wart-like bumps speckled across the flat, green nopales and the fruits' magenta skins.

The trio made their way up over the edge of the canyon rim, picking out the cattle trail that led around outcroppings of basalt and granite, then turned north where they could see a distant ridge carpeted with large prickly pear cacti. After a leisurely thirty or forty-minute ride the women drew close enough that Maggie could see the individual green pads of the prickly pear and along their rims they sported an abundance of the dark red fruit the trio were seeking.

The three stopped at the base of the steep ridge composed of loose dirt and rock and dismounted, tying their horses to the branches of several downed junipers which lay nearby. Maggie untied the saddlebags from behind her saddle, checked her pocket for the heavy leather gloves and the scrap piece of leather she intended to use to grasp the fruit, then stretched her back and turned to look at the dark-haired girl.

"Okay, Alysa. You say we just take hold of the fruit and twist? It doesn't sound too hard. And we cut the root of the pad where it attaches to the pad below it?"

Alysa nodded, her thick, black ponytail bobbing in the light breeze coming from the south. "My mother and I used to gather the fruit and nopales around this time of the year. You want to be careful of the small stickers because they're hard to get out of your hands and fingers, let alone your face, if it's windy."

Maggie cringed at the thought of those small hair-like stickers, or glochids, getting into her eyes or nose, and looked at the bright blue sky, trying to determine if the wind was likely to pick up any time soon.

Alysa, oblivious to Maggie's discomfort, continued. "The redder the fruit, the sweeter it is, but we will use everything. Just put them in the bags, and we'll burn off the stickers when we get home."

Maggie glanced over at Christina, who was also gearing up for the task at hand. Both girls had come dressed in long-sleeved shirts and each carried a pair of leather gloves similar to her own. Christina, who was as much a city girl as Maggie, was following Alysa's every move.

The three women gathered their saddlebags and headed for the nearest prickly pear, a large specimen, spreading out several feet from its origin. It seemed to be created of hundreds of the green pads or nopales, and each of the youngest pads was rimmed with magenta-red fruit. The ground below the cactus showed where several more of the fruits had fallen only to be eaten by animals. According to Alysa and O'Reilly, many of the high desert mammals, including javelina, coyotes and deer, not to mention a myriad of small rodents, enjoyed the prickly pear fruit and were not deterred by the stickers. Some even ate the nopales themselves.

After several minutes of concentrated effort, the large cactus was denuded of its fruit and many of the younger nopales, and the three had spread out to other nearby plants. Looking up, Maggie noticed several large cacti near the top of the ridge sixty or so feet above her. Nearby were several large shaggy bark junipers, covered with the green-blue berries that Maggie had also hoped to gather.

Maggie looked over to her left where the girls were busily moving from cactus to cactus, talking the whole time. Maggie shook her head, smiling ruefully to herself as she remembered what it was like to be a teenage girl talking with her friends. Of course, these two were probably talking about the garden, or the new addition to the house, or something else related to their survival, not boys as had Maggie and her friends. Maybe music. Music was always a good topic of conversation, even though they had no means of playing any recordings down at the camp. They could still talk about it though.

"Hey, guys," Maggie called out, getting the girls' attention. "I'm going to climb to the top of the ridge and start gathering the juniper berries on those trees."

"I get it," called Christina. She stood and stretched her back, grinning in Maggie's direction. "Leave us peons to gather the dangerous produce, while you take it easy gathering something where you don't have to bend down or worry about being shish kabobbed."

"Ah, the perks of being the boss," Maggie laughed back. She remembered a time only a few weeks ago when it seemed she'd never see the girls smile again. When it appeared that the haunted look would remain floating in their eyes for a lifetime. Their psyches had healed faster than O'Reilly's shoulder, however, and now she welcomed their easy camaraderie.

Taking her heavily loaded saddlebags back to where she'd tied her horse, she gathered up the empty flour sacks she'd brought along especially for the berries, then turned back to the ridge and began the upward trudge. While the hill wasn't especially high, her legs were aching when she finally reached the top. Breaking over the edge she stood for a moment, hands on her hips, breathing in the warm air, lightly seasoned with the scent of the juniper trees, dust, and something indefinable but which made her think of the coming fall.

She found herself on a relatively flat piece of land so thickly covered with trees that she couldn't tell what lay off to the west or north of her location. Looking back down the bank she could see the girls about a hundred yards away to the south, continuing to fill their saddlebags with the valuable cactus fruit. Turning to the closest tree she started to pick the waxy blue berries from the lowest branches of the large shaggy bark juniper.

The rustle of the wind and the hum of insects were hypnotic as she moved quietly among the trees. The berries, which, as O'Reilly had explained, were actually the immature cones of the evergreens, were so plentiful that Maggie didn't even make an effort to gather the ones on higher branches. Even as tiny as they were, she had no doubt she'd be able to fill her bag to the brim without risking life and limb.

She had moved to a tree about three hundred feet away from the rim, and was out of sight in the copse, when she found herself facing a small clearing. In the center, upwind from Maggie's position, a large bull elk was grazing on the sparse bunch grass growing among the malapai—the black volcanic rock that appeared across much of the Colorado Plateau. An errant ray of sunlight shown down into the clearing, illuminating the dust in the air and casting the animal in an almost ethereal glow. Maggie held her breath, watching in rapt fascination. She'd never seen a live elk before, except in zoos and animal parks, and she was mesmerized by the size and apparent strength of the animal.

Suddenly, from behind her shoulder and off to the right a shot rang out, jerking a surprised scream from her throat. The elk snorted, emitted a high strangled call and bolted for the far side of the clearing. Maggie froze for a moment then spun on her heel and started to race for the edge of the ridge, the only thoughts in her mind focused on reaching the girls and getting them to safety.

She took a dozen steps, two dozen, and she started to think she would make it, when a man stepped out from behind the low covering branches of a large juniper, bringing Maggie up short. She looked up and found herself staring into the icy, pale blue eyes of a stranger. A stranger holding a hunting rifle pointed straight at her chest.

6

"Lucas," Granger yelled from outside the large steel barn that he had turned into the group's headquarters. "Where's Daniel? Let's get going. Those deer aren't going to hunt themselves."

Two days ago Lucas had suggested going out on a hunting trip toward the Juniper Mesa Wilderness area of northwestern Arizona. Recently they'd been eating a lot of beef, having butchered several cows left behind in a nearby pasture. Many of the cattle in easily accessible areas had been commandeered by the APZs to feed the residents, but there were always a few left behind, either because they were mavericks, hiding out in the washes and brush, or because the teams detailed to accomplish this task had absolutely no aptitude for the cowboy work.

Granger and his companions hadn't grown up as cowboys either, but most of them had experience as hunters and knew how to track and kill. Granted, it helped that they also didn't have as many people to feed as the APZs. A few cows would feed their band of eighteen for quite a while, although without refrigeration the shelf life was certainly limited. Several members of the group claimed they knew how to make jerky and had attempted to convert some of the excess beef so that they would have provisions for the winter should they get deep snows. Granger confessed to having doubts, however, regarding the palatability, let alone the safety, of eating what emerged from their homemade dehydrators.

Still, a variety in protein was called for occasionally, and Lucas's suggestion of a hunting trip was a welcome change of pace. The chance to get some away time from the group was just icing on the cake, so to say.

Not that they had cake.

Or icing.

Lord, there were times that Granger found himself missing his previous life desperately with a longing that felt like a physical pain, right in the center of his chest.

Granger stood looking at the dusty green extended bed Ranger UTV standing in front of the barn, loaded and ready to head out from the secluded compound. The bed was packed with rifles and ammunition, as well as extra gas cans, tarps and other supplies the three men would need for the hunting expedition.

Granger looked back at the doorway, mouth open, ready to yell for his hunting companions again, impatient to get away from the group for a little while. Before the words were out of his mouth, however, Lucas appeared in the doorway, dressed in tattered, stained camouflage, a huge grin splitting his tanned, bearded face. His right hand gripped Daniel's elbow, holding him close to his side.

"Hey, Granger, ready to head out?"

"Yeah. I've been ready for the last thirty minutes. What's taking you guys so long in there?"

"Well, you see, young Daniel here needed some encouragement."

"Really? Why?" Granger looked curiously at the teenager. "I thought you were excited about the hunting trip, Daniel. What's up?"

The young man's head rose and he met Granger's eyes. "I just got thinkin' that maybe I should stay here for the day. Andy, he don't like it when I leave for too long. It makes him nervous."

More likely, thought Granger, Daniel was anxious about leaving his twelve-year-old brother, Andy. The youngest member of Granger's group had always impressed him as a resourceful young man, but Granger still understood Daniel's reluctance at being separated from the only family member he had left, especially considering everything they'd been through together.

Granger breathed in through his nose and out his mouth, cautioning himself to patience. He didn't mind giving Daniel the time he needed, and certainly the way the group lived right now didn't lend itself to a feeling of security, but at some point the boy had to let his brother grow up.

46

"Andy will be fine, Daniel. Kyle, let go of Daniel's arm."

Granger walked over to the pair and looked Daniel in the eyes. He could see the worry in the dark depths. "I know you only want to take care of your brother. But at some point he needs to be independent. Nothing will happen to him while we're away. The group is safe here. Linda and Allison need help with the garden, and a few of the others are going to be working on tanning hides. There's plenty for him to do here. He won't even know you're gone."

Daniel looked as though a war was going on inside. Finally, he looked at Granger. "Yeah, all right. I'm ready. Let's go." He headed toward one of the UTVs.

Lucas followed him, muttering to Granger as he passed. "You got to stop babying those kids. Stop being such a wimp."

Granger put out a hand and stopped Lucas, looking him square in the eyes. It struck him briefly that the pale blue of Lucas's eyes always seemed cold and flat. Almost reptilian, if a snake could have blue eyes.

"I'll do what I think I need to do to make sure everyone is taken care of, including them. Accept it or not, it's up to you."

A moment passed. Then two. Then ten.

Finally, Lucas broke eye contact and moved off toward the UTVs again. "Fine. Whatever you say, *boss.*"

Shaking his head, Granger turned to follow him. *Great,* he thought, *just what we need. More ego.* He ground his teeth, knowing he could have handled the situation better, but damn, he was getting tired of Lucas's unpredictability.

It took only three hours for the group to make it to the area near Juniper Mesa where they planned to hunt. The idea was to leave the UTV so that the sound of the engine wouldn't spook the animals. Then they would head out on foot, aiming for some thick juniper and grasslands that they had scouted on an earlier trip. Once they had bagged a deer or elk, one of them would return for the UTV, making it easier to pack the meat out. Lucas brought a roll of bright orange surveyor's tape he'd found in the steel barn to mark their direction so that whoever drew the short straw and had to return to the UTV would be able to find it easily in the thick brush.

They spread out as they walked through the juniper trees, making sure that each person was always aware of where the others were. The goal was to shoot a deer or elk, not one of the other hunters.

They kept the breeze to their right sides. Not as good as in their faces, but necessary since to move straight into the wind would cause them to go in a direction other than the one they wanted.

Twice they jumped a deer, but it bounded off before they could get a shot. The three had been moving for several hours and Granger was considering calling it a day. If they didn't get a deer soon they would have to spend the night roughing it. He didn't care very much about that since most of their days had been spent roughing it for the past eight months, but he knew that Daniel would struggle with being away from Andy for so long and Lucas's reaction to Daniel's worry was a concern.

The day was warm, but the thick clumps of juniper trees shaded the hunters and the breeze that wound its way through the trunks controlled the gnats. Granger thought briefly about winter, which was rapidly approaching. Arizona was best known for its hot, dry climate, but the Colorado Plateau could provide plenty of the cold stuff too, he knew. The members of the group would be forced indoors for greater periods of time, and the close quarters of the RVs and the barn would increase tensions.

A knot of frustration and worry tightened in Granger's chest, marring his enjoyment of the peaceful area. He liked Lucas, and he also felt that he owed his freedom to the tall, blond man. But, there was no denying any longer that there was something off-balance about Kyle Lucas, and that something was growing. His recent behavior just emphasized that observation, and Granger wondered, not for the first time, when that balance would finally tip past the point of no return, and Granger would find himself unable to control the man. Granger dreaded the decisions he would have to make at that time.

The trio moved onto a ridge south and east of Juniper Mesa when suddenly a clearing opened up in front of Granger and in the middle of that clearing was a magnificent bull elk. He couldn't see any others, but was sure that a herd was scattered through the trees. Raising his rifle to his shoulder, he sighted in on the animal and squeezed the trigger. A flash of color caught the corner of his eye and distracted him momentarily.

A moment was enough.

The report echoed off the trees and rock outcroppings. The elk threw up its head and sprang for the edge of the clearing, calling a warning to the herd as it ran. Granger cursed, realizing he had missed his shot. What was it that caught his attention at that critical moment? He looked off to the left just in time to catch a glimpse of someone disappearing into the junipers.

He looked back to his right and saw Daniel moving in from where he'd been flanking Granger. Ethan beckoned him on, then headed for where he'd seen the stranger vanish into the trees. It had been a few months since they had run into any other wanderers, and never had they met anyone this far out in the wilderness. The majority of the people they'd come across tended to stick to the previously populated areas where they could loot the abandoned homes and businesses. The action of the Enforcers, however, had made these encounters less and less frequent recently, not that it had happened that often to begin with.

Granger picked up his pace, holding his rifle ready, Daniel following close behind. He knew Lucas was somewhere in that direction, though he hesitated to call out, not knowing whether there were others with this stranger. Hopefully, Kyle would have intercepted this individual.

Granger and Daniel reached the far side of the clearing and moved out into the close growing clumps of junipers. They didn't have far to go, however, before they saw Lucas holding a rifle on a woman. She stood facing him, breathing quickly as though she'd been running.

"Look what I found," Lucas said in a conversational tone. "Think we ought to keep her?"

Granger looked at Lucas, startled, then back at the woman, moving around so that he was in front of her. She was attractive, relatively tall with honey blonde hair, startling green eyes and an expression that said she was afraid but ready to fight.

"Who are you?" Granger asked, causing that green stare to focus on him.

"None of your business. What are *you* doing here? Let me go now." The woman had a commanding note in her voice, as if she expected to have her orders obeyed. However, Granger could hear a slight tremor underneath the forcefulness of her words, indicating fear. He could see no weapon, so decided that her tone and stance were bravado.

"I asked who you are," Granger repeated. "And who are you with?"

"I'm on my own. You don't have any right to stop me like this. Let me go." The woman started to move gingerly away, trying to sidle past Lucas who rotated to keep his rifle pointed at her chest.

Granger debated a moment. In the past, when confronted with individuals, or small groups of people who were trying to avoid the governmental "assistance," but who also didn't have a clue as to how to live without it, he and his companions offered to take them into their own group. The way he saw it, a cluster of people wandering around clueless would end up drawing attention to the area. That was something that Granger did not want. Most had been more than willing to join up with Granger and Lucas.

On the other hand, some people were more trouble than they were worth, and several unmarked graves were the final destination of those thinking that they knew better than Granger about how to run his program. Granger didn't feel good about the decision, but he wasn't about to let some hothead jeopardize the fragile existence that he'd carved out for himself and his band.

Granger gritted his teeth as he studied the woman and he felt the scar that creased the left side of his face—a result of a confrontation with a bat-crap crazy old hermit—pull in response. It simply didn't make sense that this woman was out here in the middle of the wilderness by herself. She didn't want to come with them. If she were on her own, wouldn't she welcome the opportunity to share the burden of survival? That argued that she was lying to them. That somewhere others were waiting for her. Besides, she'd be nothing but a problem if they forced her to come with them.

Yet . . .

The snap of a breaking branch sounded off to the west, startled Granger, and caused Lucas to shift his attention briefly in the direction of the noise. Taking the opportunity afforded to her by Lucas's momentary loss of focus, the woman took off running toward the southeast, dodging under the low hanging juniper branches.

"Get her," Granger yelled, starting to run with Daniel trailing close behind.

Lucas had already bolted off after the woman, his giant stride shortening the gap between them quickly. The four broke through the junipers, and arrived at the edge of a steep embankment at nearly the same time. Small rocks and pebbles, dislodged by their feet, skittered down the steep slope, clicking and rattling against each other until they hit the bottom far below.

The woman skidded to a stop, and glanced over her shoulder at Lucas who was reaching for her arm. She turned back to the empty ranch land and yelled one word as he pulled her backward, her feet skidding in the loose dirt and grass.

"Run!"

Lucas swung his fist, and the woman dropped to the ground unconscious as that single word echoed off the surrounding hills.

7

Christina stood and stretched, wiping her face on her arm, brushing the brown hair out of her eyes. She looked at the full saddlebag at her feet and grinned at Alysa.

"Looks like we're going to be eating a lot of syrup and jam this winter."

Alysa looked up and smiled. "We've got to get the syrup and jam made first. You might not be so excited after you've spent hours working with these things." Alysa held up a deep red fruit before dropping into her bulging saddlebags.

"I've already spent hours. At least it feels . . ."

The sound of a rifle shot rang out, halting Christina in mid-sentence. She spun around, looking wildly for the source of the gunfire. Behind her, she could hear Alysa moving. Christina looked over her shoulder, her startled dark blue eyes meeting Alysa's wide brown-eyed stare.

"Was that . . . ?"

"A hunting rifle," Alysa affirmed, nodding.

"Where's Maggie?" Christina breathed, starting forward toward the spot where she had seen Maggie head up the scree.

"Wait, Christina," Alysa called after her, skirting the cactus and hurrying to catch up with her friend. "Maybe it's Maggie's rifle. O'Reilly made her bring it, remember. Did she carry it up on the ridge with her?"

Christina turned and hurried toward where the horses were tied, weaving her way between the myriad of prickly pear in her path.

Startled by her sudden approach, and already spooked by the gunshot, the horses jerked their heads against the lead ropes tying them to the fallen juniper, eyes rolling in alarm. Christina slowed, skirted the three closest horses, and made her way toward the large bay gelding that Maggie had ridden that morning. She moved around to the off side, looking for the scabbard strapped under the right stirrup leather. Her stomach dropped when she saw it right where it should be, rifle snugly encased within.

Christina looked over the horse's rear, meeting Alysa's questioning gaze.

"It's still here," she said, her voice low and tinged with fear. "It wasn't her rifle. We've got to find her." Christina turned and started toward the ridge at a run, her feet digging into the loose rock and grass.

"Wait, Christina." Alysa hissed. "If it wasn't Maggie's gun that fired, who's was it? It might be the Enforcers. What if they've come back? We'd be walking into a trap. We need to get O'Reilly."

"It will take too long to get back to the camp and O'Reilly. What if Maggie's hurt? We can't just abandon her." Panic tinged Christina's voice, fear written clearly in her eyes. She felt her heart hammering in her chest. She'd lost her mother to the influenza, her father to the Enforcers' bullets. Maggie was the only mother she had now, and she desperately didn't want to lose her too.

The sound of a man's voice raised in anger brought Christina to a stumbling stop ten feet from the horses. She looked toward Alysa where she still stood next to Maggie's gelding, then back toward the top of the ridge from which the sound emanated. No one was in sight.

Just as she commanded her feet to move her forward again, Christina saw Maggie appear from under a large juniper, and a momentary flush of relief washed through her body. She was all right. She was alive. Just as quickly as the surge of relief had hit, however, came a rush of dread as a tall, blond, bearded man wearing camouflage pants and a black T-shirt burst out from under the juniper in pursuit of Maggie.

For a moment, Christina thought that Maggie would make it. That she would reach the edge of the embankment and start her descent before the man caught her, but then Christina saw Maggie hesitate on the brink. That momentary hesitation was all it took for the man to catch Maggie, grab her by the arm and jerk her backward.

Maggie had time to scream one word before the man's fist crashed into her head, dropping her to the ground in a crumpled pile, out of Christina's sight.

"Run!"

Christina hesitated, then spun on her heel and dashed the ten feet back toward the horses, causing them to snort and jerk on their lead ropes once again. Alysa was already untying her gelding and reaching for the loose end of the pack horse's rope.

"Hurry, Christina," she called. "Just untie Maggie's horse and let him loose. Don't try to lead him. He'll only slow us down."

Alysa grabbed her horse's mane and leaped onto its back, seeming to barely touch the stirrup. Christina grabbed her gelding's reins and saddle horn, and tried to climb on, but the horse danced sideways, and she couldn't seem to coordinate her body enough to perform the task of mounting. Not for the first time, Christina cursed any situation that put her in close proximity with the four-legged mode of transportation. Looking over her shoulder, she saw another man emerge from the juniper thicket, followed by a younger man or boy, both of them holding rifles.

Christina turned and jerked the gelding's reins, grabbed for the stirrup and made a desperate lunge for the saddle horn, hauling herself up in an ungainly tangle of arms and legs. She thumped once behind the saddle as she struggled to get into the seat, causing the horse to surge forward, nearly throwing her back onto the ground. With a final lunge, she pulled herself into the saddle proper, her right foot seeking and finding the stirrup as she kicked the animal into a run.

Alysa, who had waited until Christina found her seat, also pushed her gelding into a gallop, and the two girls raced across the pitted, rocky ground, dodging rocks, cacti, and brush, heading for the narrow trail which would lead them down into the canyon.

Please, please, please, Christina thought, grabbing the saddle horn so tightly that she thought it would break off in her hand. *Please, let us make it. Please let Maggie be okay. Please God, don't let me fall off and land on a cactus.*

The sound of gunfire from behind them spooked Christina's horse, and caused it to gallop even faster than before, sending even more adrenaline through her system. A moderate horseman at best, Christina had never become comfortable with any speed over a fast walk. She glanced over at Alysa, running slightly ahead of her, saw how she bent low over her horse's neck and seemed to move as one with the creature. She looked down, then wished she hadn't as she saw the land rush by under the horse's hooves at a seemingly impossible speed, with dust and rocks kicking up in its wake.

The gelding dodged a cactus, nearly sending Christina crashing to the ground, but she managed to haul herself back into the seat and stay upright, grabbing even more tightly at the saddle horn and reins. The two loose horses, Maggie's gelding and the pack horse, raced alongside, occasionally crossing in front, or behind, causing Christina's gelding to swerve over and over.

After what seemed like hours, the girls reached the narrow trail that dropped off the edge of the cliff and wound down among the boulders toward the bottom of Adobe Canyon, where Hideaway, the ranch camp, was located.

Alysa pulled up her gelding, signaling Christina to do the same. The two loose horses which had pulled ahead of the girls on the mad dash away from the ridge slowed from a headlong run to a trot and headed down the trail, aiming for home. Alysa's and Christina's geldings followed them, nostrils wide, sides heaving. A thick foamy sweat ran from under their saddle pads and streaked their necks and flanks.

Christina looked over her shoulder as they dropped off the rim of the canyon, but they were well out of sight of the ridge and there was no sign of pursuit. Her heart ached at the thought of Maggie back with those men and dreaded the thought of facing O'Reilly and Mark without her.

She desperately held on to one thought. O'Reilly would know what to do. Maggie had to be okay, and O'Reilly would know what to do to bring her back.

He had to.

8

Granger looked from Lucas to the woman on the ground in front of him.

"Dammit, Lucas! You didn't have to . . ."

"Look!" Lucas pointed toward the bottom of the steep ridge where two people had already untied horses and were making a run for it. Two younger females, by the looks of it, and one of them none too familiar with a horse. As he watched, the brown-haired one was finally able to mount, and the pair headed east at a full out gallop.

Shots rang out, startling Granger, and he turned to look at Lucas, who was hurriedly reloading, in preparation for firing again. As he raised the rifle to his shoulder, Granger reached out and grabbed the barrel, swinging it away from the fleeing riders, wincing at the heat.

"For God's sake, Lucas. They're only girls."

"Yeah, they're only girls, but who knows who else is back at their camp. Or how well they're armed." Lucas angrily jerked the barrel out of Granger's hand, raising the stock back to his shoulder, aiming at the rapidly disappearing figures.

"Put the gun down, Lucas," Granger commanded, "or so help me, God . . ."

Lucas spun angrily toward Granger, pale eyes no longer flat, but lit by an angry light. "So help you God, what?" he demanded.

Granger glanced at Daniel, standing off to the side, eyes averted from the two angry men, staring into the distance where the girls had disappeared. Granger might have thought he was unaffected by the furious exchange except for the slight tremor in his hands, clenched at his sides.

Granger bit back an angry retort and instead lowered his voice, meeting Lucas's eyes directly. "The woman obviously has someone. That someone isn't going to be very happy."

Lucas sneered at Granger. "I'm not too worried about that someone. After all, how big a concern can he be if he lets his women go wandering around the countryside unarmed? I say we take her with us and if someone shows up looking for her, we take him out. It's just like the other times. We don't want any other bands operating in the same area and drawing the Enforcers' attention, do we? Besides, we could use some more women around the place." Lucas looked at the woman lying on the ground with an intensity that caused the warning bells in Granger's mind to ring even more insistently.

This argument wasn't new between Granger and Lucas, but Granger had always insisted that the one thing he would never accept from anyone would be rape. Up to this point, Lucas had accepted Granger's ultimatum, although grudgingly, and there were always women like Linda around to keep him occupied. But the hungry look on Lucas's face this time worried him.

Lucas had accidentally touched on a more concerning issue for Granger. Over the past weeks, he'd been feeling a growing uneasiness about the band's need to attack supply trucks and the chances that if the Enforcers decided to turn their efforts toward finding the group, they would ultimately succeed. Northern Arizona was a remote spot, but the Enforcers had the seekers, those silvery orb-like drones they used to monitor the areas around the APZs, and a determined search would be bound to find evidence of his band's camp. Anyone's camp.

Granger prided himself on how well he and his people knew the areas surrounding the compound, yet here was a woman who, with others it seemed, had apparently been living nearby, and his group had never seen any signs of it. Wherever her encampment was, it was well hidden. And if it was that well hidden, he wanted it.

Granger looked at the woman lying on the ground at his feet. The way he saw it, he had two choices . . . no three, and none of the choices sat well with him. First, he could just leave the woman here, trust that her people would come and find her before any wild animals did, or that she would wake up and make her way back to wherever her camp was located. If he made that choice, he would have a mutiny on his hands with Lucas. While it was true that for the past few months Granger had been aware of Lucas's increasingly erratic behavior and knew at some point he would have to make a decision on how to proceed, he still felt as though he owed it to Lucas to delay that day as long as possible. Besides, if he made that choice, he might never find out where the woman's headquarters was, and even if he did, her people would know about him and his group, and they might be met with resistance greater than if he made one of the other choices. She could prove to be valuable collateral.

A second choice, closely aligned with the first, was to wait until the woman regained consciousness and make sure that she was okay. From what Granger could see, while they would be able to assure themselves that wild animals wouldn't be a danger to her, the downside would be that again, Lucas would be unlikely to agree. In addition, they would be risking her people finding them there, on foot, and easy targets. He glanced at Daniel, who stood fidgeting nearby, looking from Granger, to Lucas, to the woman on the ground.

Maybe if we waited and watched from hiding and then followed her people back to their camp when they came to rescue her? He shook his head as he debated the pros and cons of that option. *No, it wouldn't work. Lucas is not stake-out material.* He quenched an internal laugh. Lucas was not "anything that requires patience" material—or a long attention span.

The third option, of course, would be to take the woman with them as Kyle wanted. Lucas had taken a liking to the tall, blonde woman for some strange reason, and when he got fixated on something, it was often difficult to shift his attention away from it. Bringing the woman would appease his obsession, but if the people she was with were well organized and armed, they might be ready to fight to get her back. Still, the three women had only been on horseback. She wasn't armed. They could get the UTV and be out of there and halfway back to Seligman before anyone even showed up looking for the woman. Once back at the compound, Granger would have help dealing with Lucas's obsession. Besides, then he would have a chance to question the woman and learn more about her people and her camp.

Finally, Granger nodded to himself and turned to look at Daniel.

"Go get the UTV. We'll start heading in that direction and meet you with the woman."

"Okay. We're taking her with us, then, Ethan?"

Granger glanced at Lucas, standing over the woman, like a wild animal over its prey.

"Yeah, we're taking her with us. Just hurry. We don't want to be caught flat-footed if her people show up to rescue her."

Daniel started off at a jog, ducking under the juniper branches, feet crunching in the dead, dry needles from the trees, and quickly disappeared from sight.

"Well, Kyle," Granger said, turning to face Lucas. "You wanted her, there she is. Pick her up and let's get out of here. You just remember our deal." The tone in his voice made it clear what deal they were talking about.

Without another word, Granger turned and started in the direction Daniel had just taken.

9

"Okay, Mark, hand me up that board." O'Reilly, perched on a ladder, gestured toward a weathered two-by-six laying on the ground next to the front door of the stone camp house built back under an overhang in the cliff wall. Back when the house was first built by miners prospecting for gold, local stone and mud gathered from the nearby creek had been the only readily available building material, and it was assembled using the same techniques as had the Anasazi and Sinagua a millennia before.

Over the intervening years, as the shelter went from miners' camp to ranch camp, the structure had been upgraded to proper mortar, windows, and an actual door. The floor had gone from packed dirt to concrete embedded with flat slabs of sandstone, horse and mule shoes, and here and there a few pottery sherds. No running water, of course, or electricity, and when much of the land surrounding the camp became designated as a wilderness area, making it even more challenging to maintain, the ranch owners decided to assign the pastures to other camps with easier access to the outside world. The camp had always been left lightly provisioned, however, and the buildings maintained in decent repair so that the cowboy assigned to the area would have a place to stay for short periods of time while working those pastures, or should someone need a place to camp out in an emergency.

O'Reilly's father had been the cowboy in charge of the abandoned camp for many years until his death. His family lived at Eagle Camp to the west, but several times during the year, they would visit Hideaway while the pastures were being worked. When O'Reilly bolted from the Laughlin Authorized

Population Zone, he instinctively headed back to this remote part of Arizona, sure that no one else would find him there. Instead, he found Maggie and Mark already in residence, and gradually, over the next few months, Alysa Thalman, Christina Craigson, her brothers, Nick and Ryan, and two-year-old Lindy swelled their numbers, making it necessary to add on to the old house once again.

Ten-year-old Mark picked up the board in question, gripping it gingerly in an attempt to avoid getting slivers in his hands. Even before the influenza pandemic decimated the population, the small camp was a long way from the nearest Home Depot. Now, since the concentration of the survivors, that popular destination wasn't just a long way away, it was entirely out of the question. That meant that any building supplies they used had to be obtained either from items left on the place, from salvaging trips to the closest ranch headquarters or camps, or the old way, though hard manual labor. In this case, there was an ample supply of old lumber sitting in a corner of the barn, probably either left over from building the corrals and alleyways, or extra boards stocked up for repairs. Many of the fences were barbed wire with juniper stays, but the alleys were sawn lumber, and by looking at some of the boards, it appeared that the occasional disgruntled cow had left her mark.

O'Reilly was glad the boards were there, regardless of the original purpose. The original house had been made of stone because that had been the easiest material available. However, he didn't relish the backbreaking effort and time it would take to gather enough additional stone to build Maggie's addition, especially since it wouldn't be tucked back under the overhang like the rest of the house. Because of that, he'd have to build a roof and three of the walls, not just the one facing outward.

Mark shoved the old, gray board up to O'Reilly, who hauled it the rest of the way to the top, laying it across the two walls which were about ten feet apart. Reaching into his pocket, he fished for a couple of nails, old and rusty, and began to hammer the truss into position. His shoulder was healing well, but he was sure that tomorrow it would be reminding him of the recent injury.

Out in the pasture one of the geldings neighed, causing O'Reilly to look up from his work. Ace, O'Reilly's buckskin gelding, stood, head up, looking toward the gate at the north end of the pasture. Surprised, O'Reilly shaded his eyes and peered in the direction Ace indicated. When the girls headed out to collect the prickly pear fruit that morning, he figured they'd be gone for several hours at least. A slight twinge of fear tightened his gut. By his estimate, they shouldn't be back for another hour or more.

Sure enough, down at the far gate, O'Reilly saw horses approaching, and a short surge of adrenaline coursed through him, along with relief. They must have just been extraordinarily lucky on their search. O'Reilly started to bend back to his work, then suddenly straightened and stared back at the gate. Four horses, check. Two riders. He craned his neck, trying to see, sure that he was missing something. No, there were only two riders. Someone was missing.

O'Reilly flung himself toward the dilapidated ladder, rushing down the rungs so quickly his feet barely had time to touch the brittle wood before he was on to the next rung.

"O'Reilly, what's . . ." Mark looked up at O'Reilly, startled green eyes wide.

"Mark, stay here," O'Reilly barked, heading for the pasture at a run, worn boots kicking up gouts of dust. Nick and Ryan emerged from the gaping door of the barn, calling out his name as O'Reilly rushed past. He didn't stop to answer; couldn't understand what they were saying.

O'Reilly's mind was reeling, repeating over and over again those two phrases. *Two riders. Someone was missing. Someone was missing!*

Who?

As O'Reilly reached the pasture gate and fumbled with the chain in his rush to open it, he looked up to see the four horses racing across the pasture toward him. The other horses loose in the pasture spun and joined the melee, rushing toward the barn, tails held high, snorting. As O'Reilly watched, mentally sorting through the scene, his heart fell. Brown hair and black flew in the wind created by the racing equines. Dark, honey blonde hair was missing. Maggie's horse was riderless.

10

A roar filled the air, making Maggie's head throb with the beat. She looked around for the source of the sound, positive that the world was being torn apart at the seams.

"O'Reilly? Christina, Alysa? Mark?" Maggie called out as she walked toward the huge barn that sat in the center of the pasture. The sound of her own voice ratcheted the banging in her head up a few more notches.

"Hey, Mom. Were you looking for me?" Mark emerged from behind a massive pile of firewood, carrying a chainsaw nearly as large as his ten-year-old body. The chain spun at a dizzying rate, making Maggie nauseous while the sight of her son wielding such a machine caused her stomach to clench.

"Mark! What are you doing? Shut it off now!"

Instead of turning off the chainsaw, Mark pressed the trigger and gripped the handle tighter, causing the entire machine to scream at an even higher pitch. Maggie closed her eyes against the pain in her head as the sound seemed to reverberate off the insides of her skull, bouncing around and around until . . .

Consciousness returned gradually. The engine scream of the chainsaw resolved itself into the deeper roar of a UTV. Maggie groaned and opened her eyes only to see a wall of black metal. She was lying on her side, folded into the fetal position in order to fit in the bed of the vehicle and covered by some type of heavy canvas tarp.

Maggie struggled to sit up, only to find her hands and feet tied. The UTV hit a rough part in the trail, and Maggie was thrown back and forth on the metal bed, her head hitting the wall with a thump, wrenching another groan from her throat.

The vehicle rocked violently, then lunged downward, then up, pitching Maggie into the front of the metal box, then slamming her back, and for a moment, she thought she'd be tossed right out onto the ground like so much garbage. The vehicle hesitated, then picked up speed on a smoother surface. Maggie relaxed onto the hard metal floor of the box, momentarily just grateful that the turbulent movement was over. She breathed deeply as the pounding ache in her head subsided from a roar to a moan. The smell of gasoline and exhaust from the UTV fought in her nostrils for dominance over some indefinable musty smell from the tarp.

Her nose started to itch, but with her hands tied behind her back, she couldn't manage to scratch it with any type of success. She tried contorting her face, hoping the movement would alleviate the annoying sensation, but it just intensified.

Seriously, Maggie thought as the UTV sped off to who knows where. She struggled to control the panic that threatened to overwhelm her. *I'm captured by violent men with guns, tied and thrown into a vehicle and hauled away to face who knows what type of fate, and dammit, my nose itches!* Maggie fought to sit up and push the tarp back to see her surroundings. She heard voices, unintelligible over the grumble of the UTV's engine, and suddenly something struck her already aching head.

"Stop wiggling," came a sharp command from the front of the vehicle. "Or I'll help you to be still."

Maggie collapsed back onto the metal surface, torn between wanting to see and not wanting to be hit in the head again. She wasn't sure how much her skull could take, in spite of having what O'Reilly identified as the hardest head in Arizona.

She took several deep breaths and started to cough. A fine dust sifted in through the tarp, making breathing uncomfortable. Her nose, which had stopped itching during the recent action, stubbornly began to remind her of its presence again. Sighing, Maggie tried once more to rub it against the rough canvas tarp covering her, then subsided. She obviously couldn't escape her current position, so the only thing to do was rest and wait for an opening. As far as she was concerned, the battle may be lost, but the war was far from over.

11

O'Reilly jerked the cinch tight, causing his buckskin gelding, Ace, to grunt and swish his tail in protest.

"Tell me again what happened," O'Reilly said. His voice was tight with worry. *Damn, damn, damn, Maggie. What the hell was she thinking wandering off like that without the rifle? I should have gone with them. I should have . . .* O'Reilly shook his head, forcing those thoughts out of his mind. They weren't going to help. He knew that from previous experience. When he'd lost Sarah and Kay-Tee, his wife and ten-year-old daughter, he'd lost himself as well, blaming his absence for their deaths. It was only recently, with the advent of his new family, that he had begun to find himself anew. He knew that if he followed those negative thoughts down the rabbit hole he'd be gone again, and he would be of no use to Maggie or the children.

Alysa spoke up in a soft, shaking voice, repeating for the third time what had happened on the ridge. O'Reilly noticed Alysa look over at Christina, their eyes meeting briefly. Both girls were pale, eyes wide and haunted.

When Alysa faltered in her narrative, describing what had happened immediately following the sound of the shot, Christina took over the story. "We started to go look for Maggie, but then she appeared at the top of the ridge. A man came from behind, grabbed her, then punched her in the head. Two more men showed up, and we ran.

"You'll get her back, right?" Christina's dark blue eyes met O'Reilly's dark brown ones. O'Reilly looked from Christina and Alysa over to where Nick, Ryan and Mark stood, watching him. The faith he saw in Mark's eyes caused another pang to wring his guts.

He hesitated for a moment, torn between wanting to reassure the children, tell them everything would be fine, and not wanting to give false hope. Finally, his throat loosened enough to squeeze out, "Yeah, I'm going to do everything in my power, Christina."

Fifteen minutes later, O'Reilly was navigating the narrow trail leading from the north end of Adobe Canyon up to the eastern rim. The thick brush grabbed at his jeans as he urged his horse into a trot, regardless of the steep trail and copious rock outcroppings. The scabbard where Maggie's rifle rested made a lump under his right stirrup leather, reminding him with every step of the dangers of living out in this empty land.

As he topped the rim, he paused for a moment and scanned the open landscape, first in the direction of the ridge where the girls had reported gathering prickly pear fruit, and then in a sweeping gaze, spreading out in all directions. He stared intently at the horizon, trying to determine if he saw any dust in the air that might indicate movement.

Nothing.

He reined the gelding toward the distant ridge and urged him into a fast trot, weaving in and out of the boulders, low brush, and the ever-present cacti. He continued to scan the horizon the entire time, looking for signs of Maggie or her captors: those mysterious three men the girls saw at the top of the ridge. The ones who hit Maggie and who presumably took her with them.

The thought that she might have been left behind briefly tickled the back of his mind, but he pushed it away. In his experience, there were two types of ghosts out here—and there was no question in his mind that these were ghosts. There were those who simply wanted the chance to live off the land without interference from the government and those who, while they also didn't want interference, had no problem taking what they wanted, either from the government or other people just trying to survive. The first wanted to be modern-day homesteaders, the second modern-day buccaneers. All indications were that these men were the latter type, and if they left Maggie behind on the ridge, it wouldn't be because they had warm, fuzzy feelings and wanted to let her return to her children. It would be because they'd taken what they wanted and thrown away the leftovers.

O'Reilly refused to consider finding Maggie broken on the hillside or having to tell Mark that he was now an orphan. Hopefully, if these men had taken Maggie, O'Reilly had time to catch them and rescue her before she suffered anything more than a clout alongside the head.

Of course, knowing Maggie, her captors might just have more than they'd bargained for when she woke up. A grim smile twisted his lips as he continued to push forward. Maggie might have been squeamish about taking the rifle with her that morning. However, there was no doubt in O'Reilly's mind that if she had the opportunity, she would use anything in her vicinity to attack anyone who stood between her and her family.

O'Reilly smiled grimly. He just hoped that Maggie was able to keep her sarcastic tongue between her teeth. He'd learned from painful experience over the last few months how she could get underneath one's skin, prodding at sensitive areas and digging up deeply buried insecurities. She could wield words like a cudgel, and anyone who crossed her could find themselves flayed and staked out for the ants. Considering the level of emotional and mental maturity displayed by many of the ghosts he'd run into, O'Reilly worried that Maggie's words could get her killed.

As O'Reilly approached the ridge where Maggie and the girls had been picking prickly pear, he slowed Ace from a fast trot to a jog. He scanned the top of the steep rock and cactus-strewn dirt bank, looking for any signs of human presence. O'Reilly knew these men had guns, and he wasn't looking to become their next target, at least not without having them in his sights as well. Reaching the base of the ridge, a pile of light colored material caught his eye. He struggled to remember what Maggie had been wearing that morning as he reined the gelding in that direction. He breathed a sigh of relief when he saw it was the saddlebags the girls had been carrying, bulging with prickly pear fruit.

Turning, he urged Ace upward, leaning forward into the horse's surging bounds as the animal's muscular haunches pushed it up the steep side of the bank. Topping out near a huge juniper, O'Reilly reined the buckskin to a stop and looked around, eyes sharp, looking for any sign of the men or of Maggie. He swung his leg over the horse's back and stepped to the ground. As he peered intently at the dry soil and broken stones, he moved slowly along the rim, leading Ace behind, looking for the place where the girls had last seen Maggie.

It didn't take long before O'Reilly saw disturbed ground, a tangle of footprints and a large area where the bunch grass was flattened and the cracks in the parched earth had been smoothed out, presumably by Maggie's unconscious body after being attacked. He cast his gaze around the area. No blood. That was good.

O'Reilly searched further out from the center of the disturbance. He located the flour sacks Maggie had brought, one partially filled with juniper berries, but he left them in place. Maggie was more important than the juniper berries at this point.

After a few minutes, he was able to pick out four sets of prints converging on the edge of the rim. One smaller set, most likely Maggie's, and three larger sets of prints, although one of those sets seemed to belong to a smaller man or boy, lighter at any rate. At a slightly different trajectory, three sets of prints left, the smaller man at a run, the toe digging into the soft ground, and the other two walking.

O'Reilly's jaw clenched as he studied the prints heading off to the northeast. Three sets of prints leaving, yet none of Maggie's smaller prints to be seen, meant she was being carried, probably because she'd still been unconscious at the time of departure. Having carried a few people in his time with the sheriff's department, he was sure that if Maggie were capable of moving under her own power, her captors would not have gone to the effort of carrying her. It just wasn't as easy as the movies made it look.

The good news, as far as O'Reilly was concerned, was that if they were carrying Maggie, they would be moving slower than if they were traveling unencumbered. Even though they had a head start on him, he had a reasonable chance of catching them before they got too far on foot. He stepped onto the buckskin gelding and started following the tracks.

At the start, the trail the men left was relatively easy to follow. It was obvious that the three hadn't been concerned about pursuit and made no effort to hide their footprints. Unfortunately, after a short distance, the trail led out of the thick cluster of junipers and into a wide, grassy meadow filled with black malapai rock. O'Reilly's progress slowed as he had to study the ground more closely, looking for subtle signs of human passage versus that of an elk or a cow; a rock shifted from its bed, the edge of a heel print. Several times he had to stop and cast in a circle to pick up the trail again. He chafed at the delay, but there was no help for it.

Finally, O'Reilly thought, as he emerged from the clearing and onto land more conducive to tracking. Sure enough, the three sets of prints continued to move away to the northeast. As O'Reilly urged Ace to a faster pace, a noise penetrated his concentration. He reined the gelding to a stop and sat listening intently. A high-pitched whine reached his ears, but it took him a moment to identify the cause. When he did, his stomach clenched into a knot.

Jamming his spurs into Ace's sides, O'Reilly took off at a gallop heading in the direction of the sound. He no longer worried about following the tracks. He didn't need to. It would be too much of a coincidence if there were more than one group of strangers wandering around this part of Arizona.

O'Reilly urged Ace even faster as he heard the whine begin to retreat and grow fainter — a whine that belonged, unless O'Reilly totally missed his guess, to a UTV. He burst out of a thick clump of juniper into another small clearing and pulled Ace to a stop. In front of him, a two-rut track trailed off through the trees. He could hear the UTV in the distance, growing fainter at a rapid rate. He wasn't as familiar with this part of the country as he was with the pasture lands down south of Hideaway, but he knew there were many small ranch and forest service roads winding their way through the areas that weren't designated wilderness. O'Reilly's heart sank as his hopes of a quick rescue disappeared with the sound of the UTV.

Damn, Damn, Damn, O'Reilly thought. His initial impulse was to head out after the UTV. He had the children to think about, however, and he hadn't packed supplies for a prolonged search. As much as he hated to admit it, he had to go back to the canyon empty-handed, inform the kids, and pick up water and supplies.

He just hoped that the time it took wouldn't be too much time for Maggie.

With one last look toward the primitive track, O'Reilly reined his gelding back in the direction from which he came and pushed him into a lope.

12

The roar of the UTV engine dropped from a scream to a grumble, and the machine lurched and turned. Maggie, who had lapsed into a semi-doze by the rocking of the vehicle, jerked back to awareness.

Quickly she ran through a mental checklist. The headache had dropped from slamming gong level to pounding nails. She tried moving her head and found that her neck apparently still attached it to her shoulders, although said shoulders were cramped from lying in the bed of the UTV with her hands tied. Hoping not to draw the attention of her captors, she slowly tried rolling her shoulders and flexing her muscles to ease the cramps. She didn't know what was about to happen, but she wanted to be ready.

Change wasn't long in happening. The UTV proceeded more slowly for fifteen or twenty minutes, Maggie wasn't sure, rocking and then surging over a rougher road, climbing, causing her to slide to the back of the box, leveling out, then crunched to a stop and the motor died. Maggie experienced a temporary vacuum of sound caused by the cessation of the engine's roar. As the ringing in her ears gradually faded, Maggie heard footsteps on the gravel surface and voices approaching the UTV.

Abruptly the tarp covering her was yanked back. Maggie squeezed her eyes shut in the sudden blinding sunlight.

"Who is she?" Maggie heard a voice filled with curiosity. She cautiously opened her eyes, squinting to allow her vision to adjust to the bright light. Standing by the box of the UTV was an adolescent boy a few years older than Mark. He didn't look threatening, and Maggie felt her lips quirk into a slight reassuring smile at the concerned look on the child's face. It was a short-lived smile, squashed flat when she saw the face of the figure who was standing behind the boy. The pale blue eyes of the man who had knocked her unconscious met her own green ones, causing a frisson of fear to tickle its way down her spine, followed by the adrenaline rush of absolute fury.

"What the hell do you think you're doing? Let me go!" Maggie struggled to sit, her tied wrists hindering her progress. From behind her, a hand grabbed her shoulder and pushed her into a sitting position in the bed of the UTV.

"Hold still," a voice commanded, and she could feel yanking at the rope securing her arms. Suddenly freed, she looked around to see the scar-faced man folding a pocket knife. Briefly, her gaze met his, then she lifted her eyes to take in her new surroundings, rubbing her wrists and trying to force feeling back into her hands.

"Where are we? Who are you people?" Maggie demanded, continuing to cast her eyes around the compound, noting the tiny cabin, old trailers and RVs, tan metal pole barn and various other small sheds that dotted the rocky ground. She realized she could see between the trunks of the surrounding juniper, piñon and white pines and off into the distance. Far off over the mountains, she saw a plume of smoke from what must be a forest fire. They were up on a mountain or a tall hill, and she could see for miles. Her heart sank. She knew of no landscape like this close to Hideaway.

More people were coming from different directions, most looking curiously at the small group surrounding the UTV. A few, however, looked worried or downright angry.

Maggie's eyes returned to the scar-faced man who was still standing next to the vehicle, studying her intently.

"I asked who the hell you were, and why you attacked me," Maggie repeated, ignoring the fact that no one had yet answered the first of her questions. Where was she? "And what are you going to do with me?"

The bearded man with the pale blue eyes was the first to answer. "You ask too many questions, bi . . ."

"Lucas! Cut it out," the scar-faced man snapped. The man whom Maggie had dubbed blue-eyes surprisingly halted mid-profanity, a scowl on his face. His eyes met those of the other man, and a staring contest ensued. Finally, blue-eyes, the one scar-face called Lucas, broke eye contact and turned his head, grumbling something under his breath that Maggie couldn't quite make out.

"My name is Ethan Granger," came the voice from her right, causing her to look back at the scar-faced man. "This is my group, and this is our headquarters."

Maggie looked around at the others who had arrived at the side of the UTV. A flurry of questions and comments floated around, pelting so fast that she couldn't quite make out who was doing the talking. She noticed that the boy who had first spoken was now standing beside the young man who'd accompanied Granger and Lucas when she first ran into them. The band appeared to be mainly men, although a few women were scattered among the group of fifteen or so. A tall, dark-haired woman had moved over to stand next to Lucas with what appeared to be a possessive air, staring at Maggie like she was some worm dug out of a rotten apple.

Great, she can have him, Maggie thought as she turned her attention back to Granger and looked him in the eye. *When in doubt,* she thought, *act like you're not intimidated and bluff like hell.*

"Okay Mr. Granger, obviously you have me at a bit of a disadvantage. I would like you to release me now and let me go about my business. My people will be expecting me, and they won't be happy that I've been detained." Her chin lifted in a defiant manner, and she kept her eyes on his, willing him to concede and let her go. The thought that she had no idea where she was or how to get home crossed her mind, but she refused to let it take root.

A wry smile creased Granger's face, the scar pulling the expression to the side. "I'm sorry, ma'am, but I don't think that's going to happen right now. Why don't you answer some questions for me and then maybe we'll talk about letting you go."

Maggie heard a shuffling behind her and looked over her shoulder to see Lucas, scowl firmly in place, leaning in toward the UTV, the black haired woman grabbing at his arm.

"Dammit, Granger! I said she's mine," Lucas snarled to the obvious surprise of the woman, who let go of his arm like it was on fire and took a step back.

"Shut up, Lucas!" Granger snapped.

It was as clear as the sky above that the discord between Granger and Lucas was having a negative effect on the remainder of the group. Several people looked down or away, and a couple began to sidle out of the crowd. Most seemed uneasy, and Maggie had the suspicion that the situation between these two men was a boiling pot ready to explode. If so, she had the uncomfortable creeping feeling that she was liable to get scalded in the process.

Deciding that the best defense was a good offense, Maggie started to push herself to her knees. "Listen, gentlemen, this is all been entertaining, but I've got to pee, so let me out of this thing, show me the bathroom, and then we can discuss how you're going to let me go so I can get back to my family."

The standoff between the two men shattered into a million pieces as Granger choked on a laugh. He hesitated for a moment, then stepped forward to help Maggie down from the UTV. Looking over her shoulder, she could see Lucas continue to watch her with an intensity that felt as though it was sending darts through her body. She wasn't happy with anyone here, but she sure as hell felt safer with Granger than she did with Lucas, and she allowed him to take her arm.

The slight, warm, fuzzy feeling that Maggie had developed toward Granger dissolved in a puff of smoke when he waved the dark-haired woman over.

"Linda, will you please take our guest to the outhouse. Do not take your eyes off her for any reason."

"You bet, Granger." Linda took Maggie's arm in a grip that threatened to cut off the blood supply, and steered her toward a small shed off behind the pole barn.

13

"**W**e've determined that the band of ghosts who hit the supply convoy two weeks ago is located about eight or nine miles south of Interstate 40, in the broken land between County Road 5 and Fort Rock Road, northwest of the Juniper Mesa Wilderness."

Dan Clements stood at the front of one of the conference rooms in the hotel turned Enforcer Headquarters. He faced the group of sixteen exorcism team members, using a laser pointer to indicate the area on a large chart where analysts believed the group of ghosts to be holed up—a small, off-the-grid property back in the mountains and valleys south of I-40.

Rickards studied the topographical map of the area, noting the steep inclines and narrow canyons surrounding and leading to the group's encampment. *If they are any kind of organized*, he thought, *they'll have sentries posted, and it won't be easy sneaking up on them. They have the high ground.*

The other members of the team must have been thinking the same thing as a voice spoke up from the other side of the room—a tall, gangly man whose name Rickards couldn't remember.

"How are we supposed to get in there without them seeing or hearing us coming?"

"The main subdivision road comes in from the northwest. However, there are a lot of interconnecting forest roads and UTV trails running through this area. The land is also heavily forested with juniper and pine, which can both help and hurt us." Clements made a circular motion with his laser pointer, the red dot inscribing a rough circle that included most of the land south of I-40 between County Road 5 and Willow Springs Road, dropping down past Burro Creek and Adobe canyons to the south.

Rickards' jaw tightened when he saw the jagged line that slashed across Adobe Canyon. He thought of the lush green meadow and the caves that riddled the yellow, red and gray stained walls of the canyon — the last place he had seen James O'Reilly. Once again, he wondered if O'Reilly had survived his injuries. Did Maggie Langton, the woman whom O'Reilly had taken up with, stay there after Rickards and the Enforcers left, or did she take the children and move to a different hidden location now that Rickards knew where they had been holed up? Questions that he'd asked himself every day since returning from the remote canyon. The one thing he was positive of was that even if O'Reilly had survived the confrontation in the caves, he would have never joined up with the ghosts who had attacked the supply convoy. O'Reilly, the deserter, the renegade cowboy, might not agree with the APZs, but he wouldn't do anything to hurt the people living there. Rickards would stake his life on that.

"We will split the group and half will come in from this direction here." Clements continued, indicating a road leading in from the west. "The remainder will come in from the south. It's a longer, rougher route, but it's probably the one they'll use if they try to escape rather than fight. It's a small forest service road, but it has tributaries that lead back out to I-40 as well as other branches which lead farther down into the ranch lands north of Prescott. We want to make sure they don't make it to those roads. That land is broken by deep canyons and tall mountains and in many places the junipers are so thick that you couldn't see an elephant if it was fifteen feet away and playing a trombone. Because of that, it would be very hard to pinpoint the fugitives' location out there, even with the help of the seekers."

Rickards could see many heads bobbing up and down in agreement and heard the low hum of murmuring between members of the team. He looked around the room, noting the men's body language. Several were leaning back in their chairs, relaxed, with their eyes half closed, although they seemed to be paying attention to Clements. The others reminded Rickards of pit bulls, leaning forward into their collars, ready to fight. It took special men, or women for that matter, although the Laughlin APZ's exorcism teams had no female officers, to become part of this elite group. Especially now that the central control had handed down the mandate that no one older than five to eight be brought back to the APZs. The remainder were to be considered enemy combatants—terrorists—and were to be terminated since they were unlikely to integrate successfully into the communities, and might spread dissension among the residents if brought in.

If Rickards was honest with himself, talking with some of the members of this team left him with a bone deep chill at times. Some had joined the Enforcers following the influenza pandemic with a deep desire to help their fellow survivors. Many of them were honest, upstanding men and women. There were others, however, who seemed to have a darkness deep inside, and many of these men had gravitated toward the exorcism teams. From talking to the Enforcer heads at other APZs, he knew they were experiencing the same thing—some of these people thrived in the violent, bloody missions of the exorcism teams, but Rickards always felt like he was keeping a tiger on a leash of thread when dealing with them.

Rickards didn't usually sit in on the exorcism teams' meetings, although they technically fell under his purview. He trusted his men and preferred to allow them to handle their business as they saw fit. However, the attack on the convoy two weeks ago had been a hard blow to the APZ.

Two drivers had died, all of the supplies they were transporting had been destroyed, including a tanker of fuel that the APZ desperately needed, and a wildfire larger than any Rickards had ever seen had swept across the land north of I-40, destroying everything in its path. In fact, the fire was still burning, although much of it had moved into the grasslands, slowing its forward movement. A recent storm had slowed things even more, but it appeared that small fingers of flame might not burn themselves out until they reached the Grand Canyon.

True, Rickards acknowledged to himself, the houses and towns in that area would have been scheduled for destruction in the near future, but there were supplies that could have been harvested from them first if the band of ghosts, or others, hadn't looted them already.

When Rickards initially heard about the attack on the supply trucks and the subsequent fire, he had to admit to himself that he hoped that the band of ghosts responsible for the attack had been caught in the conflagration. As far as he was concerned, that would have solved a number of problems.

Unfortunately for him, the seekers, those spherical drones that the Enforcers used for security, couldn't find any sign that the group had fallen victim to their own lawlessness. Then, just a few days ago, a remote seeker patrolling in the area had picked up a flash of light from a location where no light reflection had been on other passes. Closer examination of the video showed the glint had come from some chrome on an old, red quad parked next to a windmill in an open pasture. It was also possible to make out the tire tracks behind the vehicle, indicating that it had arrived in that location not long before. Tire tracks might last a long time in Arizona's dry season, but the recent storm that had helped slow down the fire would have also eradicated any tracks older than a week.

A study of satellite photos from before the pandemic showed the presence of several secluded homes in the area, but only one seemed to fit the requirements necessary for a group the size that Clements' team estimated this band to be. It was nestled on a plateau near the top of some low, rough mountains, thickly blanketed with pine and juniper. The satellite had barely picked up several trailers or RVs and a large steel building of some type, as well as an extensive bank of solar panels sitting out in an open area on the south side of the mountain, clear of encroaching trees.

When Clements had first come to Rickards to notify him that the tech department thought they'd narrowed down the location of the band of ghosts which had attacked the convoy, the two of them had debated the benefits of trying to send a seeker out for more accurate surveillance. They had decided against it since the small drones carried with them an unmistakable whine, and there was a risk of it notifying the fugitives that they'd been found. If spooked, the band could make a run for it into the ranch land south of their hideout. If that were to happen, it would require a greater allocation of manpower to track them down than the Enforcers had readily available and was more likely to result in a firefight. The Enforcers were already undermanned and couldn't afford the losses that might result from such a battle.

Rickards also wanted to make sure that the Enforcers stayed as far away as possible from that hidden meadow deep in Adobe Canyon northwest of Prescott. If it became known that Rickards had walked away from Langton and her band of children, leaving them alive, his career would be over, if not his life.

"We'll head out tomorrow morning," Clements continued, pulling Rickards mentally back to the meeting. "We'll be taking eight four-wheel-drive jeeps and the small refueling truck. Each jeep should carry two five-gallon jerrycans of gasoline. We'll park the tanker off Fort Rock Road, in a pole barn near the highway. I don't think we dare go any closer by vehicle using the main roads in case the band has lookouts posted to notify them of convoys traveling toward Seligman. They must have some sort of alert system. Their attacks have been too well thought out and coordinated, even if this is the first that has done real damage." Clements indicated the small ranch road on the map.

"Once there, we will head farther into the ranch land using the jeeps, following Fort Rock Road. We will split into two groups here." He indicated a point where two forest roads diverged, then traced a line heading east. "Alpha team will leave their vehicles here." Another red dot on the map followed a different route, "And Beta team will leave their vehicles here. We will move on foot from those locations. It will take longer, but we will have a greater chance of taking the band by surprise. Communication will be key. Make sure the radios are charged and turned to channel 17. Keep chatter to a minimum. We don't know if they have access to radios, but they might. They've been tracking our supply trucks somehow. There is a chance we'll lose the radios in the hills, so we'll also take cell and satellite phones and hope that something works. Check your signal constantly. Several men will stay with the vehicles in case the fugitives make a run for it. That way those men can get some jeeps up to the front line quickly. If we do this the right way, though, we'll hit the band at sunrise or before and run over them like a tsunami."

"This is the desert, Clements," a voice called from somewhere in the group of men, "we'll run them over like a haboob!"

A roar of approval erupted from Clements' audience at the mention of the towering dust storms that rolled through the Phoenix Metro area every monsoon season, dropping the visibility to within a few feet and bringing much of the valley to a standstill until the air started to clear. At least it had when Phoenix was one of the most populated metropolitan areas in the United States. From what he heard, the clouds of choking dust still rolled through the valley last summer, but they didn't have the same widespread impact on the Phoenix area as they had on the sprawling city before it became an APZ. Limited visibility caused little disruption when no one was going anywhere.

"All right, Ruiz. A haboob it is." Clements laughed, and the gathered men whooped and whistled and stomped their feet.

Rickards imagined that within a few years, as the bare agricultural land between Tucson and Phoenix started to be overcome with weeds, the haboobs would dissipate, new roots holding the topsoil down. He remembered that during the first months of the pandemic, the news reported a drastic reduction in air pollution as people had sheltered in place in an attempt to avoid the influenza. The confinement of the population was good for the air but didn't work as well for many of the people who had brought the virus into isolation with them or, having been jaded by past pandemic scares, had ignored the warnings this time until it was too late. Now, he imagined, with the drastic reduction in the Earth's population, pollution was probably diminishing all over the world, and it could be a very long time until it returned to pre-pandemic levels—if it ever did. He thought briefly of the file hidden in his office.

Reduction of Population.

Was that what the governments of the world wanted? Or at least planned to take advantage of? Solving the planet's pollution problem by eliminating the polluters? His mind veered away from that thought.

The noise was deafening, again pulling Rickards back out of his thoughts. He had to fight down an internal shiver. They were heading out tomorrow to kill their own countrymen, but it sounded like they were gearing up for a football game. His eyes narrowed as he ruthlessly suppressed a feeling of distaste, the bile rising in his throat, threatening to overwhelm him. O'Reilly's face flashed into his mind. O'Reilly had recognized the direction the exorcism teams and their missions were taking, and he ran. Would Rickards himself eventually do the same?

We've gotten used to seeing our neighbors as enemies during the last decade or so. Can we survive that type of conflict? he wondered.

He thought about Ludeman and his group. Rickards had heard through the grapevine that the man was still stirring up feelings of discontent among other members of the APZ. His fists clenched in his lap, knuckles popping with the strain. This whole tangled mess was moving toward an explosion like a herd of stampeding bison, and he had a feeling it would be just as difficult to stop.

Clements raised his hands, calling for the group to settle down. Gradually the men silenced, avid eyes focused on the tall, thin man standing at the front of the room.

"We meet tomorrow morning at four, and plan to head out by four-thirty. That's zero four hundred to you military types," Clements added to laughter from his audience. "If we do this right, we should be back in two days, but bring gear for a week just in case. Are there any questions?"

No one spoke up, and after a short wait, Clements dismissed the men. The noise rose as the members of the team started talking among themselves while they moved out of the room. Clements began to fold the large map, stopping briefly to talk to several of the men who approached him.

The men laughed, and Clements clapped the nearest one on the shoulder as they turned and headed out of the conference room door.

Once they were alone, Rickards approached.

"Good job with the meeting, Dan," Rickards said. He put out his hand to the man.

Clements put the map on the table and took Rickards' hand, giving it a firm shake. "Thanks, Seth. Glad you could sit in on the briefing. They're a good team. We'll nail these guys to the wall when we catch them, don't you worry."

He radiated the confidence and determination that had made him a natural leader. Rickards knew that his exorcism team ran much more smoothly than many of the similar teams in other APZs, and that was in large part due to the strength of

Dan Clements' ability to rein in some of the more aggressive tendencies of his subordinates. Clements had chosen each member personally, and with the exception of James O'Reilly, they worked smoothly together.

"I'm sure of it," Rickards said, dropping Clements' hand and stepping back. "If you don't mind, I think I'll be going along on the mission."

Clements' light brown eyes widened in surprise, then he frowned as he studied Rickards. "Are you thinking I can't handle the operation, Captain?" There was a new tension in the man's voice that set off warning bells in Rickards' mind.

He noted the shift in Clements' body language. He stood straighter, making the most of his over six-foot height compared to Rickards' five-ten, and his shoulders were thrown back. He reminded Rickards of one of those lizards that puffed its body out to make itself look larger to potential enemies.

Rickards noted that Clements had addressed him by rank instead of using his first name as the team leader had earlier and knew he was treading on thin ice. Rickards was in charge of the APZ, and as such, was Clements' superior and had the right to do what he proposed, but he also didn't want to alienate the man.

"No, no, no, Dan. You're the best at this job. You run the strongest exorcism team in all the APZs." Rickards noticed a wave of conflicting emotions wash through Clements' eyes—pride, suspicion, a touch of anger.

"It's just that. . . uh. . . I knew one of the convoy drivers personally. We grew up together," the lie flowed strangely off Rickards' tongue. He wasn't accustomed to telling anything but the truth, and he wondered for a moment if Clements would see through his words to the deception underneath. One look, though, and Rickards could tell that the team leader was buying into the vengeance scenario.

"Ah," Clements said in understanding tones, and some of the tension melted out of his body. He ran a bony hand through his thinning brown hair. "You're welcome to come with us then. You can work with Alpha team. Just remember, I'm calling the shots. We can't have two dogs trying to wag the same tail." Clements chuckled, nodding vigorously, but Rickards could still hear a hint of doubt.

"Absolutely," Rickards affirmed. "They're your team. I just hope to get a shot at the bastard who took out. . . uh. . . my friend," he stammered, stumbling over the driver's name, which he didn't know, having never met the man before in his life and not remembering from the report. In the post-pandemic era, the odds of any two people who had grown up together both still surviving were infinitesimally small—something which fortunately hadn't occurred to Clements, Rickards thought.

"We'll see you tomorrow morning then at four. I hope you remember how to pack a go bag." Clements laughed at his own joke, then put out his hand once again to Rickards.

"I think I can figure it out." Rickards said in gruff tones and gave Clements a smile that he hoped didn't look as artificial as it felt. He took the team leader's hand and gave it two vigorous shakes, then turned and strode across the conference room toward the marked exit, eager to be away before the man realized he was being deceived. Rickards was walking so quickly when he hit the double doors that they flew open and slammed into the walls with a bang.

As the large doors swung shut behind him, Rickards jerked to a stop and stood, looking around the lobby of the hotel the Enforcers used as their home base. The soft red-browns of the saltillo tile and warm earthy tones of the walls and furniture failed to soothe him. His jaw clenched, and he felt an overwhelming urge to punch something . . . or someone. He glanced back at the doors to the conference room, half expecting Dan Clements to burst through and demand to know what was going on. When the doors remained closed, Rickards released a pent-up breath with a sigh. He hoped that Clements was so involved in contemplating the implementation of his plan that he spared little thought to Rickards' abrupt departure, chalking it up to the captain having places to go, people to see, an APZ to run.

Rickards walked slowly across the expansive lobby of the hotel, heading for his office and the ever-decreasing level of antacid in the bottle sitting on his desk. He reminded himself that he needed to find out if there were any additional bottles of the liquid available in the heavily guarded supply stores. He moved almost mindlessly; his thoughts drawn back into the mental whirlpool that had been plaguing him for weeks. One idea kept swirling to the surface. He had to keep the exorcism team away from O'Reilly's canyon.

14

Ace was lathered and blowing hard when O'Reilly finally arrived back at the gate into the home meadow. In spite of the loose footing and steepness of the trail that led into the canyon, he had pushed the horse relentlessly forward, winding between the cacti and boulders. Loose rocks rolled out from under the animal's hooves, making the hillside sound like a giant-sized pinball machine. Several times, as the footing became more tenuous, the gelding slowed, dropped his head and picked his way with care. The delay stretched O'Reilly's nerves to the breaking point, but he realized that pushing the horse too quickly could wind up with them both landing in a heap at the bottom of the trail. He couldn't afford to lame Ace or himself if he had any hope of rescuing Maggie.

Once on the narrow track which traced the rock-strewn floor of the canyon, O'Reilly urged Ace back into a long trot and arrived at the home pasture within a few minutes. The twisted loop of smooth wire that held the gate shut fought him for a moment, sticking on the rough juniper fence post, and he felt his frustration level rise. Finally, the galvanized steel strands pulled loose and slipped over the top of the post. He started to throw the length of wire and juniper stays back out of the way to let the horse through. Then he stopped himself. He knew from long experience that a gate opened in that way tended to tangle, and it would take him even longer to get it straightened out and shut again. He contemplated leaving it open since he would be heading back out in short order. However, life on the ranch had taught him that cows had a radar system built into their brains that allowed them to target open gates and downed fences within seconds, and he couldn't afford the time it would take to chase down the escaped livestock.

He stepped back, pulling the end post of the gate with him. He chucked Ace's reins and the gelding stepped through the gap O'Reilly had created, then turned and faced his rider, leaving the opening clear so that O'Reilly could shut the gate once again. Cattle escape route thereby barred, O'Reilly remounted and pushed Ace into a gallop across the flat, grassy surface, reining toward the gate near the barn. He could see the children running from different locations around the camp—the garden, the barn, the stone house tucked under the cliff—all making beelines toward the same gap in the fence he was targeting. He felt a knot grow in his chest, knowing that the news he was bringing them was not the kind they wanted to hear.

Mark and the two Australian Shepherds, Gypsy and Jack, were the first to reach the large wooden gate next to the barn, running up just as O'Reilly reined to a stop. Mark pulled the heavy, wooden gate open wide enough for O'Reilly to ride through. Mark's green eyes, so much like his mother's, met and held O'Reilly's, fear clearly written across his ten-year-old features.

"O'Reilly, where's Mom?" burst out of the boy in a high, thin voice, as though he didn't have enough air in his lungs to make the words audible. "Didn't you find her?"

O'Reilly stepped off the gelding and looked up to see the remainder of the children converging on his location. He could see the same questions and fear that Mark voiced moments before on each of their faces.

"Let me tie up Ace, and we'll talk. I'd rather tell everyone at once, instead of repeating the story over and over." O'Reilly led the buckskin over to the hitching rail in front of the barn and fitted the rope halter he'd left hanging there on the gelding's head.

"Do you want me to unsaddle him," Mark asked, his voice a little stronger than before, although it still held a tremor that let O'Reilly know that the boy was fighting his emotions and trying to remain calm.

For the briefest of moments O'Reilly considered switching horses. He would need two this time, and Ace had already had a hard ride out and back, even though it hadn't been a long trip in terms of miles. Then O'Reilly shook his head. Maggie's horses, and those that Alysa, Christina and her brothers had brought, had started to acclimate to a barefoot existence, but he didn't want to rely on their chances of staying sound if he had to ride long distances or travel through rocky land worse than that around the camp.

He would take Ace and the gentlest of the other geldings he'd brought with him when he'd first arrived at Hideaway. None of those horses were exactly dude broke, but Maggie's riding skills had progressed, and he hoped he'd take the fresh out of the gelding before he found Maggie and she needed to mount. The thought of her being bucked off and hitting the ground in a cloud of dust *after* being kidnapped and beaten flashed through his mind, and for a moment he reconsidered. He could throw shoes back on Hank, Maggie's gelding, in short order. It didn't have to be a neat job. They just had to stay on. Then he discarded the idea. He didn't want to waste even that time, and Hank had always been a "backyard" horse, born and raised in a pen and always shod and only used for the show ring or a few hours out on the trails. He was adapting and hardening up, but Ace and O'Reilly's other horses had been barefoot when pulled out of a rocky ranch pasture north of Laughlin and seldom took a sore-footed step.

"No," he told the boy. "I'll be heading straight back out. I'm going to need Jimmy as well," he said, referring to a blaze-faced bay roan with an ugly head and a sensible disposition. "Wait, though, until I fill you guys in on what's happening."

By this time, all the children were gathered around the buckskin gelding. Only Lindy seemed unconcerned. She flopped down into the dust and started playing with Gypsy's ruff as the dog—the little girl's self-proclaimed guardian—stood over her, tongue lolling.

O'Reilly looked at Christina, then Alysa, and finally he met Mark's wide, green eyes staring out of his white face. "I was able to find the tracks of the men who attacked your mother," he said, addressing his remarks to the boy. "I followed them to where they had a UTV, but they got away before I was able to catch them." The last words felt as though they'd been torn out of his throat, dropping his normally raspy voice to a rough growl, sounding like a garbage disposal on the fritz. O'Reilly knew he probably looked calm to the children. However, inside he felt a churning well of anger, desperation and fear—the same mix of feelings that had nearly overwhelmed him after Sarah and Kay-Tee had been killed by the drunk, wrong way driver that terrible New Year's Eve. Once again, he ruthlessly forced that black well of emotion down, clamping a lid on the pit.

"I know they headed north, and I'm going after them. It's just going to take a little longer than I'd originally planned." He fought to maintain the professional tone he'd used as a sheriff's deputy when talking to distraught family members. He needed to keep the children calm.

"I'll be heading out within an hour. I just came back to get an extra horse, some supplies and to let you know what's going on. You're going to have to make do for a few days on your own." O'Reilly shook his head slowly. This was a decision that had plagued him all the way back to Hideaway. In order to save Maggie, he had to leave the kids alone, an idea that clawed at his guts like a mountain lion disemboweling a deer. If something happened to him and he wasn't able to return, the kids would be left completely on their own and, other than Alysa, none of them even remotely had the skills to try and survive out here on their own. He felt squeezed between the proverbial rock and hard place—abandon Maggie and protect the kids or go after Maggie and potentially leave the kids without protection.

"I want to come with you," Mark said, eyes on O'Reilly's face. Tension radiated from his small body, and O'Reilly was reminded forcibly of those moments in the caves when Mark had taken it upon himself to try to save his family because of an overwhelming feeling of guilt and responsibility.

O'Reilly stepped forward and laid a hand on Mark's shoulder. He could feel faint tremors shaking the boy, and O'Reilly squeezed softly, trying to provide some level of consolation no matter how thin.

"Not this time, Mark. I don't know what I'm riding into, but I sure don't need to be rescuing two people and I've got to move fast. The more people we have, the slower we'll be moving, and the more likely it is we'll be discovered. I don't think that these men can have gone too far—probably not more than thirty or forty miles, but even that's going to take me a day or more, and I don't know how easy they will be to find."

O'Reilly lifted his head and looked at the other children. "Mark, I need you, Ryan and Nick to take Ace down for water. Catch Jimmy and get him saddled. Then find my saddlebags. I'm going to have to take enough food for both your mom and me for several days. I need my bedroll and grab one of the sleeping bags. Several canteens as well." He paused for a second, thinking, "and make up a first aid kit. Some bandages and iodine, things like that, just in case."

O'Reilly made a quick mental note to check what the boys packed. Even though Mark, Nick and Ryan had been forced to grow up much more quickly than they would have prior to the pandemic, they were still young boys and who knew what they would consider appropriate food or supplies for a rescue mission. At least their current lifestyle meant there wasn't much around that could be considered "junk food." He recalled a story he'd read that mentioned a man who headed off on the Iditarod dogsled race with nothing but a bag of candy bars, and O'Reilly tried to remember if there was anything like that at the camp that might wind up filling the saddlebags. Nothing that he could think of. Their diets had been simple by necessity. Still, he'd better check.

The boys given tasks to keep them busy for a little while, he turned to the girls.

"Christina and Alysa, come with me for a moment," O'Reilly started for the house without waiting to see if they were following. He could hear them coming behind but didn't turn back.

Once inside the house, O'Reilly turned and studied the two fourteen-year-old girls. Lindy was cradled in Alysa's arms, and she struggled to get down. Alysa stooped and placed the toddler on the floor, where she immediately sped off, looking for a doll Maggie had made out of one of O'Reilly's old shirts—the one shredded when O'Reilly had been trapped in the cave-in. A pang stabbed him once again. Each of these children, with the exception of Mark, was an orphan, and Maggie had stepped into the role of their surrogate mother and he, their father.

Again, the doubts about leaving the children alone flooded over him.

"While I'm gone, you girls are going to be in charge and I'm going to be relying on you to keep things going around here. You'll need to keep the younger children calm and everything operating as close to normal as possible."

Christina and Alysa nodded in unison.

"We'll be fine," Christina said, and O'Reilly could see the determination in her deep blue eyes and the set of her chin.

"I don't like leaving you alone here, but I don't see another choice. I . . .," O'Reilly started.

"We've been on our own before," Alysa pointed out in her soft voice, but a hint of steel surprised the man. "We came all the way from Laughlin by ourselves."

O'Reilly knew well that it was solely due to Alysa that the group of children had made it to Wikieup without mishap. She'd been raised out on the ranches of Arizona and Nevada, her mother, a member of the Navajo Nation, had been raised on a sheep camp on the big reservation in the four corners area, and her father, an Apache cowboy, had been raised in the wilds of the White Mountains. She had learned much about living off the land from them. Christina may have masterminded the plan that got the children out of the APZ, but it was Alysa's knowledge of the land and horses that got them through the Hualapai Mountains and to Wikieup.

"I know, Alysa. If it weren't for that, I don't know what I would do right now. Still, there are some things we need to go over."

O'Reilly walked to the door that hid the room where Maggie and Lindy slept and stepped into the dark chamber. Due to its construction under the overhang of a cliff, the interior rooms of the house had no windows, and without a flashlight or lantern, the innermost rooms of the house were as dark as the depths of a cave. Still, O'Reilly knew exactly where he was going, and he strode across the small chamber to a set of shelves that Maggie used to store clothes and other items. He reached above his head for the upper shelf and ran his hand over the rough lumber. Finding what he wanted, he turned and headed back to the front room to where the girls waited with confused looks on their faces.

"You remember Maggie telling us about her discussion with Rickards, right? Well, when he left, he dropped this phone on me." O'Reilly held up the small cell phone for the girls to see—a brand common in stores prior to the pandemic. The screen was cracked, and looking at it, O'Reilly could forgive the kids for thinking it was a piece of junk.

"You mean he lost it—dropped it by accident?" Christina said, her eyes narrowing in suspicion. Christina had interacted with Rickards more than anyone here other than O'Reilly himself, and she had good reason to distrust the man.

"No." O'Reilly was glad to hear that his voice was calm and in control. "He left it with Maggie and told her that if she ever needed anything she was to send him a message." He powered on the phone and hit the icon for the contacts. Scrolling through, he found the one he wanted and extended the phone out to the girl, waiting for her to take it from his hand.

"If I'm not back in two weeks, you need to contact Captain Rickards," O'Reilly said, looking at Christina and Alysa, his brown eyes intense. His voice had the solidity of the cliff walls that surrounded the home pasture, leaving no room for argument.

Predictably, Christina argued anyway.

"We're not going back to an APZ, O'Reilly. You know they won't let us come back." Christina's narrowed eyes met O'Reilly's with unflinching directness, but O'Reilly could see the glint of tears unshed. Her fists were clenched at her sides, and his memory flashed back to the angry girl he met in the APZ. The one who had been locked up in the cell in the basement of the Nursery because she refused to play the game—to stop criticizing the governmental leaders and the decisions they'd made to concentrate the remaining population of the country.

O'Reilly closed his eyes for a moment, then opened them and looked at Christina and Alysa. He had underestimated the girls' understanding of their predicament when the Enforcers had followed them to Hideaway weeks ago. He thought they probably understood that it was life and death for O'Reilly, but he didn't realize that they'd known their own lives would be forfeit if they were captured.

Still, things had changed now. Rickards had handed Maggie a lifeline, and they might need to take him up on the offer.

"If I don't make it back with Maggie, being in an APZ is the only safe place for you. Rickards will make it happen. He made that clear to Maggie. You can't stay here. You won't survive." O'Reilly closed his eyes once again, not wanting to meet the girls' stares and prayed that he was right.

"We have the garden," Alysa started, "and you've taught us to hunt. We can feed ourselves."

"You might make it for a while." O'Reilly focused on the dark-haired girl and nodded, a slow motion as he fought to control the knot of conflict he felt growing in his chest. "You might make it for a long time if food was the only thing you were worried about. It's not." The last two words were uttered in a flat voice, the bleakness O'Reilly was feeling leaking out. He could see the girls' eyes widen in response.

"Those men who took Maggie know there are people in this area now," O'Reilly continued, in the same voice, devoid of emotion. "And they saw you girls. They're going to know that whoever lives here is going to have supplies, weapons, ammunition. I've had experience with men like these and they won't hesitate to take what they want."

Christina started to open her mouth, but O'Reilly held up his hand and continued, a thin thread of frustration and anger entering his voice.

"I believe that I'll be able to find Maggie and rescue her. I wouldn't leave you kids otherwise, but I've dealt with groups like this before and I know how they operate."

He paused for a moment. He had no intention of telling the children that he had been part of an Enforcer's exorcism team when he'd run into groups of ghosts, some of them violent, and that none of those men or women had come out of that interaction alive.

"Things happen, though," he continued. "And I'm not going to lie to you. What I'm about to try is dangerous. If I get caught or killed, you have to assume that at some point those men will be coming back this way, looking for Hideaway and intending to take whatever they can.

"Just think about what you saw them do to Maggie," he said, the intensity in his voice increasing. "They're not going to let a group of kids stop them from taking what they want and they're either going to take you, too, or worse." O'Reilly didn't elaborate on what he meant by worse, but he could see that both Christina and Alysa understood his meaning. He hated to see the fear return to their eyes. There had been a time, following the confrontation with the Enforcers, that O'Reilly had wondered if he'd ever see the girls free of the specter of fear, but it had faded much more quickly than he'd expected. Now he was bringing it back with a vengeance, and he felt badly about that, but he also knew that the fear might be the only thing that would keep them alive in the upcoming days.

The girls remained silent; eyes fixed on O'Reilly. He looked down and away for a moment, gaze seeking out Lindy, who was sitting in front of the fireplace, playing with the rag doll Maggie had made for her. Gypsy, who had followed the small group up to the house, lay close behind her—Lindy's own personal guard. A small, sad smile twisted his lips.

He looked back at Alysa and Christina. "That's why if I don't return in two weeks, you will contact Rickards and he'll get you back into the APZ." He spoke with a confidence he didn't feel, knowing that the older children were beyond the age that the administrators generally saw as able to adapt to the conditions of the restricted community. Besides, they'd already run away once. "If Rickards tells the authorities that I kidnapped you. That you escaped and returned to the APZ because you knew that's where you'd be safe, there shouldn't be a problem." That was a stretch, considering Christina's history, but it had to work.

It was the only thing he had.

O'Reilly could see he'd made an impact on the girls and that even Christina couldn't find a good argument, although he knew from past experience she was probably trying to think of one.

"The caves . . ." she started. "We could hide in the caves like we did when the Enforcers came and wait until Maggie's kidnappers left."

"*If* they left," O'Reilly stated. "Hideaway is quite a prize, even though it's a long way from their supply routes. They may just decide to stay around and utilize the garden and the other supplies we've gathered. Even if they did leave, they for darned sure wouldn't leave you with any of the provisions you need to survive the winter, and there's no time to plant a new garden.

93

They'd also probably use the camp as a fallback location if ever they were on the run. You'd never know when they were coming, and sooner or later, they'd be bound to catch you.

O'Reilly could tell from the look on Christina's face that she still wasn't convinced, although he could also see that his argument had shaken her confidence. Alysa was harder to read. She always seemed passive, her face closed off from her emotions, but he knew there was a rock-solid core to her personality.

He held out the phone, and after a moment, Alysa reached out and took it, looking at the cracked screen as she did so.

"Power it down and put it in a safe place," O'Reilly said. "Maybe up in the caves. I'd like you guys to sleep up there until I get back anyway, just to be safe. The phone won't get reception in there. Hell, it won't get a signal anywhere in this valley, but it will be safe. If you need to call, you'll have to go to the rim."

Alysa tucked the device into her shirt, securing it under her bra strap, just as the boys burst in through the front door.

"O'Reilly," Nick started, speaking quickly in excited tones.

"We have Jimmy saddled and Ace is watered. Here are the saddlebags. Do you want us to start packing for you?" Ryan finished, his voice nearly identical to his twin's in both sound and emotion. A more genuine smile, the first of the afternoon, tweaked O'Reilly's lips and lit his dark eyes. Regardless of how much time they'd spent together, he continued to have some difficulty in telling the difference between the boys and, on several occasions, jokingly threatened to ear tag them so that he could tell them apart.

Mark had followed Nick and Ryan more slowly, and the look on the boy's face quickly erased the smile from O'Reilly's once again and reminded him of what lay ahead.

He turned back to Nick and Ryan. "Boys, pack some jerky and maybe some of those granola bars that we've been saving and see if there are any of those freeze dried meals I brought back from Wikieup. Canteens and water. Bedroll and sleeping bag. Got it?" he rapped out, giving them a mock stern look.

Nick grinned at O'Reilly, then looked over at his brother. As if they'd spoken, one headed toward the pantry and the other toward the bedroom. O'Reilly shook his head. He'd worked with a few horses with which he'd had a nearly telepathic connection, who seemed to know when he was going to ask them to turn, to speed up or slow down so that he could rope a calf or drive a maverick steer out of the thick brush and into the open, but never another human. Even he and Sarah hadn't had that level of communication, and he found he envied the twins a little.

"Mark, come with me for a moment." O'Reilly motioned toward the open door. Mark turned and went back out to the flat, hard-packed dirt area in front of the house, followed closely by O'Reilly, who closed the door behind them. He stood facing the boy who looked back up at him, misery written clearly across his face.

"Come here," O'Reilly said, his gravelly voice a low rumble.

Mark took a step and then, after hesitating for a moment, another. Two more steps and O'Reilly enfolded the boy in a hug, holding him for a moment, then pushed him back and looked down into the boy's green eyes, his own face serious. "I'm going to find her, Mark. I know you're scared. Hell, we're all scared," O'Reilly's voice broke on a slight laugh. He coughed to clear his throat, then continued. "It will be fine." He tried to put all the confidence he didn't feel into his voice.

"Okay," Mark said so softly it was almost inaudible. His eyes continued to search O'Reilly's face. A light breeze ruffled his honey blond hair, the same color as Maggie's.

O'Reilly placed his hand on Mark's shoulder again, and the two turned and watched the chickens scratching in the yard in silence for a moment. Houdini strutted among the multicolored hens, one yellow eye toward the sky as he watched for hawks and eagles. He paused and raised his beak in an earsplitting crow, then ruffled his black and white hackle feathers and scratched the ground several times, snapping up some form of insect dislodged by the action of his claws. He raised his head and examined his surroundings once again, then headed for another area of the farmyard.

Mark looked back up at O'Reilly. "I trust you." His voice was stronger. Determined.

The three words stabbed another arrow into O'Reilly's chest. He stayed silent for a moment as he continued to watch the chickens. The image of Houdini and Maggie's ongoing feud flashed into his mind's eye, and he smiled softly to himself.

Looking back down at the boy, O'Reilly squeezed his shoulder again. "I'll do my best."

Another moment of silence, then O'Reilly drew in a deep breath. "I'd better make sure Nick and Ryan have gotten everything ready. I need to get going."

He took his hand off Mark's shoulder and turned toward the door of the house.

15

Mark opened the gate at the far end of the home pasture, pulling the mass of wire and juniper stays back with him so that O'Reilly could ride through, leading the second horse. Christina could see the man pause for a moment as he bent down to say something to the boy. Then he straightened and urged the buckskin gelding forward, chucking the second horse's lead rope. The small figure stood as if frozen to the spot, watching the tall man as he disappeared around the gray rock outcropping that marked the spot where the canyon bent to the east. Then, hanging his head, Mark turned and started back across the grassy expanse, walking toward the other children, the two dogs bounding at his side. Several times Christina could see the boy raise his arm to his face, and she was sure he was trying not to cry. She knew she felt the prickling in her eyes that warned of her own impending tears.

Christina sighed and looked over at the other children.

"What do we do now, Christy?" Nick asked, using the pet name that he and Ryan had always called their sister. Christina disliked the diminutive and refused to answer to anyone else who used it. However, when Nick and Ryan were toddlers, it was the best they could come up with, and she had given up trying to get them to change a long time ago.

"O'Reilly is going to expect us to take care of everything while he's gone, so we're going to do the chores just like every other day. We've got to water the garden, pick any of the ripe vegetables, milk Lizzie, and take care of the chickens."

"Do you know what's ripe?" Ryan asked. Doubt was clear in his voice. Christina's gardening skills were well known to everyone at the camp.

"I—um . . ." She looked over at Alysa, who dropped her head. Christina didn't miss the slight smile on her face, however. Alysa almost certainly knew that Christina wouldn't recognize a ripe vegetable if it bit her on the nose, but she was kind enough not to point it out to the other residents of Hideaway.

"I'll look, but I also think I should go back to the ridge and pick up the saddlebags with the prickly pear fruit and nopales," Alysa said. She looked up at Christina with a frown on her face. "We can't afford to lose those saddlebags and we may need the fruit and pads."

Christina momentarily felt as though the ground had been pulled out from under her at Alysa's comment.

"Nothing's going to happen to those saddlebags up there," Christina protested. She could hear both panic and anger in her voice, and she fought to get it under control. "We can wait until O'Reilly gets back."

Alysa looked at Christina, the frown deepening and storm clouds were building in her dark eyes. "Javelina, bears, coyotes or rodents will chew up the saddlebags trying to reach the fruit inside. It will be fine. You heard O'Reilly. Those men have left so there's no danger of running into them again. I'll just go up, grab the bags and ride straight back. We don't know when O'Reilly and Maggie will return."

She left the "or if" unsaid, but Christina heard it loud and clear. She thought again about O'Reilly's orders—that they were to call Captain Rickards and return to the APZ if he or Maggie had not returned within two weeks. Christina looked at her brothers and could see them watching her and Alysa with identical worried expressions.

"You guys go and start watering the garden." Christina looked toward the pasture and saw that Mark was almost back to them, no sign of tears on his face. His ten-year-old features were set like stone, and Christina wondered at his self-control, unusual in someone so young. At least, it was before the pandemic.

"Okay, Christy," Nick said. He turned to look at Alysa. The boys held an admiration that bordered on hero worship for the girl. "Are you coming with us, Alysa?"

Alysa looked over at Christina, who tried to give the girl as imperceptible a shake of the head as possible, crossing her fingers, metaphorically speaking, and hoping that it wasn't *so* slight that Alysa didn't catch it either.

She didn't need to worry as Alysa gave Nick a warm, reassuring smile but shook her head. "I'll be there in a little bit, *shitsilí*," she said, using the Navajo word for a younger brother. "Don't pick anything until I'm there, okay? I don't want to be eating green squash this winter. I can go for the saddlebags after I show you what to pick."

"I thought the squash were supposed to be green," Christina blurted out, frowning as she struggled to remember her mother bringing squash home from the grocery store. She wasn't sure it had ever happened. Her mother had embraced all of the quick-fix prepackaged foods available in the frozen foods aisle and the "be your own chef" websites and food delivery services, and Christina wasn't sure that she'd seen many vegetables in their original skins—at least not in their kitchen.

"Some squash are green, but not butternut, and that's what's in the garden," Alysa said with a laugh. Christina, Nick and Ryan's lack of knowledge had provided a great deal of amusement for the girl over the weeks since their escape from the APZ.

Christina remembered back to the time when she had been assigned as Alysa's roommate following her own release from the isolation cell in the basement of the hotel the APZ called the Nursery. She'd thought at the time that Alysa had been totally indoctrinated into the new, post-pandemic lifestyle. Once they'd broken free from the APZ, however, Alysa had been loosening up, cracks appearing in the rigidly reserved shell that the girl had adopted in order to survive in the drastically altered world of the Authorized Population Zone.

"Okay," Ryan said, and the two boys took off toward the garden.

Christina looked over at Mark, who was climbing the wooden gate leading out of the pasture rather than pushing it open. Typical boy, she thought. "Hey Mark, go help Nick and Ryan water the garden. Alysa and I will be over to help in a minute."

Silently the boy nodded and turned to trudge across the barnyard, heading for the plot of green plants that were supposed to feed their patchwork family for the winter.

"They're gone," Alysa said in her soft voice. "What's up?"

Christina turned back toward the dark-haired girl and examined her. Quizzical dark eyes looked back.

"What do you think about what O'Reilly said?" Christina started, glancing over her shoulder to make sure the boys were really gone. She kept her voice low just in case, although she was sure there was no way they could hear her all the way from the garden. Lindy had toddled over toward the chicken coop where Houdini could be seen preening his glistening black and white feathers.

"You mean about us going back to the APZ if he doesn't return in two weeks?"

"Yeah, that," Christina said, and she could hear the anger and frustration in her voice.

There was silence for a moment as the two girls looked at one another. The stoic curtain was over Alysa's face once again making its expression unreadable and, for a moment, Christina didn't think she was going to get an answer to her question.

Then Alysa shook her head, her dark ponytail flying side to side, like one of the horses switching its tail at flies.

"I'm not going back to the APZ," Alysa said with rock solid determination. "I think O'Reilly is probably right, and if he doesn't return it may not be safe here any longer, but I won't go back."

Christina's eyes widened in surprise at Alysa's answer. She knew that the girl had hated being locked into the APZ, although she hadn't shown it at the time. However, Christina hadn't expected an endorsement of O'Reilly's concerns about an attack from those who kidnapped Maggie.

"Where will you go?"

"I'll go to my mother's people—to *Dinétah*." Alysa had a set to her jaw that silenced Christina. There was no question that the Native American girl had made up her mind.

"Di . . . dine e tah?" Christina tried the unfamiliar word. It sat strangely on her tongue, and she could tell from the slight smile that lightened Alysa's features for a moment that the girl found her pronunciation somewhat lacking.

"*Dinétah*," Alysa repeated, speaking more slowly. "The big reservation at the four corners. You know, where Arizona, Colorado, Utah and New Mexico touch?"

A shiver of fear ran through Christina. She had counted on Alysa being on her side when it came to not going to the APZ, but she also knew that without the girl, Christina and her brothers, as well as Mark and Lindy, were doomed. She had thought they'd all stay in the canyon or maybe move up to one of the other camps or even a local ranch headquarters if O'Reilly and Maggie failed to return. She'd never considered that Alysa would want to leave them.

"Why there? What makes you think any of your family is still alive on the reservation and not in some APZ somewhere," Christina stammered.

Alysa was silent for a moment, dark eyebrows drawing together in a frown, as though she were picking her words with care.

"I remember my mother saying that during the last pandemic the reservation got hit really hard. She said that this time they locked the roads down early to keep others who might be carrying disease out. There were even reports of people being shot at the border of the reservations if they tried to get past the roadblocks. It was one of the reasons we didn't go there when everyone started getting sick. That, and they started getting really strict about the shelter-in-place orders, arresting people who went out without permission."

Alysa lifted her head and looked up toward the rim of the canyon high above their heads, her eyes distant, and Christina knew she remembered the panic that engulfed the country and the world at the start of the H5N1 influenza pandemic.

"My mother told me a number of the reservations around the country were taking the same actions. The states fought the tribal leaders on the road closures, saying the tribal councils had no right to block the roads even though it was reservation land. I guess I'm hoping that they were able to keep the virus away. That they learned enough the last time to be able to stay healthy now, even though this disease was much worse."

Alysa sighed, then looked back at Christina with a half smile and lifted her shoulders in a slight shrug.

"What about the concentration, though? Once the influenza was gone, didn't the members of the reservations get pulled into the APZs?" Christina tried to remember anyone talking about the various reservations around the Southwest. Nothing.

"I don't know," Alysa admitted. "But if they were able to close the reservation land off from the disease, then maybe they were also able to resist concentration as well."

"You've never mentioned any of this before," Christina said, her voice barely above a whisper. She studied the girl. She could hear the hope in Alysa's voice. And a yearning. The urge to find out if she had family left alive.

"I like it at Hideaway and the reservation is a long way away from here," Alysa continued. "I knew Maggie and O'Reilly wouldn't let me leave by myself, and I thought there was no rush. I'm not sure I can reach the Rez, but I'm not going back to the APZ either."

Christina was silent for a moment. If O'Reilly didn't return, what would she and the boys do? She didn't like the idea of reentering the APZ any more than Alysa did, and she was a long way from convinced that they'd actually let them back in, no matter what O'Reilly said. The caretakers at the Nursery would remember her, of that she was sure. Still, the journey that Alysa was proposing didn't have a guaranteed outcome either. Could they get on to the reservation land if they were even able to reach it?

She made a decision.

"Can we come with you?" Christina asked, the intensity in her voice surprising her. From the look on Alysa's face, it surprised her as well.

Alysa chewed her lip, face creased in concentration as she studied Christina and then looked over toward the garden where the boys were watering the plants.

"Yes," she said finally, drawing the word out, making it clear that she had doubts. "You can come with me. It would be a hard ride, though. A lot harder than what we've done so far. The reservation is on the far side of the state, and it might snow on the way. It's already late September or early October. Even if we get there, I'm not sure if they'll let you past the border of the reservation. You're not Navajo."

"Can't we ask for asylum, or something like that? It's not like the influenza is still active, is it?" Christina asked, frustrated at the possibility of being locked out just because of her heritage. In her whole life, as the daughter of academics and scientists, highly educated and well off, if not rich, Christina had never been denied access to anything. At least not until she'd been locked into that cell in the basement of the Nursery.

"I don't know," Alysa said simply. "We won't know until we get there."

"But what if they turn us away?" Christina knew she was on the verge of tears, her eyes feeling as though ants were crawling across them, and she scrubbed her face with her forearm and looked back at Alysa, who had been studying her with a frown settling on her copper penny face.

"There's an APZ in Albuquerque, I think," Alysa said softly, sympathy clouding her dark eyes.

Christina felt her heart drop to her feet at Alysa's words, knowing that there might be no choice, and if there was one thing Christina didn't like, it was feeling like she had no choice.

"We may not have to worry about it," Alysa continued. "O'Reilly will be able to rescue Maggie and will get back here before two weeks is up."

Christina could see that Alysa was trying to put more confidence into her voice than she really felt, but Christina felt reassured nonetheless.

"You're right," Christina said with a sigh. "My dad always told us 'don't trouble trouble until trouble troubles you.' O'Reilly will take care of everything." She gave Alysa a small smile, then looked over at the boys, who had apparently decided that a water fight would be an effective strategy for watering the garden. At least it was a warm day. "I guess we'd better go help the boys. Otherwise, I'm not sure there will be any vegetables left for us to pick."

Alysa scooped up Lindy from the ground where she'd been playing with several small stones, and the two girls turned and started toward the garden.

16

Maggie pulled the door of the aged wood shed the group was using as an outhouse closed behind her and took a deep breath. She immediately regretted the action since the air in the unventilated building was fetid. She started coughing, which only made her headache worse. A banging on the door didn't help matters much.

"What do you want?" Maggie snapped, raising her voice to make herself heard, then coughed several more times.

"What's going on in there?" The woman's voice was muffled but intelligible.

"What do you *think* is going on in here?" Maggie growled back, although she was sure the woman outside couldn't hear her clearly. "I'm having a blasted tea party in this fine establishment."

More banging on the door. "What did you say? I can't hear you. Hurry up in there!" The annoyance in the woman's voice was increasing, and, for a moment, Maggie debated on the wisdom of irritating her captors. For some reason the old movie, *The Ransom of Red Chief,* flashed through her mind, but she had the feeling that Lucas would never pay O'Reilly to take her back. The blue-eyed sociopath would be more likely to shoot her and leave her body out for the coyotes and the vultures after he'd raped her. She made a face. She did *not* want her final moments on this planet to be as food for one of those ugly, bald, red-headed birds.

Maggie stepped forward and, with a shiver of trepidation, peeked into the hole covered by the broken toilet seat and wrinkled her nose. It was about what she expected—a malodorous pit. It didn't seem to be as deep as she would have thought necessary for its function, but it didn't appear as though there were any snakes ready to leap out. No black widow or brown recluse spiders had spun their webs across the hole, waiting for the bounty of flies that the outhouse was attracting, or Maggie's rear end, for that matter. She shivered at the thought. Being stung on the butt by a black widow would certainly put a cap on a bad day.

She wondered why, with the various motorhomes around the compound, the group wasn't using the built in bathrooms. If they were having to resort to outhouses, though, it didn't bode well for the possibility of a shower. Come to think of it, the people she met upon her arrival did seem to have a pungent odor about them, although she'd been focused so much on her captivity that she hadn't paid it much attention at the time.

"Will you hurry up! And don't use all the toilet paper!" came the loud, irritated voice from outside the building, and the woman crashed her fist into the door again, shaking the shed to the point that Maggie was worried the entire structure would tip over with her in it.

Maggie's eyes widened, and she glanced around the closet-sized outhouse, smell forgotten for the moment. There it was, perched in a position of glory on a dowel poking out from the wall—a half-roll of quilted two-ply, squashed looking, but undeniably toilet paper. She froze for a second, then reached out and ran a finger over the tissue. She couldn't remember the last time she'd seen toilet paper. It had been in short supply during the height of the pandemic when people in a panic had cleared the shelves. When she and Mark arrived at Hideaway, they'd had to go back to the pioneer era as far as hygiene went. O'Reilly had managed to bring back a roll or two here and there, but it didn't last nearly as long as Maggie would have liked.

Bang, bang, boom!

The outhouse shook violently once again, jerking Maggie's attention back to the needs at hand.

"Okay, okay!" she called back, fumbling at the button of her jeans. "Just give me a moment, and I'll be finished."

Two minutes later, Maggie pushed the outhouse door open and stepped out into the fresh air. She took a deep, grateful breath and looked around the compound. A sound from her right caused her head to whip around, and her neck popped, the headache making itself known once again. For a moment, the ground tilted, and she wobbled on her feet.

Linda was leaning against the wall of the shed, arms crossed, a disgusted look on her face. She pushed her body away from the wood siding and squared up to Maggie.

"What's wrong with you?" the woman said, her chin jerking up slightly in Maggie's direction and her voice making it very clear that she wasn't really very concerned about her prisoner's condition except in relation to how it might affect the dark-haired woman herself.

Even though Maggie knew Linda didn't care, she chose to answer. "The gentle ministrations of your boyfriend have left me with a bit of a headache," she said in conversational tones, swallowing the more bitter words she wanted to say. No point in irritating the woman even further. "What now?"

Linda nodded toward and open area Maggie could see on the far side of the compound. "I suppose you can help out in the garden. If you're going to be here, eating our food, then you have to work." The derisive note in her voice made it clear what Linda thought about Maggie being within fifty miles of the encampment.

Maggie's jaw creaked with the effort needed to keep from telling the woman what she thought about being there and eating the group's food. She forced her muscles to relax, wondering if she could fracture her teeth if she ground them any harder, and where she'd find a dentist if she did.

Linda stopped and examined Maggie. Her brown eyes narrowed, and her lip curled as though she smelled something nasty, and Maggie didn't think it was the outhouse, standing in solitary, odiferous glory next to them. Linda hesitated for a moment, then, as if deciding there was nothing to lose, she spoke.

"I know Kyle is obsessed with you right now, but he'll get over it. He's mine, and he's going to stay mine. You just remember that."

The menace in the woman's voice chilled Maggie. She wasn't sure who was more dangerous—the blue-eyed man who seemed to be teetering on the edge of insanity, if not actually sliding down into the pit, or the woman who wanted him.

Linda turned and gestured for Maggie to move in front of her. Together the two walked toward the far edge of the compound where the band of ghosts had planted their garden.

Or what they think of as their garden, Maggie thought as she stood staring at the plot of land. Even to her inexperienced eyes, the plants in front of her wouldn't feed anyone for very long, let alone a group the size of this. O'Reilly had taught her a great deal about gardening for survival since he arrived at the camp, and although she readily admitted that her thumb was still probably more of a muddy-brown color than the true green thumb of a master gardener, even she knew that what she was looking at barely qualified as a garden.

The soil of the fenced-in area was yellowish-orange in color, as opposed to the rich dark brown of their garden at Hideaway. She knew from what O'Reilly had told her that the camp had good soil for growing food due to the sediment deposited by centuries of floods rolling through the area and the build up of organic material, such as dead grasses, leaves and animal manure. He'd told her that many other Arizona gardeners who weren't as blessed in the soil department had to rely on augmenting their land, bringing in the humus and nutrients that nature had failed to provide. From looking at the group's garden, they hadn't been as lucky as she had been in the land's natural condition, and didn't have the experience to realize that support was needed or the means to bring in that support.

"This is your only garden?" Maggie asked although it was obvious that it was precisely that.

"Yeah, what of it?" Linda said in defensive tones. "We got a late start. We didn't move into this compound until mid-summer, so it's not like we had the entire growing season at our beck and call. Besides, when the solar system went down, the pump in the well stopped working and we had to start hauling all our water, other than what we could collect from the rain."

She threw her arm out, indicating a large storage tank stationed next to the tan pole barn. Gutters had been hung under the roof, and a down spout had been rigged to the corner of the structure and led into the tank. They'd had a decent amount of rain this past monsoon season, so Maggie thought they should have caught a fair amount of water, although she had no idea how much a setup like that could collect.

"You'd be surprised how much water comes off the roof during even a small storm. The big, green tank was almost full," Linda continued, her voice dripping with disgust. "But there's a leak and we lost nearly everything. We haven't had much rain this last month either."

"No well pump," Maggie said, almost to herself. "That's why you're using the outhouse instead of the bathrooms in the motorhomes." She'd been right that the delightful condition of the facilities, not to mention the aromatic state of the group's members, was due to a lack of water.

"The solar system took a hit in a thunderstorm. No electricity, no pump. No pump, no running water. For that matter, we don't know if the electric pump took a hit as well. It might be fried. They're trying to get a windmill hooked up to the well to pump water, but that will just fill the little tank, not get water into the RVs. They're uphill from the well and the booster pump won't work on wind, even if it didn't get fried." She indicated a second, smaller tank sitting a few feet away from the one rigged to the runoff system of the barn. "We can use gravity to water the garden when there's enough water in it, though."

Maggie nodded. They had to haul water by bucket when Maggie and Mark first moved to the camp. However, O'Reilly had been able to liberate a hose from the ranch headquarters he'd raided, and between that and some hand dug irrigation, watering the garden had become much more manageable. Still, gravity didn't run uphill, so the house itself, tucked as it was up under the cliff, still had no running water.

"Aren't there other homes in the area that have solar systems and wells that work? Why can't you use them?" Maggie asked, her natural curiosity overriding her fear and anger for the moment. Why, with all of Arizona to choose from, did the group insist on remaining in this mountaintop camp if there were properties with more accessible water nearby?

Linda studied Maggie for a moment, her jaw working as though she was trying to trap the words behind her teeth, but they were fighting to get out. "Here we can see if anyone is coming.

We're on top of the mountain—the high ground you know," she finally spat out. "Besides most of the places around here hauled water from a community well closer to Seligman, so we'd be in the same position there as here. We've tried to bring up other solar systems, but so far haven't been able to make them work."

Maggie looked off toward the rim, and the open juniper-filled valley to the west, thinking about the situation the group found themselves in. She was familiar with having to choose between "modern conveniences" and safety. She'd chosen safety, going to ground at Hideaway Camp with its lack of running water and electricity instead of staying in a more accessible location or even going into an APZ which still had most of the conveniences people thought they couldn't live without. Still, it seemed strange to choose to remain in a place without water, regardless of the view. The group's leaders must really be worried about being hunted down by the authorities. Then she remembered the story O'Reilly had told her of his time with the exorcism team and thought maybe she could understand that fear.

"I suppose you have a garden where you live," Linda said, jerking Maggie back to the here and now. She made it a statement and not a question. "You can help pull the weeds. We'll water when we're done. We're waiting for Joe to bring up a load from the windmill in the valley. Just make sure you don't pull out any of the vegetable plants."

Linda reached out and pushed Maggie's shoulder, propelling her into the garden. She stumbled and nearly wiped out a pitiful tomato plant that sported several tiny orange tomatoes.

"I *said* don't damage the plants," Linda snapped.

Maggie straightened and turned to face Linda, her temper finally to the boiling point.

"Listen, Linda," Maggie saw the woman bristle at the use of her name and continued on, feeling a stab of satisfaction that she'd scored a hit. "If anyone here has the right to be pissed, it's me, not you. I was out there minding my own business when your boyfriend attacked and kidnapped me. It's idiotic for you to be blaming me because your *boyfriend* is an ass."

Linda's hands bunched into fists, and she raised her right arm. Maggie realized that the woman was going to attack her. She had braced herself for the blow when she heard someone call Linda's name from across the compound. The dark-haired woman spun around, looking for the speaker. Maggie took a step back out of arm's length and to the side so that she could see around Linda's slender frame.

The man who called himself Ethan Granger was striding across the compound with a furious expression.

"What the hell is going on, Linda?" Granger asked as he came to a stop at the edge of the garden. His dark blue eyes snapped in anger, and Maggie noticed that Linda immediately dropped her fists and stepped back, crushing the pathetic tomato plant, finally putting it out of its drought-ridden misery. The anger remained clear on her features, however, even though her attention had been diverted from Maggie for the moment.

"Why do we have to have this woman here, Granger?" Linda's lip curled, and she jerked her thumb at Maggie, making it sound as though she was a scraggly, flea-bitten dog that someone had dragged home from the local garbage dump.

If it weren't such a serious situation, Maggie thought, Linda's reaction would be funny. Sure, Maggie was pretty grubby at this point in time, but nothing compared to the people she'd seen in the group. Yet, from Linda's reaction, you would have thought that Maggie stank to high heaven.

"We have enough people to feed without her. I thought it was up to the group to approve new additions. Not just one person. Especially after what happened to your cheek," Linda spat.

"Enough," Granger said in a cold, calm voice. "I don't have to explain myself to you, or to anyone here. If you don't like what I say, you're welcome to go take your chances in an APZ at any time."

Linda opened her mouth to argue, but Granger put up his hand, stopping her; argument caught in her throat, unspoken, clearly choking her.

"If you want to know why this woman is with us, then ask Lucas," Granger continued, "I'm warning you, though, you may not like his answer." His expression made it clear what he meant by the comment. "At this point, however, I would like to talk to our guest myself." He held out his arm toward Maggie, gesturing for her to come with him.

Stepping around the wilted and now squashed tomato plant, Maggie walked to his side, watching Linda out of the corner of her eye, ready to duck if she seemed likely to swing. The woman seemed to wilt as badly as the tomato plants at the man's words, however, apparently knowing that Granger was right about Lucas but not wanting to admit it to herself. It was much easier to blame Maggie or Granger for her problems.

"Come with me and we'll talk," Granger said, ignoring Linda. He put his hand behind Maggie as though to touch her back, and she flinched away. He quickly dropped his arm and started toward the pole barn, glancing over to make sure that Maggie was walking with him.

"I'm sorry about Linda's attitude just now," Granger said in conversational tones. He turned his head, and gave Maggie a sideway glance.

"I'm not feeling especially fond of her either," Maggie said with acid in her voice.

Granger picked up on the sarcasm, and a small smile pulled at the corner of his lips. "No, I imagine not. Still, you're here now, and I'd like to talk to you — get a little information."

"Are you going to let me go?" she asked. "That's all the information I'd like to get. Take me back to where you found me and I'll forget all about you people." She tried to soften the anger in her voice and adopt a persuasive tone. The mix was less than convincing, even to her own ears.

The two had reached the tan pole barn, and Granger pulled open a small, human-sized single door next to the large white garage-style door. Instead of answering her question, he held out his arm and ushered Maggie inside. She stepped into the large, cool interior of the barn and looked around. Several men were working at the end closest to them. Maggie couldn't tell what they were doing, but it involved manhandling a pile of large pieces of sheet metal, pipes and bars. A long truncated triangle of grayed, black stained galvanized steel reminded Maggie of the windmill at Hideaway, and she decided this was the windmill they were trying to get attached to the well. Other than that group of men, no one else was in the barn that she could see, and she looked back at Granger with a question in her eyes.

"At the back." He pointed to the rear wall of the barn, where she could see a second door. Skirting a pile of metal, Maggie walked to the door Granger indicated, aware that the other men had stopped whatever it was that they were doing and were staring at her. She felt tiny clawed feet of fear scamper up her spine, and she shivered slightly.

Granger reached the door and pulled it open, standing aside for Maggie to walk through into a wooden-walled lean-to built onto the back of the barn. She jerked to a stop just inside the opening and looked around the rough room. She found herself in a long, narrow space. One wall was the tan powder coated steel of the barn's outer surface, and the other three were untreated wood, the studs exposed. To the left of the entrance, the walls were lined with plywood shelving which held several large boxes. On her right, the end of the room closest to the door, there were several folding lawn chairs and an old, ratty, brown couch positioned under a large, barred window which provided the only light for the space.

Granger pointed to the couch, his meaning clear. Maggie walked over to the dilapidated piece of furniture and sat, stifling the cough triggered by the dust that floated into the air at the introduction of her weight. The man moved over to one of the folding chairs and lowered himself onto the stained plastic straps. He leaned forward, elbows on his knees, as he studied Maggie.

Maggie fought to remain relaxed under the scrutiny. She didn't want him to see how frightened she was, or how angry.

The room was silent except for the muffled sounds of the men in the main expanse of the barn. Maggie watched Granger, determined not to be the first to talk.

The man who sat in front of her didn't look intimidating, other than the scar that creased his left cheek. His sandy brown hair was long and unkempt, and Maggie was aware of the strong scent of unwashed human. Without thought she reached toward her own honey-blonde hair. She hadn't had it cut professionally since shortly after the start of the pandemic, at which point most of the businesses had been shut down in a futile attempt to halt the spread of the influenza. Other than a time or two, when the condition of her hair drove her to desperate means, she'd resisted the urge to become her own barber, and as a result her hair was much longer than she wore it before the world fell apart.

She had insisted on cutting Mark's hair and that of the other children once they arrived in the canyon. O'Reilly had even submitted to her scissoring skills after resisting for a month or more, proclaiming his intention of letting it grow as long as Rapunzel's before he'd let Maggie near his bare neck with sharp implements.

At Hideaway, they'd been lucky, though. They had water from the windmill, and during the summer they could bathe in the nearby creek, so they'd been able to remain reasonably clean, and O'Reilly had produced a few sticks of deodorant following his trip to Wikieup. Laundry had been a challenge, however, and she guessed that she had some of the same mélange of odors surrounding her that she'd noticed in the members of this group, even if not as strong. She wrinkled her nose, then fought to get her expression back under control, hoping Granger hadn't noticed.

He had. When Maggie looked at the man, he had a slight smile on his face, as if realizing what she was thinking.

"We stink, huh?" he said with a faint chuckle. "We need all of our water for drinking, cooking and the garden. There's a well a couple of miles away, at a windmill in the valley, but most of us have gotten out of the habit of bathing regularly." He rubbed his stubbled chin. "If we don't find a new supply of razors soon, I'll be giving up on shaving, too. Some already have. If things continue on this way for much longer, we'll be a fine group of mountain men." He paused for a moment, then nodded to her. "And women." The smile became a grin, as if he were inviting Maggie to join in the joke. She bit the inside of her lip, refusing to give him that satisfaction.

Sighing, the grin faded from Granger's face, and he looked at her. Once again the seriousness of the situation fell on Maggie like a ton of rocks.

"We find ourselves in an awkward situation. I've introduced myself, but I still don't know your name. Why don't we start there?" Granger finally began, breaking the standoff.

Maggie sat in silence for a moment, eyes narrowed, biting down hard on her words as she debated how much information she should volunteer. Deciding that her name couldn't make much of a difference, she spoke.

"Maggie Langton."

Granger nodded slightly in acknowledgment of the crack in her wall of resistance. "Thank you, Ms. Langton." His voice was formal, as though he was conducting a job interview.

An interview for a job Maggie definitely did not want.

"I've got a number of questions. Let's start with how many people are in your group."

Maggie choked on a bitter laugh. "You don't really think I'm going to answer that question do you? Or, if I do, do you think I'm going to tell you the truth? Let's say there are fifty people. That sounds like a good number, doesn't it?" She saw a spark of anger in Granger's eyes and could hear the derision in her own voice. Maggie struggled to get her temper under control. She was at this man's mercy, and she didn't need to antagonize him needlessly.

"We're not interfering with you," she said. She tried to adopt a placating tone that threatened to choke her. She took a deep breath and continued, "We're not competing with you for food or resources. You can still just take me back to where you found me and let me go. Your people don't want me here. Linda made that very clear."

"Linda doesn't make the decisions," Granger said, his voice hardening into ice.

"Linda said the group makes decisions. Not just one person. What was it she said—'especially after what happened to your cheek.' How *did* you get that scar?"

Granger raised his hand to his face and fingered the still angry red mark, rubbing it lightly, a distracted look in his eyes. "We were north of Seligman, and came across a bunker in the forest. Not surprising up here. We'd run into a number of shelters and bunkers. Most of them empty. A few of them had the bodies of the people who had built the shelters or at least found them and moved in. It appeared that some of the people who had retreated to the hideouts to try and save themselves from the influenza virus actually sealed themselves in with it.

"The old guy who was living in this bunker seemed glad to see us." Granger stopped for a moment, his eyes looking off into the distance. An uncomfortable grimace twisted his features as he shook his head. "I guess he thought it was best to welcome us instead of trying to fight us off. There were twenty-six of us then, and we could have taken both him and his supplies easily."

"Why didn't he just hide in the bunker?" Maggie asked. She had become caught up in the tale in spite of herself. In her mind she saw a potential story, crafting the hook, feeling the flow of words like a deep river of energy—a hold over from her journalism days. She shook herself mentally. There were no magazines or newspapers any longer, or at least none that would print any story she wrote. Even before the pandemic, her profession had been under fire from those in power who desperately didn't want word of their corruption to get out or at least be believed. And with the horrors of the disease ravaging the planet, many governments, including theirs, had tried to clamp down on the spread of stories which put their conduct in a bad light. Still, she couldn't shut off that part of her brain.

"We caught him while he was out hunting. He couldn't make it back to the bunker in time. He'd gotten careless too, probably figuring everyone was gone. He'd started a garden near the hideout, and when we came across his place, we stopped, figuring to harvest whatever was ready to be picked. He was blocked from returning to the shelter, so I guess he decided to bluff." Granger shrugged. There was a sadness in his eyes that Maggie couldn't define. She was unable to pull her gaze away from the man sitting across from her.

"I felt bad for the old fart. From the looks of him, he hadn't had it easy since the concentration and I invited him to join us, even though many of the others in the group didn't like the idea of adding any other mouths to feed, especially an old guy like this fella. Lucas was the leader of that faction." Granger uttered a bitter chuckle. "You may have noticed that Kyle Lucas isn't overly blessed in social skills, but he's a good man." Granger hesitated, then added, almost under his breath, "or was."

Maggie thought briefly about her and Mark's experiences when they first moved to Hideaway and the challenges of keeping the two of them fed. Of course, they didn't have a stocked bunker. Still, the chores of survival became much easier as more hands shared the work. She could see the other side too, however. Too many mouths to feed and not enough resources could be a problem. A density-dependent limiting factor is what the scientists had called it when she wrote an article on the reintroduction of the Mexican gray wolf to Arizona several years back. Unfortunately for some, the wolves tended to broaden their diet to include cattle, horses, dogs, cats and other domesticated animals before the increased density resulted in situations that would naturally decrease the population.

Sometimes she wondered if the recent upsurge in pandemics during the past thirty years or so was their own density-dependent limiting factor. Without a doubt, it had become nearly impossible to halt the spread of any determined viral contagion, as they'd found out in the past few pandemics.

Granger continued, unaware of the shift in Maggie's thoughts. "That night, when we were all asleep, the guy attacked us with everything he had. A pipe bomb, I think, and an AR-15. Thank God the gun jammed. I looked at it afterward and he hadn't loaded the magazine carefully enough." Granger shook his head. "When the weapon malfunctioned he went after us with a knife." He gestured toward the scar. "I was lucky," he continued on a flat note. "We lost eight people, and another five were injured. Since then we've agreed that the entire group would vote on new members."

"How did you survive? You must have lost a lot of blood." Maggie asked, curious in spite of herself.

"Kyle Lucas saved me. The second time that happened. The first was when he got me out of the Phoenix Metro area without being trapped into an APZ or shot by the Enforcers."

The faintest note of frustration in his voice spoke to Maggie of his internal struggle. He felt he owed Kyle Lucas his life twice over, but it was clear he didn't totally trust the man any longer.

Granger's eyes sharpened, and he looked back at Maggie again. "Now it's your turn." His voice now held a hint of steel that left little doubt that he intended to be accommodated.

How much, Maggie thought frantically, *how much can I tell him that won't compromise us. How much can I lie and still convince him that I'm telling the truth?*

"There's only me and six children," Maggie started, speaking slowly. A quiver gathered in her voice, and she allowed it full rein. This man seemed to have a conscience, even if it was battered by what he had been forced to do to ensure his group's survival. He was much different from Kyle Lucas. That man was dangerous.

"We escaped from concentration in Prescott, stole horses and moved north onto a ranch," she carefully left out the fact that they were at a remote, hidden camp in a canyon. Hopefully, he would think they were on one of the big ranch headquarters farther south and east. "We've been trying to gather enough food for the winter, but I don't know if we're going to manage it. I've been thinking that we would have to go to one of the APZs, or join up with another group like yours." She prayed that Granger would think that they had nothing that would be worth stealing. She also hoped that the mention of a group of children who now had no one to look after them would pull at his heartstrings.

She tried to keep her thoughts from settling on O'Reilly. She couldn't afford for Granger's sharp instincts to pick up on any subtle tells in her body language. Tells that might alert him to O'Reilly's presence. She couldn't help but wonder, however, what O'Reilly had done when the girls returned without her?

A worm of fear slithered around her heart, tightening. Alysa and Christina must have returned to Hideaway. Neither Granger nor Lucas had mentioned them. They must have heard her warning and run. *They had to have escaped.* The alternative was too terrible to think of, and she jerked her thoughts away and back to the small room.

Still, O'Reilly snuck back in, like he always did. Was he coming to rescue her, or had he decided that he couldn't leave the children unprotected? Her chest tightened again at the thought, and she wasn't sure which scenario she preferred. She knew she was in danger—at the very least of rape at the hands of Kyle Lucas, if not outright death—and she'd give anything to see O'Reilly riding over the hill, coming to her rescue, her knight in cowboy boots and dusty jeans. However, the thought of Mark, and the rest of the children, left alone if something happened to both Maggie and O'Reilly, terrified her.

Maggie became aware that Granger was leaning forward in his chair, studying her with an intensity that felt almost like a physical touch.

She cleared her throat and continued, "So, no supplies. No guns or ammunition." That part was true, at least, unless you counted her one rifle. "Nothing that would benefit a group like yours, Mr. Granger. Just more mouths to feed." She ended with a shake in her voice that was only partially feigned.

Granger took a deep breath and sat back in his chair. A frown clouded his expression as he examined Maggie. The silence dragged on until she was ready to scream at the delay. *He doesn't believe me,* she thought. She cursed mentally, nearly choking on the words she wanted to scream at him.

"You're a lousy liar, Ms. Langton," Granger finally said in a soft voice. "We may have to do something about that. For now, however, you'll stay right here. I suppose we'd better increase our lookouts, just in case your people come after you." He pushed himself to his feet and looked down at where she sat on the dusty couch. "You'll sleep in here since the door can be locked."

"What about blue-eyes—the one you call Lucas? The man who hit me. He's a raving lunatic and he seems to have other plans for me," Maggie said, her temper beginning to flare once again.

"It was necessary to let him have his way when it was just he and I. As you've noticed, he's been . . ." Granger paused, as if trying to think of the correct word or phrase. "He's not as stable as I'd like lately, but he and I have a deal, and he'll live up to it or else."

"And what exactly is this deal?" Maggie said in acerbic tones, "and how does it affect me?"

Granger pushed himself to his feet, the rickety lawn chair creaking and moaning, and walked to the door. He put his hand on the knob, then turned back and looked at Maggie. "The deal is that he is not allowed to rape anyone. I had a wife and two daughters, you see. I made it clear to Lucas early on in our partnership that if he rapes a woman, I'll kill him myself." Granger turned, pushed the wooden panel open and left.

The door closed behind him, and Maggie heard a scraping sound. She rose quickly and walked to the entryway. Grabbing the knob, she tried to push the door open only to find it able to move less than an inch. It wasn't actually locked, as Granger had referred to it. Instead, something was blocking it, which made sense when she thought about the situation. If someone in this group hadn't actually owned the property prior to the pandemic, and it didn't seem like anyone had, then they wouldn't have the keys to any of the locks unless they happened to get extraordinarily lucky when they arrived and found them in the barn or one of the trailers.

Stooping and bringing her face close to the wood, she peeked through the crack between the door and jamb. It appeared that a board had been slid across the doorway, preventing the wood panel from swinging open. There was no time for them to have arranged the impromptu lock since her arrival, so this room must have been used as a prison before. She felt a frisson of fear. If the lock keeping her in was so simple, what would keep Lucas from opening it and attacking her at night when Granger was sleeping? Would he really trust that a few *words* would keep someone as sociopathic as Lucas seemed to be in line?

She walked over to the barred window. She could slide it open and get fresh air if she wanted, but the bars a few inches beyond the window screen appeared solid and would prevent her from crawling out that way.

She chewed her lip and turned her head and looked at the door, then back to the window, contemplating the wisdom of tearing the screen so that she could see how solidly the bars were attached to the wall of the lean-to. Maggie turned and walked to the far end of the room, where the wooden shelves lined the walls. Most were empty, although there were several cans and jars of some sort of food, two vacuum sealed packs of toilet paper, which caused her to pause for a moment in surprise, and three boxes of what appeared to be old, greasy car parts. Nothing struck her as something she could use to break out.

She returned to the couch and sat. Another gout of dust puffed into the air, sparkling in the light from the window. The headache continued to throb, and she felt as though her brain cells had gone on strike. Finally, she decided that it would be best to tear the screen and test the bars after dark, when the others in the compound had gone to sleep. She hoped that any sentries that Granger posted would be overconfident and under-vigilant and that all the area's mosquitoes had died off as winter approached.

She had been sitting there for close to twenty minutes, as near as she could tell, when she heard scraping at the door.

The board being removed.

She leaned forward and rose rapidly to her feet, turning to face the sound, mentally telling her body to relax, trying to keep from telegraphing her emotions to whoever was going to appear and praying that it wasn't Lucas, intent on breaking his deal with Granger.

The dark-haired young man who had been with Granger and Lucas when she was captured walked in, carrying a bucket and a plastic jug of water. The younger boy followed him, carrying a large plate with a cloth draped over it.

Her eyes narrowed briefly, and she felt her body tense. She might be able to take out the two boys and make a run for it, but then she noticed the muffled sounds of male voices and banging from the main room of the barn, and she shook her head, almost to herself. Breaking out of the door right now would be a case of out of the aquarium and into the river filled with piranhas.

"Got some water and food, Miss," the oldest of the two boys said, holding the jug out toward her. He seemed afraid to meet her eyes, looking everywhere in the room except at her. He shuffled his feet on the dirty floor, giving every indication of extreme discomfort. *Maybe feeling guilty?* Maggie thought with a tickle of hope. Guilt was powerful and could be used to her advantage. Maybe he wasn't on board with her abduction—or maybe he knew something she didn't.

The younger boy didn't seem to have any misgivings and studied her directly. Both boys had the same dark, copper-brown skin and intense brown eyes. *Hispanic? Maybe Native American?* she thought. So far, the boys were the only children that Maggie had seen in the group, and she wondered about the eight people killed by the old man north of Seligman. Were there children among them, or had this group always been just adults other than these two? It was obvious they were brothers, and she wondered about their parents.

Maggie hadn't realized how thirsty she was until they showed up with the water. She stepped forward and took the jug. "Thank you. I appreciate it," she said, trying to sound as friendly as she could. "What's the bucket for?"

The boy set the bucket on the ground, turned and took the plate from his younger brother. He walked to the closest set of shelves and placed it carefully on the bare plywood, then turned and looked at Maggie, more directly this time.

"It's for if you need the outhouse, but no one's around to take you."

Maggie couldn't tell for sure in the dim light from the window, but it seemed that he flushed a little at the statement, and it brought a slight smile to her face—that was until she processed what he'd said fully. This filthy, plastic five-gallon bucket was her toilet. She thought of the fetid outhouse wistfully. *You should never be ungrateful for what you have because it can always get worse,* she thought and sighed.

The older boy took his young brother's shoulder and propelled him back toward the door. "Come on, Andy. We've got to go."

The younger boy resisted for a moment and kept his eyes fixed on Maggie. "Why are you in here, Miss?"

"I don't know, Andy," she said in a sad, soft voice.

"Come *on*," Andy's brother said, his voice sharper than before, a frown making his eyes even more intense. "You don't want to be making Lucas angry."

The older boy pushed Andy out of the door then paused in the opening and looked back at Maggie. He reached out for the door and started to pull it shut, his eyes never leaving her face. Just before he stepped back to finish closing the door, he said, "Sorry, Miss." His voice had turned as sad as hers. Then the door finished its arc, clicking into place, and Maggie could hear the board being slid back into its brackets.

Maggie returned to the couch and sat. A tear trickled its way down her face, ignored, soon followed by another and then another.

17

The convoy of jeeps pulled off I-40 onto Fort Rock Road, west of Seligman, at 7:39 a.m., according to Rickards' watch. Twice they'd had to stop to change flat tires—punctured by debris left over from accidents that had happened months ago. During the peak of the pandemic, there weren't enough tow trucks—or tow truck drivers—left to fully remove vehicles that fell victim to accidents. Often, they were pushed to the shoulder of the highway so they wouldn't impede progress from other vehicles. Small shards of plastic and metal still tended to migrate onto the road due to wind, rain or wildlife, however, and the few cars and trucks left that traveled the pavement did so at risk of their tires.

Rickards climbed out of the battered dark green Jeep Wrangler he was riding in and stretched. Dan Clements slid out from behind the wheel and walked around to stand next to him. Together they watched the small tanker, filled with gasoline that the group would need to get home, pull up to the pole barn just visible from the highway and stop in front of the double-height garage doors. As the remainder of the four-by-fours pulled in and parked in the flat area in front of the barn, the tanker driver climbed out of the cab and made his way over to where Rickards and Clements were waiting.

"Want me to top off the jeeps before we head out?" the driver asked as he stopped next to the two men.

Clements nodded absently as he looked around the area, shading his eyes as he stared east, toward their target, unseen in the distance. After a moment, he turned back to the tanker driver. "Yeah, we'll do that. Wait for a moment, though."

Clements raised an arm, put his hand to his lips and blew out a whistle so loud Rickards thought it would break his eardrums. He instinctively looked toward the east even though he knew they were much too far away for the band of ghosts to hear Clements—at least if they were camped out in the mountains southwest of Seligman as the seeker images seemed to indicate.

The men, responding to the piercing sound, walked over to Clements and Rickards, laughing and joking as they moved. None of them seemed too concerned about the upcoming mission, even though each one was outfitted as though heading to war. As they gathered around, Clements gestured for everyone to settle down. The sixteen men quieted quickly, all eyes fixed on the leader.

"I need everyone to line up their vehicles and fill the tanks from the truck. Once you're topped off, pull out onto the flat area over there." He pointed toward the large graveled lot to the west of the barn. "We also need to get this garage door open so that we can pull the tanker inside when we're done. We have no idea how widely these ghosts are patrolling. If they've seen us pull in, we can expect to find their compound empty. I'm betting that they're not coming down this far, but I also don't want to take a chance on them coming across the tanker in the open while we're gone. We'll need the fuel to get home. I'd like to head out in twenty. Any questions?"

"You buying the beer and pizza when this is all over?" came a voice from somewhere in the cluster of men.

Rickards looked for the speaker and saw a short, heavily muscled man with dark, close-cropped hair and a happy-go-lucky grin on his face. A tall, lanky man standing next to him shoved his shoulder, and the entire group laughed. Pizza and beer had been in short supply for months. With no one running the breweries or making cheese, much of the supply that had been on the shelves at the height of the pandemic had been used up and never replaced.

Sure, Rickards had heard of several people trying to build their own stills at both his and other APZs, in spite of the shortage of fermentable grains and fruits within the communities. A few of the more industrious ones sneaked out of the APZs to scavenge the desert for the abundant local plants, such as prickly pear fruit and agave. Some of these do-it-yourself distillers had been successful, at least based on the visible results, many of whom had been arrested while causing intoxicated brawls. Other experiments, unfortunately, had resulted in alcohol vapor explosions, poisonings and death. The owners of those stills, as well as others in close proximity, had paid dearly for their desire for a drink.

Surprisingly, the cheese for the pizza was almost more difficult to come by than the alcohol. With a shortage of people to run the dairy farms, and, even more importantly, a lack of people skilled in making cheese from the milk, not to mention the shorter shelf life of the product, most people hadn't had a *real* pizza for a very long time and weren't likely to indulge any time in the foreseeable future.

Unfazed, Clements grinned. "You bet, Ruiz, pizza with all the fixin's *and* anchovies and pineapple." He laughed at the groans from the crowd. Apparently, putting fish or fruit on pizza was not popular in this part of Arizona. "Plus all the beer you can drink, *if* you're able to find any at the compound."

The men cheered, in spite of knowing perfectly well the reward for a successful mission was more likely to be water and jerky. Unless, of course, this was an industrious band of ghosts, and they'd figured out how to make their own beer or other forms of alcohol from local plants.

For a moment, Rickards got lost in dreams of a bottle of well-aged whiskey, or even a bottle of mezcal, although the agave based drink was not usually high on his list of preferred beverages, with or without the worm. Still, agave, or maguey plants, were readily available in much of the desert southwest, giving newbie distillers plenty of material for their experimentations in fermentation. He looked over toward a gigantic century plant he'd noticed twenty feet out into the pasture behind the barn, and a small smile played on his lips.

" . . .do you think, Captain?"

Clements' voice jerked Rickards' attention back to the here and now. The men had moved off to start filling the jeeps. Two were working on the padlock affixed to the barn door with an industrial, shark-sized set of bolt cutters. Rickards coughed to hide his surprise, then looked at the team leader. The tall man was staring at him with his strange, pale brown eyes. A frown creased his forehead.

"I'm sorry, I missed that, Dan. What did you say?" Rickards asked, raising an eyebrow in question, trying to gloss over the fact that he hadn't been paying attention.

"I was saying that I can lead Alpha team and you lead Beta team. What do you think?" Clements repeated.

Rickards could hear a faint note of misgiving in Clements' voice, and he understood immediately. Even though they had established that Clements was in charge of the mission, the man still had some doubts that Rickards would follow his command and had made some changes to the original plan. Rickards had no experience on the exorcism team operations, however, and was wise enough to recognize where others knew more than he did. It was one of the things that made his law enforcement career so successful, not to mention his marriage to Marie. In spite of their earlier agreement, Clements was trying to find a balance between ensuring the team's mission went well, and no one was injured — except for the ghosts, that is — and deciding to throw a bone to Rickards' authority.

"I appreciate your confidence in me," Rickards said, a wry note in his voice. "But I'm not going to fool myself. Your team is well trained and I'd be a liability. Keep your normal group leaders as we discussed. I'm just along for the ride."

Rickards saw Clements begin to relax, a smile slowly spreading across his face. He ran a hand through his thinning hair, put on a stained gimme cap and pulled it down over his eyes.

"Was it that obvious?" Clements chuckled.

"Yeah, well I won't hold it against you." Rickards took a deep breath. "I appreciate your including me." He held up a hand to halt Clements as he started to protest. "No, I know I'm your superior, but as I told you at the meeting, you're the one who has been running these missions. So, accept the thanks and drop it."

Tension loosened its final hold on Clements' shoulders. He laughed, a rumbling sound like thunder, a deep resonance incongruous in someone so thin, and nodded. "Consider it dropped. Get the jeep topped off and be ready to head out in twenty." He laughed again, turned and strode off toward the rest of the group, calling to them as he went, making ribald comments and eliciting laughs and similar observations in response.

You'd think we were at a deer camp, Rickards thought, shaking his head with a slight smile on his face as he started to follow the team leader. *No one watching us would have any idea that we were getting ready to kill the people who used to be our neighbors, people we'd see on the streets and wave at or meet at the local bar and share some drinks.* The smile slipped off his face like snow sliding off a tin roof in the sun.

Twenty-five minutes later, the line of four-wheel-drive vehicles was heading down the small dirt road, leaving behind a cloud of dust boiling up from the tires in spite of the slower speeds Clements had demanded in order to minimize the easily visible evidence of their travel.

The road wound its way through juniper and boulders, devolving from a well-maintained gravel road to a primitive dirt track and eventually to a two-rut trail. With each transformation, the speed of the convoy decreased to accommodate the rougher surface, finally slowing to a fast crawl. The high clearance vehicles pitched and yawed as they traversed the boulder strewn route, and several times Rickards grabbed at the door frame to keep from being flung from his seat.

In spite of the remoteness of the area, signs of human encroachment were still easily visible in places. Rickards started in surprise as they rounded a curve in the road only to be faced with a dilapidated, twenty-five-foot sailboat docked between a giant granite boulder and an ancient alligator juniper. He was torn between disgust at the people who dumped their trash out in the wilderness and impressed someone had actually managed to get the large boat back this far on the ranch and forest roads.

The track smoothed out, and the jeeps picked up speed again, although Clements, the leader of the pack, kept the amount of dust strongly in mind. Several times he muttered about wishing there had been rain more recently.

Finally, after Clements had glanced back, released the accelerator, and grumbled about his desire for some of the wet stuff for what seemed like the tenth time, Rickards asked,

"Wouldn't a wet surface make things worse—I mean wouldn't the mud be harder to get through?"

Rickards was genuinely curious. He'd been raised in Los Angeles and had moved to Laughlin when he'd begun his law enforcement career thirty years ago. He'd seldom been hunting, despised hiking, and unless you counted the shooting range, he rarely left the city limits. By all the criteria he knew of, he considered himself a city rat, not a country mouse. Still, he'd seen enough accidents caused by rain on pavement over the years, and it didn't make sense that rain on dirt would be any better.

Clements looked over at him, and Rickards could see pity touched by derision in his eyes—the expression someone comfortable with camping, hiking and living in the wild gave another whom he felt had been woefully disadvantaged in his youth.

"We don't want muddy roads, but if there'd been some rain in the last twenty-four hours we wouldn't have to worry as much about visible dust. There would still be enough moisture in the ground to keep dirt in place."

Rickards didn't answer, just nodded once, sharply, and turned to face the track in front of them, feeling foolish he hadn't thought of that himself.

Another curve, and they were faced with several strands of barbed wire strung across the road.

"Passenger gets the gate," Clements said, giving Rickards a sideways look and a grin, the earlier pity missing from the expression.

Rickards gritted his teeth, then, feeling the ache in his jaw, he forced his muscles to relax. Sighing, he swung himself out of the jeep. *Clements is getting entirely too much enjoyment from this being in charge thing,* he thought. There had been no doubt in his mind when he'd told Clements that the exorcism leader was in charge on this operation, and there still wasn't, but the man didn't need to rub it in.

Rickards walked up to the twists of wire, noticing that they connected two juniper stays, one on either side of the road. Each stay was fastened to the fence post next to it with strands of smooth wire. The loops of galvanized steel that secured the branch of juniper on the right of the track were above and below the top and bottom wires of the fence, making it possible to slip them off. However, on the other side, the attaching wires were between the strands, making that post permanent. Rickards grabbed the juniper stay on the right and pushed it toward the post, trying to get enough slack in the upper loop to slip it over the top of the branch. The wire of the gate was stretched tight, and Rickards finally had to reach around, grasp the fence post in his right hand and pull it toward his chest, using his shoulder to squeeze the smaller stay forward. At that point, the top loop loosened, and he was able to push it up and out of the way. He then lifted the branch out of the wire loop at the bottom of the gate and walked the entire mass of wire and wood back to the left side of the road, dropping it in a heap, not caring if the wire tangled. No one was left to complain if the gates were left open.

Clements had driven the jeep through while Rickards had been dumping the useless wire gate and he braked so that the captain could climb back in. The road continued a short distance to the edge of a canyon, then dropped down, traversing a steep hillside at a forty-five degree angle, emerging on a lower plateau. There, some enterprising hoarder had parked a variety of old campers and vans, none of which had intact windows, and few had actual doors. The hoods of the vans were raised in what Rickards had been told was the "Arizona salute," used by people to try and avoid a pack rat invasion into the engine compartment. Loveless had told him stories of the devastation a pack rat could wreak on the wiring of a vehicle, but Rickards had never seen it for himself, pack rats being relatively uncommon in the middle of Laughlin.

From what he could see of the conglomeration of vehicles, the war on pack rats had been lost years ago, and the rodents had taken no prisoners. The campers appeared to be infested, and Rickards felt an internal shiver of disgust that made its way out to his face as they drove the hundred feet or so through the compound.

"Hantavirus Hilton, there," Clements said conversationally, nodding toward a beat-up pickup camper, garbage and other debris protruding through the broken windows.

"Huh?" Rickards said, surprised at Clements' comment.

"Hantavirus. That disease carried by rat pee?" Clements clarified. "There's been enough rats in those campers to probably infect the remainder of the Earth's population."

"Actually, it's deer mice that carry that particular virus," Rickards said, although he knew he sounded distracted as he watched the last of the detritus from the garbage dump drop behind. He looked over his shoulder and saw some of the other vehicles slow, then accelerate after the lead jeep.

"Oh," Clements said, and he spared a quick look at Rickards, then back at the trail, which had turned and headed up the hill, gaining in roughness and altitude at the same time. "I didn't know that. I thought it was any rat."

Rickards gave him a half smile. "My wife was a nurse. She told me. She was paranoid about any rodents getting into the house." He felt a sharp pang of loss lance through his chest at the mention of his wife. He was also aware of a gnawing feeling of guilt. When Marie died, it was in the midst of the full explosion of death that followed the influenza pandemic like a shadow. As a Laughlin police officer, he'd been inundated and overwhelmed with the needs of the people he had sworn to serve. He'd been forced to build walls around himself as thick as the Grand Canyon was wide just to be able to face the dead and dying every day.

Marie's death had been the last time he'd cried. It hadn't placed the final brick in that wall, but it was close. The day he held a one-year-old little girl who was gasping for her final breaths and stood looking at the child's dead mother, knowing there was nothing he could do, knowing no matter how quickly he rushed the baby to the Laughlin hospital, there was nothing *anyone* could do, that was the final brick. That day he felt an overwhelming calm flow over him. It felt as though he'd been wrapped in a thick blanket, and nothing could touch him.

Others looked at his stone-like visage and called him cold — unfeeling. Only he knew about the boiling emotions trapped within that wall. He knew he hadn't had a chance to grieve for Marie, and at times he felt guilty he could go for days without thinking of her, lost in the immediacy of the pandemic and the reorganization that followed.

That woman in the canyon — Maggie Langton, she'd said her name was — had been the only real crack in his fortress for months, and Rickards felt guilt about that too. Guilt that he thought more about her than about his wife. Still, the woman was alive, and

Marie was not. He could help the woman as he hadn't been able to help Marie or the little girl, or so many others.

The jeep jerked to a stop, and Rickards looked up, pulled out of his thoughts. They were sitting at a fork in the track. One set of ruts led east, while the other southeast.

Clements gestured out the open door of the jeep, indicating that Alpha team was to follow him and Beta team was to head to the southeast. Their handheld radios were already set to channel 17, but Clements had reminded the men they were to remain radio silent as much as possible just in case their quarry was monitoring radio activity in the area.

Rickards thought this was a bit of overkill since the odds of someone in their vicinity being on a radio was almost as likely as a snowstorm in Phoenix during the summer, but Clements was the leader, and he had no intention of questioning the man. Besides, the precaution couldn't hurt anything.

The eastern track became rougher, and the shortened line of vehicles crawled over boulders and up steep banks. Rickards found himself gripping the grab bar tightly several times as he was sure the vehicle would turn turtle, rolling down the mountainside, spitting out men and equipment as it went. On the periodic breaks between cliff sides and rocks, the abbreviated convoy picked up speed, passing windmills, feeders and the occasional small herd of cattle, several of whom raised their heads and stared at the humans as they drove by. Rickards made a mental note of the animals as he figured they could provide some necessary protein should the APZ's other supplies fail and the herds closer to the city be depleted.

In spite of the slow speed, it wasn't long before Alpha team reached a wash that fed a large grove of cottonwoods whose branches spread out and covered the vehicles from prying eyes. The men climbed out of the open doors of the jeeps and started pulling out packs and weapons without waiting for Clements' command.

Rickards looked over at the leader of the exorcism team and found the tall man watching him. His pale, brown eyes were sharp, and his bony face somber. Rickards felt slightly uncomfortable under the intense scrutiny.

"You ready for this?" Clements asked, and there was a new, unfamiliar note underlying the man's normally casual tones. Rickards realized that in spite of Clements willingness to welcome him on the mission, the leader still wasn't entirely sure Rickards could cut it.

Neither was Rickards, for that matter.

Rickards nodded and swallowed hard before he answered, "Yeah, ready when you are."

A crooked smile took over Clements' stubbled face, and he turned and slid out of the jeep and walked to the back of the vehicle to retrieve his pack and weapon. Rickards started to climb out on his side when a soft *burring* at his hip caused him to pause. He fished the satellite phone from his pocket, mentally cursing himself for not putting the device on silent. A mistake like that at the wrong time could give away the entire operation and result in loss of lives. He glanced at the screen and saw a message waiting from Knox.

Ludeman demanding to meet again. Threatening revolt.

An involuntary growl of frustration escaped his throat, and he punched in his message, hitting the screen so hard an observer might have been excused if he thought the Enforcer captain was trying to drive his thumbs through the glass and into the guts of the device.

Tell him out of town. Arrest if becomes a problem. Do it quietly.

Rickards put the phone on silent and shoved it back into its case, then turned and pulled out his backpack and rifle. Looking around at the other members of the exorcism team, he saw a variety of weapons. Several automatic and semi-automatic rifles were in view, as well as one or two other older hunting rifles. Since the turn of the century, there had been many converts to the assault-type weapons, proclaiming their value for self-protection. From what Rickards heard, some even liked to use them for hunting. Rickards had trained on one and knew it had strengths and weaknesses. For his money, however, he wanted the old .30-06 hunting rifle with the high power scope left to him by his father, knowing he could do the damage with a few well-placed shots that some of the others could do with a spray, and he didn't need to stockpile as many resources. It might be "old school," but it was his school.

He was aware that prior to the pandemic—well, for that matter, probably for the lifetime of the country, if not longer—

there had been a faction who believed that survival in a disaster, be it natural or man-made, depended on who had the most ammunition, the largest stockpile of weapons, and the greatest ability to kill their fellow man. It didn't matter if the target in the crosshairs was the family from the next town who came looking for help, or maybe the guy next door who had come to the Fourth of July barbecue without the potato salad. There were also people who believed in creating a community of like-minded individuals who would support each other in staying fed and protected, but many others prepared for solitary survival. He'd always figured the ones who would survive would be the ones who focused on skills and supplies more than the weapons and ammunition, although the latter was certainly important. For one thing, the ammunition could become a valuable trading commodity if there was enough to spare, while most of the hunting could be done using bows or crossbows.

Years ago, he'd been fascinated with what was called "post-apocalyptic" fiction, and some of the premises made sense to him, although he found others laughable. The idea that old, pre-computer day vehicles would function for an extended time and distance on just the amount of gasoline left in underground storage tanks and the tanks of disabled vehicles abandoned on the roadways confused him. Hell, what kind of mileage could those things get? If you were driving around the way they described in some of those books, the available gasoline would evaporate faster than a drop of rain on a June day in Arizona.

Since his own experience with several comparatively minor pandemics and now the post-apocalypse—real life and not fiction— he looked back at those books from a new perspective. Of course, they weren't surviving an EMP or a mutant, zombie-creating rabies virus, just a shortage of resources due to a lack of skilled labor—a shortage that would be rectified soon, he hoped. Some people had died due to a shortage of medications or skilled medical care, but at least here in the West, food had not been a significant issue. Nor had water. At least not in the Laughlin APZ, thanks to the Colorado River running practically across the front porch. That was the point of the APZs—make sure everyone was treated equally.

He thought about the band of ghosts they were chasing and sighed. There would always be some, however, who felt like they had priority over everyone else. They would take what they wanted and to hell with anyone who got in their way. He'd seen it in both of the major pandemics he'd survived. From everything he'd heard from the exorcism teams and the heads of other APZs, the bands of ghosts had a much rougher time than those who had submitted to concentration. It was the price of going it alone, in his opinion. From what he could see, the social order had not collapsed, as many had predicted, and while there had been some skirmishes among the people in his care—he thought sourly of Ludeman—by and large, everyone cared for everyone else.

Phase One: Reduction of Population. Phase Two: Consolidation of Population. The APZs had done that. But would this new organization last? The thought flashed into his mind, and he felt a knife-blade twist of doubt in his gut.

He felt his hip and found the handgun still snugly tucked into its holster. He hoisted the pack over his shoulder and walked over to where the rest of the small group was gathered.

"Jacobs, you and Alvarez are going to stay with the jeeps," Clements was explaining, gesturing to the two men he'd named. They nodded attentively. "Monitor the radios, and if we call, get two vehicles up to us ASAP. Bring the biggest ones." Clements' voice was intense, and it was obvious from the posture of his audience that the seriousness of his message was getting through. "Alvarez, you've got a phone with GPS, right?"

"Yeah," the man pulled out what appeared to be a standard cell phone and glanced down at the screen.

"Got a signal?"

Alvarez squinted at the screen, hesitated, then nodded. "It's got one bar, but it's going in and out."

"We'll have to hope one bar is enough." Clements stated, a frown on his face, frustration audible in his voice. "We'll also have to hope the radios don't get blocked in the mountains. You'll have to be on your toes."

The phone Rickards left in the canyon with the Langton woman was a traditional cell and hadn't gotten any signal, but he'd figured she could go up to the rim if she needed to call. It was registered to Rickards, and he hadn't reported it missing so that it wouldn't trigger the alarms if she had to use it. Upon the return to the Laughlin APZ, Rickards had quietly liberated another phone from the stash collected by the Enforcers following the concentration—either taken from empty homes where the owners had died, or turned in by citizens when the Enforcers explained the need. Of course, Rickards wasn't fool enough to believe that everyone had turned in their phones, especially considering the tech addiction that afflicted so many people prior to the pandemic. The lock down of the internet had solved that problem. Enough techies had survived to help with the new restrictions on the world wide web, and to come up with a way to get the seized phones reprogrammed and "registered." In their area, the cellular service was pretty spotty due to the failure of maintenance on the cell towers and other equipment needed for that technology, but the authorities had been trying to get new technicians trained and climbing the towers to repair those damaged by the elements.

Clements had finished giving everyone their marching orders, then shouldered his pack. "Come on, we'd better get going. We need to be in position well before dawn. Remember you're on radio silence and keep your talking to a minimum. We have no idea where they may have posted sentries."

With that, Clements stepped out, heading for a narrow cattle or game trail that led off down the wash.

Rickards picked up his pack and rifle and fell into step behind the team leader, maneuvering carefully over the rocks and boulders in his way. In spite of the shade in the wash, the early fall day was warm, heading for hot. Unless there was a late monsoon storm, they were in for a long, sweaty walk. He could hear the steps of the men behind him and felt reassured, as though there was a wall of protection at his back. With that comforting thought, he focused on the back of the man ahead of him and put one foot in front of the other, praying he wouldn't slip in any of the fresh cow pies that liberally splattered the ground in and around the wash.

18

Ethan Granger stood on a granite boulder looking out over the valley west of the compound. A few clouds dotted the intense blue of the early fall sky, but he could feel heaviness in the air—increased moisture. Maybe there'd be some rain coming in spite of the nearly empty horizon. It wasn't normal this time of year, but occasionally Pacific hurricanes threw a lot of moisture into Arizona in the early fall.

He'd spoken to people who had moved to the Phoenix area after living in more humid climates, be it hot or cold, and to a man, they all were surprised at how the dryness of the desert manifested itself. Many talked about how they couldn't seem to get enough water or how they'd suffered from dehydration for not drinking adequate amounts. They complained about the dryness of their skin and hair. But mostly, they talked about how even a slight rise in humidity during the summer felt as though a heavy, wet, wool blanket had been thrown over their shoulders and stuffed in their faces. Arizona's perpetual summer marketing tool—but it's a "dry" heat, often accompanied by a picture of a skeleton in a blast furnace—held a modicum of truth, and newbies often found themselves overdoing it in the summer because they underestimated the actual temperature and its effects.

Behind him, he could hear members of the group going about their morning chores, voices subdued, none of the usual joking and laughing he was used to. He wasn't surprised after the night before.

"Get out of my way, Granger!"

Kyle Lucas stood four feet outside of the door to the pole barn, looking at Granger, who was standing in the opening, blocking the blond man's entrance. Lucas's ice blue eyes lit with the fire of rage. Although, if Granger was honest with himself, that frozen flame was starting to look more and more like insanity rather than anger.

Granger glanced over his shoulder at the large west-facing window in the steel pole barn. About a half hour until sunset, he estimated, based on the color of the glow at that glass portal. He felt the momentary urge to look at the screen of his cell phone to check the time. The feeling was so strong he was aware of the muscles in his arm tightening in preparation for the movement, his fingers trailing across the pocket of his grubby jeans. Of course, the phone wasn't there, and even if it had been, never again would anyone be able to use it to tell the time. The battery had been on life support for months following his and Lucas's flight from Phoenix, and Granger had developed the habit of only turning it on for a few minutes at a time in order to look at pictures of his daughters, his ex-wife, his previous life. Occasionally they would come across a car or truck that still had a battery with power, and he would recharge the device, but those opportunities were few and far between and becoming even rarer as lack of maintenance was the death knell for many car batteries in the hot summer months of Arizona. Then a month ago, the phone's screen had been shattered, his memories relegated only to the recesses of his mind.

Old habits die hard, however. Granger had never realized how compelling the urge to know the time could be. It didn't matter anymore. They were back to judging the time of day by needs instead of hours. If the sun was up, he needed to work in the garden, or prepare food, work on the shelter or go hunting. If the sun was overhead and he was hungry, it was time for lunch. If the sun was sinking into the western mountains, it was time to get ready to sleep for another night—if he could manage that without nightmares ripping him out of slumber.

Granger mentally forced his hand and arm to relax and waited for the urge to pass. He wondered how those who had been so obsessed with their electronic umbilicalis and the ever-present connection with others had managed since the cord had been cut.

The first group he and Lucas encountered after finding Lucas's bolt hole violated included a woman who sat staring at the black screen of her dead phone. Occasionally she tapped on the broken glass with her thumbs or swiped her fingers across the flexible surface. Watching the woman absorbed in her device, laughing on occasion, or smiling, or frowning as though reading a text, sent sandpaper chills up Granger's spine. Nothing, it seemed, could penetrate the woman's delusion that the device was still working.

That woman hadn't lasted long, wandering off one night while the others sat around the fire. They found her the next morning at the bottom of a cliff, shattered cell phone still in her hand. It was sad, Granger had thought at the time, but they'd always said texting while walking could be dangerous, if not downright deadly.

Granger looked back at the angry man standing a few feet away from him.

"We have a deal, Lucas. I let you bring the woman with us because we need to know about her people and where they are hidden." Granger tactfully avoided also saying that he had allowed Lucas to bring the woman back mainly because he wasn't convinced he could control the man out in the wilderness with no backup. "We agreed there would be no rape, though," said Granger, not bothering to pretend he didn't know what Lucas intended to do with Maggie Langton.

"Dammit, Granger. That woman is mine." Lucas paused for a moment as though he was thinking, then a sneer settled on his face, temporarily transforming the fury but making Granger even more uncomfortable. "Besides, you haven't gotten any information about her people or her camp yet, have you?" he said, his voice making it clear what he thought of Granger's questioning techniques—an opinion he'd expressed several times during their friendship. "You'd have said if you'd learned anything. You need to let me interrogate her. You know I can get it out of her. What do you care what happens to her after that?" It was obvious he thought Granger would acknowledge that the need to know more about Langton and where she came from was of higher importance than what would eventually happen to the woman during the learning.

"We may need her in one piece," Granger stated flatly, hoping the roiling of his stomach didn't show on his face. He had a feeling Lucas was like the beta wolf who would kill the alpha male if it became weak.

Lucas opened his mouth, preparing for another argument, then paused. Granger saw an expression flicker into the man's eyes. He glanced over his shoulder, his manner furtive, looking to see if anyone was nearby.

In a soft, husky voice, much lower than the one he had been using, he said, "I'll give you some of my stash, Granger. You know what I mean, right? You're the only one who knows." Lucas's voice had dropped to a near whisper, and he glanced over his shoulder once again, eyes darting from side to side, making sure no one was listening to them. They were still alone. Most people made themselves scarce when Lucas was in one of his moods. Granger wished he could do the same.

Granger knew exactly what Lucas meant by his *stash*, and the thought of the small canvas bag the blond man kept hidden in his pack nauseated him.

The first time Granger had seen Lucas's stash was at a small homestead buried in the thick junipers northwest of Seligman. As Granger, Lucas and their slowly growing group wandered around northwestern Arizona, it was depressingly common to find remote homes where the residents had attempted to isolate themselves from the virus, only to find they'd brought the disease with them.

At this particular cabin, the group found only one corpse, to Granger's relief—an older man who had passed while laying on a worn, blue denim couch and had collapsed into a desiccated piece of human jerky in the dry Arizona climate.

As usual, the group raided the man's kitchen, taking whatever supplies they could find. Lucas, who proved to have a nose like a truffle pig when it came to secret hideouts, discovered the man's main supply cache in a nearby cave.

That evening the group gathered around the fire and enjoyed a feast unlike anything they'd experienced for several weeks.

Without discussion, the small cluster of survivors had set up camp near the man's barn in tacit agreement that the house be left to its owner. As the satiated members drifted off to find their sleeping bags or bed rolls, Granger noticed Lucas was no longer among them. He looked around the fire. Andy and Daniel were curled up in their blankets near the barn wall, a soft snore indicating one or both of the boys had already fallen asleep.

No Lucas, however.

Finally, Granger decided he must have gone off to water a tree and started to roll himself into his own sleeping bag. Just as he was pulling the edge of the bag up to his neck, he saw a glint of light in the front window of the house and froze.

The faint glimmer flashed again, so brief Granger wondered if he was seeing things. He threw back the top of the sleeping bag and quietly crept across the yard to the cabin's front window.

What he saw chilled him to his core. Lucas was at the old, denim couch, yanking on the old man's head. For a moment, Granger thought Lucas was actually trying to decapitate the corpse, then the man jerked back, and Granger saw a pair of needle nose pliers in his hand. Something yellowish glinted between the jaws of the pliers and Granger realized Lucas had just pulled a gold crown from the body's mouth. Lucas picked up a small canvas bag that had been sitting on the floor next to his knee and dropped the crown inside, then bent back to the remains. Granger could see in the harsh glow from the flashlight that the lower jaw had been forced open and probably broken or dislocated to give Lucas better access to the molars.

Granger felt as though his recent meal was going to make a reappearance, and he stepped back from the window. Lucas must have caught the movement from the corner of his eye, and he straightened and looked over toward the window, a furious expression on his face. When he saw it was Granger, however, his features eased into a smile, and he held up the pliers, a second tooth clearly clenched between the jaws, then dropped it in the canvas bag. Granger staggered backward, then turned and stumbled back to his sleeping bag. No one else was still awake, or if they were, they didn't seem to notice Granger's disappearance and reappearance.

It wasn't much longer before Lucas also walked back into the circle of firelight, stretching and scratching his belly. He looked over toward Granger, caught his eye and shot him a grin and winked, jiggling his shirt pocket. Granger could clearly hear the click of the teeth rattling together, but he pretended he heard nothing. He turned over in his bag, pulling the edge over his head and tried to sleep.

Over the following weeks, Granger occasionally caught sight of the canvas bag, growing slowly in size as the group came across more abandoned homes. Granger never saw Lucas performing his macabre dental work again, and they didn't come across many other corpses since most people had abandoned their homes as the pandemic progressed, either for the hospital, the morgue or the APZs. There still were many other small items such as rings or other bits of jewelry, however, left behind when the residents departed.

Granger never mentioned Lucas's desecration of the corpses they found, and for his part, Lucas had never brought up the subject again, either.

Until now.

Now Lucas was standing there, fumbling to untie the knots in the string that held the dirty canvas bag closed, the contents clattering and ticking inside.

"Dammit, Lucas, cut it out!" Granger barked at Lucas, his tightly controlled temper flaring, his fists clenched at his sides. "I don't want any of your morbid *stash*. I should have left that woman out where we found her regardless of what you said. Regardless of what you did. You and I have a deal and you will live up to it."

Lucas froze, his eyes narrowed, and Granger didn't know whether the blue-eyed man was about to back down or attack him with full, insane fury.

"You owe me," Lucas finally snarled. "If it weren't for me you'd still be stuck down there in Phoenix. You'd be living in an APZ, crying over your dead wife and kids . . ."

Granger drew in a breath with a hiss and took a step back, feeling as though he'd been punched. His eyes met Lucas's, and for a moment there was silence. Granger fought the roiling emotions threatening to overwhelm his self-control.

Lucas had halted mid-sentence and was now watching Granger warily. A small noise behind Ethan broke his focus, and he looked over his shoulder and into the barn. Andy, the younger of the two brothers, was standing in shadow near the back wall of the building, a terrified look on his face, several plates in his hands. Granger realized he must have been collecting the empty dishes left over from the prisoner's meal when the confrontation began and had been afraid to make his presence known.

"This isn't over, Granger," Lucas said in a flat voice, causing Granger's head to snap back around. He saw Lucas, still standing a few feet away, but whereas before he had seemed consumed by a white-hot flame, now he seemed cold and calm as ice. He turned and stalked off across the compound, heading toward the nearest of the motorhomes.

"I know, Kyle," Granger said to his retreating back, his voice soft—not a whisper, but close. His chest felt tight, and he wondered for the briefest of moments if he was having a heart attack and then debated whether he might prefer that to whatever else this post-pandemic world had in store for him. He felt a prick of tears and fought them down. He had sobbed over the bodies of his daughters as he'd buried them in the backyard, furious at himself and his ex-wife for failing to keep them safe. He was damned sure not going to cry now, not over a taunt from someone like Kyle Lucas.

He turned to find Andy rooted to the same spot on the concrete floor, still watching Granger with wide, dark eyes, plates clutched in his hands.

"What are you doing there, Andy?" Granger called. He could hear the hoarseness in his voice and cleared his throat. He saw the boy flinch at the sound, but he also took a step forward.

"I set the lady's dishes on the shelf and forgot them when I left. Jackie told me to get them. She was pretty pissed off that I left them here. You didn't see me, though, when you and Lucas started talking, and I didn't want to let him know I was here. I don't like him much." The snap of anger in his dark eyes and the level of venom in Andy's voice surprised Ethan. He knew Lucas tormented the boy—both boys, truth be told—giving the excuse that Granger, and some of the women, babied them too much. Granger had thought maybe Lucas was right at the time—but he hadn't realized how much it had affected the younger boy.

Then Granger frowned, and his gaze shifted to the barred door of the back room. He wondered at the silence behind it. Sure, he and Lucas had been standing at the front of the barn, and the lean-to was at the back, and their voices had been kept low for the most part. Granger's because he didn't want to draw the attention of the rest of the group to the argument, although he was sure they were aware. Lucas's voice had been low and menacing the entire time. He debated on going to check on the woman, then stopped himself. After the confrontation with Lucas and the dilemma he found himself in, he just didn't have the courage to look into those bright green eyes again, at least not yet.

Turning to Andy, he beckoned the boy over. Andy approached, shuffling his feet, his reluctance obvious and tearing at Granger's heart.

Granger put his hand on Andy's shoulder when the boy finally got close enough. "You okay?" he asked softly.

"I'm okay, Ethan," Andy said, avoiding looking into Granger's eyes.

"How much did you hear?" His mind cast back over the argument with Lucas. Did he say anything that could jeopardize his position in the band? While Granger had fallen naturally into the leadership role within their community, lately he'd been aware of a expanding sense of discordance. He'd figured it was because of Lucas's growing instability and Granger's perceived connection with him. Granger was torn. He knew the only reason he wasn't in an APZ or dead was because of Lucas. The man was right about that. At what point did loyalty to the group override loyalty to Lucas? He just didn't know. But he was afraid he was going to find out soon.

Then he thought about Linda and realized he might also find out who in the group preferred insanity, anger and vengeance over calm common sense because, from what he'd seen over his lifetime, there were people like that.

"Not much. You was talking quiet," Andy said in a voice barely above a loud whisper. He looked up, and his gaze met Granger's for the briefest of moments before speeding away once again.

"Good," Granger said, feeling a release of tension. "Don't talk about it with anyone, will ya? I'd like to keep it quiet if possible. Now, go take the dishes back to Jackie before she gets any more pissed off at you." He dredged up a grin for the boy and pushed him over toward the motorhomes where he could hear some group members talking with each other as they sat around the fire pit. The sun slipped behind the western mountains and the air turned cooler in an instant. Granger shivered.

Looking out over the valley the next morning, Granger was still unsure about what action he should take. He'd chosen to sleep in the pole barn the night before in case Lucas decided to defy Granger and go after the woman under cover of darkness. When he went to gather his blankets from the motorhome he shared with Lucas, Linda and three others, he had to pass the campfire. He could see Lucas on the far side of the flames, his eyes glinting in the flickering orange light as he watched Granger enter the RV.

When Granger emerged with his bedroll in his arms, he glanced over toward the fire to see if Lucas had taken the opportunity to return to the barn. A knot of tension eased when he saw the blond man sitting in the same spot and then tightened again when their eyes met. It felt as though an ice-cold inferno had scorched his body. Granger looked quickly away, clutched his bedding closer to his chest and strode off toward the pole barn. The urge to turn and see if Lucas was still watching was almost unbearable, and the hair on the back of his neck rippled and tickled with the feeling that he was still the focus of that laser glare.

Taking a deep breath, Granger turned away from the spectacular view and walked back toward the cluster of RVs. Seeing Linda over by the garden, Granger changed his direction and strode over to her.

"Have you seen Lucas?" Granger asked.

The woman's head snapped up, and she glared at him. "He went out early this morning. I'm not sure where." She spat out the words as though she thought Granger was responsible for Lucas's erratic behavior. "He didn't even come in to sleep last night, just sat by the fire staring at the damned barn."

"Linda, I don't . . ." The ice in his voice matched the heat in hers.

"Yeah, *you don't.* You don't understand Kyle. He's been going out a lot lately, and he won't tell me where. You've said he saved you and that you owe him, but you sure don't act like it sometimes." Linda spun on her heel and stomped away.

Granger wondered who the woman was angrier with, him or Lucas. He frowned, rubbing his hand through his sandy brown hair. Linda said Lucas had been going out a lot lately and now that he thought back, he couldn't remember seeing the blond man around the compound most days.

Of course, he couldn't actually *remember* seeing any of the members of the group at any given time if he wasn't specifically looking for them. Maybe he kept track of the boys, but as far as the other adults went, he never considered himself their keeper. Members of the group didn't have assigned activities most of the time. They naturally gravitated toward the tasks that would keep the entire group fed and sheltered. On occasion, something would arise and Granger would ask someone to handle it, but for the most part, people drifted toward those jobs that corresponded to their skills.

But try as he might, he couldn't picture Lucas working at any of the normal daily activities. Not hauling water, working in the garden, working on the windmill or repairing the buildings. He shook his head as if trying to clear the cobwebs. His fists clenched and loosened as he looked into his memory.

Nothing.

Well, hell, he thought, disgusted with his inability to remember. *Kyle's probably just going hunting, or scavenging the local homes, or something totally innocent, and I've got better things to do than worry about his feelings.*

Granger turned and stood for another minute, seeking one more sight of the morning-lit valley, trying to soak in the peace from the view. In the distance, faint over the growing breeze of morning, he heard an elk bugle, the squeaky hinge sound sending shivers down his back. Quail chip-churred nearby, and other bird life filled the morning with sound. A faint hum caught his attention for a moment, but when he looked in the direction he thought the sound came from, he saw nothing. Of course, the group used UTVs to haul water or gather items from other properties, so the sound wasn't that strange. He wondered briefly if Lucas was out there, gathering more molars for his stash, then squashed that thought down as hard as he could.

Granger took a breath and turned away from the valley. He paused for a moment and cast his gaze over the compound once again, then made his way over toward the tan steel barn.

It was time to see how their visitor had slept and whether she was willing to hand out any more nuggets of information. Not that he'd gotten much yet.

19

The sound of a coyote yipping nearby roused O'Reilly from a restless sleep. He lay on his back, head pillowed on his saddle, looking at the dark northern Arizona sky filled with stars. He remembered that as a child living at Eagle Camp, he and his brother loved watching the night sky, but even then, there was a discernible glow to the south from the Phoenix Metro area and a fainter one to the northwest, from Kingman. Now, with the recent extreme reduction in the world's population thanks to the H5N1, vehicle and electric light use had drastically decreased, and with it light and air pollution. This morning the starry sky seemed to explode into his senses and threatened to swallow him whole.

Then the memory of the day before washed over him, and he threw back the canvas top of his bedroll and pulled himself from its depths. His movement caused the horses who were hobbled nearby to shuffle their feet, and a deep nicker rumbled from Ace's nostrils, announcing the gelding's belief that O'Reilly should immediately provide the two horses with some form of nourishment other than the dry grass that surrounded the nearby dirt tank.

O'Reilly knuckled the sleep from his eyes and scrubbed the dark mahogany stubble on his face with his hands. Exhaustion felt like twenty-pound weights tied to his feet, holding him to the ground. He estimated it was four or thereabouts and he'd only fallen into a deep sleep an hour or so earlier in spite of having to pause his search as the light faded the night before. The three-quarter moon cast a ghostly light over the clearing where he'd camped. He reached for his saddlebags and, squinting in the dim illumination, he rummaged through the contents. He cursed under his breath, knowing he'd forgotten to tell the boys to pack some of the small hoard of coffee Maggie had squirreled away in the back of the pantry. Breakfast would have to be jerky and water, saddle the horses and be ready to head out at the first light.

He stared at the stars, chewing slowly on a piece of the venison jerky. He knew he was approximately twenty miles from Hideaway, and he wondered about the children, hoping he'd made the right decision in leaving them. He ruthlessly squashed down a sick feeling of dread and slowly pulled himself to his feet, and prepared to saddle the horses. A faint, almost imperceptible lightening in the east promised the day was near, and he would once again be able to follow the UTV's tracks down the small forest road and be sure his quarry hadn't turned off at any of the other cross trails.

Back at the camp, Houdini would be announcing the coming dawn. A slight smile twisted his lips. He never thought he would miss that blasted rooster, but right now, he'd give anything to hear his raucous crow. O'Reilly paused for a moment, almost thinking he could hear the rooster over all the miles. Nothing, though, except for some equally obnoxious spadefoot toads serenading each other down by the dirt tank. Damned things spent most of the year hidden in underground burrows but let a little bit of moisture show up, such as the monsoons, and suddenly you could hardly hear yourself think over the sound of their voices.

Sighing, he hoisted his saddle onto his hip and headed for the horses.

A little over an hour later, O'Reilly sat on Ace, staring at the intersection of the small dirt road he'd been following and County Road 5, the road signs incongruous, mounted as they were in the middle of the thickly forested wilderness. O'Reilly leaned over the gelding's shoulder and examined the dirt of the trail, studying the hard packed surface for evidence the UTV carrying Maggie had passed this way and whether they had headed north to Seligman or south to Prescott.

With a sinking feeling in his chest, he saw their tire tracks heading in both directions on County Road 5, both south and north. He cursed loudly enough that Ace's ears twitched, and behind him Jimmy startled, pulling back until the slack was out of the rope, the dally around the saddle horn bringing him up short.

You'd think this was a damned super highway, O'Reilly thought, clenching his jaw as he sat up in the saddle. He narrowed his eyes against the early-morning sun as he looked first north, toward the Juniper Mesa Wilderness area, and then south toward Williamson Valley Road.

As a former sheriff's deputy, not to mention growing up in this area during the time his father was one of the camp men on the S Lazy V, O'Reilly was familiar with the network of small county and forest service roads crisscrossing this part of Arizona. He knew several ranch headquarters and camps dotted the area, and any could house a band of ghosts.

O'Reilly's forehead creased in a frown. It didn't make sense. Most of the ghosts who'd had the misfortune of crossing paths with O'Reilly during his exorcism team days had set up their bases of operation close to the main highways. He acknowledged that some may have tried to retreat to the countryside, much as Maggie and he had, but on his forays to the ranches around Adobe Canyon, he had never seen signs of anyone other than Lindy's mother, the woman he'd found dying of the influenza at a nearby ranch headquarters. Lindy's mother had been too far gone to save, and O'Reilly hadn't been able to find out if she was a fugitive, or just someone who had been missed during the concentration.

He took off his sweat-stained, dusty, black felt hat, set it crown down in front of him on the saddle, then ran his fingers through his sweaty, dark mahogany hair as he continued to study the road before him. His gut told him the northern route was the most likely. Interstate 40 was the primary artery for the APZ supply trucks in northern Arizona, and there was a lot of empty land up in the Seligman area. Still, it was approximately thirty miles to Seligman and only about twenty miles south to the closest residences that could be exploited by a band of ghosts.

Thirty miles was no big deal for a UTV, however, and he knew the Prescott area was high on the list for the annihilation teams. Shortly after his arrival, he'd told Maggie her house had probably already been looted and destroyed, and he still believed that scenario was likely. Several times, when he'd been up on the rim of the canyon, he'd noticed smoke from the direction of Prescott, Chino Valley and Prescott Valley.

Prescott, however, had been the Central Control's primary focus in the tri-city area. Its position in a small bowl of land nestled in the Bradshaw Mountains, with limited ingress and egress, made it easier to defend if there were any form of large scale insurrection in the future. All populated areas had been ransacked in order to stockpile supplies for the APZs. Obtaining supplies wasn't the only goal, however. The government had also determined the structures themselves were high priority for razing using the standard explanation that many of the old buildings in downtown Prescott had been found to be reservoirs for the influenza virus.

The ghosts wouldn't know that, however, and Prescott's reach stretched a long way out Williamson Valley Road, the other name for the road at which he now sat.

Finally, he slid the hat back onto his head and reined Ace south, clucking to Jimmy. He eased the gelding along, his eyes fixed on the ground and the faint traces of the passing UTV. They had moved close to a hundred yards down the road when, to O'Reilly's surprise, he saw skid marks where the UTV pulled a sudden u-turn, the tracks doubling back on themselves.

He pulled the buckskin to a stop, then looked over his shoulder toward the intersection. It appeared the UTV driver had changed his mind and turned back to the road O'Reilly had just left. He reined Ace around and headed back to the north. It seemed they were headed for Seligman, over thirty miles away, after all. O'Reilly looked back down the small forest road he'd taken from the west, in the direction from which he'd come. He was already close to twenty-five miles from Hideaway, and Maggie had been kidnapped nearly a full day ago. If the ghosts had come all the way from Seligman, he had at least another day to go before he would find them, assuming they hadn't holed up at any of the ranches or properties that had sprawled out from the little western town.

And the horses were already tired.

While horses could go twenty to thirty miles a day over an extended period of time, Ace and Jimmy weren't in top working condition, spending much of their days out in the pasture grazing. Ace was in better condition than Jimmy since O'Reilly usually rode him when he needed a mount, but Ace was also carrying a rider.

If they had been working on the ranch, they'd usually switch out mounts in the remuda, not ride the same gelding two days in a row. No other option, though. Not unless O'Reilly came across a ranch camp or house with a quad or jeep sitting there with a full gas tank.

He pondered that thought for a moment, then dismissed the idea. He had no clue where the ghosts were camped out, and the sound of a jeep or UTV approaching would alert them to his presence well before he knew where they were. Based on their actions with Maggie, it was highly unlikely he'd be welcomed with open arms, handed Maggie and sent on his way with well wishes.

The horses would get him closer to wherever the kidnappers were hiding out without tipping them off that he was there. He had a better chance of taking them by surprise and rescuing Maggie. Even if one of the geldings happened to nicker or whinny within a lookout's hearing, it would likely be chalked up to feral horses, freed from local ranches or smaller holdings when their owners had gone into the hospitals, died, or had been gathered into an APZ.

O'Reilly pushed Ace back into a long trot, chucking Jimmy's lead rope to hurry him along. The leather of the saddles creaked in time with the muffled hoof beats on the packed dirt road.

The knot of tension O'Reilly had been living with since the girls had raced back into the camp tightened once again, and he resisted the urge to kick the horses into a lope, knowing the geldings would be able to maintain the trot for miles, unlike the faster gait. The longer Maggie was in the kidnappers' hands, the less likely she would return unscathed. Maybe Maggie would be able to talk her way out of trouble. She was good at talking. However, remembering his first meeting with her and Mark, he wondered again if she would be able to squash her acerbic, sarcastic tongue, and keep herself safe.

20

Click-click. Click-click. Click-click.
Deputy Travis Harlan sat at the scarred wood desk in the Enforcer's headquarters in Laughlin, alternately pressing the butt end of the ballpoint pen, then pressing the release button to draw the point back inside the translucent black casing. His eyes were focused on the closed door to Captain Seth Rickards' office, but he wasn't seeing the solid slab of blonde oak. In his mind, he was replaying the visit to the little ranch camp in northern Arizona.

This is bullshit, Harlan thought, his face twisting into a scowl. The clicking doubled in speed as he thought about that mission. He was positive Rickards was hiding something about the final conflict in the caves, and Harlan wanted to know what it was. They had pulled out too quickly. Rickards wouldn't let them retrieve the body of the traitor, James O'Reilly. There had also been no sign of the children, the Craigsons and Alysa Thalman, who had run from the APZ and met up with O'Reilly in the Arizona ranch land.

O'Reilly had some bullshit story about another person who had taken the kids away with him, leaving O'Reilly behind. Harlan had expected Rickards to immediately order seekers into the air to look for the fugitives or to monitor the camp to verify that it was actually abandoned. To his surprise, Rickards stated that it would be a waste of resources. The children were gone and would likely be caught by a patrol or an exorcism team from another APZ, or would die in the wilderness, and their bodies would never be recovered.

When Harlan pushed, Rickards had snapped at him, making it clear the decision had been made. It was obvious from the look in Rickards' eyes that if Harlan wanted to continue working for the Laughlin branch of the Enforcers, he was going to drop the subject.

In fact, Rickards hinted that the Miami, Florida, APZ was looking for officers for their Everglades exorcism team. Harlan had heard the rumors that large numbers of ghosts had hightailed it for the depths of the Everglades and were proving to be illusive and aggressive, striking supply convoys and even breaking into the storage facilities of the APZ itself. Plus, the Everglades were known for things that had a tendency to bite first and ask questions later: alligators, panthers, snakes, mosquitos. Being assigned to the Everglades exorcism team was not the fast track to promotion.

Maybe Rickards wouldn't want to take the chance that Harlan would start talking, and that another APZ's leadership would boot the complaints on up to Central Control. At least, Harlan tried to tell himself that was the case. However, the look in Rickards' eyes, and the knowledge that the captain was held in high esteem by the reorganized government, convinced him it wasn't worth the risk that Harlan, himself, would be branded as a troublemaker and fed to the mosquitos in the hopes that the terminal blood loss would remove the possibility Harlan would start complaining to the new administration.

And now there was this crap with Ludeman and his band of merry men. And women. Even now, one had to be politically correct.

Every person who had descended on the Enforcers' offices last week should have been thrown in jail. If Central Control knew how Rickards had pandered to the man . . . Harlan felt almost nauseous. If it had been up to him, they would think twice before questioning the people in charge. If Harlan had been appointed as captain, *he* wouldn't have kicked the can down the road with suggestions that Ludeman and his followers learn survival skills during the winter, and they'd discuss the group leaving the APZ in the spring.

Click-click. Click-click. Click-click. The frequency of the clicks increased again as Harlan thought about the things he'd do differently if he were in charge.

"Hey, Harlan. How's it going?"

A voice yanked Harlan out of his reverie, and he looked up to see Alex Donner, one of the other deputies on the Laughlin APZ branch of the Enforcers, standing just inside the doorway, utility belt in his hand, staring at Harlan, curiosity clear on his face. A bolt of annoyance seared through Harlan's chest. He didn't have much respect for most of the others in his division, but he was especially critical of Donner.

Hell, the man got spooked by a chicken and shot another deputy during that disaster of a mission to Adobe Canyon. A chicken, for God's sake. Harlan thought, remembering that chaotic scene outside the small shelter built back under the cliffs of the canyon. Harlan felt his jaw ache as he clenched his teeth, and he forced his muscles to relax.

The man should have been kicked out of the Enforcers if not actually locked up for criminal stupidity. He is a disgrace to the force, Harlan narrowed his blue eyes as he looked at the other deputy.

Donner hesitated, waiting for a response to his question, then shrugged and walked over to his station. He swung the laden duty belt up onto the scarred surface of the desk, where it landed with a thump, then turned and studied Harlan once again, a frown creating two small furrows between his eyes.

"Everything all right?" Donner asked, his voice having lost the casual tone of his first question.

Finally, Harlan loosened his jaw enough to answer, "Yeah, everything's just fine." Harlan could hear the sarcasm in his tone and saw the effects on Donner's face. Struggling to control his anger, Harlan continued, "I was just thinking about the Nick Ludeman situation. I don't know why Rickards isn't just shutting them down. Why the hell pander to them and let them think they're leaving in the spring."

Donner pulled out his chair and sat, gaze fixed on Harlan. "What would you have him do?" he asked. "Maybe he's hoping that by next spring everyone will think twice about wanting to head back out, especially since there won't be any stores or other source of supplies in most of the towns away from the APZ. Maybe once they start learning the skills they need to live out there on their own and see how tough it is, they will realize it's better here."

Harlan snorted in derision. "And if they don't? Better to put down the uprising right now instead of letting them gather more followers."

"I don't know," Donner mused, a slight frown on his face. "If it came to bloodshed, or locking people up, you'd be running the risk of creating martyrs and we'd have a worse situation on our hands than we do now. Remember the riots back a few years ago?"

"Yeah, I remember them. They're one of the reasons I decided to get into law enforcement. I saw what those mobs were doing and it seemed like almost no one had the balls to do anything about it. It's disgusting what's happened these days."

Harlan didn't mention he hadn't made it through the police academy in his hometown and had been turned down when he'd tried to enlist in the Marines. *Jackasses didn't know what they were missing,* he thought. When the influenza pandemic hit, and the various branches of law enforcement and the military had been obliterated, Harlan had seen his chance to join the newly formed Enforcers. The new agency had been cobbled together from the remainders of various military and law enforcement groups, as well as other survivors of the pandemic who had shown an interest or an aptitude for the task. They didn't have the time or capability to check everyone's background.

Donner uttered a short burst of laughter, then pushed himself out of his seat. He picked up his duty belt again and buckled it around his waist. Donner looked at Harlan with a smirk that made Harlan itch to erase it from the man's features.

"Seems like whenever people stop listening to each other, people start dying. Enough people have died lately from what I can see. I can't say as we need any more, at least not for something stupid like this."

Donner turned and headed back out of the office, leaving Harlan sitting and staring and an empty doorway, flicking the butt end of his pen, gritting his teeth.

Click-click. Click-click. Click-click.

21

The sound of voices, muffled by the wall and unintelligible, pulled Maggie from an uncomfortable sleep. She cracked her eyes, then opened them wide, surprised at the dim light shining through the dirty window in the far wall. Thanks to Houdini, she couldn't remember the last time she'd slept past sunrise–or even close to sunrise, for that matter.

She started to straighten her cramped legs, preparing to swing them off the couch and to the floor, then froze as it felt like every muscle in her body had joined a union and were engaging in concerted rebellion.

She closed her eyes again and did an assessment. Legs? *Hurt.* Back? *Hurt more.* Arms and shoulders? *Hurt like hell.* Jaw and face? *What was worse than hell?* She groaned, closed her eyes in mute prayer, then opened them again and finished pushing herself into a sitting position on the couch. Another flock of dust motes floated into the air, bringing on a sneezing fit that felt like it was going to rip her bruised ribs apart and deposit her lungs on the floor. She leaned her elbows on her knees and put her head in her hands as she breathed slowly and tried to convince herself her body wasn't going to shake into a million pieces in the next few moments.

God, she missed Houdini!

The thought took Maggie by surprise, and nearly choked a laugh from her throat. It was true, though. As much as she hated that rooster and had contemplated his demise on a daily basis and in a variety of tasty ways, right now she'd give anything to hear his crow and feel his wings and spurs beating bruises on her shins while she tried to keep from dumping her basketful of eggs on the ground and falling flat on her face.

Her shoulders tensed as she heard the rasping thud of the bar being removed from in front of the door. She raised her head and turned in time to see the wood panel swing open. Granger leaned into the room, dressed in the same grubby clothes he'd been wearing the day before, although he was freshly shaven.

She rolled her eyes at her thoughts and stifled a nervous giggle. *Who am I to criticize? I'm wearing the same clothes, and I can't even brush my hair.* Her hand moved briefly to her dark blonde braid, which was decidedly frayed and the worse for wear, loose hairs floating over its surface. She was glad there wasn't a mirror around. She'd hate to see what impact the activities of yesterday, combined with her restless night's sleep, had on her face. Her mouth felt gritty, as did her eyes, and when she rubbed her face with her hand, it felt strange, as though there was a second skin.

"Come on," Granger said, with no greeting or preamble.

Maggie froze for a moment, then pushed herself slowly to her feet, stumbling a little as her muscles rebelled once again.

"Good morning to you, too," she said, her voice sounding as gritty as she felt, and she cleared her throat, fighting the urge to spit. "I had a lovely night's sleep. Thank you for asking."

Granger's head jerked up, and he choked back what might have turned into a laugh, biting it down hard, but then a smile tilted his lips, and his expression softened.

"I'm sorry, Ms. Langton. Please forgive my appalling manners. If you would, please join me out on the patio . . ." Granger said with exaggerated formality, sweeping his right arm toward the open door and the barn beyond.

"For mimosas and brunch?" Maggie filled in, making her way toward the door, feeling her muscles start to loosen with the movement. "Sure, I haven't had a good mimosa since before the influenza hit."

Granger's features lightened even more, and he stood back as Maggie made her way through the door and into the main body of the barn. There were three other men down at the far end, near the pile of scrap metal. *The windmill*, she thought again, studying the tangled mound of dull gray metal. *It's definitely a windmill, and if these people are counting on it to produce water any time in the near future they're all delusional, not just Lucas.*

"We can absolutely provide you with a mimosa, if you don't mind using powdered orange drink instead of orange juice." He paused, then continued, the smile expanding into what Maggie might have called a grin. "And an old bottle of sparkling apple cider instead of champagne."

"Oh, gack!" Maggie said. She made a gagging sound, and Granger started to laugh. He turned toward the front of the barn, and stepped up to Maggie's side.

"I do need to hit the outhouse on the way, though, and freshen up you know," Maggie said. "I don't suppose any of your people have a comb they'd be willing to loan me? And maybe a washcloth?" She could hear a wistful note creep into her voice and ground her teeth, biting down on the feeling.

"I will see what we can do," Granger said, appearing oblivious to her internal battle. He gestured for Maggie to walk in front of him and then pointed toward the front door of the barn.

Maggie lifted her chin and walked with purpose toward the small single door. She saw the three other occupants of the barn staring at her. One licked his lips then turned to talk with the man standing next to him. Anger filled her, washing out the laughter from a few moments before and making her feel as though her chest was going to explode, spewing fury and gory slime all over the inside of the barn. Lip-licker caught her glare and quickly looked away, picked up a wrench and pretended he was working on a leg of the defunct windmill.

Maggie turned her head back to the open door and stepped out. The breath of fresh mountain air eased her chest, and she paused for a second, the mixture of pine duff and fine, dusty earth feeling almost soft under her boots. She looked around, noticing once again the pine and juniper forest on either side of the compound. For the briefest of moments, she wondered what would happen if she just high-tailed it into the nearest trees— whether they would come after her or whether they'd write her off as a bad investment for their time and resources. Then she shook her head slightly, and her shoulders drooped. They'd never let her go, and even if they did, she had no idea where she was or how to get back to Hideaway. She'd been unconscious too long while the UTV had carried her away from home, and she didn't know if they'd gone north, south or east. At least, she thought, she could write off west. She wasn't sure how far Adobe Canyon went up toward I-40, but hopefully it was far enough that it would have blocked her captors from heading in that direction.

For some unexplainable reason, it didn't feel much like Prescott, so maybe she could eliminate having gone south as well. Most of the trees here were juniper, piñon and white pine and not the towering ponderosa pines that grew around Prescott. The landscape just didn't look right either, with the remote valley showing little sign of habitation. She knew there were some long looks off Mingus Mountain near Prescott, but if that's where they were, she should be able to see Granite Mountain or the San Francisco Peaks. Besides, it just didn't seem as though they could have come that far while she was out cold, not without attracting some attention from the authorities.

Damn O'Reilly, she thought angrily. *I bet he'd know where he was if he'd been knocked on the head and driven off into the wilderness blindfolded. You could probably throw him out of a helicopter over an unfamiliar desert anywhere in Arizona, and he'd find his way out within half a day without breaking a sweat.* She fought down the voices in her head reminding her that O'Reilly had been raised riding horseback all over this country, so of course he'd know where he was. She didn't want to hear it.

North toward Seligman and Ash Fork, then, or maybe they *had* circled around the northern reaches of Adobe Canyon and the Juniper Mesa Wilderness area and headed back toward Trout Creek and Wikieup. Regardless, it would be foolhardy to try to escape and make her way home until she knew exactly where she was. If she took off, and *if* she didn't get recaptured—and that was a big *if*—she'd probably fall into the Grand Canyon or bump into an APZ before she found her way back to Hideaway. There would be a good chance she would die before she ever found home. Trying to follow the tracks of the UTV wouldn't help because they'd expect that and be looking for her on the roads. She sighed, feeling deflated.

"Ahem."

The sound of Granger clearing his throat came from behind her, and she startled, realizing she was blocking the door from the barn. Quickly she took a couple of steps forward and spun, looking at the man who was staring back at her, a quizzical expression in his eyes.

"Planning your escape?" Granger asked in conversational tones as though he took it for granted escape was exactly what she'd be contemplating, and he knew she realized how hopeless it was.

Maggie paused for a moment, annoyed at his perspicacity as a thousand possible answers flew threw her mind. Then she decided it was pointless to deny it.

"Naturally. Do you mind telling me where we are so I don't go off in the wrong direction?" She bit down on her tongue. She really had to start controlling the sarcastic attitude that had a tendency to surface when she was feeling threatened.

"Information has to flow both ways, Ms. Langton — Maggie," Granger said in soft tones. A sardonic smile twisted his features and tightened the scar across his cheek.

Their eyes met once again, dark blue to bright green. Maggie's jaw tightened as she refused to break the look and let Granger think she was weak. The screech and crash of metal from inside the barn jerked Granger's eyes away from hers, and she let out a breath. A long string of curses emerged from the doorway, and Granger turned and looked back into the cool darkness of the building.

"What the hell is going on in there?" Granger called, annoyance obvious in his voice. Clearly, he hadn't wanted to be the one to break the staring contest any more than Maggie had, she thought with a malicious interior chuckle. It might have been a small victory on her part, but it *was* a victory, and she savored it.

The reply was unintelligible, but Granger nodded and then turned back to Maggie, a frown on his face. His eyes met hers once again, and she could see the mask of calm authority slide back into place as clearly as if it was a physical part of his body.

"Come with me, Ms. Langton, and we'll get you something to eat and try to round up that comb and washcloth you were asking for." Granger started to move off toward the campfire.

After a brief detour to the outhouse that left Maggie contemplating the continued health of her lungs and sense of smell should she remain long with the group, the pair arrived at the fire pit. At this time of the morning no other members of the band were present. She looked around the compound again, noticing a few people working in the garden, but there were nowhere near the number of individuals Granger had said were with him.

"Where is everyone?" Maggie asked. "You said there were eighteen members of your group. With you and the men in the barn, plus those people over there, Lucas, Linda and the boys I met last night, you're only at about ten."

"You have a lot of questions, Ms. Langton." Granger offered a smile that fell somewhat short of genuine. "I guess it can't hurt to tell you, though. The others may be off hunting or they might be searching for houses that we, or someone else, haven't looted yet. Have a seat," he motioned toward an old, nylon-webbed lawn chair sitting next to the soot stained stones encircling the fire pit.

Maggie sat. The chair creaked and sagged slightly, and she stiffened, wondering if it was about to dump her to the ground. The chair's complaints subsided, however, and Maggie started to relax, keeping her gaze on Granger the entire time, feeling somehow that if she took her eyes off him, he might strike like a rattlesnake.

Granger sat on a nearby log and studied Maggie, much as he had the night before, saying nothing.

Maggie shifted in her seat, the old chair grumbling once again, then finally took a deep breath and said, "What's it going to take to get you to let me leave. You've had the night to think about your options." Maggie looked around the compound once again, then back at Granger, making it clear she didn't think much of their location. "Seems like keeping me captive creates a world of complications for you, regardless of what your blue-eyed sociopath wants."

At the term, *blue-eyed sociopath,* she felt the skin on the back of her neck prickle as if said *sociopath* was standing behind her, listening to every word, even though she knew she and Granger were alone. Regardless, she'd had a sleepless night to think about the situation, trying to piece together the things she'd seen in the compound with what little O'Reilly had told her about ghosts and the exorcism teams. For a moment, she wished desperately O'Reilly hadn't been so reluctant to talk about the APZs and his time in the Enforcers, other than the bare minimum required to convince Maggie to do what he said was necessary to avoid capture. Even then, he'd focused more on the law enforcement side of the coin than he had on the bands of ghosts.

"The way I see it," she continued, deliberately allowing a disparaging note to enter her voice after getting no response from Granger following her barb. "You've got a pitiful garden and lack the skills and resources to make it better, so you have to be keeping everyone fed, clothed and healthy from supplies taken from houses in the area." She paused for a moment before adding, "Or maybe supply trucks headed to the APZs?"

She held her breath, waiting to see if Granger would take the bait. If he admitted to the supply trucks, she would know they were fairly close to I-40. O'Reilly said the major supply routes between APZs were on the interstate highways such as I-40, I-17 and I-10. They were wide enough that it was less likely they'd be completely blocked by stalled cars or accidents that hadn't been cleared, although he did say the debris from any accidents tended to be murder on the truck tires. And if they were close to I-40, then they were at daily risk of the Enforcers locating them. A tremor ran down her spine as she remembered O'Reilly's story of the eradication of one of those particular bands of ghosts that had been unable to hide their existence from the government.

"I did say some of the group may be out looting," Granger said in mocking tones, appearing unaware of the uncomfortable turn of Maggie's thoughts.

"And the supply . . ." A second thought struck Maggie, freezing her mid-sentence. "You want to know about us because you have been raiding supply trucks, and you know you're at risk of being hunted by the Enforcers. You want to know if my camp is better hidden than yours? Lucas may have forced your hand in kidnapping me, but since I'm here, you want to determine whether or not we have enough food and supplies, and whether we're well enough hidden to make it worthwhile attacking us. That's why you wanted to know how many are in my group, not because you were worried they were coming after me."

Granger stared at her for what seemed like minutes, although it was likely only a few seconds. She could see a myriad of expressions flickering behind those blue eyes. She'd nailed it. She was positive.

Finally, Granger took a breath and said, "You told me there was only you and six kids, though," he said. "If that is true, then anything you have, food, shelter, water, would hardly be able to handle a group this size."

"But you didn't believe me! You said I was a bad liar," Maggie exclaimed, leaning forward in the chair and gripping the arms. She looked over Granger's shoulder and saw several of the people who had been working in the garden stand and turn to look in the direction of the campfire. One woman, not Linda, Maggie was happy to see, lifted her shovel and started to walk toward them.

Granger, seeing the direction of Maggie's gaze, looked over his shoulder, then stood and faced the garden, totally regardless of having turned his back on Maggie. She felt a quiver wriggle down into her stomach and then another bloom of anger. He didn't think she was any danger to him. Her fists balled as she fought the urge to show him exactly how dangerous she could be. Then she forced her hands to relax, reminding herself that, at this moment in time, he was right. She wasn't dangerous. He was the only thing standing between her and an insane mountain man and a group of ghosts who didn't want her eating their food and drinking their water.

Granger was calling to the woman who had started in their direction, reassuring her that all was well. The woman turned back to the garden, calling something to one of the other workers. Then Granger returned his attention to Maggie and sat on his stump once again, bland expression firmly in place.

Neither spoke for what was probably two or three minutes, but to Maggie it seemed like at least twenty. Her mind whirled as pieces of the puzzle fell together.

"You have been going through the houses in the area, but not finding enough supplies, have you?" Maggie started, her gaze fixed on his face, watching for signs she was right.

"Even though many people in the more remote areas of northern Arizona believe in prepping, in living off the grid, the influenza pandemic, and the food shortages that started occurring in the stores as it went on longer and longer, disrupting the supply chains and production facilities, caused people to start to dig into their reserves. By the time people were forced into the APZs, there wouldn't have been much left, and the authorities would have taken anything they could find. So, you've had to start raiding supply trucks heading to the APZs, and now you're worried they're going to come after your group because they'll know you must be camping near the highway." The words flowed from her in a torrent as she became more convinced that her hypothesis was true.

Maggie remembered O'Reilly telling her that in the Southwest, the ranchers were, in his admittedly biased opinion, some of the ones in the best position to weather the storm of the pandemic since they were used to living out in remote areas, were often completely off the grid and accustomed to providing much of their own food through gardens, flocks of chickens, dairy cows, beef and hunting. Many of those living on the ranches could make due for an extended period of time without needing to go into town, which was important because sometimes the weather would sock them into their camps or headquarters for weeks on end.

However, he said, many other people who aspired to the survivalist lifestyle simply focused on guns and ammunition and self-protection. They worked hard to put up canned and freeze dried food, but didn't stockpile seeds. Some of these people didn't take the time to develop the skills necessary to take over once the stockpile of food was gone. Not everyone, by any means, but many. Often their preparations were designed to last for several weeks or months, figuring that any "SHTF" scenario, as they called it, would last at most a few months, not years . . . or eternity. And they focused on things that were luxuries, not necessities. *Like toilet paper*, Maggie thought, biting her lip to keep from smiling at the memory of the vacuum sealed rolls in the lean-to where she'd spent the night. Maybe there'd been food there when the group moved in, but not now, that was for sure.

Unfortunately for many of this type of prepper, storing food and weapons was of minimal protection against a virus as contagious as this H5N1 influenza had proven to be, especially when the world was weary of taking health precautions due to the frequency of the pandemics in the early 21st century. In fact, Maggie remembered rumors that those earlier, relatively minor viruses had been specifically utilized, whether natural or not, to desensitize the population—essentially to teach people to ignore reports and doubt health experts and recommendations. That meant when an infection developed that had catastrophically high morbidity and mortality rates, it had a greater chance to get a toehold in those populations who might under normal circumstances, be more likely and better able to take rapid protective action.

Images of the protests that peppered the beginning of the worldwide spread of the influenza swept through her memory—people angry about the steps the governments of the world required to attempt to halt the spread of the new H5N1 virus. Thoughts of the mass graves being dug a few weeks later, filled with the bodies of those who died from the influenza that spread so easily as the virus caught a ride on all the droplets expelled by those yelling in the mobs, packed together as tightly as sardines. Then there were the images of piles of bodies laying on the side of the streets as the population started to drop to the point where no one was left to remove the dead. Then the images stopped all together.

Her eyes met his, and she caught a brief flash of something—she wasn't sure what. Maybe fear, maybe desperation. It disappeared as quickly as it arrived, leaving her wondering exactly what she had seen.

After a long moment, Granger nodded, his chin moving so little Maggie wasn't sure whether he had meant a gesture of assent or had just moved his head. Then he spoke.

"You're right, Ms. Langton, to a degree. There are not as many supplies, or at least valuable supplies, in the area's houses as we'd thought there would be, and other looters have been through the vicinity before we got here which decreased the quantity even more. We've also had some challenges as far as getting a solar system moved up here."

And, Maggie thought, they couldn't move down to more fertile, open land where there were functioning wells with an adequate supply of water because those areas would also be more visible to the watching eyes of the Enforcers. Lucas's mind might be focused on immediate gratification, but Maggie was sure Granger was playing a long game.

A small, wry smile crossed Granger's face as he continued, apparently unaware that Maggie's thoughts had jumped out in front of his own. "And some of the enduring skills, like gardening or raising livestock, are not our strong points. Maybe we just want to talk with your people—ask them to help us develop those skills?"

Maggie refocused on his words, her eyes narrowing.

"Or take over what we have," Maggie said, the sharp note in her voice making his smile grow, although the look in his eyes made it clear the smile was sarcastic, not humorous.

A sudden gurgling from Maggie's mid-section broke the tension, and Granger laughed at the shocked look on her face.

"I'm sorry, Ms. Langton," Granger said, his voice filled with a mock formality once again. "I invited you to brunch not an interrogation, and it certainly wasn't my intention to starve you into cooperation."

He leaned over, picked up a stick laying on the ground next to his seat and used it to lift the lid off a large, cast iron Dutch oven that had been sitting unnoticed next to the coals of the campfire. Setting the lid off to the side, he peered inside.

Gingerly he reached into the black pot and picked up something that looked to Maggie like a cross between a hockey puck and a petrified cow patti. He picked up a blue plastic bowl from a stack of dishes sitting beside his stump and set it on the ground next to his foot. The fire pit must be where the group did most of their cooking, she thought, then realized that even if the RVs had stoves, the propane that fueled them had probably run out long ago. Either that or they were saving it for winter when the mountains in northern Arizona could become bitterly cold.

He dropped the dubious source of nutrition into the bowl, where it landed with a hollow *clunk*.

He glanced up at Maggie. "Biscuits and gravy?" he asked, nudging the bowl with his toe.

"Really," Maggie said incredulously. "You call that a biscuit? I value my teeth more than that, not to mention my stomach."

Granger gazed down into the plastic bowl, a considering look on his face, then he looked back at Maggie and shrugged.

"It was Jake's turn to cook this morning." He looked back down into the bowl once again, then reached forward and prodded the charred lump with a forefinger and slid it back and forth with a rasping sound. "I can't say this was his best effort, although learning to use the Dutch oven has been a bit challenging. Not to mention trying to figure out how to use pine nut flour instead of the real stuff." He looked up and gave Maggie a crooked smile. "Still, soaked in gravy it softens up. Your dental work should be safe."

"I don't see any gravy," Maggie said, but her stomach chimed in once again, declaring its willingness to try anything. She thought with longing of the fresh vegetables from her garden, the venison and beef that O'Reilly brought in, the milk from Lizzie, their milk cow, and the newly laid eggs from Houdini's flock of hens.

Granger leaned over and lifted the lid from another Dutch oven that Maggie hadn't noticed, camouflaged as it was in soot and ashes from the campfire.

"It hasn't got any sausage, of course," he said, giving it a stir with a spoon that had been left propped against the side of the pot. "But Jake used some powdered milk and the pine nut flour, and there are chunks of beef or venison in there." He paused for a moment, then continued, "At least I think that's beef or venison. It might be squirrel, I guess. It could be worse." Granger picked up a dripping spoonful of the "gravy," and the brown sludge dripped slowly back into the pot, making soft plopping sounds that reminded Maggie of the soft splat of fresh cow dung hitting the ground. Granger picked up the bowl and spooned more of the thick gravy over the hockey puck.

A smell reached Maggie's nose, causing her stomach to reissue its demand for sustenance. The aroma wasn't exactly Gordon Ramsey gourmet. It wasn't even ten-year-old Mark Langton gourmand, and the greasy brown sludge falling from the spoon made her think of mud pies and botulism, but she didn't hesitate when Granger held out the bowl.

She lifted the spoon to her mouth and took a tentative taste of the tepid mush. She must have made a face because Granger started laughing.

Maggie glared at him and dropped the spoon into the bowl with a clatter. She leaned forward with a creak from the lawn chair and set the bowl carefully on the ground, then used her toe to push it toward Granger. Her stomach issued a mewl of disapproval, which she ignored with steadfast determination.

Granger stopped laughing, but she could see it wasn't far from the surface, and it infuriated her even more.

"Ms. Langton, starving yourself as a grand gesture won't help." He pushed the bowl back toward Maggie, using his own toe.

Maggie refused to look at it and instead kept her eyes focused on his. She could feel her anger coming to a boil once again, the roller coaster of emotions she'd been riding on since waking rising to new heights, and even her stomach quieted as if quelled by the fury that was burning inside.

"Mr. Granger. . ."

"Why don't you. . . ?" His voice trailed off as if suddenly realizing he was in danger of a flashover rivaling that of the largest inferno if he pushed her much farther.

Maggie gritted her teeth and started again. "Mr. Granger, I am done with this dance. I'm not doing it anymore." With every word, her frustration, fear and fury started to spill, out and she no longer tried to stem the tide. With a violent move, she kicked the bowl, sending it spinning off away from the fire pit, splattering brown muck in an arc, the so-called "biscuit" flying off into the dirt a few feet away.

"I'm stuck here because of you! I'm away from my son because of you! *I may never see him again because of you*! And you don't even know what you're going to do with me." The rage that had exploded inside died as suddenly as it had erupted, and Maggie sank down to the dirt and buried her head in her hands, tears hot and wet on her fingers.

Maggie didn't know how long she'd sat there, but gradually she resurfaced from the well of desperation that had swallowed her, and she realized Granger hadn't spoken but instead was sitting, watching her, a look of sympathy on his face. When he saw her looking at him, however, his expression quickly shifted to a stony impassivity.

"You're right, Ms. Langton. We need to make some decisions, and you may not believe it, but I am sorry you became caught up into this maelstrom." His voice was low but without emotion—almost cold, as though he'd squashed out all the empathy she had seen seconds before. "But you're also right that we do need a better location, and we need skills you and your people may have. And make no mistake," his voice became colder, if that was possible, and Maggie suppressed an internal tremor, "with or without your help, we will find your camp. What happens next will be up to you and whether you told me the truth about your group . . ."

His voice trailed off, and he looked at her with a quirked eyebrow. Another shiver tickled its way down her spine and out to the tips of her fingers and toes, and she fought to keep it from showing on her face.

"I . . ." she started, but Granger put up his hand with an abrupt jerk.

"About Lucas," Granger continued, "I meant it when I said I owe him, but he owes me as well, and we have the deal, as I mentioned before." He paused for a moment and lifted his head to the sky as if the words he needed were trapped in the brilliant blue. Then he looked at her.

"Have you ever seen a cat play with a mouse?"

This non sequitur threw Maggie, and she looked at Granger with confusion.

"My wife used to have this scroungy looking orange cat that would go hunting in the neighborhood and bring back live mice and lizards. Drove my wife up a tree. The cat would bring them into the house and let them loose." Granger's voice had taken on a dreamy note. Maggie shook her head, the confusion growing, and she could feel frustration mounting once again at this strange diversion.

"The thing is that when these mice or lizards lay still as if they were dead, the cat left them alone. It just sat and watched until they moved, and then it would pounce again. However, if the mouse remained still, the cat would lose interest pretty quickly." Granger's look sharpened, and he met Maggie's eyes once more.

"In this case you're the mouse. Lucas doesn't have the longest attention span and if you lay still, he'll move on to something else."

"But then what?" Maggie said.

"Maybe we let you take your son, and these other children you spoke of, and leave safely, if you've told me the truth."

And maybe we find other uses for you if you've lied, Maggie thought. Granger seemed as though, in his former life at least, he was a good guy, but she'd be lying to herself if she thought he'd protect her over his own people. And what would happen to O'Reilly if he had remained in the camp instead of following her? There was no doubt that if Granger and his band of merry men descended on Hideaway by surprise, O'Reilly would not make it out alive if he were there.

Maggie tightened her fists. She had to escape, but she didn't dare escape. Damned if you do, and damned if you don't. The reality of her situation crashed down upon her once again, just as it had upon leaving the barn. Her chances of surviving on her own, on foot, lost in the wilderness of the northern Arizona ranch land with no water, no food, no weapons, and no idea where to get any of those things, were less than spit on a Phoenix sidewalk in July. At least when she left Prescott with Mark, heading for Hideaway Camp, she had the horses, food and water, a map, and the knowledge of her starting point. Even then, they'd gotten lost several times before finding Adobe Canyon. Besides, if O'Reilly was hunting for her, what would happen if he got here and she was gone. He might never find her.

She looked up at Granger. He was still studying her. The frigid distance of the few minutes before had thawed somewhat, and she saw a faint echo of the previous empathy lurking in his eyes. Neither spoke.

A woman's scream ruptured the silence. Maggie's head whipped around, looking for the source of the sound. Beside her, Granger had jumped from his seat and taken several steps toward the garden before stopping.

Linda was running toward them, calling Granger's name, a note of panic in her voice surprising Maggie. She hadn't known the woman for twenty-four hours but had somehow developed the idea that Linda had two settings—pissed and crazy. Maggie was surprised anything could shake the woman to the point of the hysteria she could hear in her voice now.

Behind her, two men were supporting a petite blonde woman between them. Something had happened to cause the woman to struggle to walk, her right leg dragging.

"What happened!" Granger barked out, catching Linda's arms as she raced up to him.

"A snake! A rattlesnake bit Jackie!" Linda gasped, her eyes wide.

The two men had caught up to Linda and stood there with the blonde woman, Jackie, still supported between them. It was clear from the look on her face that she was experiencing a great deal of pain. Her face was ghostly white, and tears and sweat ran down her cheeks.

"Put her down," Granger commanded, then snapped, "No, here by the fire. There's not enough room to move around in the RV," as the men started for the nearest camper. "Don't move her any more than necessary."

As the men obeyed Granger, he turned to Linda. "Go get the first aid kit. Barn. Back on the left wall."

Linda stumbled the first few steps, then appeared to grow stronger with her mission, and her stagger became a sprint as she headed for the tan steel building.

Maggie looked away from Linda's exit and back toward Granger and the woman who had now been placed on the ground next to the fire, one of the men's T-shirts pillowing her head. Everyone's attention was focused on the inner surface of the woman's right leg, where two puncture wounds and a trickle of blood just above the knee and below the edge of her shorts pinpointed the location of the bite.

No one was paying any attention to Maggie. She glanced around the compound. Everyone's attention was focused on the woman, and slowly an idea started to take root. While escaping on foot would be almost certain death, escaping on a UTV might just be possible. She looked over toward the barn where several of the vehicles were parked. A million things could go wrong with the plan, she knew, but just maybe.

With a slow, deliberate movement, she began to rise to her feet. Not one look flashed her way. She took a step backward, careful to avoid the old lawn chair and some branches lying on the ground. Then another.

"Granger, it was a Mojave. I saw it. Jackie flipped a big rock over, and it hit her! Bam!" The man, a big, brown-haired guy Maggie couldn't remember seeing the afternoon before when Lucas and Granger brought her back to the compound, was speaking in urgent tones.

"Aww sh . . ." Granger started before being interrupted by the other man who had helped Jackie to the campfire pit.

"Ya gotta put on a tourniquet and cut her leg before the poison spreads!" the darkly-tanned man with long, greasy black hair said.

"You idiot," brown-hair retorted, snapping his head around to look at black-hair, and Maggie froze. "That's not the way to treat snakebite anymore. That's an old wive's tale."

"You got a better idea? It's not like we have any of that antivenin they have in the hospitals."

"You're sure it was a Mojave green?" Granger broke in. Maggie took another step backward unnoticed.

"Yeah," brown-hair said. "I saw the greenish color. I . . ."

"I've got the first aid kit, Granger!" Linda yelled as she came running back, the three men from the windmill project in the barn following close behind. "What do you need?"

Maggie took another step backward. She glanced around, noting two UTVs near the barn. Yesterday, when they'd gotten to the compound, she was sure Lucas had left the keys in the UTV's ignition. If she had a vehicle instead of traveling on foot, maybe she had a chance. Not much of one but maybe . . .

Almost as if he'd read her thoughts, Granger half rose and looked around, his eyes coming to rest on Maggie. "Ben," he indicated one of the men who had been working in the barn, "take our guest back to her room. Make sure the door is locked."

The man Granger called Ben walked over to Maggie and grabbed her arm. He turned her toward the tan steel barn, propelling her in front of him. She looked over her shoulder at the small crowd of people around Jackie and tripped over a pine tree root running along the surface of the ground. Ben roughly jerked her upright in a move that felt like he'd ripped her shoulder apart, and pushed her back toward her prison.

22

Blades of bunch grass, pine duff, brittle sticks and small collections of malapai rock crunched under O'Reilly's boots as he moved slowly forward. A battered double-wide trailer and several outbuildings were visible through the junipers and brush ahead, and he paused, studying the building. No sign of movement at this one either, and he felt the now common sense of disappointment.

A few more steps and the home came fully into view, and he shook his head, lips pursed.

Another dead end.

O'Reilly's day had proceeded much more slowly than he had anticipated. It had been several years since he had traveled the Williamson Valley corridor between Prescott and Seligman, and to his frustration and disgust, many more properties had been developed along the road than he expected, especially the closer he got to the small western town on Route 66. He eliminated many of the side roads and homes he passed, as there were no new tire tracks from a passing UTV. No one had visited these holdings during the last week, and O'Reilly was grateful that the recent storms that blew across northern Arizona narrowed his search options. It was clear, however, that *someone* had visited a number of the properties since the rains, if not the last day or two.

Even with the storm erasing tracks and reducing the number of homes he had to check out, he still found himself sneaking through the brush to spy on too many abandoned properties, and the wasted time ate away at any patience he had left.

The sun was past its zenith as he came to another long driveway that showed signs of recent intrusion. He slipped through the brush toward the house, boots crunching softly in the dry grass and juniper duff. A sound caught his attention, and he paused and listened. Off in the distance he heard the harsh scream of a red tail hawk hunting, the call starting as a high-pitched screech, like a rusty screen door, then dropping in tone and trailing off in its characteristic fashion. Without thinking, he looked skyward, searching for the bird. Another answered, and he finally saw them, high in the sky, flying lazy circles to the left of the hill behind the abandoned home.

Rabbit hunting, he thought as he trained his attention back on the driveway. He'd tied the horses in a clump of brush and junipers well back from the property so the sound of their approach didn't alert anyone who might be staying in the home, but he could tell now that no one had lived in the house for some time. The door of the double-wide trailer hung open, and several of the windows were broken.

Sighing, O'Reilly turned and headed back through the brush to collect the horses and continue his search. A banging from over toward the gray, wooden hay barn drew his attention, and he saw a small, brown Jersey cow standing at the gate staring back at him.

She lowed plaintively, then started rubbing her bony head up and down on the pipe gate that led to a brushy pasture that extended out behind the barn. O'Reilly stared at her in surprise. Too many times in the last few months he had come across the carcasses of horses and cattle that had been trapped in pens and small pastures when the people they depended on died. In his experience, the cows seemed a bit better at breaking down fences and escaping when lack of food and water drove them to it, but just that morning, he had passed the headquarters of a large ranch that had a hundred or more mummified cattle and horses littering the ground of several large feed pens that had exceptionally well-built sucker rod fences.

The cow mooed again, and pushed against the gate, then snorted and shook her head, flinging cow snot out in an arc. She looked shiny and well enough fed, from what O'Reilly could tell, and he looked around the compound again nervously. Was someone in the house watching him? Waiting to see if he'd leave or looking for a good shot? The hair on the back of his neck tickled, and he hunched his shoulders, then he looked again at the cow and relaxed. While she hadn't broken out of her pasture, from what he could see, she had broken into the hay barn and had been helping herself. A windmill about a hundred yards out onto the rocky, barren ground must have kept her water trough filled.

Well, the least I can do is let the lady out before the barn runs out of hay, he thought, chuckling a little, and he headed across the barnyard. He didn't know if a Jersey could survive out on the range, but she sure as heck couldn't survive in that pasture once the hay ran out.

The brown cow pushed into the gate, making it hard to get the chain unhooked, and he shoved her back. She crowded the gate again, and he slapped her nose, causing her to retreat, blowing more cow snot.

"Move it, mama! Get out of the way unless you want to starve in there." His voice sounded loud and harsh, startling him, and he realized he probably hadn't spoken more than one or two words since leaving the children yesterday.

The cow came back in close, rubbing her black and brown head into his hand, and he shoved her away once again, fumbling with the latch on the chain encircling the gate and fence post. Finally, it came loose, and O'Reilly pulled the green pipe gate open with a creak. The cow ambled through the gate, walked up to O'Reilly and rubbed her bony head against his arm hard enough to cause bruises.

Laughing, he rubbed her poll, admiring her huge brown eyes. Jerseys were dairy cows, not beef as were most of the cows on Arizona ranches, but his mother had a Jersey when he was growing up. He remembered the rich, creamy milk the cow produced for ten months of the year, and the butter and cheese his mother made that tasted so much better than anything that came out of any grocery store. Maggie's cow, Lizzie, was also a Jersey, although O'Reilly had always thought she was crossed with beef. She didn't have the animated, hair-covered, skeleton look of some of the purebreds.

Stepping back, he examined this cow. Like most Jerseys, she wasn't overly large but she had a shining red-brown coat and good feet. She appeared to be heavy in calf, although that didn't hide the bony frame. For a fleeting moment, he thought he should bring the cow back to Hideaway for Maggie. She'd like its personality. Then the memory of the purpose of his journey crashed back down on his shoulders, and he gave the cow a last pat and turned to head back to where he had left the horses tied.

He had covered half of the hundred or so yards to the copse of junipers where he'd left the horses when he heard the thud of hoof beats from behind him. It was obvious that the origin of the sound was in a lumbering gallop, and O'Reilly jumped to the side just in time to miss becoming pasture road kill as the Jersey charged by. She stopped and swung around, swinging her head and butting him in the chest, nearly knocking him down in the process.

"Knock it the hell off! I have to go!" O'Reilly snapped, pushing the cow's head away. Unfortunately, she took that as a signal he was ready to play and immediately pushed back in again. He slapped her with his open hand. *Whap!* "I said knock it off!"

The cow took a step back and watched him for a moment, then turned her attention to a tuft of sideoats grama grass nearby, ripping out a chunk with an abrupt upward jerk. O'Reilly waited for a few seconds to make sure she was fully distracted by the new food source, then continued on his way to the horses.

Untying the geldings from the juniper branches, he stepped back on Ace, chucked Jimmy's rope, urging him to follow, and they continued down the road. They had traveled nearly a half mile when a soft moo from behind caught his attention, and he turned his head. The Jersey was in an ungainly trot, heading after them, huge belly bouncing and flaccid udder swinging. It didn't take long before she caught up to Jimmy and dropped into a walk, breathing hard and blowing more clear slime.

Great, he thought, *just what we need.*

O'Reilly turned to face the road ahead of him again and kept riding, studying the tracks of the UTV. *At least if she makes any noise, people who hear her will think it's just a random cow in the pasture.* He glanced back. The Jersey ambled along behind Jimmy as if tied. O'Reilly just shook his head and faced forward again. He'd deal with the cow later.

O'Reilly figured he'd gone about fifteen miles since dawn and the afternoon was dragging on toward evening when the tracks he'd been following suddenly veered off to the left, heading down a smaller forest road toward a mountainous area southwest of Seligman. With the feeling that he was getting close, he reined Ace onto the new road and glanced over his shoulder. The cow still followed along, stopping periodically to help herself to the roadside buffet, then lurching into a trot to catch back up to the horses. Somewhere along the way, she had ceased to become "the cow" or "the Jersey" and had become Thelma. He had no real idea why, but she seemed like a Thelma and appeared to be content to answer to the name.

He halted the horse and sat studying the distant low mountains on the edge of the Colorado Plateau. He estimated the closest range was maybe four miles away as the crow flies, with another range just visible beyond. Maybe seven or eight miles.

"If I was a betting man, Thelma," O'Reilly said softly, "I'd be taking the high ground." He focused on the farthest mountains. As a sheriff's deputy in Yavapai County, O'Reilly had occasionally traveled the small roads that meandered through the various developments along Anvil Rock Road, so he had a general idea of the layout. He debated on the best move. If he stayed on the roads, following the tracks, he would be guaranteed not to miss the signs if the vehicle turned off in an unexpected direction. That meant he wouldn't have to backtrack if he lost the trail.

On the other hand, if his quarry was up on the far mountain, and he was riding down the middle of the road, they would likely see him well before he arrived. If any one of them was a decent shot, he could be picked off before he even knew exactly where they were. There were plenty of junipers, scrub oak and other cover in the area, however, and moving cross country would both get him to the mountains more quickly, and make it much less likely the kidnappers would see him approaching.

Trust his gut, or follow the road?

As he sat on Ace and tried to mentally track the potential consequences of his two choices, a faint sound drifted to his ears, and he straightened in the saddle. Nothing but bird song and the breeze whispering through the juniper boughs. Just as he thought he'd imagined it, his ears caught the faint sound again. He looked at the landscape, trying to determine where it came from or what it was. O'Reilly's common sense told him the sound of a scream couldn't carry that distance. However, he could swear it sounded like a woman's scream, although it was so faint that it could have been the red tailed hawks again, or a mountain lion, or maybe an elk bugling.

But it could have been a woman screaming. And if it was a woman, that woman must be in a world of hurt for her voice to carry that distance.

Gut it was.

O'Reilly pulled Ace off the road and headed straight for the low range of mountains in the distance. He knew the road would take a much more circuitous route, and he wanted, no, he needed, to get to that plateau as quickly as possible.

Three hours later, O'Reilly was approaching the foot of the range of squat mountains. He had only paused in his chase once, stopping at a dirt tank so the horses, as well as Thelma, who followed persistently in spite of the pace, could take on some much-needed water. Twice during the ride, he had heard the sounds of UTVs in the distance and had taken cover in the thick groves of junipers and scrub oak that covered the area, waiting to see if they came in his direction. Each time the sound drifted away, and he was able to continue on. Several times the wind shifted direction, and he could swear that he could smell wood smoke but he wasn't sure if it was from a campfire or from the remains of a forest fire whose smoke he could see far in the distance to the north.

As the ground grew rougher, O'Reilly started watching for a good location to leave the horses. He had no choice. He needed to proceed on foot if he wanted to sneak into the ghosts' camp. The fly in the ointment, so to speak, was that he didn't know the exact location of the hideout. However, he also knew that if the mountaintop was more pine than juniper and oak brush, it would be very hard to creep up on it with two 1,100-pound horses in tow, not to mention a cow with the grace of a hippopotamus on ice skates.

He had passed several homes, some of which had pipe corrals, and he thought the best solution might be to find something like that and turn the horses and Thelma loose in the pens. The thought nagged at him, though, that he had no idea how many were in this band of ghosts—was it just the three men whose tracks he'd seen on the ridge, or were there more? The largest group he'd come across was twenty-five, but he'd seen many smaller, especially at the start of the concentration. If this band was a large one, he thought, might they have spread out into some of the nearby homes, and if so, would he advertise his presence if they suddenly noticed two horses and a cow in one of their corrals? No, it would be better to hide the horses in the trees as close to the base of the low mountain range as he could get safely, and hidden from any potentially occupied homes.

He hadn't heard the screams again and still wasn't positive that what he'd heard earlier was human in origin. Still, his memory played that sound over and over again, and in his mind's eye, he saw Maggie, mouth open, agony on her face.

He examined the ridge of the mountains before him and picked an area rimmed by an escarpment of volcanic rock. Below the outcropping, the cliff fell away for around fifty or sixty feet until it hit a more gentle brush and tree-covered slope. As that particular hill reached the plain below, it folded into several arroyos or washes, like a pleated skirt, divided by ridges of land covered with dense brush.

O'Reilly urged Ace forward, heading for the closest of the arroyos. The wash bed was choked with scrub oak and other vegetation with a few junipers clinging stubbornly to the steep sides, but O'Reilly pushed through. Close to the head of the arroyo, the sandy bottom widened out in a fan and the sides of the wash flattened, blending into the surrounding land.

Dead end, he thought grimly. He pulled Ace to a stop and studied the evening sky. Birds were busy hunting for some last minute insects to carry them through the night. He heard the hawk scream again, and after a moment, was able to locate it circling over some land a short distance to the north. He nodded to himself and reined Ace in that direction, pulling Jimmy after him.

It didn't take long to cover the half mile to the head of the next arroyo. To his relief, he found himself sitting on the edge of a steep bank, a dirt tank below him filled halfway with muddy water. A small, poorly maintained catch pen encircled both the tank and about a hundred yards of grass and brush. A meager trickle of spring water emerged from a rock outcropping that poked out of the nearby mountainside like a volcanic wart.

"Come on, Ace," O'Reilly said, the tension in his shoulders loosening a tiny amount. This would be a perfect place to leave the horses. They could drink and graze until he and Maggie returned. He had to assume they'd be pursued, and the horses had to be ready to go.

O'Reilly urged Ace over the edge of the sandy bank of the wash. The horse tucked his rear legs underneath him and shifted his weight backward as he slid downward in the loose footing. Jimmy hesitated for a moment, pulling back on the lead rope, then plunged over the bank, slid down the slope, and broke onto the bottom of the wash in a trot, shaking his head, black mane flopping, head nodding up and down. O'Reilly glanced behind him. No Thelma. He felt a small trickle of disappointment. He'd gotten used to the bony, brown bovine tagging along, but had to admit to himself, he'd been surprised at her tenacity.

O'Reilly dismounted and led the geldings to the gate of the water trap while studying the fence that encircled the area. It wasn't perfect by any means. Many of the stays were broken, and he could see an area where the top two wires had snapped, probably when some cow or elk decided to take a shortcut to the outside world. In spite of its deficiencies, it was probably good enough to hold the horses for a few hours. It wasn't visible from outside the wash, but it was easy to find, even in the dark, if you knew what you were looking for.

O'Reilly unsaddled the geldings and placed the rigs outside the gate. Happy for the break, Ace moved off several yards, then dropped to his front knees in a sandy patch, back legs tucked under him. He was suspended for a moment, back legs shaking with the effort, then with a loud *whump* he fell over onto his side and started vigorously rolling, wriggling his side and back into the coarse sand. With a groan of pleasure, he gave one last convulsion, then lunged back to his feet, shook the dirt from his coat and wandered over toward the water tank where Jimmy was already drinking.

O'Reilly was letting himself out of the wire gate when he heard a low moo. He looked toward the bank of the wash and grinned when he saw Thelma rushing down the steep side, dirt and rocks flying in all directions as she slid and scrambled, hitting the bottom of the wash at a clumsy trot. She rushed up to him, and he jumped back when it looked like she wouldn't stop before she ran him over.

He opened the wire gate again and walked into the catch pen. Thelma followed close behind, then passed him and trotted over to the dirt tank, where she waded in knee deep, buried her muzzle in the brown water and started sucking in huge gulps, her ears rowing back and forth with the contractions of her throat muscles.

For a moment, O'Reilly smiled, then the seriousness of his mission settled on his shoulders once again, and he closed the gate and walked to his gear. He gathered his canteen and several pieces of jerky. He pulled the rifle from the scabbard that was nestled under his stirrup leather and placed some extra ammunition in his breast pocket.

With a final deep breath, he looked back at the catch pen. The horses, thirst slaked, had moved into the grassy area. The sound of grass being torn from its roots, followed by rhythmic chewing, came to his ears, a peaceful music in his opinion, soothing his soul and preparing him for the night ahead.

He glanced at Thelma, who had finished her drink and now stood, chewing her cud, and looked to be deep in bovine meditation. Her sides jerked as the calf readjusted its position. The cow's udder was flaccid. She wasn't yet producing milk for her calf, or springing as it was commonly known, due to the udder suddenly increasing in size before calving, so he knew she was a ways off. Good. A newborn calf was all he needed on this mission.

With one final, longing look at the grazing horses, O'Reilly turned, climbed the sandy wash bank, then turned his attention toward the mountain where he was sure Maggie's captors were hidden.

The mountainside was in shadow, and the light in the sky above was yellowing as evening approached. O'Reilly made his way up the rough rock-covered slope, staying in the cover of the trees wherever possible. He moved slowly and deliberately, studying the terrain above and below while climbing steadily upward. Several times he was sure he heard a UTV, but it was hard to pinpoint the exact direction of the vehicles as the surrounding hills, valleys and mountains bounced around sound waves like ping pong balls.

He was heading in the right direction, though. He was sure of it.

The color had leached from the sky, but it wasn't fully dark when O'Reilly topped out. His breath rasped in his lungs, and he stood for a moment surveying the land in front of him. He regretted not having scaled the mountainside more quickly as he now found himself faced with an uneven area of smaller rolling hills and valleys, all covered with the ubiquitous juniper and pine trees—and cacti. A lot of cacti. Right at the perfect level to perforate his shins above his boots.

He felt his pocket, searching for the tiny LED flashlight he carried with him, then hesitated. They were currently in a waning three-quarter moon phase, and moonrise wouldn't happen until well after night had fallen, which meant he found himself at risk of getting up close and personal with a number of the mountain's cacti population if he was wandering around blindly, but the flashlight had two-fold disadvantages. First, it would make it easier for any lookouts to see where he was, and second, it would make it harder for his flashlight-adapted eyes to see the sentries before they saw him. He left the little tool in his pocket. He wasn't sure how much battery power it had left anyway, and he wanted to save that for a true emergency.

Breath caught and ready for the next stage of his rescue mission, he stepped out, heading farther onto the mountaintop where hopefully, he'd find a road or trail that would point to the location of the ghosts' hideout.

Two steps, and he felt the needles of an unseen pincushion cactus puncture his shin. He pulled his leg back and swore.

Half an hour later, he had covered the distance of a football field, the equivalence of three stories in steps while hiking up and down the slopes of three washes, and removed approximately fifty cactus spines from his legs and then from his fingers.

Full dark had fallen, slowing his search even more, and he felt the nagging fear that he would fail Maggie, Mark and the rest of the children, raise its head once again. He had just tripped over another outcropping of the black volcanic rock that formed the bones of this mountain range when he heard the clatter of stones falling down a hillside somewhere off to the right. O'Reilly froze.

Deer? Javelina? Bear? Coyote? Insanely large squirrel?

Or a man?

He waited to see if the sound came again. Just as he had decided the rocks had fallen naturally or due to wildlife movement, he saw the briefest of red glows off to the right, immediately extinguished.

Ah hell. This whole mountaintop is alive, he thought.

O'Reilly focused on the area where he'd seen the red light. It didn't come again, but he knew that light, or at least one like it.

It looked to him like the power indicator on a handheld radio or some other electronic device. It wasn't a laser sight. He was sure of that. He blew out a slow breath he hadn't been aware he was holding.

Sentry, he thought. He waited a few minutes. The red glow didn't appear again.

Just as he was about to continue forward, he heard a soft footstep coming from the direction where he'd seen the light. Maybe fifty feet away, he thought, but it was hard to tell up here. That first step was followed by a second, and then a third. It sounded as though the lookout was moving away, farther toward the interior of the mountaintop.

O'Reilly turned and headed off at a forty-five degree angle to the line he had been taking, moving closer to the rim of the mountain but still heading in the general direction he'd been walking before.

He stopped and listened frequently. There was no way to know how many sentries this group had posted. It was unlikely there were more than one or two, and it was sheer bad luck he'd tripped over the one in this quadrant, but he couldn't afford any more bad luck of that kind.

Twenty minutes later, O'Reilly couldn't tell for sure any longer, he stumbled over the edge of a dirt road. The gap in the trees gave him slight illumination from the three-quarter moon, which was just rising in the east, and he could see the faint tire marks from passing UTVs, although the light wasn't bright enough to tell how recent the tracks were. The rough track disappeared off to the southeast, and he thought it was the narrow line he'd seen from the base of the hill. Looking west, he could dimly see the gravel surface curve to the left. He was sure he was approaching the southern edge of this little range of low mountains and was positive he was getting close.

He crossed the road and was stepping into the trees on the far side of the narrow track when a shot rang out. He froze mid-step and looked around wildly. Within seconds a fusillade of shots shattered the peace of the mountain night. Shouts and screams tore through the thunder of the weapons. O'Reilly started to run toward the chaos and immediately slammed into an exceptionally large pincushion cactus.

23

Maggie fought the urge to flip over in an attempt to try and find a more comfortable position on the old couch. There wasn't one, and any movement would just produce a new cloud of dust. *Where did all the dust come from?* Maggie wondered for a moment. With the amount of time she'd spent on this couch in the last day and a half, you'd think the state's dust reserves would be running empty, but no, every movement produced more.

She sighed, then immediately regretted it as the deep breath brought in more of the small particles, tickling her lungs and triggering a reflexive cough which strained her still sore ribs.

She wanted to sleep so badly, both because she needed the rest to keep her mind clear, but also so she didn't have to think. Didn't have to remember.

She was afraid she'd never be able to close her eyes again without hearing the screams and cries of the woman who had been bitten by the rattlesnake.

Stop! she told herself mentally. She squashed the audio track that played in her brain on a loop. *It's not helping you, get rid of it.* She attempted to empty her mind and consciously tried to relax all her muscles. She took a deep breath, fought the urge to cough, then released it, counting to five. Another breath, another stifled cough, and another controlled exhale. She focused on her body and relaxed the muscles, starting at the toes and moving up her legs into her body. She relaxed her fingers, and mentally traced a path up her hands, then arms, feeling the muscles let go. She felt herself drift off toward sleep.

Her mind released the rigid bonds of control . . . and the woman's screams came back unbidden.

Maggie ground her teeth and started all over again.

It didn't help she'd been left on her own to cool her heels in the lean-to for the majority of the day. She'd opened the window for some fresh air, but that had allowed in all the sounds from the compound along with the oxygen, and those sounds were not comforting. From what Maggie could tell, the woman's death wasn't peaceful—it was agonizing, and Maggie's mind started to dart off in other directions. Why hadn't she done more to protect Mark from rattlesnakes?

Her imagination, more fertile than was good for her even at the best of times, heard Mark's cries instead of the woman's. She had the irrational thought that right now, that second, Mark was suffering from a snake bite, his small body wracked with pain, and O'Reilly and the girls were unable to soothe him because his mother wasn't there.

She shook herself mentally. Firstly, just because this woman got bitten didn't mean that Mark had. O'Reilly had taught the kids about snakes, especially when they'd started venturing into the caves. Secondly, even if Mark had been bitten, she had no doubt that O'Reilly would pull out some time-tested, ranch-based treatment that would have him cured and on his feet in thirty minutes flat.

If O'Reilly was at Hideaway, of course. If he wasn't chasing after her and the kids were alone. Home alone. Her exhausted mind jumped to scenes from the old movie she'd seen as a kid. She beat down the ideas again.

Why can't I just fall asleep? Maggie begged and tried the muscle-relaxing, mind-clearing process once again.

Her stomach growled.

Shut up! she told it. *You've been fed. I don't want to hear any more from you.* Then, *great, now I'm talking to myself, or at least to my body parts. Maybe I should just embrace insanity and get it over with.*

Maggie finally gave in to the urge and turned over. Sure enough, the predicted wave of dust puffed into the air, and she sneezed.

She had been fed, albeit many hours ago. The boys had come in once again with a plate and another jug of water. By then she had been so hungry that she'd been regretting her outburst that morning with the biscuits and gravy, and was wishing she'd waited at least until after she'd eaten to melt down. By the time the boys showed up in the late afternoon, she was sure she'd been forgotten by the entire crew and was growing concerned she'd be forced into some sort of drastic action—like eating one of the many mice she saw ducking in and out of the corners of the lean-to.

When Andy and his brother, she still didn't know his name, showed up with the food, Andy was looking frightened and as though he had been crying. She'd tried to get the boys to talk with her, tell her what was happening outside her prison, but both were close-lipped. They put down the food, exchanged her bucket for another equally dirty specimen, and left her with no more information than she'd had before.

She picked up the plate and found some sort of stew. Stirring it with the spoon provided, she saw what looked to be pine nuts and some sort of meat. She spooned out a chunk and studied it. It was white and had a small bone, maybe a rib bone, sticking out of it. Not beef or venison. Both of those meats had much more color. For a brief, panicked second, she wondered what mouse meat looked like, then dismissed that idea. She took a tentative bite. It didn't taste like anything, although it was a bit tough. It looked like cod, catfish or Tilapia, and she wondered if the group had come across a frozen fish stash in a local house. Then a thought skittered across her mind, and her stomach clenched. She eyed the rib bone and was sure of it. She was eating the snake. Someone must have killed the reptile after it bit the woman and, in the true spirit of "waste not want not," had skinned it and decided to serve it up for dinner.

She ate all of it, down to the last drop of gravy and morsel of snake.

Apparently, snake meat didn't have a lot of carrying power, however, and now her stomach was complaining once again.

She wondered what time it was, aware it didn't really matter, and hadn't really mattered for months, if not years. Time was a prepandemic concept.

She started to go through the muscle relaxing technique again, *because it had worked so well before,* she thought sarcastically.

Maggie was starting to drift off into a light sleep when a hollow thump from the barn jerked her back awake again. She heard a muffled voice raised in anger and agitation but couldn't tell what it was saying. Then another voice answered the first, and Maggie thought she recognized Granger. He sounded much closer to the door of her prison, and she wondered what he'd been doing there.

The two men were in some sort of argument, and Maggie shivered. She struggled to sit upright and pulled on her boots. If that lunatic broke into the lean-to, she wanted to be ready to fight or run, and she darned sure wasn't doing either barefoot.

The door to the lean-to was abruptly pulled open, and Maggie rose to her feet, braced to fight if needed. In the dim light, Lucas—she could see the light glinting off the long, blond hair and beard—rushed in and grabbed her arm in his iron hand, jerked her forward, savagely twisted it behind her back before she could react, and forced her toward the door.

24

Granger lay awake, staring toward the roof of the steel barn hidden in shadow.

Every time he closed his eyes, he saw Jackie, wracked with pain, as the venom from the Mojave green rattlesnake moved up her leg and into her body. *She shouldn't have died, dammit!* Granger said to himself. He wanted to hit something. His fists balled at his sides, and he ground his teeth.

Rattlesnakes were a constant danger in places like Arizona. He'd seen them frequently growing up. He'd even had a friend who had been bitten when he tried to show off for some girls and pick up a snake they'd found in the school playground. The yellow lab his family had when he was a kid had been hit in the chest, and it had survived, although it had lost a lot of tissue from the venom.

She shouldn't have died! Before the influenza pandemic, a bite would have been serious, of course, but a very small percentage of people actually died. *You take them to the hospital, they give the person some antivenin, and the person recovers. She shouldn't have died!* He repeated the mantra in his mind over and over, although it wasn't doing him any good. Jackie had died, and died in agony, and he couldn't get it out of his memory.

Of course, it had to be a Mojave green, and, from what he could tell, one of the Mojaves that had both a blood and a neuro poison. In the past twenty years, this particular species of rattlesnake had made its way from the low desert land up into the mountains. It was considered more aggressive and likely to strike than some of the more common species found in the area.

Not that Arizona was short of rattlesnakes, of course. He'd heard once that over thirteen different species made Arizona and the other southwestern states, and Mexico their home. Why couldn't it have been one of those?

Of course, Jackie also had the bad luck to be kneeling down as she moved the rock the snake was hiding under, and it appeared to have hit an artery on the inside of the knee. That the venom of the Mojave green could interfere with the blood from the wound clotting complicated things badly.

Still, if it hadn't been for the pandemic, the concentration, and the lack of hospitals with antivenin, the odds were that Jackie would have lived instead of dying the way she did. God, there were days he just wished he'd been taken by the pandemic with his ex-wife and their daughters. He pulled his arm out of the sleeping bag and draped it over his eyes as if trying to block the sight from his mind's eye.

The sound of the door to the barn being thrown open jerked Granger out of his thoughts, and he sat up, struggling out of the sleeping bag.

"Granger? Where are you Granger?"

The voice was Lucas's, and he sounded agitated—well, more agitated than normal for him—and Granger rose to his feet and braced for whatever madness Lucas was running on now.

"I'm here, what's going on?" He paused, waiting for Kyle to restate his demand to be allowed access to the woman and wondering what he'd be willing to do to protect her and live up to his word.

"They're here, dammit. They're in the trees, I know it. We need to get out of here. Now!"

"Who's here?" Granger was taken aback. This was the last thing he expected. "The woman's people? Are they here for her? How do you know? How many?" Questions swirled in his mind as he fought to make sense of the situation. He hadn't heard anything. Maybe Lucas had finally gone totally mad and was hallucinating.

"No, not the woman's people, dammit! Think! It's the Enforcers. They're here to take us out. Come on, grab the woman and let's get out of here."

"Just stop, Kyle! I need to make sense of this. How do you know the Enforcers are here? I haven't heard anything. No one else has raised an alarm. Did you tell the others?" Granger's frustration was rising, and his surprise was beginning to transform into anger. He reached out and grabbed Lucas's shoulder, bringing him up short.

Lucas shook off Granger's hand and sidestepped, moving past Granger and reaching the door to the wooden lean-to where the Langton woman was being kept. Granger took a giant step and blocked Lucas once again.

"Lucas, cut it out. You can't have the woman. We have the agreement, remember. What's all this about Enforcers being here? Have you warned the group?"

Lucas turned to look at Granger, pale blue eyes almost glowing in what little moonlight shone through the translucent fiberglass panels that were spaced regularly along the roof of the building. The effect chilled Granger to the bone, and he stepped back.

Lucas yanked the bar out of the brackets attached to the door jamb, threw it backward and opened the door with a bang. He barged into the room where Granger heard a muffled scream. Seconds later, Lucas rushed out the door, twisting the Langton woman's arm behind her back. She stumbled, but he jerked her upright again, looking as though he'd rip her arm from its socket.

The paralysis that had seized Granger broke, and he reached out and grabbed the woman's other arm, stopping both she and Lucas in their tracks.

"What the hell are . . ." Granger started.

The sound of a shot interrupted him, causing all three to look toward the open door to the barn. Within seconds more shots followed, so many and so fast Granger couldn't count them. Couldn't tell what direction they were coming from.

"Come on," Lucas urged, pulling Langton out of Granger's hand and pushing her toward the exit. "If we don't get out of here . . ."

"Ethan! Ethan, where are you?" Daniel Espitia came running through the doorway and skidded to a stop when he saw the shadowy forms of Lucas, Granger and the woman coming his way across the barn.

"Daniel, what's happening?" Granger snapped.

"I don't know, Ethan. I gotta find Andy. Have you seen him?"

"Get out of the way, kid," Lucas growled and shoved past him, pulling Langton behind.

"Lucas, stop!" Granger said, frustration clear in his voice. He ran after Lucas and Langton, catching them just as they reached the front door of the steel barn, and Lucas plunged through, pulling the woman after him. Shots continued to ring out, punctuated with screams. The compound was chaos as members of the band grabbed their weapons and tried to determine where the attack was coming from.

One of the members of the group, a man standing near the road, suddenly howled and fell backward. Granger's eyes widened, and his heart rate, already elevated, escalated to the point he thought it would burst from his chest. The faint, acrid stench of gunfire was adding itself to that of the wood smoke from the campfire.

Lucas bared his teeth in a humorless grin and snarled, "Not now! If we don't go we're dead! Come on!" He pulled the woman toward the woods, away from the light of the compound.

Granger hesitated for a moment, then looked over his shoulder at the camp.

"Please, Ethan, where's Andy? I need to find him. I . . ." Daniel had followed the men through the door. His eyes were wide, the glow of the flames from the compound reflecting in their horrified depths.

Lucas stopped and rounded on Daniel so quickly that the boy shrank back, dark eyes widened even more in fear.

"Your brother is dead, kid. I saw his fucking head blown off! Now if you want to join him, keep wasting our time."

Daniel staggered backward, and Granger grabbed his arm to steady him. Then the boy straightened, his hands fisted at his sides, and he started to advance on Lucas and the Langton woman.

"Not now, Daniel," Granger hissed in his ear. He saw another member of his group fall, a hole in her chest, and he felt a knot tighten in his gut. It was Linda, he thought. These were his people, and they were being slaughtered. "Lucas is right. We have to go."

He looked wildly around in time to see Lucas disappear into the trees on the southeastern edge of the compound, dragging the Langton woman after him. Grabbing Daniel by the arm, Granger ran after the man and the woman, following them into the pines and away from the compound.

25

O'Reilly rushed through the trees as quickly as he could, ignoring the cactus and rocks that grabbed at his legs, the pine branches that ripped at his face and hair. The night had splintered into bursts of muzzle flash and a cacophony of gunshots, shouts and screams. O'Reilly felt the flush of adrenaline course through his blood as he realized what was happening.

Enforcers. An exorcism team, it had to be.

Not only was he going to have to battle a band of ghosts, but he had stumbled into the middle of an exorcism. Maggie wasn't safe either way. The exorcism team wasn't going to ask for identification and release Maggie because she wasn't part of the group. To them, she would be just another ghost and treated in the exact same way. If he didn't get into that camp, find Maggie and get out fast, neither of them would survive.

He felt something whiz past his ear, then smack into the tree behind him. He realized it was a bullet and ducked reflexively, then charged forward once again.

O'Reilly could see a vague glow not far ahead and slowed, realizing he was coming up to the ghosts' camp and not wanting to rush out in full view of the inhabitants or the attackers. He heard hurried footsteps to his left and froze, peering through the trees. O'Reilly saw several dark shapes making their way through the forest to his left, then disappear. Some of the ghosts, he guessed, trying to escape the exorcism team's bullets. He didn't have time for them. He had to find Maggie, and now.

The gunshots were slowing, although the screams from the wounded and dying didn't diminish. O'Reilly crept to the edge of the trees and looked at the scene in front of him, rifle ready if he was seen and recognized. These men would likely be some of the same ones he'd served with when he was on the Laughlin APZ's exorcism team. He knew how they worked. O'Reilly also knew that past friendships wouldn't save him if he were caught.

Ahead of him was a tan steel pole barn with a large water tank attached. A few RVs were scattered around. Two men in dark blue Enforcer uniform shirts walked across the compound, headed for a small, dilapidated cabin on the edge of the trees. He could see several bodies on the ground.

Where would they have kept Maggie? *Please let her be all right.* There's no way she would have been out with the main members of the compound. She would have been kept captive somewhere.

He studied the buildings again, evaluating which would make the best prison.

The barn would be a good bet, he thought. It was large enough that there might be a locked storage room in it. Of course, she could have been secured in one of the RVs, or the cabin, but the barn was closest and in the best condition.

Rising to his full height, black hat pulled low over his face, and rifle gripped in his right hand, O'Reilly stepped out of the trees. He was wearing a dark blue shirt, similar to the uniform shirts worn by the exorcism team, and he counted on being mistaken for one of the members should he be seen.

"Hey, Aiken, that you?" a voice came from over near where the road entered the compound. O'Reilly held his breath and glanced in that direction. He saw one of the exorcism team members standing there, an assault rifle cradled in his arms. He was looking toward the first of the motorhomes, where another man was going through the pockets of one of the bodies that littered the ground. O'Reilly let out the breath and continued to the barn, trying to walk as though he was exactly where he belonged and not as though every hair on the back of his neck was erect and his shoulders tense, waiting for the shot he wouldn't hear. The one that would drop him in his tracks.

O'Reilly made it to the smaller of the two barn doors and stepped inside the cool interior of the building. The fiberglass panels in the roof let in dim moonlight, and the light from the campfire and the exorcism team's tac lights added their own faint glow through the windows. There was just enough light so that he could see the pile of metal on the left hand side of the barn—the top of a windmill tower. More tools were stacked at the far end of the barn, along with a cot. He could also see a door in the back wall but couldn't tell if it was open or shut. A storage room would be a perfect prison.

He cast his gaze around the barn once again, looking for any sign of a trap. Seeing none, O'Reilly started across the concrete floor, rifle held in front of him. The muffled sounds outside were dying away, and the light from the windows was growing. It was standard operating procedure to burn the unusable belongings of a band of ghosts—as well as the bodies of the ghosts themselves. This appeared to be a large group. They would have a lot of belongings to burn.

And a lot of bodies.

O'Reilly reached the end of the barn, and his heart dropped to see that the door to the room was ajar. There's no way Maggie would have stayed in a storage room, he thought, if she wasn't locked in.

Unless she was tied—or hurt or dead.

He stepped forward and pulled the door all the way open. The room was darker than the barn itself, having only a single barred window and no ceiling panels. He looked around for signs that someone had been held captive. Nothing, although there was a blanket and pillow on the nasty old couch. He picked it up and examined it. He held it to his nose and inhaled deeply, willing himself to be able to pick up Maggie's scent.

No such luck.

He stepped back out the door and stood looking around the barn, a feeling of desperation rising in his chest. Was Maggie's body one of those being piled on the pyre out in the compound? And if so, how would he ever know.

A small whisper of sound to his right caused him to step back and raise the rifle, pivoting in a smooth, practiced movement.

"Who are you?" he snapped. "Come on out and let me see you. Let me see your hands."

Several sheets of plywood had been leaned against the back wall of the barn, leaving a triangle of darkness between them and the wall. From within this shelter, a quivering voice emerged.

"I'm coming out. Don't shoot me."

A child's voice.

O'Reilly didn't lower the rifle, but he relaxed slightly. *Great. Another kid. Maggie is going to kill me this time.* The thought escaped his unconscious mind before he could stop it. Followed by the thought, *if I can find her.* Ever since O'Reilly had brought home Lindy after finding her with her dying mother, and then Alysa Thalman, Christina, Nick and Ryan Craigson after a salvaging trip to Wikieup, Arizona, whenever O'Reilly left Hideaway, Maggie would look him in the eye and tell him he couldn't have any more kids in a joking voice.

Now, here was another kid at risk.

The boy had crawled out from behind the plywood and stood before O'Reilly. He appeared to be slightly older than Mark, maybe eleven or twelve, and in the growing light from the fires outside, he looked to be either Hispanic or Native American.

O'Reilly lowered his rifle, although not entirely, and took a step toward the boy. The child took a quick step backward, and O'Reilly thought he would retreat back under the plywood.

"Wait," O'Reilly said, softening his voice. He transferred the rifle to his right hand and reached for the boy's shoulder with his left. "I won't hurt you. I'm looking for a friend of mine." He felt as though he were trying to calm a wild horse. "Her name is Maggie. She's a bit shorter than me with dark blonde hair in a braid?" The inflection made the statement into a question. He let go of the boy's shoulder and gestured toward his own head with his left hand.

The boy studied him for a moment, then said, "She was here. Lucas, he and Granger, they took her when the shooting started. I was hiding behind the barn when they left, but the shooting got bad." His voice quivered again. "They took my older brother, Danny, too."

"Aw, sh . . ." O'Reilly started. If Maggie had left the shelter of the barn, she would have been outside in the compound during the worst of the gunfire. He thought of the pyre—of all the pyres he'd seen during the time he was with the exorcism team, and he felt as though he'd vomit.

The boy was continuing, however, and O'Reilly's attention was jerked back to him and what he was saying.

"Repeat that!" He commanded and then softened his voice again when he saw the boy flinch. "Please, I didn't hear exactly what you said." O'Reilly looked over toward the barn door. From the sounds of it, the exorcism team was still feeding the bonfire, but at some point the looting would start in earnest, and he didn't want to be in the barn when they showed up.

"Lucas, Granger, the lady and Danny ran out of the barn when the shooting started. I saw them leave and tried to catch up, but the everyone was screaming and the shooting was bad. I saw Linda shot dead, and I ran back into the barn. Lucas and them, they ran into the forest over there." The boy pointed toward the right front corner of the barn, southeast of the compound.

The boy's words took O'Reilly's breath away. Maggie was alive, or at least had been only a short time ago, and he still had a chance to rescue her. He thought of the people he'd heard running through the forest, away from the camp, as he was approaching. It might have been them. *Damn!* O'Reilly took a deep breath and blew it out, willing his heart to beat slower. The boy was watching him warily, and O'Reilly gave him a smile.

"What's your name? I'm Jim O'Reilly."

"Andy Espitia," the boy said. "I . . ."

The sound of a voice near the front door of the barn surprised O'Reilly, and Andy turned and scurried back under the plywood. O'Reilly squatted in the shadow from the lumber, but he wasn't small enough to crawl into the burrow with the boy.

"I'll just be a moment," called the person silhouetted in the open door of the barn. "I thought I heard something." It was a deep voice. Male. Something about it rankled at O'Reilly's memory. Not surprising, he thought. He likely knew at least half of this particular exorcism team.

The man entered the barn and paused. He seemed to slump slightly and lowered the muzzle of his rifle toward the floor. O'Reilly tried to sink into the wall, willing the figure not to look too closely toward the back of the barn. The individual stood, gazing back out the door for what seemed like forever. Just as O'Reilly thought the exorcism team member would never leave, he raised his rifle again and started back outside. O'Reilly took a deep breath of relief. He shifted position on his aching knees and accidentally bumped the stock of his rifle into the sheet of plywood, which emitted a hollow *thunk.*

The figure at the door spun, raising the rifle he was carrying. "Who's there?" he snapped out.

O'Reilly's heart sank. The odds were that the man would recognize him and know he was a fugitive. The boy hidden under the plywood would be killed. He thought about shooting but knew if he opened fire, the remainder of the exorcism team would descend on the barn before he and the boy could make it out.

His best chance, and the best chance for the boy behind him, would be to get the man talking, and pray for an opening where he could knock the team member unconscious and make a run for it. O'Reilly rose to his feet slowly and carefully. The silhouetted figure took a step forward, then another. He stepped into the shaft of orange firelight shining through the window, and O'Reilly's eyes opened wide. His mind raced, and then he decided to roll the dice.

Forgive me, Maggie, if I'm wrong, O'Reilly thought, and he took a step forward.

26

Alpha team took all afternoon, and a fair share of the night to reach the ghosts' encampment. The team set out from the riparian area where they left the jeeps, and through the afternoon they hiked across the rough, brush covered country finally making their way up the west side of the mountain where the team had pinpointed the compound's location. Several times Clements had checked in with Beta team on the radio and learned they were making good time coming up from the south. The remainder of the afternoon the, two bands maintained strict radio silence, as well as restricting talk among themselves, and Rickards was repeatedly impressed with Clements' leadership as they navigated the rugged terrain.

Rickards, city rat that he was, had never had to hike long distances over rough land, and he hoped he never had to do it again.

He had to admit to himself the landscape, was beautiful—for the first hundred yards or so, while they were hiking through the riparian area. The afternoon sunlight filtered through the brilliant green leaves of the cottonwoods and sycamores as they walked through the darker green grass that grew lush and tall along the banks of the creek bed. As they moved, Rickards studied the canopy of foliage above him and noticed a few patches of yellow that heralded the coming of fall. He knew the Seligman area was at an elevation that would receive snow in the winter, and he wondered for a minute what that would be like. He'd never lived in an area that had much snow, although he had visited it a few times. *Pain in the ass to drive through*, he thought.

He found himself thinking about many random things that afternoon—anything to keep his mind off his feet, his burning legs and shoulders, and the upcoming attack on the compound of ghosts.

Once the team climbed out of the coverage of the trees and into the sun, the coolness was a memory. It may have been early fall, but in the harsh sunlight, it was hot, and Rickards found himself mopping his forehead with his shoulder many times as he readjusted the pack. It didn't help that Clements seemed determined to take the most circuitous route he could find. Rickards respected Clements' leadership, and agreed that a low profile and secrecy were important, but he wished for the jeep and a smooth road. He remembered the approach to the hidden canyon south of his current location. In that case, they hadn't been forced to resort to walking until close to their quarry.

And, more importantly, that was hiking downhill, into the canyon, not uphill, onto a mountain. He was beginning to hate mountains.

When evening fell, Rickards welcomed the coolness of the night sky. This was Arizona, however, and the lack of humidity meant things cooled off quickly when the sun went down. He didn't mind the cooler air much while moving, but once they reached the mountaintop, and Clements had stationed them around the encampment, ready for the final attack, Rickards quickly found himself getting uncomfortably cold.

Damn, I'm getting to be a wimp in my old age, he thought and sighed again, rubbing his back.

The orders were to wait for Beta team to get into position on the south side of the mountain and encampment, low enough to be out of danger from crossfire. Then, after they were sure that the members of the band of ghosts had settled for the night, the Enforcers would attack. If the band posted lookouts, Clements' team would try to identify and eliminate them quickly and quietly, but if something went wrong, they would attack hard and fast.

Of course, Rickards thought later, something went very wrong.

Rickards groaned and stretched, wishing he were back at the APZ in Laughlin, sitting at his desk in his comfortable chair instead of sitting in the dark, on a rock, on the top of an Arizona mountain, shivering with cold and watching the dim glow from a fire a hundred yards or so away. *What the hell possessed me to do this?* he thought. He pushed the night vision goggles he'd been assigned back on his head in frustration. The things were uncomfortable, and he had trouble adjusting to walking in the alien world he saw while wearing them, but at least they kept him from bumping into the innumerable cacti that littered the ground on this mountain.

He figured it was approximately one or one-thirty in the morning, not that it made much difference. It had been at least an hour since he heard indistinguishable voices coming from the direction of the encampment, and the fire glow was getting ever dimmer, filtered through the trunks of the sparse pine trees. He checked his rifle once again. He knew they were waiting for Beta team's final signal that they were ready, and then Clements would give the order to attack.

Rickards was still sitting and staring at the distant firelight playing in the pine branches when he heard a noise off to his left, toward the southeast side of the plateau. He rose to his feet, moving slow, trying to avoid making any noise. His knees popped so loudly that he froze, fearing that if the ghosts had posted any lookouts, they would have been alerted to his presence at that moment.

He listened, but the sound that caught his attention didn't come again, and he wasn't really sure if he'd heard anything to begin with. He turned, peering into the dark woods. He knew where the other team members were stationed in the silent blackness, but he couldn't see them, and soon every night noise of the high desert sounded like an attack.

The sound of a stick breaking caused him to spin quickly back toward the compound, rifle at the ready. Nothing. A scurrying behind him brought his heart rate to that of a jackhammer.

Dammit, this mountain is messing with my mind. The light from the compound's fire was so faint now Rickards could barely distinguish it from his position.

The sound of water falling on leaves and pine duff caused Rickards to frown, and he glanced toward the sky. The three-quarter moon wasn't providing much light through the pine branches, but he could see stars and knew the sky wasn't overcast. Then the acrid smell of urine drifted over him, and he stiffened.

Rickards pulled the night vision goggles back down over his eyes. Their light-multiplying technology caused the trees to pop out in eerie blue-green, and he was aware of a slight sense of vertigo as he looked for the source of the sound and smell. Just as he'd decided that a deer had chosen to take a leak nearby, he heard the faintest of scratching sounds from a zipper being raised, short-lived and easily missed. He zeroed in on the tree from where the sound seemed to originate and could faintly see the shape of an arm and a leg of someone standing on the other side. A shiver of adrenaline ran down his back—any closer and the guy would have peed on him.

Rickards took a step to the side in an effort to see the individual better. It had to be a lookout from the encampment, as none of the other exorcism team members should be in that quadrant. He took another step, and a stick emitted a large *crack* as his weight came down on it. Rickards froze.

The sound galvanized the figure behind the tree, who stumbled backward into full view. Rickards raised his rifle and trained it on the man—because it was clear now in the alien night vision world that it was a man, not a woman—and waited to see if he realized Rickards was there or if he would attribute the noise to the area's wildlife.

To Rickards' shock, the lookout, at some point in his stumble, tripped on something, probably a branch or a rock—or a cactus, Rickards thought wryly—and fell over backward. He caught himself with his right hand, the one holding the gun. He must have had his finger in the trigger guard, and when the weapon he was carrying slammed to the ground, it fired a wild shot off into the trees.

Rickards waited a beat, then a second. The radio at his belt, set low, emitted one word. "Now." Then the night air was ripped apart by the gunfire of the exorcism team as they fell upon the sleeping encampment.

The next fifteen minutes was hell on earth, thought Rickards later. At the time, he wasn't thinking—he was reacting. When it was over, he stood looking at the ghosts' compound and experienced a strange form of double vision. He could see the tan pole barn, the RVs and the cabin in both cases, but superimposed over the hellscape of dead bodies, broken glass, overturned chairs and bullet-riddled metal, was an image of people going about their lives, preparing food, growing a garden, laughing, fighting maybe, but living for sure.

He felt a moment of vertigo again and swayed on his feet. He thought about James O'Reilly, who had broken following an exorcism like this—albeit one that included children—and he thanked God there hadn't been any children here. He remembered the dead truck drivers and others this band had killed ruthlessly. The vertigo worsened, and he felt as though he had to get away and clear his head for a moment.

Rickards looked around and his gaze fell on the large barn. He stumbled in that direction, desperate to escape, if only temporarily. Unfortunately, one of the other team members noticed and called out to the captain.

"Rickards, where you going?"

Rickards paused for a second, thinking wildly for a response. He didn't want any members of the exorcism team to see his weakness.

Rickards unclenched his tongue from the roof of his mouth and called back, "I'll just be a moment." He was both pleased and surprised he didn't hear any quiver in his voice. "I thought I heard something."

He walked more quickly to the barn, praying no one else would notice his departure.

The interior of the barn was even darker than outside, other than the glow of the campfire shining in through the windows. That glow, which had been dying away prior to the start of the attack, was growing once again, and Rickards tried to block the reason for the increasing flames from his mind.

His shoulders dropped, the muzzle of the rifle dipped toward the ground and he felt some of the tension run out of his body. He stood for several minutes, sheltered by the barn but staring back out into the forest. The orange-gold of the flames was beautiful, flickering off the trees as it was, almost as if some king sized glow worms were throwing a rave. *Strange how something can be both so beautiful and so terrible at the same time*, he thought.

After what seemed both hours and seconds simultaneously, in keeping with the duality of the night, Rickards took a deep breath and headed back through the open door. Just as he was stepping outside, a loud *thunk* from the back of the barn caused him to spin on his heel, raising the rifle barrel as he moved.

"Who's there?" he barked.

No answer came from the deeper darkness at the back of the barn. Rickards reached for his night vision goggles, then swore under his breath when he realized his head was bare. They must have fallen off at some point during the chaos of the battle.

The light from the fire made the back wall of the barn retreat even farther into the darkness. Rickards took several slow steps forward, moving into the light from the fire beyond the window, aware that it illuminated him even more than his silhouette in the door had, and started to take another step forward when he saw the darkened figure of a man step toward him—a different layer of dark from the wall itself—peeling away and approaching.

Rickards' finger tightened on the trigger, and he prepared to fire when a voice caused him to take a sudden step backward, then stand as if paralyzed—turned to stone by shock. His mind struggled to make sense of what he was hearing. He recognized the voice, although the last time he heard it, the words had been filled with pain and roughened by the dust from a cave-in.

The voice was familiar, however, although it was one he never expected to hear again, let alone in this remote barn on a mountain outside of Seligman.

27

"Seth," O'Reilly said in his soft, gravelly voice, dragging the name out. A statement, not a question.

The man took a step backward, then froze. The two stared at each other for a moment, then Rickards said, "O'Reilly? Is that really you? Dammit, you're supposed to be . . ."

"Dead?" O Reilly said in wry notes. This situation was quickly becoming one of those farces he'd been involved in too many times since meeting Maggie.

"Yeah, dead," Rickards responded, his wry notes matching O'Reilly's. "Why aren't you? Dead, I mean."

"You met Maggie Langton." O'Reilly's voice was so dry at that point that it made Death Valley seem like a tropical oasis.

Rickards choked back a laugh.

A large *thwump* from outside caused everyone to look toward the window. The light from the pyre was gaining in brilliance, and O'Reilly figured they'd poured some form of accelerant on it—gasoline or oil, maybe. He knew by the time the team pulled out, nothing would be left.

"Seth, I've got to get out of here." He heard a sound behind him and glanced back. The boy had crawled out from under the plywood and stood behind him. "*We've* got to get out of here." He reached back and pulled the boy up to his side.

Rickards looked at the boy with surprise, then his eyes met O'Reilly's again, and in that instant, O'Reilly knew he'd made the right choice. Rickards may have originally hunted O'Reilly with the intention of capturing or killing him, but that encounter with Maggie in the caves, as well as whatever happened after he returned to the APZ, had changed the man.

"What are you doing here anyway?" Rickards asked.

"Maggie was kidnapped." O'Reilly's voice was matter-of-fact.

"What?"

"Maggie was kidnapped and brought here by some members of this band of ghosts. I came to rescue her."

Rickards turned and looked toward the window and the ever-increasing glow beyond, then back at O'Reilly. Even in the dim light, O'Reilly could see the look of horror on Rickards' face, and he knew why. He rushed to push his words past his lips as he continued.

"Andy here says that when the attack from the exorcism team started, two men and his brother grabbed Maggie and made a run for it. I was just getting ready to go after them when you showed up."

Rickards didn't move for a moment, and O'Reilly was just preparing to speak again when a look of determination took over the man's face. He nodded once and said, "I'm going with you. You're going to need help."

O'Reilly had been shocked when he saw the Enforcer captain walk into the barn, but it was nothing compared to what he felt at Rickards' words now. He didn't have time to argue, however. Still, he had to ask, "What will you tell the APZ afterward . . . I mean if we make it out alive?"

"Easy, I'll tell them I was kidnapped by one of the ghosts and taken hostage. Eventually I escaped, killed the man and I've now returned."

O'Reilly snorted in derision. "Think they'll believe you?"

"I think enough will." Rickards spoke quietly, with a conviction that O'Reilly didn't feel about the plan. It would be good to have help, however.

There was another large *whump* from outside, and O'Reilly started for the end of the barn, pulling the boy behind him.

"Fine, I accept your assistance. We've got to go now, before someone realizes you're still in here and comes to find out why. Give me your arm."

Rickards gave O'Reilly an uncomprehending stare, unmistakable even in the dim light. Then his expression cleared, and he held out his left arm. O'Reilly quickly fished his knife out of his pocket and grabbed the man's wrist, felt for a second, then, with a quick, experienced slice, removed the chip buried under the skin, dropped it on the floor and ground it under his heel. Rickards hissed in pain.

"It was shallow," O'Reilly said. "They didn't get it in very deep. It will heal fast, but we don't want them to be able to trace you past this barn."

Rickards nodded. "It was a new technician who didn't know exactly what he was doing. I actually meant to have it reinserted. I'll just tell the authorities my kidnapper noticed it under my skin and removed it because he was afraid it was a tracker. Which I guess it was, come to think of it."

O'Reilly looked up and saw Andy practically vibrating with impatience. He nodded toward the boy, and they started for the door of the barn.

Rickards fell in behind O'Reilly and the boy. O'Reilly glanced out the window as they moved past. The size of the pyre roiled his stomach, and he fought to keep down what little he'd eaten that day.

The three got to the small door, and O'Reilly started to step out, rifle at the ready. Rickards stopped him with a hand on his shoulder.

"Let me. If they see you and realize you're not a member of the team, we're in trouble." Rickards moved around O'Reilly and stepped outside, scanned the area, then walked to the left corner of the barn—the one closest to the compound. He peered around the edge of the building. O'Reilly could see him check the vicinity carefully, then he motioned for O'Reilly and the boy to go. O'Reilly tapped Andy on the shoulder and the two of them ran for the trees in the direction the boy had said Maggie had been taken. O'Reilly could hear Rickards following close behind.

Just inside the trees and past the glow from the fire, they stopped. Rickards stepped up next to O'Reilly, breathing heavily from the sprint, and O'Reilly wondered if the man would be up to what was ahead.

"Now where?" Rickards asked. "We don't want to stick around here too long. He chinned back toward the conflagration. One of the RVs, the closest to the pyre, had been torched, and they could hear shouts from the members of the exorcism team.

O'Reilly stood for a moment, weighing his options. The chances of tracking and catching the men who had Maggie in the dark were so small as to be virtually zero. However, if they went back and got the horses without knowing where Maggie's captors were taking her, they would spend a lot of extra time hunting for the small group once the sun came up—in a forest that might still have members of an active exorcism team looking for possible escapees from the attack. It would also give the kidnappers a head start, and it would be that much more difficult to track them if they weren't using a UTV. He . . .

"Betcha they're going to Lucas's hideout." Andy said, seemingly unaware of the mental battle O'Reilly had been fighting.

Rickards and O'Reilly both stared at the boy who was starting to walk off through the woods with a sureness that spoke to his knowledge of the direction their quarry had taken, as well as the location of any obstructions. In spite of the multi-layered darkness, the child wasn't hitting a cactus every other step, O'Reilly noticed with envy.

"Wait," O'Reilly hissed after the boy, rushing to catch up to him. "This man you call Lucas, he has a hideout . . . from *this* hideout?" That was a level of paranoia that made O'Reilly nervous. That type of man could be very dangerous because he would be suspicious of everyone and everything, and willing to act on his suspicions.

"Yeah, he's been going there for weeks and stockpiling things like food, guns and ammo. Even has a UTV with gas in it. Danny and I followed him one time for the fun of it, to see if we could, and we checked the cabin out when he left. Sometimes we go back to see what he's been doing." Andy made a face barely discernable in the tree-filtered moonlight, and O'Reilly realized the boy didn't like this man, Lucas, very much.

Andy sounded calm, although eager to get going. *What must this kid have gone through,* O'Reilly thought, *that the horrors of the last half hour have rolled off his back-and he is in control of himself.*

"All right, Andy," O'Reilly said. He nodded toward the forest and motioned for Rickards to come. "You're in charge, kid."

"Dammit," said Rickards, and O'Reilly saw him pawing at his head in an agitated manner.

"What?"

"I had night vision goggles. I forgot I lost them in the attack, I guess. I pushed them back on my head when the light from the fire was so bright. They must have fallen off. I realized they were gone earlier, but I keep forgetting and reaching for them again."

O'Reilly looked back at Andy, who was disappearing into the deeper darkness of the forest.

"I guess you'll be at the mercy of the cacti the same as me. Now come on."

O'Reilly turned and hurried after Andy.

28

With Lucas leading, dragging Maggie behind, the small group moved more quickly than was safe through the pine and juniper forest. Granger found himself struggling to keep up with the blond man as he followed some invisible game trail to the southeast of the encampment. The sound of gunfire faded as they made their way through the trees and over the rolling terrain that marked the top of the mountain range.

Damn Lucas, he moves like a mountain goat," thought Granger as he tripped and nearly fell for the twentieth time. The Langton woman did fall, uttering a small scream of surprise as she pitched forward to her knees. Only Lucas's grip on her arm kept her from going flat on her face. Lucas jerked her back to her feet and cuffed her, demanding silence.

It dawned on Granger that the woman actually had been surprisingly quiet during the escape, and he wondered about it. Then he realized she must have recognized the attack as Enforcer led, not a rescue attempt from her people. It also showed that she knew what her chances were in the hands of the law enforcement officers. Lucas may be a sociopath, but based on the rumors Granger had heard from individuals they had met who had escaped "exorcisms," being "rescued" by the teams would have meant immediate death.

Granger's breath burned in his lungs, and his back and legs were screaming when Lucas halted a few minutes later.

Daniel skidded to a stop behind him. They were on the edge of the volcanic rock rim that circled the southeast side of the mountain, a sharp drop in front of them disappearing into the strange moonlit landscape below. He could still hear occasional shots and screams from the compound and felt a well of fury rise within his chest. He wanted to cry and to wail, and to kill every single one of the members of the exorcism teams. The chaos of those minutes following the attack began blurring together into a confused, undefinable maelstrom of fear and fury. He ground his teeth and focused on controlling his emotions.

Daniel stood beside him, breathing heavily, but not nearly as heavily as Granger. In the dim moonlight, Granger could see a trickle of tears running down his cheeks, although he made no sound. The loss of Andy tore at his heart too, and he felt for the boy.

"Where are we going, Lucas?" Granger asked.

Lucas looked over his shoulder at Granger. A small smile cracked his beard, and the moonlight did startling things to the pale blue eyes. Granger took a small step backward and came up short against a pile of the black rock that created this little mountain range.

"You owe me again, Granger," Lucas said. "I saved your worthless life again." He laughed as though they'd just gotten out of an escape room where they'd been in danger of nothing more than being ridiculed because they couldn't solve the puzzle.

"But, where are . . ." Granger started. His breathing was nearly back to normal, and his heart no longer felt as though it was going to explode from his chest.

"Say it, Ethan! Say I saved your life. Even after everything you've done the last few days." Lucas laughed again, and the note of insanity in his voice chilled Granger and made him feel slightly nauseous. He glanced at the Langton woman, still tight in Lucas's grip. She stood silently, her breath coming fast. She stared at her feet, her blonde braid falling over her shoulder, glinting in the pale moonlight. As Lucas laughed again, she raised her head, and even in the nearly non-existent illumination, Granger could see the hate-filled stare she turned on the blond man. Granger half expected Lucas to burst into flames. Lucas caught the glare, and his grin turned malicious.

"Fine!" Granger snapped, losing his temper with the insane man. "You saved my life. Again. Thank you. Now, where are we going?"

"I got me a bug out location," Lucas said, clearly proud of himself. "It's a little place about five miles from here. Come on. We need to get there before it starts getting light in case the Enforcers are still looking for anyone who might have escaped the attack." Reaching into the pocket of the light jacket he was wearing, he pulled out a short length of nylon rope and tied it around the woman's wrists, keeping them in front of her so her balance wouldn't be impaired.

He turned and winked at Granger, jerking the woman's arms to make sure the knots were secure, then he turned and started to pick his way down the mountain, following a barely discernible trail that led off the rim and downward at an oblique angle.

For a moment, Granger didn't move. His mind boggled at the information that Lucas had been creating a bolt hole. Who in their right mind created a bug out location for their bug out location? He looked at Lucas and revised the question. Obviously, Lucas wasn't always in his right mind, but this time the man's paranoia had been justified. Of course Lucas had a bug out location.

Granger shook his head, and feelings that swung between amusement and admiration temporarily pushed down his wary distrust of the man's sanity. Granger started down the trail, following close behind Daniel. It slowly dawned on him that the boy had shown no surprise at Lucas's disclosure, and wondered if the brothers had discovered the man's secret while out hunting or just exploring. He doubted Lucas had ever knowingly shared the existence of his private hideout with Daniel and Andy since he'd never shown anything but annoyance and disdain for the youngest members of the band.

The small group moved in silence for the next twenty minutes or so, following the trail through several switchbacks, winding slowly downhill through the rocks and trees. As they got closer to the floor of the valley, the trees transitioned from primarily pine to primarily juniper, and Granger found himself relaxing. The thicker juniper foliage provided greater cover than did the tall, spindly white pine trunks, and as the eastern horizon began to lighten with the coming of dawn, he wanted all the coverage they could get.

Once in the valley, Lucas struck out toward the southeast. Granger hurried to catch up with the man, Daniel trailing behind.

"Lucas," Granger started.

The man was still moving quickly, although hampered by his grip on the short rope he'd tied to the woman's wrists. Occasionally he'd yank her arms and tell her to hurry. Maggie Langton seemed to be holding up at least as well as he and Daniel were, and other than occasionally stumbling over a branch or a rock, eliciting another yank from Lucas, she didn't fight back.

"Lucas!" Granger said, raising his voice a few decibels. Even as he did so, he glanced around, irrationally expecting every Enforcer in the state to have discerned their escape route and be hiding behind the trees, ready to pounce.

Lucas glanced over at Ethan, a frown on his face. The exaltation he'd shown earlier after their escape had been replaced by a dogged determination to reach his bug out location as quickly as possible.

"What do you want?" Lucas snapped.

"Why did you bring the Langton woman? Isn't she just slowing us down?" In truth, Granger had mixed feelings about Maggie Langton being included in the escape. He knew if she'd been left behind, she almost certainly would have been slaughtered with the rest of his people. His chest clenched at the thought, and he prayed some of the others had escaped the massacre. She also had information that could potentially benefit them, especially now that he, Lucas and Daniel were alone once again. However, considering Lucas's obsession with the woman, he knew he was going to have to fight to keep her from being abused by Lucas as he'd promised.

"Her?" Lucas said casually, yanking Langton's arms again, although she was already moving as fast as they were. "She's going to show us where her camp is. Isn't that the information you were trying to get out of her?" Lucas grinned at Granger and ignored the look of pure hatred Langton shot in his direction.

"We don't know how many are in her group, and there are only three of us now," Granger protested. Yes, he'd wanted to know where her camp was and take it if possible and if it seemed safer and better hidden than their own mountaintop encampment. He coughed back a harsh laugh. It seemed like just about anywhere would have been safer than his group's compound. He fought down bitter regret. Granger knew his decision to start hitting the supply trucks led directly to the group's discovery and ultimate destruction, and the guilt ate a hole in his gut.

If only they had left the APZ supplies alone. He knew, however, that the group wouldn't have enough food and fuel to make it through the winter if they didn't raid the convoys. In spite of that, he felt strongly that the blood of his people was on his hands.

"We also had to leave most of our armament behind when we were attacked. If Langton's camp is any size whatsoever, we don't have the firepower to take it, and I don't really think they'll welcome us with open arms, considering how Ms. Langton here came to be in our company."

Lucas was silent as he strode along, pulling the woman periodically, forcing her to keep up in the growing pale dawn light, and Granger began to wonder if the blond man had heard him.

The small group continued for another hour, staying off the roads but paralleling them, from what Granger could tell. They were moving steadily east-southeast according to the rising sun when, without warning, Lucas turned south and struck off on a cattle track. They walked for five minutes, topped a small hill covered with juniper and live oak, as well as yucca and mormon tea and the ubiquitous prickly pear, and found themselves looking down upon a small wooden cabin. A large, rusty steel shed sat about thirty feet away.

"C'mon," Lucas said, shooting Granger a grin and started down the hill, tugging the woman behind him. Granger and Daniel looked at each other, and Granger shrugged and followed Lucas.

The weathered wood cabin was the definition of minimalist, Granger thought as he looked around the open room. In the right corner of the back wall were several pine boards resting on concrete blocks with a large, stainless steel sink nestled into a hole cut out of the yellowed lumber. Between some blue cloth curtains strung under the boards, he could see white PVC piping draining into an old five-gallon bucket. A ladder led up into a loft above, where Granger figured the owners slept when in residence.

The front of the one room cabin had been used as a living room, but Granger could see Lucas had been busy stockpiling everything he could find and piling it in the space. Several boxes of food sat on an old plaid wool couch, and a collection of rifles and handguns, as well as boxes of ammunition, were lying on the scarred coffee table next to eight or nine bottles of whiskey and tequila. A few piles of medical supplies were stacked near the food. More items, such as clothing and boots, were scattered about the room.

Granger stared around the space, his mind whirring. *Exactly how long* has *Lucas been working on this stash?* Then he answered the question for himself. Lucas must have been provisioning this bug out location since the day their band chose the mountaintop encampment. Probably every time he went out looting, he skimmed off the best of his take, bringing it to this secluded location. When he returned to the compound, he had many different excuses for not bringing in much. The houses had already been looted. The people who owned the homes had used up the supplies before leaving — or dying.

Granger took several steps into the room, turned his head and took in everything. He was aware of a growing fury. He turned on Kyle Lucas, his hands in fists. It felt as if all the pain, despair and fear of the night had collated into an overwhelming chamber of magma in his chest, ready to erupt at any moment.

"What the hell, Kyle! We could have used this stuff at the camp, and you've been hoarding it here? What other secrets are you keeping?" He saw both Daniel and Maggie Langton watching him warily, the way they usually watched Lucas. He fought to control his anger and frustration. He could see Lucas's expression flow from pride to confusion and bloom into anger at Granger's tone, and he fought to rein in his fury. He couldn't afford to alienate the man right now. He took a deep breath and tried to calm his heart, which felt as though it was beating through his chest.

"I'm sorry, Kyle," Granger said, "I shouldn't have reacted that way."

To his ears, his voice still sounded brittle, and he was surprised when he saw Lucas begin to relax, and the insane fire begin to drain from his pale blue eyes.

How many times am I going to play this game? Granger asked himself. *When will I finally have had enough of this man and cut him loose? Or will I wait too long, and when he goes completely over the edge, be caught in the whirlwind?*

The smile was back on Lucas's face, although a wary look still lingered in his eyes.

"I also got a four-place with a trailer in the barn out there, with some extra tanks of gas. Plenty of water in jerrycans, too. I've got weapons and ammo here. I say let's take this lady back to her people."

His words dripped with derision, and Granger knew what he meant. He also knew the odds were good that if any of Langton's people resisted, none would walk out alive, at least if it was a small, poorly armed band, as Langton had indicated.

A sudden wave of exhaustion swept over Granger, and he wanted nothing more than to climb that ladder, lay down on the bed, if there was one, and sleep for eternity. He knew Lucas was right, and after all, he himself had been trying to get the information on Maggie Langton's camp with the idea of appropriating it for his band. Now that his group was only three didn't mean they needed a safe spot any less. And, with the Enforcers likely to be patrolling the area, looking for any possible escapees from the massacre, that safe spot wasn't anywhere around Seligman.

Granger realized with surprise that he was no longer the "leader." It almost seemed as though they were back at the beginning, with Lucas guiding him out of the Phoenix Metro area and up into the mountains.

"All right, Kyle," Granger said on a sigh. He realized he'd been feeling off balance since Jackie's death earlier in the day. Hell, it seemed as though everything had spun out of control since the hunting trip and kidnapping the Langton woman.

"Daniel, start moving the guns and the ammo out to this four-place Kyle mentioned." Granger motioned toward the table. "Those are the most important items. Then pack whatever food and medical supplies will fit."

The boy nodded, went to the coffee table and started loading his arms. Kyle had been very busy indeed, thought Granger, and apparently, the residents of the subdivisions south of Seligman had been very well armed. For a second, he wondered, with a bitter resentment rising once again, whether having those weapons up in the encampment would have made a difference when the Enforcers fell on them. The next second he told himself that no, it just would have meant that the team that attacked would have had that many more guns to take back to the APZs. Every member of his band had possessed at least one assault or hunting rifle and one handgun, and while ammo wasn't plentiful, they still had enough. Adding this lot would have made no difference as, ultimately, you could only accurately shoot one weapon at a time. Granger fought down a feeling that said the guns and ammunition could have made a difference, but they would never know for sure. He knew he'd always have that feeling of doubt—of "what if."

Lucas said he'd warned them, didn't he? Granger could remember asking, but couldn't remember what Lucas answered. What did he say? Granger tried to remember the specific events at the beginning of the attack. He . . .

"I'm taking the woman out to the UTV," said Lucas, interrupting Granger's thoughts. "We need to be ready to go fast. They might hear the UTV engine up at the camp. I don't think so, but maybe." Then he laughed, his short, crazy-loon laugh. "You all didn't hear though, did ya? All that time when I was preparing my bolt hole, you never suspected." He laughed again, sending shivers down Granger's back and reminding him once again that while Lucas was calling the shots right now, he still wasn't the man who had led him from the Valley—he was insane, and only a fool trusts an insane man.

Lucas jerked on the rope tied to the Langton woman's arms and led her out of the cabin toward the barn. Maggie Langton looked over her shoulder as she was pulled along, a mix of fear and anger in her eyes. *Help me!* she mouthed, then snapped her head back around as she stumbled over a loose board and nearly fell. Lucas yanked on the rope again, and Langton regained her balance and followed quickly lest she be pulled down and dragged through the gravel and cactus.

Dammit! Granger thought. His priority had to be *his* people—Daniel, and Lucas, crazy though he was. Langton was not his, and although he hated it, if she had to be sacrificed to protect his people, so be it.

Turning on his heel, he grabbed a nearby pack of food and strode out of the cabin, heading for the storage shed where he could see the UTV waiting. He stopped for a second and looked toward the mountain to the northwest. In the pale, dawn light, it sat silently. All shooting was over, and a narrow wisp of smoke flowed into the sky from the southern edge, hinting at the activities now being conducted. He thought he could smell that smoke and shook his head, forcing his imagination to drop the idea. He knew what burning flesh smelled like—although, in the past, it was he and his band doing the burning.

The low, plaintive moo of a distant cow reached his ears from somewhere north or east of him. He wasn't sure of the direction, but it felt like he was hearing Odysseus's sirens calling them out and away. He knew it was time they got out of there and headed back for the area south of Juniper Mesa, where they had found Maggie Langton.

29

O'Reilly followed the young boy through the trees almost by sound, it seemed. Even though he knew dawn was approaching, it sure hadn't gotten there yet, and several times he had to call out for Andy to slow down as he tripped again over a pile of rocks, a log, or another damned cactus sitting dimly in the path. He could tell from the sounds behind him that Rickards was having no easier a time, and he fought down a laugh when the Enforcer let out a faint yelp and swore profusely.

Andy paused at the escarpment of rock that marked the edge of the mountaintop, staring at the ground as if looking for something. Across the valley to the east, the horizon paled in the coming of the dawn, and O'Reilly was able to see the ground much more clearly in the growing light. He knew that would make it easier to navigate the steep trail past the pile of rocks but it would also make it easier to be seen if any of the exorcism team had missed Rickards and begun a search for the Enforcer captain. He knew the aftermath of many of these raids was chaotic, and if they were lucky, they might think Rickards had been killed and accidentally thrown on the pyre.

Lately, he hadn't felt very lucky.

"The trail's here," Andy indicated a faint indentation in the ground that wove between two rocks and then disappeared down into the pine forest that covered the steep slope. He ran lightly down the trail, disappearing quickly over the edge of the escarpment.

O'Reilly looked back at Rickards, who shrugged and gestured for O'Reilly to go ahead once again. *Just let Maggie be safe*, he thought, probably for the thousandth time that evening.

He was getting close. He knew it. Maybe in the next hour or two he'd have her with him once again, and they could go home to the children.

The light grew steadily stronger as the three made their way down the steep slope, the trail cutting back and forth in shallow switchbacks instead of moving straight. Twice, when the path widened, O'Reilly could pick out the occasional footprint that didn't belong to Andy. Larger prints. Men's boots. There weren't enough prints for O'Reilly to be able to be certain how many people they were following, or even if Andy was right and this was the man, Lucas's, secret trail instead of some regular path to a windmill he could see off in the distant valley to the southwest.

What he did know was that the prints were fresh, and he was determined to hold on to the belief that they were close on the trail of Maggie and her captors.

The sun was fully above the horizon when the three of them hit the bottom of the valley and struck out across the juniper-studded grassland. O'Reilly felt as though eyes were burrowing a hole between his shoulder blades, and he glanced up toward the mountain behind them. Pale streams of smoke continued to drift upward, and he wondered briefly if another wildfire was brewing.

In his time with the exorcism team, fire was a perpetual challenge to the cleanup process. The teams didn't exactly try to start a wildfire, but if one did ignite, no one tried hard to put it out. Fire was seen as the ultimate in environmental cleansers, and if it didn't endanger the team's retreat, or put an APZ, travel route or needed power transmission lines at risk, then no effort was made to extinguish it either.

"Do you think they're watching?" Rickards asked, eerily echoing O'Reilly's thoughts.

"If they are, it won't be long before they're after us." O'Reilly's voice held a grim tone that made it clear his and Rickards' chances if the exorcism team did come after them were not good.

"We'll be out of sight soon," Rickards said, and O'Reilly could hear in the gruff notes that the man was also concerned about being observed from the mountain. He was right, however, that if they made it to the next copse of junipers and over the small ridge, they should be out of sight of anyone on the mountain who was studying the valleys below, looking for Rickards or escapees.

A thought crossed O'Reilly's mind, and he jerked to a stop, turned and looked at Rickards, meeting the man's questioning gaze. The captain had not yet put on the sunglasses that hung by a bow from the collar of his shirt, and his hazel eyes met O'Reilly's dark brown stare without flinching.

"Seth, I need you to make me a promise," O'Reilly said, the words sounding as if they were being squeezed from his throat.

Rickards' eyes narrowed in apparent suspicion, but he answered without hesitating, "I will if I can. No *carte blanche*, though."

O'Reilly paused for a moment, and with surprise, he felt his jaw moving as if he were chewing on his words. He made a face, finding them bitter.

"If the exorcism team comes after us . . . I mean if they catch us, you have to tell them that I captured you and Andy."

Rickards' eyes went from narrow suspicion to wide-eyed surprise in a fraction of a second, and the man reared back as if struck.

"What the hell?"

"Wait and hear me out. If . . ." O'Reilly turned his head, realized Andy was nearly out of sight, turned and started walking quickly after the boy while raising his voice so Rickards could hear him.

"If we are found and trapped by a large force, we are not well enough armed to shoot our way out, and besides, that would blow your story of being captured. How many in that exorcism team? Fifteen, sixteen? Did they lose any members during the raid?"

"Sixteen men and the captain, Dan Clements," Rickards said, obviously thinking about the attack on the compound. "I didn't hear of any members of the team being killed, but I also didn't stick around long after the attack. I don't think any one was lost, but I can't be sure," he continued after a brief pause.

"Clements is a good man," O'Reilly said. He wasn't lying. When he'd worked with Clements, he had liked the guy and respected his leadership skills. He just hated the mission and couldn't understand why men like Clements were okay with the situation. Then he reminded himself that throughout history, good men had been persuaded to do terrible things for the "common good" if the propaganda was convincing enough.

"If Clements and his team realize you've been 'taken' and come after us—maybe find and catch us in a location where we can't get away, you tell them that I captured you and the boy. Stay close to the story you were planning on anyway. Tell them the ghosts were holding the boy captive as well. That way they 'rescue' you and Andy and I'm the only one killed."

"O'Reilly! Jim . . .!" Rickards started, protesting O'Reilly's plan.

"No, listen to me. If you live, you can maybe get away later. Say you have to visit the Phoenix APZ or something. Find a way to save Maggie."

"I won't know where they are," Rickards sounded frustrated, anger growing in his voice.

"I think they'll be heading for Hideaway," O'Reilly said, his voice dropping low as he felt the growing desperation. "They have lost their group, and if Andy is to be believed, this Lucas man has put away enough supplies to reach the camp. Even if Maggie doesn't tell them exactly where it is, if they just start from where they took her, they'll find it soon enough. Promise me that if I'm killed or taken, you will do whatever it takes to find her."

For a moment, neither man spoke, but then Rickards responded, "I will," his voice also low.

Suddenly O'Reilly laughed. "Four months ago did you ever think we'd be working together?"

"Four months ago I wanted nothing more than to put a damned bullet in your head after I'd tortured you into telling me why you'd bolted and ran from the APZ."

"You know now?" O'Reilly asked, looking over at Rickards, curious to hear what the man had to say. The humor had left his voice.

"Phase One," Rickards offered, his words dripping with sarcasm.

"Did you ever find out exactly what it means? The *Phase One* I mean. The *Reduction of Population.*" O'Reilly could feel his curiosity growing as they trudged after the boy. The sun was becoming warm in the early fall air, and O'Reilly worried it would become one of those Indian summer days that would make you wonder if winter would ever come again.

"No, I . . ." Rickards started but the sound of a UTV's engine, loud and close, cut him off.

Both men looked toward the sound. Maybe a half mile or a mile away, in O'Reilly's estimation, and he started running. Andy met O'Reilly, racing back toward him, an excited look on his face.

"Hurry up! They're leaving!" Andy turned and ran back toward the sound again, O'Reilly and Rickards following close behind.

After five minutes of dodging juniper boughs, cacti and mounds of black and red hardened volcanic excrement, the trio burst out of a final cluster of junipers and scrub oak at the top of a gentle rise which led down to a small cabin with a larger, dilapidated steel shed sitting behind it, nearly buried in another copse of junipers.

Just in time to see a four-seat UTV pulling a small trailer race away east down the dirt two track that served as the cabin's driveway, a thick cloud of dust boiling up behind it.

Maggie Langton sat in the back, driver-side seat, and her eyes met O'Reilly's for a moment, then they were gone.

How many curse words are there in the English language? O'Reilly thought. He was aware of a strong desire to use every single one of them. Repeatedly.

O'Reilly, Rickards and Andy stood in front of the small cabin, looking down the two-rut driveway that led off to the east.

"Now what?" Rickards said, tension thick in his voice.

"Now we get the horses and we go after them." O'Reilly looked over at Rickards from the corner of his eye. "Do you know how to ride?"

"Nope, never sat on one of the beasts in my life. I suppose there's no better time to learn. We're never going to catch them in time on horses, though. Even if they're nearby, which I suppose they aren't." Rickards' voice still sounded tense and angry although he was making a clear effort to reinstate the icy level of control he'd been known for when O'Reilly was a member of the Enforcers.

"The horses aren't too far away. More importantly we know where they're going, and the horses can take a straighter line back to Hideaway than that UTV which will have to stick to the roads and trails. I don't have to track them any more. I just have to get back to the canyon as quick as possible."

O'Reilly had thought this through as they followed Andy down the trail from the mountain to the bug out location. He had been hoping to catch the people they were chasing at the hideout but was convinced that if he didn't, they would head for Hideaway.

And if Maggie's captors were heading for the camp, and he was certain they were, then with the horses, he had the advantage of being able to move, if not as straight as the crow flies, then darn close to it. At the same time the UTV would be forced to follow the ranch roads, which swung wide to the east and around a rough wilderness area that had no roads before heading back to the west and closer to Adobe Canyon, where this whole thing started. The UTV would move faster, but by moving straight overland, maybe he and Rickards would get to camp not long after Maggie and her kidnappers.

"Come on Seth, grab what you need from the cabin. Andy, get a canteen and some food, put it in a pack and let's go. We're heading back across grassland and are going to pray no one is watching."

30

"Holy sh . . .!" stammered Ramon Martinez, his voice tailed off, a look of shock on his face as he looked around the main office of the Laughlin APZ branch of the Enforcers.

"What? What's going on, Ray?" Alex Donner asked, as he rose from where he sat at his desk.

Travis Harlan looked at Martinez with a mixture of curiosity and disgust. *Probably found out that they ran out of tacos for dinner,* he thought with derision. *The guy looks absolutely floored.*

"Ray, what happened?" Donner asked again, his voice tense.

Martinez made an urgent "quiet" motion while clutching the phone to his left ear. "Okay, what do you need from us?" he asked the unknown caller. "What can we do?" Pause as the other person spoke. Harlan could hear the unintelligible voice at the other end of the call raised in excitement. Maybe something was going on that would break the mind-numbing monotony that had settled on the Laughlin APZ over the last few days.

"Just let us know." Martinez hit end on the call and stood looking for a moment at a blank screen. Then, taking a deep breath, he turned and faced the others in the office.

"Captain Rickards is missing," Martinez said. "That was Dan Clements, head of the exorcism team the captain was with."

The office erupted into chaos, with everyone asking questions at once, except for Harlan, who stood there, thinking.

What Harlan really wanted to do was shout for joy. *The old man is missing? Great! Maybe things around here will change when Central Control appoints a new commander.*

Knox looked as though he'd been hit by a baseball bat. His pale eyes were open wide, and his Adam's apple bobbed as he swallowed hard. Harlan fought to keep his lip from curling in disdain. Rickards' assistant was one of those by-the-book, suck-up jokers, and he couldn't stand being around the man. Harlen felt his lip start its upward climb again, and he forced it back into a facsimile of shock and outrage.

Martinez motioned for everyone to quiet down, and slowly, his voice dead of emotion, he related what Clements had told him on the phone. Rickards had been with the Alpha team, the one led by Clements himself, when they launched the attack on the band of ghosts who had struck the supply trucks a little over two weeks ago. There had been a snafu at the start. A sentry wandering into the trees looking for a good place to piss had tripped across one of the team members and let off a shot. This had triggered the full-scale attack much earlier than intended.

According to Clements, Rickards had been seen on the northeastern edge of the assault. No one had seen him fall. One team member said that he'd seen Rickards go into a large steel structure located on the southeastern edge of the compound to investigate a noise. No one could recall seeing him after that.

"The bodies and unuseable property of the ghosts were burned. Clements said it was SOP for these missions," Martinez said, his voice becoming colder as he neared the end of his recitation. "They don't think that Rickards was among the bodies, but it's sometimes hard to tell. Seems the ghosts will collect clothing from wherever they find it, and occasionally they'll find bodies wearing Enforcer uniforms. Besides, Clements said the exorcism team wasn't in full uniform anyway."

"Do they think he was captured by ghosts who escaped?" Knox asked. "Some of us could go join a search and rescue effort."

Suck up, Harlan thought.

"Clements said they don't think anyone got away, but they're going to send out some searchers just in case, and they've put in a call for some seekers. Right now he wants us to stand by. He just wanted us aware of the situation."

The room was silent for a moment as everyone digested the information they'd been given. Then Martinez, who had been left in charge during Rickards' absence, much to Harlan's annoyance, spoke up again.

"We need to disseminate the information to those officers who are off duty. For now we will continue as we were until it's determined exactly what has happened to Captain Rickards, and whether he will be returning."

Nods from around the room as the on duty officers took in their orders.

"Harlan," Martinez continued, "You've been the communications officer on duty today. Contact Central Control and let them know the situation. Inform them that at this time everything is under control."

Harlan fought down exultation at the assignment, giving Martinez a short nod of assent. *I'll absolutely give Central Control a call, and while I'm at it, I might drop a few hints about how things have been running here the last few months under the command of Captain Rickards.* He wanted to whoop and fist pump the sky. *Rickards can't have me sent to the Everglades if he's missing in action. I'd like to buy whatever ghost accomplished that little trick a drink. Hope they dropped him down a mine shaft somewhere.*

With Rickards gone, there would be a new person appointed to lead the Laughlin branch of the Enforcers, and who better than Harlan if he played his cards right. If they don't choose him—chose Martinez, maybe—well, there might be other exorcism teams and missions.

31

Maggie tried to stretch—to ease a cramp in the muscles of her back. The UTV ride back to the area south of Juniper Mesa was more comfortable than her ride away from it two days before, she thought—at least as far as seating went. Her mind, on the other hand, was screaming—cannibalizing itself as it went over the events of the past twenty-four hours. And over, and over and over.

O'Reilly came to rescue me.

The thought both thrilled her and made her sick to her stomach. *He came, and he'd been so close.* But now, because he came after her, no one would be at Hideaway to protect the children when Lucas and Granger found the canyon. Because they *would* find the canyon, and they *would* realize that it would make a good headquarters. It wasn't like a gigantic gap in the ground would stay undiscovered for long. It might take them a little more time to find the trail into the gorge, but, while it was narrow, it wasn't exactly hidden. And once within its walls? Well, you couldn't exactly get lost in a canyon like Adobe. There were only two ways to go.

A bone-cracking yawn pulled at her facial muscles and made it feel as though her jaw was going to dislocate like a snake eating a rat. The previous night she had fallen into an uneasy sleep only moments, or what seemed like moments, before Lucas had burst into the lean-to, grabbed her arm, and forced her out into the barn. He was saying the Enforcers were there, that they were attacking . . . Something pestered at the back of her mind. Something about that moment.

She glanced over at the boy who sat next to her. He was staring out the right side of the UTV, watching the trees and brush fly by as they covered the dust choked miles along the dirt road, heading south toward Prescott, at least according to the signs she could see occasionally marking various tributaries to the main road. The signs had surprised Maggie, as they seemed an incongruous intrusion into the forest and wilderness areas they were racing through.

The boy's shoulders slumped, and several times Maggie saw him dash a tear away with the back of his hand. She thought of his brother, the young boy who had brought her food and water, and felt her heart break at the thought of his death at the hands of the exorcism team. She wished she could reach out to Daniel, to comfort him, but Lucas had made sure to tie her hands tightly to the back of the driver's seat. She had been working on the knots, trying to loosen them, with no success. It didn't matter when it came down to it, she thought. There was nowhere to go.

Yet.

Her legs ached, and she desperately wanted to get out of the UTV, to get away from the noise and the vibration. The escape down the mountainside in the dark had taken its toll in bruises, scratches and a few punctures from the occasional cactus, mescal or yucca growing next to the blasted goat trail they'd used to reach the valley. The entire walk Maggie had fought the urge to scream or call out. However, drawing the attention of the Enforcers would have been the literal definition of out of the frying pan and into the fire, she thought, remembering what O'Reilly had said the exorcism teams did with the bodies following an attack.

She hated the band of ghosts and their belief that as long as they had what they wanted, no one else mattered, but she wouldn't have wished their fate on anyone. *Well, I might make an exception for Kyle Lucas,* she thought as she shot a venom-filled glare at the back of his head.

They had been traveling down the dirt road for over thirty minutes, from what Maggie could tell, when Lucas braked and examined a small track leading off to the west. She wished desperately she had been conscious on the earlier trip. She didn't know if they'd used this road or a different one. Then another thought blew through her mind. Was O'Reilly tracking her still? Would he know if they turned off?

She rolled her eyes. Of course, he would. If he'd been able to find the compound on the mountaintop and then track them to Lucas's hideout, he'd for sure be able to follow them back to the canyon. He'd probably be there before her.

Before. That tickle at the back of conscious thought once again.

Making a sudden decision, Lucas wheeled the UTV onto the track. After less than a quarter of a mile, winding through rocks, brush and trees, they drove out into an open area. A dilapidated double wide was sitting back near a cliff of black basalt that was liberally splattered with florescent yellow lichen. The door hung open, and the windows were broken, giving the house a sad, abandoned air. To the left was a pasture with a windmill and water tank. Leading into the meadow was an older wooden hay barn. The green pipe gate to the weedy meadow hung open, and Maggie couldn't see a single living thing in the area except for some mourning doves perched on the edge of the tank.

"Where are we?" Granger asked. His voice held simple curiosity and weariness. It appeared, however, that Lucas also heard suspicion and distrust.

"Another bug out location," Lucas answered, his voice surly.

"How many of these damned things do you have?" Granger started, then quickly modulated his tones, as if remembering Lucas wasn't handling questioning very well at the moment.

"That's my business," was the only reply.

Lucas climbed out of the UTV and stretched. He looked over at Granger, and suddenly Maggie noticed dark shadows under his eyes, highlighting the dull glow of insanity that burned there.

"We'll be safe here for now."

Granger, moving as though he was an old man, slid out of the UTV and walked over to Lucas. Daniel stayed in his seat but watched them apathetically.

"What do you mean, 'safe here'?" Granger asked, swinging his arm around, indicating the house and the barn. "We're going to find the Langton woman's camp."

"Easy. I'm tired. If we continue right now, we'll reach the spot where we found the woman around noon. We don't want to attack the camp until dark or dawn, when they're not expecting us." Lucas gave a laugh, although it was a cruel mimicry of humor. "We've seen how well that works, yeah? Might as well get some sleep here in comfort instead of in the wilderness. We've come far enough that those Enforcer seekers won't find us. They don't even know anyone escaped."

Without waiting for a response, Lucas went to the back seat where Maggie was tied, loosened the knots and pulled her from the UTV. He dragged her over to the house, where he pushed the door the rest of the way open. Once inside the cool, dim living room he turned toward one of the attached bedrooms.

Maggie started to struggle. *I refuse to have gone this far only to be raped now!* she thought as Lucas dragged her into the small room and threw her on the bed.

"Don't worry," Lucas snarled. "I'm not interested in anything but sleep and food right at the moment. Later though . . . After we've taken your camp. Then we'll see." He tied her rope to the headboard of the twin bed, turned and stalked from the room.

Maggie didn't think she'd sleep, but exhaustion won out, and when she woke, she could see from the light outside the window it was early afternoon. She stretched and came up short against the rope holding her arms to the bed frame. She hadn't thought she could be any more sore, but that slight movement had proven her wrong. She lay on the bed for a moment, wanting to find some enjoyment in its softness but so worried about what would happen next that the comfort of the bed dimmed in comparison.

Would O'Reilly come? Was there any chance he'd catch them here? She felt a little thrill of hope in her chest, knowing he was out there, looking for her.

The door banged open, and Granger strode in. He looked slightly more rested than before, although still tired and sad.

"Come on," he said, "Dinner is served."

"How do you expect me to do that?" Maggie asked. She raised her arms, pulled back against the bed frame and shook them. The metal headboard rattled.

Granger shook his head as if trying to get his thoughts back in order. "Sorry, I forgot." He stepped forward to untie the rope, then led her back out into the main room where he pushed her down into a wooden kitchen chair.

Lucas was nowhere to be seen, but the boy, Daniel, was sitting at a kitchen table eating something that looked surprisingly like scrambled eggs from a blue plate. The way he was shoveling it in reminded Maggie how hungry she was, and when Granger brought a chipped china plate over to her, she took it eagerly.

"Where did you find the eggs?" Maggie asked. She took in the delicious smell of the meal, and her mouth watered in anticipation. With the first spoonful, she closed her eyes, lost in the moment.

"Lucas found a store of freeze dried supplies. A couple cans of scrambled eggs and bacon, some of powdered milk. A few other things."

Maggie ate another bite and savored the rich taste. It wasn't as good as the fresh eggs from Houdini's flock, although the savory, salty bacon pieces went a long way toward enhancing the palatability.

The front door banged open, and Lucas strode in, an agitated look on his face.

"We have to go, Granger. Get the woman and come on."

He turned and went out again before anyone could ask a question. Granger looked at Maggie and shrugged. "You heard the man. Come on, Daniel. Finish off those eggs and let's get going." Granger took Maggie's rope and waited for her to rise after finishing the final bite of eggs. Then the three of them left the house.

Lucas was standing next to the UTV, jittering with impatience.

Granger led Maggie around to her seat and waited for her to get in. Then he tied the rope to the seat back in front of her. At the same time, he looked at Lucas, confusion written on his face.

"What's the hurry, Lucas?" Granger asked with impatience. "You thought it was safe enough several hours ago."

"Someone's been here. I thought maybe when we first got here, but now I know for sure."

"How, who?" Granger asked.

"When I was here before, there was a brown cow in that pasture. I just left her here since there was hay and water, and I thought maybe we'd need her."

Maggie could see the annoyance on Granger's face, and a flash of anger at that remark, although he tried to hide it from Lucas. Maggie knew why. Granger's band of ghosts didn't have much, and a milk cow would have been a welcome addition, even if watering her would have been complicated. Lucas didn't keep the cow at this distant property because he thought "they" might need her. He kept her here because he thought *he* might need her.

"So, she got out," Granger said. "Cows get out."

"Cows don't wear size eleven boots, though," Lucas sneered. "Someone has been here, and it's time we go." Lucas climbed back into the driver's seat and waited with annoyance while Granger walked back around the vehicle and got into the passenger seat. Daniel was already in the back next to Maggie. Lucas turned the key, revved up the engine, and raced out the driveway. He didn't slow as he turned right onto the dirt road, and Maggie glanced behind. The trailer made the turn without flipping, but just. Once heading south again, they rocketed toward Prescott.

Maggie gritted her teeth and shifted in the black vinyl seat as she tried to find a more comfortable position. *This damned UTV must have dysfunctional shocks*, she thought. They hit another hole in the road, and she felt as though her tailbone had been driven up to her neck. She squirmed in her seat once again. It had only been thirty minutes since they'd left the house, but it felt like she'd been sitting on the black vinyl so long that she was in danger of fusing to the plastic.

After an additional ten minutes, she felt as though she couldn't take it any longer and pounded her hands against the seat back.

"Hey," she said, raising her voice to carry above the roar of the UTV engine. Neither Granger nor Lucas responded although Daniel turned in his seat to look at her. She was appalled at the difference the last day had created in him. In spite of their break at Lucas's second bolt hole, sooty smudges encircled his haunted eyes. His nose and lips looked chapped, as though he had been rubbing them on something rough, like sandpaper, not a shirt sleeve. Maggie knew what misery looked like, and this was it. However, it was misery touched by a bone deep loathing whenever he looked at Lucas.

Maggie hit the back of the driver's seat with her fists once again. "Hey, Granger, Lucas!" she shouted, and this time Granger looked back at her, a question on his face. His dark blue eyes didn't hold the same broken soul, gut-wrenching despair that Daniel's brown eyes did, but Maggie could see profound sadness all the same.

"What do you want?" Granger asked, also raising his voice to be heard over the UTV's engine.

"Can we stop? I really need to go to the bathroom," she answered back. Granger nodded and leaned over to Lucas. She had trouble hearing what he said, but she saw Lucas shrug, and the UTV slowed, then stopped near a large clump of juniper trees and scrub oak. Several large yuccas and a couple of century plants also dotted the landscape of the area to the east, while the area to the west was shadowed by the rise of Juniper Mesa. At least Maggie assumed it was Juniper Mesa.

Lucas climbed out of the driver's seat of the UTV without saying a word. Apparently, his nap hadn't improved his mood much. Either that or he really missed that cow. Lucas moved to Maggie's seat and started to untie her hands from the steel frame of the front bucket seat, impatiently jerking several times on the rope as he tried to gain enough slack to work the knots loose.

Maggie's bladder was making its desires known, and she shifted in her seat.

"Sit still, or I'll let you piss in your jeans." Lucas growled as he yanked on the rope once again.

"Lucas!" Granger snapped. "What's your problem?"

"Maybe I'm tired of always keeping you out of trouble, yet you never even say thank you," Lucas answered back, the surly tone grating on Maggie's nerves. "And now I'm stuck with you two sad sacks, whining about some little kid who was just slowing us down." He shot a pointed look at Daniel, who blanched and took a step forward, only stopping when Granger put a hand on his shoulder.

The knot tying Maggie's arms to the seat came loose, and he pulled her from the UTV. She stumbled and nearly fell. She put both hands out in front of her and caught the downward momentum on a handy boulder on the side of the road. She pushed herself upright and faced Lucas, pulling back on the rope, trying to free it from Lucas's grasp.

"Let go," she demanded. The way Lucas had spoken to Granger and Daniel about Andy made her queasy. If he felt that way about the boy who had lived as a member of his camp for months, how would he feel when he found Mark and the other children at Hideaway? She felt hot and chilled at the same time.

"Why, so you can make a run for it?" Lucas said. He sounded almost bored now as if his casual cruelty was getting old, even for him. Maggie felt her jaw muscles tense and worried her teeth would shatter into a million pieces, piercing her tongue and cheeks with the shrapnel. The crazy mood roller coaster Lucas was riding didn't show signs of pulling into the station any time soon.

"Lucas," Granger said, his frustration clearly mounting. He left Daniel and strode around the front of the dusty green UTV. The exhaustion and sorrow were still clear upon his face, but it was now overlaid by aggravation. "What's she going to do? Even if she ran, we'd catch her quickly with her arms tied. Just let her go to the bathroom and stop tormenting her."

Maggie shot a surprised, grateful glance at Granger, although it did annoy her that he was referring to her almost as if she was some dog Lucas was enjoying pestering.

Lucas looked at Granger, shrugged and dropped the rope. "Have it your way." He climbed back into the driver's seat of the UTV and leaned his head back on the headrest. "Just don't take too long or I'll come and get you." Lucas's voice held a threat that chilled Maggie in spite of the rapidly warming day.

"Go on," Granger said to Maggie. "We need to keep moving."

Maggie hurried toward the clump of juniper and yucca. She looked over her shoulder to see what the males of the group were doing and tripped over a large rock. She caught her balance just before impaling herself on a nearby century plant, then scurried around the trees and out of sight of the men.

Ten minutes later, Maggie walked back to the UTV. Lucas was still sitting as though asleep in the front seat. Granger stood on the far side of the road next to Daniel. His hand rested on the boy's shoulder, head bent down, talking to the young man. Maggie was too far away to hear what they were talking about, but she saw Daniel wipe his eyes on his shirt sleeve, and she could guess. Granger looked up and saw her approach. He pushed the boy back toward the UTV, then walked around the vehicle to where Maggie now stood.

Maggie slid into her spot and held her hands out to Granger, who once again tied the rope to the metal frame of the driver's seat.

"Make sure you tie her good," said Lucas from the front seat. "Don't want her jumping out and running away when we get close."

"Don't worry so much, Lucas," Granger growled. Maggie told herself she needed to watch for more opportunities to put a wedge between these two. If she was lucky, maybe they would get into a fight and take each other out.

Granger pulled on the rope to make sure the knots were tight, gave Maggie a stiff smile, and then walked to the passenger side and slid back into his seat.

Maggie blew out a slow breath of relief. He hadn't noticed that the ends of the rope were now being held between Maggie's clasped hands to make it look as though it was still tied around her wrists and that the rusty spike she'd used to abrade through the rope was now securely tucked into her boot.

The four traveled another ten minutes along the dirt road before Lucas braked again, the sharp movement throwing Maggie forward hard enough that she almost lost her grip on the ends of the rope as she tried to keep herself from slamming into the seat back. Before the UTV had slowed sufficiently, Lucas turned right onto a small forest road so hard that Maggie feared that they would roll. Carefully she readjusted the rope ends. She glanced over at Daniel to make sure he hadn't noticed, but the boy continued to stare out the right side of the vehicle.

The noise of the engine droned on, and Maggie began to doze in spite of the roughness of the smaller track. Several times she jerked back awake just as she was in danger of dropping her hands and exposing her secret. She bit her lips, trying to stay awake. She rubbed her right ankle with her left foot, digging the spike into her leg—a reminder that she had a weapon, and now she had a chance.

When Maggie had gone around the trees earlier in the day with the intention of emptying her bladder, she found a rusted ruin of some piece of machinery. She had no idea what it had been in its former life, but now it was simply a pile of twisted metal and rotted wood, with a few spikes and iron straps scattered around it on the ground. She had peeked around the huge mescal plant to see what was happening back at the UTV and whether anyone was coming after her. No one was, and she quickly squatted to urinate. Then, upon finishing, she examined the scrap metal. On the ground near a three-inch-wide iron strap she found a large, pitted and rusted iron spike.

Carefully holding the spike between her knees, she rubbed the rope sharply against its surface and was elated to see the fibers start to part and fray. It took almost no time before she was able to finish the job, yanking her wrists apart repeatedly to break the last few strands, and she was free.

But she was still a long way from home and didn't know whether O'Reilly was following behind the UTV or whether he had surmised where they were going and had decided it would be faster to go cross country.

No, she decided, it would be wiser to let her captors think she was still tied and wait until they were closer to the canyon before she made her escape. And if Lucas gave her a chance, she was sure she could find a new sheath for the spike—preferably in his throat, she thought, teeth clenched.

It was mid to late afternoon, as far as Maggie could tell, when the UTV pulled to a stop in a clearing surrounded by junipers and a few pines. Lucas climbed out from behind the steering wheel and stretched, while on the other side of the vehicle both Granger and Daniel were also disembarking.

They had left the dirt road and been moving cross country for close to a half hour. Avoiding rocks, cacti and low hanging tree branches had slowed them to walking speed, and she wondered where they were going.

Now, as Maggie looked around, something seemed familiar. She frowned and dismissed the idea as wishful thinking. After all, one juniper looked like another, and there was an abundance of the species all around the clearing where Lucas had parked. Then it struck her. The clearing was the same one where she'd seen the elk. The same one where she'd first had the misfortune to run across Lucas, Granger and Daniel.

She stared at the surrounding clearing, realizing she was looking at it from a position opposite where she'd stood two days before. It seemed like she'd been gone for weeks, yet it was only a little over forty-eight hours.

"What's our plan, Lucas," asked Granger as he moved to the trailer hitched behind the UTV and started to untie the brown oiled canvas tarp covering the guns and other supplies Lucas had collected. Daniel walked over to help him. Maggie rotated in her seat, careful to keep the rope between her hands. She needed to see what the men were doing. Houdini had taught her to never turn her back on an enemy, and she'd learned that lesson well.

Lucas reached into the small utility trailer and pulled out an older looking AR-style rifle. He handed it to Granger. He studied it, scrutinizing the scratches, a little surface rust and other signs of poor maintenance. He looked at Lucas, eyebrows quirked.

"Think this thing will fire without blowing up in my face?" he asked.

"Yeah, it's fine," Lucas said, the dismissive tone in his voice telling Maggie he hadn't thought too much about it. "It's not like I could do a lot of test firing, you know. The group would have heard and investigated. The gun is okay, but if you're scared, you can choose another if you want." Lucas made it clear he thought Granger was being a wimp.

Maggie twisted the other way in time to see Granger pick two magazines from the pile of weapons and ammunition. He examined one of them, nodded and slid it into the gun Lucas had given him. He raised it to his shoulder, sighted, then lowered it again.

"It'll do," Granger said, although it was clear from his voice that he still had some doubts. He reached back into the trailer and pulled out a handgun in a black nylon holster. He slid it out, checked the magazine, then replaced it within its secure nest. He fastened the holster to his belt, then stepped back from the UTV and trailer.

Maggie shifted her legs, feeling the weight of the spike in her boot. *Wait for the right time*, she told herself. *It will come. Just wait.* She relaxed her shoulders.

Daniel had chosen a rifle of some sort. It looked similar to O'Reilly's hunting rifle, as well as the one she'd brought with her from Prescott, but she didn't know whether it was the same or not. All she knew is it had the same dark wood stock. The boy loaded the gun, then filled his pockets with extra ammunition. Meanwhile, Lucas had selected another AR-style rifle. Maggie noticed it seemed in decidedly better shape than the one he had handed to Granger. He already had a handgun in a holster at his waist, but he opened a box of ammunition, and filled his pockets.

Oh, my God, Maggie thought, with a feeling of despair. *They are preparing for a war, and there are only children waiting for them.* She told herself that Granger and Lucas didn't know there were only kids in the camp. Granger hadn't believed her when she told him it was just her and the children. He must still have some doubts about her story, or they wouldn't be preparing to storm the ramparts.

She knew there was no possible way O'Reilly could have made it back to Hideaway before her. He had to be horseback. He might have found a quad, truck or UTV at one of the ranches or homes he'd passed, but she couldn't believe he would have taken it. It would have been too risky, not knowing where he was going, how far or how much fuel he'd need. No, he'd stay horseback. The horses were slower, but it was easier to "fuel up" when all you needed was grass and water.

O'Reilly was probably at least a day behind them based on when he'd showed up at Lucas's first bolt hole, and now she was going to be forced to take three armed men—well, two armed men and one armed boy—into a camp of unarmed children.

If she ran, there was a chance they would shoot her, and they still would find her camp and her kids. However, if she could get back to the camp before them, she and the children could hide in the caves. It had worked before. They could do it again, she thought. She could feel her heart racing and began to fear she would have a heart attack. She moved her leg again and felt the spike rub on her calf, a heavy, reassuring weight. Her heartbeat slowed.

They were planning on attacking at night, or maybe at dawn. The same as the exorcism team had done to them. The same as Rickards had done to her. She realized that O'Reilly almost certainly would have told the children to sleep in the caves. They should be safe if Lucas and Granger stuck to their plan. It was mid or late afternoon, though. Plenty of time to find Hideaway and attack them before nightfall if they realized how poorly protected the camp was. She had to slow them down—to make sure they didn't find the canyon meadow before the children went into the caves for the night.

Apparently unaware of the direction of Maggie's thoughts, the men were discussing their next moves.

"The UTV and trailer will be safe here," Granger said. He slung the rifle over his shoulder and pulled the tarp over the guns and supplies. "We can't take it any closer without risking alerting the camp. Make sure you have water and food, but don't weigh yourself down."

Lucas nodded in agreement. He also slid his rifle's sling over his shoulder, collected a canteen and walked over to where Maggie was still sitting in the UTV, tied to the driver's seat. He untied the knots, then stepped back, preparing to yank her from her seat once again.

Maggie was ready for him this time, and as soon as he stepped back, she slid out of her seat and released the ends of her bonds so that when Lucas jerked the rope, he had more slack than he expected. He stumbled backward, releasing his end of the cord in the process. Maggie realized she may have made a mistake when she saw the unhinged rage on the man's features. He charged toward her, arm upraised, hands clenched.

Maggie felt the blood drain from her face, and she ducked moments before his fist came crashing down where her head would have been. His hand grazed her shoulder, and he cocked his arm again, ready for a second attempt.

It felt as though she was trapped in a whirlwind—things moving both too fast to make sense of, and in slow motion at the same time. Granger was shouting at Lucas not to hurt her, that they needed her. In the same instant, Maggie crouched, pulled up her jeans leg and grabbed the rusty spike from her boot.

Lucas's fist came down, aiming for her head once again. Simultaneously, she reared up to meet him, spike held in both hands, and she slashed at his face, trying for his eyes. She missed, and the dull, rust-pitted edge of the spike laid open a deep gash that extended from the side of his nose across his cheek to below his left ear. Lucas fell backward, reaching for his handgun. Blood was running down his face and into his beard. His pale eyes burned with an insane fire.

Maggie launched herself at him, spike raised over her head for another strike. She swung again, trying for Lucas's throat. Out of the corner of her eye, she saw Granger lunge for her. She flinched away and missed her strike, hitting Lucas's shoulder instead of his neck. The spike snagged in his shirt and was pulled from her hands. The blow was hard enough, however, that it jarred his right arm, causing him to drop the weapon.

Maggie fell back, then scrabbled on the ground, trying to reach the gun before Lucas was able to retrieve it. Granger reached for her arm, and she jerked it away before he could get a good hold. She heard high-pitched screaming and with shock, she realized the sound was coming from her own throat. Her outstretched hand landed on the weapon, and her fingers wrapped around the barrel.

She fumbled the firearm and nearly dropped it while trying to get a proper grip. Lucas charged her again, and she pointed the gun and pulled the trigger. Nothing happened, and she realized the safety was on. With a growing desperation, she felt for a button or toggle but couldn't find it.

With a final cry, Maggie turned and ran for the ridge where, only two days before, she and the girls had been collecting prickly pear fruit and nopales. With a feeling of *deja vu,* she ducked branches and dodged the trunks of the juniper trees, expecting every second to feel a bullet between her shoulders or a hand on her arm, spinning her, punching her in the head again. Two shots rang out, but neither found its mark.

Maggie raced out from between the trees and threw herself over the edge of the bank, struggling to keep her footing on the steep slope of loose rock and dirt. Her breath rasped in and out, and her chest felt as though it was on fire. She hit the bottom of the bank close to where the horses had been tied, but instead of heading directly for Hideaway, she turned west and ran for her life.

She fought the urge to look over her shoulder, knowing it would slow her down, and positive that if she tried, she would trip over a rock and face plant into a boulder, a cactus or a fresh cow pie. She tried to dodge from tree to tree, yucca to mescal, in an attempt to make shooting her at a distance much more difficult. She knew she had injured Lucas, but not nearly severe enough to keep him from coming after her. She just prayed it was serious enough to slow him down, and Granger as well, since he'd stop to help the blond man, she hoped.

Maggie was heading for an arroyo that she knew led to the northeastern most tip of Adobe Canyon. She and Mark had found it while exploring the area during the first few weeks after arriving at Hideaway. The narrow fissure in the land deepened rapidly and included a few big drops which were challenging to navigate. Part way down, a spring fed Adobe Creek, creating a small waterfall. During the monsoon storms of the summer, the arroyo turned into a raging river, overrunning the spring and turning the trickle of Adobe Springs into a torrent.

Mark and Maggie had never made their way from the floor of the canyon up to the rim above by following this wash, but Maggie was counting on gravity helping her in this case—that going down would be easier than going up. And that she wouldn't break a leg or her neck in the process.

She could see the arroyo well ahead of her. It felt as though she'd been running forever. That her lungs were going to burst from her chest. Black spots swam, clouding her vision, as she continued toward the brush-rimmed crack in the ground, stumbling now and then as she felt the adrenaline drain away.

Just when Maggie thought she couldn't run one more step, the wash was at her feet, and she went down the steep bank, falling to her knees on the gravel and sand bottom of the ravine. She knelt there, arms wrapped around her chest as she heaved in gulps of air. Her heartbeat was thundering in her ears. She listened for the steps of her captors but was afraid she wouldn't hear them over the pounding.

As both heart rate and breathing slowed and some strength returned to her legs, she turned and crawled back up the bank slowly. She peeked over the edge, half expecting to see Granger and Lucas only five feet away, hot in pursuit. She blew out a relieved breath when no one was there. Maggie lifted her gaze, studying the land between her hiding spot and the ridge where she had descended, almost indiscernible off in the distance. At first, she saw nothing and a cold bolt of fear stabbed through her. When she'd run, she'd counted on their following her to this northern trail. Not only would it give O'Reilly more time to catch up to them, but the narrow slot canyon might present her with some options to attack them while they were trapped between the two walls.

Just as she was beginning to panic, afraid they'd gone the direction they'd seen the girls go horseback two days ago, she saw the barest hint of movement in the distance. The figure was so tiny she wasn't sure what she was seeing at first as the dark speck made its way down the ridge she'd slid down not long ago, then another figure joined the first and she was sure it was them. They must have had to deal with Lucas's injuries before coming after her.

Maggie held her breath. Would they follow her, or try and follow the tracks left by the girls.

Please, please, please, let them follow me, she begged silently.

The third figure joined the other two, and they dropped out of sight behind the brush and trees at the bottom of the ridge. Just as she was contemplating screaming or making some noise to let them know where she'd gone, she saw them emerge from behind the trees and head in her direction.

Thank you! She sent up a silent prayer, then slid back to the bottom of the arroyo. She crouched down and studied the handgun she'd taken away from Lucas, trying to determine how it worked and how to deactivate the safety. Finally, she found the desired button and tested it, clicking it off and on several times. Satisfied she could turn the safety off quickly, she held the gun in both hands as if she were going to fire. She'd never touched a handgun before, although, like most people in the United States, she had watched TV shows that demonstrated a two-handed grip. She tried to point the firearm and aim it as she'd seen in police procedurals. The gun was huge and much heavier than she'd expected. She was sure her aim would be off, but the weapon was better than the spike by a long shot.

She had no idea how many bullets were in the magazine and didn't have time to try and figure out how to eject it so that she could check. She tried to tuck the gun in her waistband, finding it so heavy it nearly pulled her jeans down.

Great, she thought, *I'll be really scary if my jeans fall to my knees as I try to draw my weapon. I won't need to shoot them. They'll die laughing.*

Finally, she shoved the gun, barrel first, into the front of her bra and climbed the bank once again. For a moment, she couldn't see the three men. Just as she was becoming worried they'd changed direction, she saw one of the figures—Lucas, she thought, since the sunlight glinted off the pale blond hair—move from behind a large mescal. They were still coming, and they were moving faster than she'd expected.

She scrambled back down to the floor of the wash and started toward the main canyon, moving at a fast walk. The men weren't running, and her legs still ached from her earlier frenzied dash across the ranch land. For a moment, she wondered about the shots she heard. Two of them. She hadn't even reached the ridge yet.

Who shot? Did Lucas have another gun other than the rifle? It didn't sound like what she thought an assault rifle should sound like but he was the most likely. They didn't even start pursuing her for at least ten or fifteen minutes, based on when she saw them come down the bank. Why . . .?

Then Maggie froze, the answer to the question that had been teasing the back of her mind since the middle of the night before exploding in her brain.

Lucas had come in, grabbed her, yanked her out into the barn and told Granger that the exorcism team was there before a single shot was fired. Before the attack ever happened, he knew they were out there. How? Had he seen someone in the woods? If he had, why didn't he warn the rest of the group so they could defend themselves?

Did Granger realize the timing inconsistency of Lucas's warning, or had the ensuing chaos and the need just to survive muddy the waters? Confuse his memory the way it had hers?

Maggie pushed herself faster, jogging again, feet sinking into the sandy floor. The arroyo was deepening, becoming something closer to a canyon. Towering rock walls were replacing the brush-covered dirt, sand and clay banks that she had descended back near the head of the wash. She had never explored the canyon from this end and was relieved that, while it had some brush and trees growing in it, for the most part, the watercourse was clear of anything but rocks and sand.

That sand, though.

Maggie was already tired and aching from the attack and being tied in the UTV two days before, and even more so from the run down the mountain last night and then the mad dash across the grasslands only a short time ago. Where it was deep, the sand made it feel as though she was running with fifty-pound weights on each foot. The sand dragged at her, and she quickly was gasping for breath once again and had to slow to a walk.

For the next ten minutes, she switched between jogging and walking. The watercourse moved in a rough curve, heading northwest with little deviation. Several large cottonwoods had planted themselves in what dirt was left along the bank. Each time Maggie reached one of those trees, she stepped into the shelter of the trunk, turned and studied the canyon she had just passed through. None of those times did she see the men but she had to assume they were still behind her. She worried that her labored breathing would drown out the sounds of pursuit and the first warning she would have would be a bullet in the back.

Then she wondered if they wanted to use her as a hostage and if she was of greater worth to them alive. If that was the case, they might just count on trying to run her down—wear her out.

They knew she had Lucas's handgun, but they also knew that she was ignorant about how to use it based on her performance at the UTV.

She tripped on a pile of rocks and caught herself just before she fell. She cast her mind around for something else to focus on instead of the ache in her legs and the burning in her chest.

There were two shots. What were those? For a moment, she felt a thrill of fear. What if O'Reilly had surprised the men, and they shot him? It would be just her and the children. She thought that she had no more adrenaline left in her, but another blast coursed through her body.

It couldn't have been O'Reilly, she told herself, sternly marshaling her thoughts. *He couldn't have caught up this soon if he was horseback, and if he'd been driving a quad or a UTV, they would have heard it when they stopped.*

She took a deep breath. She'd wanted a distraction, but not that kind.

The ravine took a turn, and Maggie was faced with a widening horizon as the watercourse started its fall into the main body of Adobe Canyon, and she could see across to the far rim. Several large, reddish-tan boulders, worn smooth with hundreds, if not thousands, of years of water and sand washing over them, lined the rim of the first drop. Maggie walked to the edge slowly, as her breathing started to steady. Her legs still twanged with fatigue, and she had a mental picture of her falling to her death if they finally gave out while climbing down the rocky precipice.

The first drop was a nearly horizontal fall of what appeared to be about eleven feet, ending at a pile of boulders rimming a sandy basin. Darkness in the sand and a few pools showed where a small spring was leaking water from the canyon side. Farther down, a larger spring was pumping even more water into the creek below.

The drop looked intimidating, and Maggie hesitated. A shout rang out behind her, and she looked back up the wash just as Lucas, followed closely by Granger and Daniel, came around the curve. Maggie stepped backward, bumped into the boulders that lined the wash, and fumbled the handgun out of her bra. Pointing it, she thumbed off the safety. Lucas let out a shout, and he, Granger and Daniel dove back behind the bank of the arroyo as Maggie pulled the trigger of the heavy handgun.

The noise was deafening in the steep-sided wash, and Maggie thought both her wrists had been broken. To her surprise, instead of only one shot, the gun had apparently been modified for automatic fire, and seven or eight shots rang out. She nearly dropped the weapon as her hands went numb, and pain shot from her wrists to her neck.

If an elephant had been standing in front of her, it would have been completely safe, except for a ringing in the ears. If there had been a barn, she might have scored one or two hits—if it was an exceptionally large barn.

The barrel swung wildly, and Maggie saw spirts of sand explode from the arroyo floor and a few chips from the rock walls.

Without waiting to see what Lucas would do, she stuffed the gun back into her bra, cringing from the barrel's heat, and turned back to the watercourse. She slowly let herself down over the boulder that seemed to offer the best hand holds. Her now throbbing hands felt unstable on the rock, and Maggie was afraid she would be making a completely uncontrolled descent. When she couldn't hold on one second longer, she let go and fell the last few feet to the sandy basin below.

Maggie hit the damp sand, her exhausted legs buckled under her and she stumbled backward, nearly falling off the next ledge. She sat down hard, jarring her tailbone and a bolt of pain zinged up her spine. She glanced up at the top of the wall and scrambled to her hands and knees. The next portion of the watercourse was a steep, undulating, smoothly worn slope of rock, broken by several eroded shelves and basins, curving out of sight down between the steep walls.

Maggie didn't wait, sure that the men would be following close behind. She sat on the edge of the sandy basin, swung her legs around and started scooting her way down the sixty-degree incline, wincing at the pain in her tailbone as she slid over unseen bumps.

She prayed the children had heard the gunshots and had realized that they needed to hide in the caves now and not wait for darkness. If they had, and if she could get to the camp before the men caught her, she might have a chance to hide as well.

The steep slide lasted only about two-hundred feet before it reached another sandy basin where the larger spring resulted in a pool of clear water. Maggie paused for a moment, dipped her hands in the liquid and drank, then splashed her face, wincing when the water washed over myriad scrapes. She didn't care if there were bugs or algae. She desperately needed water after her exertions. Maggie didn't dare spend too long, however, as she was sure the men were close behind. She knelt by the puddle's edge, head uplifted. The ringing in her ears from the earlier gunfire had abated somewhat, and now she could hear sounds from above, telling her the men had not stopped at the first eleven-foot drop and certainly would not at the incline.

Maggie hurled herself over the next ledge, landing only five feet below on a strip of stone that ran between two piles of boulders. She knew she was nearly at the bottom of the canyon as the gorge was shallower at this point than it was farther down by the camp. Trying to keep her balance on the wet, water-smoothed stones, she made her way down to the bottom of the wash, turned left and ran down to the first of several doglegs. Once around the first rock outcropping, she paused and looked back toward the fall of rock she had just descended, wet from the stream of water that fed into Adobe Creek. Within seconds Maggie saw Granger, followed closely by Lucas and then Daniel. To her annoyance, the men seemed in better condition than her, and they navigated the final drop and then the rock-strewn slope easily.

From her place of concealment, she pulled the gun from the front of her bra and pointed it at her pursuers. Taking a deep breath, she flicked off the safety once again and pulled the trigger.

Even though she was expecting the recoil and the noise this time, it still felt as though she was hanging on to some wild animal, fighting to free itself from her grasp.

Her aim still left much to be desired. However, in an extraordinary stroke of good luck, one bullet ricocheted off one of the rock slabs that made up the wall of the canyon at that point and struck Granger in the leg. He staggered, fell to his knee, then straightened once again. Voluble cursing broke through the ringing in Maggie's ears, and she felt a brief thrill of satisfaction. Annie Oakley she was not, but it felt good to be on the offense if only for a moment.

That moment didn't last long, however. The men, who had taken brief cover behind some of the larger boulders on the slope, had split up and were now moving downward once again. They scrambled swiftly, from boulder to boulder. Granger was limping, and Maggie could see the dark stain of blood on his jeans, pinpointing the location of the wound on his right thigh.

Why couldn't it have been the knee? she thought, although grateful that anything had been hit other than the rock walls of the canyon.

Maggie lifted the gun once again, and once again prepared for the recoil as she pulled the trigger. Three more shots fractured the peace of the canyon air. The men dove for cover. Lucas—at least she thought it was Lucas—returned fire, hitting the rock just over her head with a *twing.*

And then the gunfire stopped. Maggie pressed the trigger. Nothing happened, and she realized with a sickening drop in her chest that the gun was empty. The automatic fire made it easy to expend many bullets quickly, but also meant she would need to reload more often. And she had no more ammunition.

Lucas must have realized what had happened. He knew weapons much better than she did and knew how many bullets the magazine of the handgun held. He emerged from behind a large, black basalt boulder that had washed down from somewhere, a lopsided grin on his face. She could see the bloodstains in his beard and on his shirt, left from the injury inflicted by the rusty spike. Someone, probably Granger, had patched it up with a large pad of gauze and tape, but he still made a terrifying image as he strode forward.

Maggie turned, threw the useless handgun into a tangle of thorny bramble vines and ran.

32

O'Reilly felt as though there was a clock in his head, ticking away the seconds, minutes and hours. Maggie was alive. She appeared to be safe, albeit bedraggled and bruised, but definitely alive. He had been so close.

So close, so close . . . the mantra played in his mind all the way back to the catch pen where he'd left the horses. *If I'd been five seconds earlier, I could have shot out the tires. The chase would be over. It would be . . .*

Then he reminded himself that if he had shot the driver, Maggie could have been badly hurt in the ensuing crash. He didn't have a shot at the other man and he wouldn't shoot Andy's brother, even if he'd had a chance. Not unless he had no other choice in order to save Maggie or the children. Besides, if he'd shot any of them, or even shot out the tires on the UTV, it would have alerted the exorcism team in the mountaintop compound that there were still ghosts around, and the team would not hesitate to hunt them down, especially if Rickards had been missed.

It took over an hour to reach the horses, but it was still early morning when O'Reilly, Rickards and Andy headed out. On the way north, O'Reilly had been forced to stick to the roads that Maggie's captors had taken since he wasn't sure where they were going. Now, he was positive they were traveling back to the ridge where they found Maggie and ultimately to Hideaway itself. He figured if he stuck to smaller roads and bee-lined it where no road was available in the Juniper Mesa Wilderness area, he could cut ten miles or more off the trip.

His biggest worry was the horses. They'd rested for the past twelve to fifteen hours and had plenty of grass and water, but he'd covered a lot of miles in the last day and a half, and another twenty miles or more were ahead of him.

He glanced over at Rickards, who was sitting in the saddle as though it was strapped to a landmine. Andy was riding double behind him, a decision O'Reilly questioned repeatedly. However, Jimmy had made the journey north without any burden other than his saddle and bridle while Ace had carried O'Reilly. Jimmy was fresher, which in O'Reilly's mind, was both good and bad. Jimmy would have an easier time carrying both the man and the boy, but Jimmy also might have an easier time acting up if he didn't like the burden.

Andy was much more comfortable horseback than Rickards, and, after the first fifteen minutes during which the boy's excitement nearly got both he and Rickards bucked off when he kicked Jimmy in the flanks, he had settled down and had actually started to nod off, arms wrapped tightly around the Enforcer captain's middle.

The horses were moving out at a fast walk, with Thelma continuing to follow along, stopping periodically to grab a few mouthfuls of dry grass and brush. Whenever O'Reilly thought they'd lost her, she'd come trotting up from behind, mooing low and shaking her head, huge belly bouncing gently.

The two men didn't talk much, and Andy was dozing behind Rickards. O'Reilly was feeling the lack of sleep from the night before. He cast his mind about, looking for something that would keep him awake now that the adrenaline of last night and this morning had worn off.

Rickards must have been feeling the same way because suddenly he asked, "Why aren't we running the horses. You know, like they do in the movies—although I guess I just answered my own question there." He laughed a low, deep chuckle.

O'Reilly turned to Rickards, a tired grin on his face. Rickards might be more of a gunsel than Maggie and Mark had been, and that took some doing.

"Horses can cover the most ground in a day at a walk," O'Reilly said. "Lope and gallop are fine for short distances, like if you need to get around a cow that's breaking from the herd, but if you need to cover a lot of ground, you need a fast walk and a long trot." He gestured at Ace and Jimmy, "These two got a good rest and a good feed last night, but they were pushed hard yesterday and the day before and now again today. We'll be doing a lot of walking and trotting."

O'Reilly had a sinking feeling, knowing he was demanding more from the geldings than was good for them, and he mentally promised them a good, long rest when they got back to Hideaway and rescued Maggie.

When we rescue Maggie! Not if, when!

O'Reilly felt an overwhelming rage washing out the momentary ease from before—a rage he couldn't control. He had to move faster. He urged Ace into a long trot. He glanced over at Rickards again to make sure the captain was keeping up. Jimmy was trotting, but it wasn't the smooth, long trot of a seasoned ranch horse. Rickards was jerking the reins and holding them too tight, causing Jimmy's trot to become short and choppy, throwing the man around like a sack of potatoes. Jarred awake, Andy had a stranglehold around Rickards' waist, which was complicating the man's balance.

"Get off his head, Seth," O'Reilly said. Impatience jangled his nerves. Ace picked up his anxiety and broke into a short lope until O'Reilly shifted his weight back, sat down, and forced himself to relax. *It will be a miracle if Rickards makes it alive to the camp the way he's riding.*

O'Reilly clenched his teeth, then forcibly relaxed his jaw once again. "You need to relax your legs, sit in the saddle, and loosen your reins. Don't lean forward," he said, looking over at the man riding beside him.

"What the heck do you think I'm doing?" Rickards growled, almost to himself, but O'Reilly could see him try to relax his legs and sit back in the saddle. He dropped his hands, allowing more slack in the reins, although O'Reilly could see that giving the horse its head went against Rickards' desire for control.

With his rider sitting deeper in the saddle and not balancing on the reins, Jimmy's trot evened out, and the two rode in silence for fifteen minutes until, pent-up anxiety dispelled for the moment, O'Reilly pulled Ace back into a walk.

He looked over at Rickards and attempted to determine how the man was holding up. He tried not to make the scrutiny conspicuous, but apparently wasn't successful.

"I saw that," Rickards said.

"What?"

"That look. The one that said 'this guy has never been on a horse before and is just going to slow me down.'"

"You haven't, and you are," O'Reilly said. His lips quirked in a smile, and his eyebrows rose inviting a response. Nothing in his tones held condemnation, however.

"Yeah, well, I may never walk again after this," Rickards said. "I don't know how you cowboy types do this every day. Everything below my waist is being pulped into applesauce."

O'Reilly snorted a burst of laughter, surprised he was capable of the emotion after the last two days.

"Are you wishing you were riding your desk chair back in the APZ?" O'Reilly asked. "It's an easier mount, but the herd may be a bit harder to control." He shot Rickards another grin. It felt good to have some laughter, some uncomplicated lightheartedness. He'd need the energy it gave him in the hours or days ahead, so he nursed it as he might the smallest ember in a dying campfire, feeding it, nurturing it.

The question had the opposite effect on Rickards. The smile slipped from his face, replaced by a frown.

"You have that one right," Rickards said, a distant note in his voice, a faraway look in his eyes. Then his gaze sharpened, and he looked up at O'Reilly, a rueful smile returning to his lips. "Right now, I've got a group headed by this guy named Ludeman, and they're arguing that they should be allowed to return to their homes. They're also demanding to be given whatever they need—as far as food and medical supplies—from the APZ supply stores."

O'Reilly's good feelings started to melt away as he looked over to Rickards, and he wished he hadn't made the comment. The man was adjusting himself in the saddle, then patted Andy's hands where they gripped his middle.

"Are you going to let them?" O'Reilly asked, sure he knew the answer.

Rickards emitted a noise that was somewhere between a growl of anger and a snort of derision. Jimmy jigged, startled by the sound, and his ears twitched back and forth. Rickards snatched up the reins, and the horse threw its head.

"Loosen the reins. Get off his head," O'Reilly snapped again, and then "good" when Rickards followed directions.

Once the gelding settled back into a smooth walk, Rickards continued, "I haven't decided. Central Control is adamant that the remaining population of the country are to live in the APZs. You know as well as I do that we can't provide medical services, supplies or protection out away from the population zones. We don't have enough manpower. They'd be living like pioneers out there."

O'Reilly thought, for a moment, then said, "What would happen if you let the ones who want to be pioneers go ahead and live like pioneers?"

"Many would die. Some would come back to the APZ because life out there was too hard. Others would figure it out and make a living off the land," Rickards answered in matter-of-fact terms. Then his lips twisted with a wry smile. "And Central Control would have my ass."

O'Reilly laughed, although there was little humor in it.

They rode on in silence for a few more minutes, both lost in their own thoughts.

"As far as supplies go," O'Reilly said, picking up the conversation minutes after it had seemed to die, "those people who are living in the APZ work, correct? Their pay may not be in money, but it's in a place to live, food, medical care."

Rickards nodded but didn't say anything. He knew O'Reilly had lived in the Laughlin APZ, so was perfectly aware of how the economic organization of the population zones worked. There was a barter system in place for certain things, but by and large, everything necessary for survival was provided by the APZ in exchange for working at an individual's assigned job.

"You could do something similar with the pioneers. They'd be out growing food, right? Well, they can bring their surplus to the APZ and trade for the medical supplies and other items they can't create." O'Reilly shrugged. He thought the plan made sense and would be a step back towards returning the country to normal. He just didn't know if the current government wanted a return to a way of life closer to what had been the status quo only a few years ago.

Phase One: Reduction of Population. The line ran through his mind. Considering the degree to which pollution had diminished during the pandemic, he wondered whether the governments of the world would want to do anything to move back toward the old ways.

Then again, considering all of the conflict and hate that had washed over the country and the world during the past few decades, maybe the status quo wasn't all that great after all. *Besides, how close to normal can you get with such a small percentage of the population left alive?* he thought.

O'Reilly pushed Ace back into a long trot. He checked over his shoulder to make sure Jimmy hadn't left Rickards and Andy sitting in the dust. Nope, Rickards and Andy were still in the saddle, although the expression on Rickards' face made it clear he wasn't too happy about it.

It was late afternoon when O'Reilly, Rickards and Andy emerged from the Juniper Mesa Wilderness and dropped down to the small forest road O'Reilly had started out on the day before yesterday. He pulled Ace to a stop and studied the ground. Sure enough, there were the tracks of the UTV heading out, overlaid by fresher tracks heading back in. Here and there, he could see hoof prints left by Ace and Jimmy that hadn't been wiped out when the UTV returned this way.

Got them! he thought.

"They're here," O'Reilly said, looking over his shoulder at Rickards and Andy. "They've come back this . . ."

O'Reilly froze as he heard faint, muffled gunshots off in the distance to the west of where he was sitting. He was confused for a moment and thought the lack of sleep had addled his brain. The shots, indistinct and echoing off the hills as they were, did not come from the direction of Hideaway.

"Gunshots," Rickards said succinctly.

"Yeah," O'Reilly said, his voice grim. "And they're not from camp. Sounds west of here, or at least southwest and the camp is much farther south, although it's hard to tell."

He reined Ace toward the west and followed the tracks of the UTV, even though he was positive he knew where the vehicle was going—back to the ridge where Maggie and the girls had been picking prickly pear.

An unknown number of minutes later—maybe fifteen or twenty or more—O'Reilly thought he heard additional shots over the hoof beats on the dry ground, but this time he wasn't positive. Regardless, he pushed Ace faster, even though the gelding was nearly done in. Foaming sweat dripped from the saddle pad, and more foam fell from his mouth. His buckskin coat was soaking wet, but the gelding was still willing to give it his all. O'Reilly mentally thanked the horse and promised him a good long recovery.

Jimmy was also coated with sweat, his bright bay roan coat dark red. Andy, who was still riding behind Rickards, had the horse's sweat coating the inside of his lower legs. O'Reilly was sure his skin was chapped by this point, but the boy never complained.

The UTV tracks veered from the road, heading southwest to where they'd been parked before. This time, however, O'Reilly could see the driver had taken the vehicle beyond their previous location, and he was sure they'd been heading for the prickly pear ridge, if not farther. Of course, the UTV was too large to take the trail to the bottom of the canyon, and O'Reilly had found no indication these men had ever been beyond the ridge at the time of Maggie's capture, but they saw the direction the girls had ridden two days before.

The land became rougher, rocky and brush covered with the junipers growing thicker and closer together. However it was still open enough that the horses had no trouble maintaining the trot and soon they were moving through a thickening forest of juniper. The trees formed close packed clusters interspersed by single, or sometimes two or three trees growing together. A glint of silver in the distance caught O'Reilly's eye, and he pulled Ace to an abrupt stop. The horse's flanks were heaving, and he bobbed his head, mouthing the bit with a *clink* and *rattle*.

Rickards rode up alongside and pulled Jimmy to a stop next to Ace. The captain had a pained look on his face as he shifted in the saddle.

"What is it?" Rickards asked as he leaned forward, peering toward the speck of silver, although O'Reilly thought he was just using it as an excuse to take the weight off his aching rear end.

"UTV," O'Reilly said, his words clipped. "The one we've been following." O'Reilly dismounted and stepped in front of the gelding. He studied the terrain, searching for signs of Maggie or her captors.

Meanwhile, Andy wriggled around and slid off Jimmy. He landed with a thump which caused the tired gelding to sidestep, but he was no longer fresh enough to raise much of a fuss. The boy ran up to O'Reilly, an eager look on his face.

"Are they there? Do you see my brother?"

"Shhhhhh!" O'Reilly said, gesturing sharply to the boy.

Andy's questions subsided, but he was nearly thrumming with excitement. O'Reilly gave him a stern look, afraid that if their quarry was with the UTV, they would hear him. The memory of those distant shots plagued his thoughts. He could swear they weren't from an area this close.

O'Reilly looked back up at Rickards, who was continuing to sit on Jimmy. "Are you getting off that horse?"

Rickards gave him a sardonic look, then said, "I'm not sure I can get back on if it becomes necessary."

Surprised, O'Reilly choked and started coughing, burying his face in the crook of his arm to muffle the sound. They hadn't dismounted often during the ride back to the camp and never for long. O'Reilly couldn't say he'd paid much attention to how Rickards had remounted any of those times, but he imagined that by now, the man was fairly uncomfortable, if not in a great deal of pain.

"You're too big of a target horseback," O'Reilly said. He privately wondered whether the captain would be so stiff and sore he would become more of a liability than an asset in the coming hours.

Rickards took a deep breath, slowly swung his leg over the horse's back and gingerly lowered himself to the ground. His muscles were visibly quivering, and ultimately they abandoned all semblance of support and dropped the captain the last few inches. He pulled his foot from the stirrup and staggered backward. Then he straightened with obvious pain and walked over to O'Reilly, Jimmy's reins in his hand and the gelding following close behind. Andy was standing next to Ace, bobbing his head back and forth as if trying to see between the trunks of the juniper trees.

With shock, O'Reilly realized Thelma was no longer with them, and he felt a surprising pang of intense disappointment. Without conscious thought, he looked back toward the road and Juniper Mesa. No cow. No mooing. He wasn't sure when they'd lost their bovine shadow. He promised himself that once Maggie was safe, he'd go back and find her. Still, losing the cow at this moment felt like an ill omen for the future.

"Any movement?" Rickards asked. He studied the distant speck of silver.

O'Reilly carefully assessed the area. He knew the ridge was a short distance away. He didn't see any sign Maggie or her captors were still in the area, but they could be sleeping. *Did they post a lookout?* he wondered. *There are only three of them. They've got to be as tired as we are.*

Making a decision, O'Reilly turned to Rickards, "You go that way," he pointed to the left. "Stay in the shadow of the trees. You have plenty of ammunition?"

"Yeah," Rickards responded, patting his pockets.

"I will go to the right. We come in at forty-five degree angles. I'll signal you when to move. Andy, you're going to stay here, keep the horses quiet and out of sight behind these trees."

The boy nodded. "Do I get a gun?" He sounded eager.

"No, I only have my rifle, and Rickards only has his weapons. Besides, if you shot by accident, you might hit Seth or me."

The boy's face fell in disappointment, but O'Reilly didn't budge. He knew this area was backed up to the ridge, which would complicate their quarry's retreat if they were nearby. If Maggie's captors came out toward the boy and he opened fire, there was too much risk of he or Rickards being caught in the crossfire. Besides, he didn't think Rickards would be willing to hand over his handgun or his rifle.

Then a wave of anxiety washed over Andy's face. "You're not going to shoot Danny are you?"

O'Reilly looked at the young boy who stared back at him, chewing his lip, dark eyes wide with worry. O'Reilly realized the boy had been showing a resilience few adults would be able to demonstrate in a similar situation. His only family member was with Maggie's kidnappers. Lucas and Granger, the boy had called them. Was Daniel working with these men, or had he been taken as Andy seemed to think? If he was working with Lucas and Granger, it was possible he was as much of a danger to Maggie as the men were, and it might be necessary, if it came down to a firefight, to kill him.

If he was another victim, though. God, O'Reilly's head was hurting.

"No, Andy, we're not going to shoot your brother," O'Reilly said, mentally crossing his fingers that he or Rickards wouldn't be forced to shoot the boy. He looked up, met Rickards' eyes and saw the captain knew as well as he did that this type of promise should never be made because there was no guarantee they could keep it.

The boy seemed pacified, however, and took the reins the men handed him.

O'Reilly looked at Rickards and nodded. Then, using the trees as a screen, he circled out to the right. He stopped frequently and studied the speck of silver as it increased in size, then signaled Rickards to move forward. Within five minutes, the two men were standing, looking at the silver UTV and trailer and examining the clearing.

"They left us the keys," Rickards said, reaching into the UTV and plucking a key from the ignition. He held it up, the silvery key dangling and clinking against a circular gold fob with the manufacturer's logo.

"That's nice of them," O'Reilly said, a grim smile on his face. "They also left us quite an armory." He had pulled the tarp back from the box of the utility trailer to expose rifles, magazines, knives and ammunition, along with some food and medical supplies. "This Lucas fella must have been hitting all the houses and vehicles in the area and keeping any weapons he found instead of taking them back to his people. Heck of a guy!"

Rickards came over and inspected the haul. "You know, if the group had all that food and those other supplies we found in the house, as well as these weapons, the exorcism team might not have succeeded, especially if the band had a decent plan for responding to an attack."

During the ride from the Seligman area, O'Reilly and Rickards had questioned Andy about the men the boy had identified as Kyle Lucas and Ethan Granger. According to Andy, when he and his brother first ran into the pair, it was somewhere down by Phoenix. Andy said Lucas scared him, and Daniel didn't like him much either, but that Granger was nice, and had protected them as much as possible. Whenever anything bad happened, Lucas was usually involved.

Andy said he had heard a lot of the other members of the band talking about Lucas. They said he was crazy, although some of the women, someone called Linda for example, liked him.

To O'Reilly's surprise, Andy said Granger was the leader of the band, even though Lucas was the one who had gotten the four of them out of Phoenix. When he thought about it, though, it made sense. While throughout the ages some insane people had become leaders, it didn't sound as if Lucas had the charisma necessary to command a large following, especially with a group of people who were likely craving safety and stability after the chaos of the pandemic and the subsequent concentration.

Rickards had walked off and was surveying the area, moving in slow concentric circles out from the UTV and trailer. He kicked at a piece of rope, studied it, but left it on the ground and walked on. He came to a sudden stop, bent, then squatted with a groan, and O'Reilly thought the captain would fall to his knees. He maintained his balance, but just. Rickards reached out, touched something, then brought his fingers to his face, a frown creasing the area between the sweat stained bill of the gimme cap he'd found at the cabin and his eyes.

"There's blood here, O'Reilly." Rickards gestured at the disturbed earth he'd been studying. "Quite a bit."

O'Reilly's gut clenched as he thought back to the earlier shots. He still could swear that the gunfire hadn't been this close.

But was he mistaken?

O'Reilly strode to where Rickards was squatting and looked at the ground. Sure enough, there were liberal splatters of blood turning the yellow-red earth dark. Rickards touched another spot and raised his hand to O'Reilly.

"It hasn't fully dried yet," the Enforcer captain said as he started to rise to his feet. He collapsed again with a creative curse aimed at horses and those people who force others to ride the beasts. O'Reilly put out an arm and helped Rickards back to his feet.

"If the blood isn't fully dry, they weren't here too long ago," Rickards said, gesturing toward the dark patch with his dirty hand, then wiping it on his jeans as an afterthought. "What's that over there?" He pointed to an object a few feet away, and O'Reilly went to pick it up. It was some sort of spike, much bigger than a nail. Maybe it was as big as a railroad spike, but he didn't think so. It was the same shape, though. It was old, rust-pitted and rough.

And covered in blood and strips of skin and hair.

O'Reilly was confused. The men who took Maggie should have returned to this clearing before noon. They should have been gone from the area hours ago unless they were specifically waiting for nightfall to attack the camp. But they had Maggie as a hostage and a shield, and if they wanted they could have walked into Hideaway during the daylight, although they probably didn't realize there were only children present. The whole thing just didn't make sense.

Whose blood is this? If the spike was used, Maggie was probably the attacker since the men had access to the knives and guns in the UTV. That meant the blood came from Lucas, Granger or Andy's brother, Daniel. The timing confused him, though, and the confusion was rapidly turning into frustration.

O'Reilly turned abruptly, and walked past the UTV. He beckoned for Andy to bring the horses. At first, he didn't see movement and took several steps forward and motioned again.

He didn't dare whistle or shout to the boy because he had no idea where his quarry was. Just as he thought he would have to walk all the way back to where he'd left Andy and the horses, the boy stepped out into sight and started toward him, leading the geldings.

O'Reilly turned around and walked back to the UTV, where Rickards stood, studying the contents of the bed.

"We've got to get going. We've wasted too much time and it's making me twitchy. I can't figure out where they've been that got them here so late in the day. I don't think those shots came from here, but they didn't come from the direction of camp either—and this blood wasn't from a gunshot."

"What about the UTV and the guns?" Rickards asked.

O'Reilly thought for a moment. "We leave the UTV and trailer here. You've got the key, right?"

"Yeah, right here." Rickards patted his jeans' pocket.

"Okay," O'Reilly said. "Help me wrap the guns in that tarp, and we'll hide them under some brush so if they come back this way they've got nothing. Do you need anything before we wrap them up?"

"No, I grabbed some extra ammo that fits this rifle. You?"

O'Reilly studied the stash, found a box of ammunition for his rifle, and a 9 mm handgun in a black nylon belt holster. He found some ammunition for that as well. He strapped on the holster and checked the weapon.

"That should do it," he said.

By this time, Andy had come up with the horses and was looking curiously at the UTV and the collection of items the men were laying out on the tarp.

"Do I get a gun too?" he asked once again.

O'Reilly examined the boy. The argument of not having enough weapons or ammunition was out the window now. "Do you know how to shoot a gun?" he asked. Even he could hear the doubt in his voice, and Andy bristled at the perceived insult.

"Of course I can. Granger taught me. I can shoot a bow and a crossbow too." Andy's indignant tone rocked O'Reilly, and Rickards shot him a grin.

Of course he can, O'Reilly thought. *He's been living in the wilds, being hunted with the rest of the ghosts for close to a year, if not more.*

If this Granger is any kind of a man, he will have taught these kids how to protect themselves—even if ammunition was in short supply and Lucas had hidden away all the guns he found. He, himself, had been working with Mark, Nick and Ryan, teaching them to shoot both the rifle and the bow, and all three of the boys were younger than Andy. He shouldn't be surprised that someone had taken the time to teach this boy. Hell, his own father had taught him and his brother, Jason, to shoot a .22 when they were only seven or eight, although his dad had also been very strict on teaching safety and responsibility. To his father, a gun was a tool, not a toy, and he enforced those lessons physically if needed. Target practice was meant to sight in the rifle, and to build their skills, not a fun pastime activity. At the same time, his mother enforced the idea that "if you kill it, you eat it." There may have been a few minor exceptions to that rule, such as with a coyote that was trying to get the chickens, but not many. Both O'Reilly and Jason had become darned good shots, but there were other things they valued more about their ranch life.

O'Reilly looked at the pile of weapons sitting on the tarp and picked out an older .243 with a shoulder strap and found some ammunition for it in the collection. He handed it to the boy, who examined it critically. O'Reilly bit his lip to keep from laughing.

"You understand you do not point it at anything or anyone you don't intend to shoot and kill, right?"

"Of course I do." Andy said, looking O'Reilly in the eyes, a serious expression on his face. "That's the first thing Granger taught Danny and me."

O'Reilly saw him check the safety, raise it and look through the scope. Then with a nod of satisfaction, he slung the rifle over his shoulder.

"Are we ready to storm the castle?" Rickards asked. He gestured toward the sky, which was taking on the yellower light of early evening.

O'Reilly gave him a shocked look. "Your taste in movies leaves something to be desired, Seth."

"What's it say about yours that you knew the reference." Rickards laughed, and O'Reilly felt some of the tension drop away, although not for long.

O'Reilly and Rickards each took an end of the tarp and carried the guns about fifty yards to a heavy growth of scrub oak. Braving the sharp leaves and branches, they secreted the bundle in the middle of the clump, then threw some of the old dead leaves over the dark brown canvas. Standing back on the outside of the brush, O'Reilly was satisfied that he couldn't see any indication that something was hidden inside.

The men walked back to where Andy stood, holding the horses. O'Reilly was preparing to mount when he noticed Rickards staring at Jimmy with disfavor.

"Do you need a leg up?" he asked in a joking tone, although he could feel the building tension in his chest. They had taken too long, and he needed to see what was happening in the camp.

"Shut up," Rickards said conversationally, then he took the reins and led Jimmy over to a fallen tree. He walked the gelding alongside, then stepped up on the tree trunk and mounted. O'Reilly hid a smile. At least he was on board. Andy scrambled up behind Rickards and, with O'Reilly in the lead once again, they headed across the clearing toward what he'd begun to think of as the "prickly pear ridge."

O'Reilly studied the tracks leading to the west, away from the trail that led down into Adobe Canyon and then to Hideaway, trying to make sense of what he was seeing. O'Reilly had easily tracked the men over to the ridge. However, instead of going straight down the bank, the tracks veered off toward the northwest, reaching the bottom of the ridge more than a hundred feet away from the original trail. Once on the flat ground below the bank, the tracks continued to move away from the original trail. He could see the tracks left two days ago, first by Maggie and the girls coming to the ridge, then the girls racing away back to camp and finally his own tracks as he headed out initially looking for Maggie, back for supplies, then out again on his rescue mission. These new tracks, however, headed off toward the northwest, instead of toward the trail to Hideaway.

Then all the pieces came together in his mind.

"Maggie escaped," O'Reilly said, both wondering and worried. "She must have gotten that spike somewhere, attacked one of the men and wounded him, then made a run for it."

Rickards nodded, forehead furrowed in concentration as he contemplated the scenario O'Reilly described.

"I can see it, but why head in that particular direction?" Rickards asked. "They're too close to the camp. The men would still find it with no problem. What did she hope to accomplish?"

O'Reilly thought a moment, then answered, positive he was right. "She was trying to delay them. Probably realized I would have told the kids to sleep in the caves at night, so wanted to make sure she kept the men from getting there before the children had gone to ground. Maybe also to give me a chance to get here. For some reason, they're much later than they should be. Maybe they had a mechanical problem or a flat tire, or maybe they stopped at a house to rest, thinking they were far enough away from the mountain to be safe. Then they moved on in the afternoon. I don't know, but Maggie must have realized I'd still be following her and wanted to give me more time.

"There's a ravine up in that direction, several miles away." O'Reilly chinned off in the direction the new tracks took. "It leads down into the main body of Adobe Canyon. There's a steep drop as it falls off the rim, but I think someone could make it if they were careful. From there, the canyon curves off to the northwest, then down to the southwest."

"Think she's armed?" Rickards asked.

"I don't know." O'Reilly thought about Maggie and her current aversion to guns. "She's been pretty much against handling a weapon since I was wounded, but I suppose if, when Maggie attacked whoever she attacked, she was able to get his gun, she wouldn't hesitate.

"Of course, then she'd have to figure out how to use it, especially if she grabbed one of those assault rifles. That arroyo would make a good place to bottleneck the men, though, and maybe be able to get off some shots and slow them down."

O'Reilly nodded as if to himself, certain he had figured out the basics of what had happened. Those shots he and Rickards had heard may have been Maggie and the men exchanging fire in the ravine or close to it. It had sounded like automatic weapon fire, which worried him as he was positive she'd never touched an automatic gun in her life. He'd known men who had no training, and no common sense, who needed medical and dental attention after using a fully automatic weapon for the first time.

"Come on, we need to hurry," O'Reilly said, his decision on direction made. He reined Ace toward the camp, and away from the tracks leading to the ravine, and pushed him into a long trot once again. The horse was tired but had caught his wind during the stop at the UTV and stepped out willingly.

Rickards and Andy caught up and the man looked over at O'Reilly.

"You think they're at the camp already?" Rickards asked with difficulty, considering the jouncing he was getting at the horse's trot.

"I hope not, I don't know if the kids are in the caves yet. It's still pretty light out, but if they heard the shots, I hope they went right away."

"Are they armed?"

"No." O'Reilly didn't explain further. His gut twisted at the thought of these armed men descending on a camp of children with no protection other than some bows. Especially a man like this Lucas seemed to be. A man who would keep back needed supplies from his own people so that he felt well provided for. A man like that wouldn't hesitate to kill some unknown kids and keep all they had for himself.

O'Reilly pushed Ace harder, pulling ahead of Rickards and Andy. He had a knot in his gut that felt as though it was the size of a watermelon, and with every step the horse took, it got bigger and tighter.

33

Christina stood and rubbed her back. She was hot and sweating, and her brown hair stuck to her face. She was just not cut out to be a gardener, she thought. She wiped her sleeve across her cheek, trying to blot away some of the moisture, but from the looks of the cloth, all she'd managed to do was smear more dirt onto her face. Her eyes stung from the salty liquid, and she carefully dabbed at them.

Alysa was working a few rows of vegetables away from her, looking fresh and relatively clean, although there was a smear of dirt across the bridge of her nose. She was so darkly tanned that it was almost invisible.

The boys were also helping out in the garden, although that term was loosely applied to what they were actually doing. Nick and Ryan had been assigned to weed duty while Mark was ensuring the ditches O'Reilly had dug to water the plot from the windmill tank were all still clear of debris so that water could flow to every thirsty plant. Lindy was following Mark with the two dogs in attendance, and Christina cringed when she saw all four of them covered in mud to the eyeballs since doing the laundry at the camp was a challenge at the best of times.

She missed Maggie and O'Reilly. She couldn't believe how badly she missed them, considering she, Alysa and the boys had only been at the camp two months give or take. She told herself sternly that she didn't just miss Maggie because the woman was the one who normally would have taken charge of bathing Lindy and making sure that Mark and the dogs didn't track dirt into the house.

Come to think of it, why was she so worried about the introduction of a little dirt into the old stone structure, considering that the floor was just rocks, old Sinagua pottery sherds and horseshoes cemented together. It couldn't be exactly swept clean since the surface was so uneven. Last week Maggie had even found a snake hole near the wood stove—complete with a snake wriggling out of it. Maggie screamed, bringing O'Reilly, who looked at it, and proclaimed it to be an Arizona mountain kingsnake and not a deadly coral snake. He did say it was an unusually fine specimen and that it would keep any rattlers away from the area since a kingsnake's preferred diet was lizards and other snakes.

Maggie relented and allowed Mark to pull it from the hole and take it outside. The hole itself was immediately packed full of dirt and rocks.

The wind was starting to pick up, as often happened during the heat of the afternoon, and the breeze felt good on her skin. For once, it was coming from the southwest, hitting the canyon just right. If the breeze came from any direction other than southwest or northeast, it tended to skip over the deep gorge, and they only got a little hint of it down on the canyon floor. O'Reilly said that Hideaway could be viciously cold in the winter because cold air sank, and the wind wouldn't stir it up much. It could also be wickedly hot in the summer, not because of the hot air sinking, of course, because it didn't, but because once again, the wind didn't always reach the depths of the canyon.

Christina bent back to her row of beans, picking the ripe ones and dropping them into a basket, when a faint popping noise reached her ears. She looked around the home pasture. Nothing.

"Alysa, did you hear anything?" Christina called over to the other girl.

"Like what?" Alysa straightened up, setting her container of peas on the ground. She looked around, a question on her face.

"I thought I heard something popping. Sort of like popcorn, only a fast *pop-pop-pop-pop*. I haven't heard anything like it before, and I don't know where it came from. Things echo so much here." She threw out her arm, gesturing at the walls of the canyon.

"Woodpecker maybe? I heard a couple of sharp pops about twenty minutes ago. I figured it was a woodpecker somewhere up the canyon."

Alysa didn't seem very interested, which strangely comforted Christina. If Alysa didn't think there was anything to be worried about, then there probably wasn't. Christina looked down toward the creek where several large cottonwoods had taken root over the years, as well as a few sycamores. Could the sound have come from that direction?

Yes, she decided. It was possible. She wished the sound would come again so she could be sure, but all she could hear was the wind blowing, the windmill creaking, and the boys talking and laughing.

Christina sighed and bent back to her work.

She picked beans for another five minutes or so when she heard the popping sound once again. This time it seemed closer, and she stood and looked back at the trees by the creek. Alysa had also heard the sound this time and had left her pea picking to study the area.

"Was that a woodpecker?" Christina asked as she tried to determine which tree it might have come from. Of course, there were more trees growing up and down the canyon, not in the meadow itself, and it might have come from one of those. Somehow the explanation just seemed wrong to her. The sound made her nervous.

"I don't know," said Alysa, stepping over a row of beans to come stand beside Christina. The wind blew her black hair over her shoulder and in a cloud around her head. "I can't tell where exactly it came from. The breeze is confusing things."

Christina stood, listening for the popping sound again. It didn't come, but she felt a growing anxiety nonetheless.

Finally, she turned and looked at Alysa. The Native American girl also looked concerned, although she didn't display any of the panic Christina was feeling.

"Do you think we should take the boys to the hideout? It's almost evening." The kids had spent the last two nights sleeping in the caves and used the small, triangular hole to check the camp before coming out in the morning.

"Over a woodpecker?" Alysa looked surprised.

"Are you sure it was a woodpecker?" Christina asked, although she couldn't think of any other explanation. It was too muffled and indistinct. And they were in a canyon in the middle of nowhere. If she'd been in the city, she would have thought someone was nailing shingles on a roof, or building a house, although anyone who could swing a hammer that fast could give a comic book superhero a run for his money.

"I guess not," said Christina. She looked around again. Alysa's comment made her feel better, but there was still a thread of disquiet tickling away. Of course, ever since they'd come out to Hideaway, things had been so strange and unfamiliar that she often felt unbalanced. This was probably just more of that same feeling.

No more woodpeckers or any other strange noises disturbed the late afternoon air as the children finished working in the garden. Mark, Nick and Ryan headed down to the creek, screeching and shouting as they pushed at one another, each trying to be the first one into what they called the swimming hole. Jack tore along beside, the Australian Shepherd barking and making feints toward their ankles, herding them like an unruly group of cattle. Christina wondered what the fish thought about the whole thing. Not that there were a lot of fish in there, and she wasn't exactly sure where they came from since the stream didn't flow above ground the entire distance. O'Reilly said something about it actually flowing heavily on the surface of the creek bed during in the spring and early summer, but she'd never seen it.

Christina and Alysa walked toward the strange little home built under the overhanging cliff. Alysa was carrying Lindy with Gypsy, the toddler's self-appointed guardian, following close behind. Christina had the day's collection of beans and peas, as well as some late tomatoes. Tomorrow they would prepare the food and put it outside into a frame O'Reilly had created to protect vegetables and fruits while dehydrating. Maggie was determined to can some of the garden produce since she thought she could preserve greater amounts in a shorter time, but dehydrating took fewer resources and, as long as they could keep the results dry, lasted longer.

Christina eyed the chickens that were still scratching in the barnyard. They had been one of the greatest challenges to the solar drying enterprise since they seemed to think the drying pans were put out specifically for them. Houdini, in particular, seemed drawn to the dryer trays when squash was on the menu, causing yet another point of contention between the rooster and Maggie.

Christina looked over at Alysa. The girl was talking to Lindy, making the toddler laugh. She jounced the child up and down.

"Where do you think they are now?" Christina asked. She glanced toward the creek to make sure the boys were still engaged in their water sports.

Alysa looked at Christina. In spite of the smile playing with Lindy had put on her face, there was a dark worry deep in her gaze, and Christina remembered her plan to head up to the big reservation if Maggie and O'Reilly didn't return.

"It's only been two, almost three days," Alysa said, and Christina could hear the worry there as well, even though the dark-haired girl tried to control it. The toddler-induced happiness was starting to fade from her face, and Christina felt a small shiver of guilt for being the cause.

"I know," Christina looked toward the north end of the home pasture, now shrouded in shadow as the sun dropped low enough it could no longer illuminate the floor of the canyon.

"I just . . ." Christina's voice trailed off. Movement from the far end of the meadow caught her eye, and she came to an abrupt stop.

"What?" Alysa said. She swung her head around to look in the same direction as Christina.

A figure had emerged from the bend in the canyon and made its way toward the gate at the end of the home pasture in a halting run. The figure fell, pushed itself back to its feet and came on again. Christina could hear a high, thin cry, but it was too far to make out the words. The light falling into the canyon became brighter as the walls opened up, and Christina could make out a blonde, tangled braid. It was Maggie Langton.

Christina let out a wail, dropped her boxes of beans and peas and raced for the meadow gate. Maggie was running through the grass, the few cows and horses who resided there spooked and bolted out of her path, tails and heads held high and snorting. Christina made it to the gate next to the barn shortly before Maggie, with Alysa close behind in spite of being burdened with Lindy.

As Maggie got close, Christina stopped in shock. The woman looked terrible. A dark purple bruise and black eye had blossomed on the left side of her face, and she was covered with scratches and cuts. Her braid was frayed, and damp, sweat-darkened, honey blonde hair draggled onto her shoulders and into her face. Still, it was Maggie, and after a moment's hesitation, Christina threw open the gate and rushed out into the pasture to meet her.

"Christina, where is Mark? Where are the boys?" Maggie gasped in between ragged breaths.

"Down by the stream," Christina started, "They . . .,"

"Get them and take them to the caves now. There's no time to explain. They're coming," Maggie said. She was bent over, hands on her knees, braid hanging over her shoulder.

"Who?" Christina started to ask.

"Now!" Maggie snapped. She straightened and started for the pasture gate. Alysa was already running for the caves, Lindy bumping on her hip, impeding her movement.

Christina turned and ran for the creek.

"Nick, Ryan, Mark! Where are you?" Christina yelled as she raced through the tall, creek-fed grass that grew near the water hole.

She saw Mark's head pop above the rock covered berm along the creek's edge. He was soaking wet and laughing. Then he saw his mother who was following Christina as quickly as she could, and the laughter was wiped off his face.

"Mom!" Mark scrambled up the bank, barefoot and dressed only in his underwear, and ran for his mother.

"Nick, Ryan!" Christina called, panic rising in her voice. The boys both appeared over the bank, wide-eyed, clutching their clothes in their hands.

"Come on. Maggie is here and she says we have to go to the caves now." Christina said, stopping next to the two boys.

"Can we put on our shoes?" Nick asked. "There are stickers in the field."

"No—I mean yes. Hurry! Don't take time to put your shirts and pants on." Christina snapped. She looked toward the north end of the pasture and froze.

Alysa, who had left first with Lindy and Gypsy, was walking back across the pasture toward the barn.

Behind her were three armed men, one of them pointing a rifle at Alysa's back.

Maggie looked in the direction Christina was staring.

"No," Maggie whispered in desperation. "No, no, no."

34

Granger staggered and fell to his knee as a hammer crashed into his right thigh. At least it felt like a hammer. A ricochet. The woman couldn't shoot worth crap, but he gets hit by a damned *ricochet* of all the luck. He cursed — loudly. Then he pulled himself back to his feet and continued descending the slope, wary of any more shots.

Several more reports rang out — three from the woman and one from Lucas. Granger looked back up the slope and saw Daniel was moving carefully between the boulders, unhurt from the barrage of bullets and ricochets. How could the woman blast off that many shots in a narrow canyon and still only hit one person, and that by accident?

The gunshots stopped after only that short volley, and Granger realized the woman's gun was out of ammunition. He crouched behind a refrigerator-sized boulder that had been washed down the ravine and peered around the edge. The woman was gone.

Farther down the slope, Lucas cackled with glee. *It appears the chase has restored Lucas's good mood,* Granger thought sourly. The man was lucky. When Langton had attacked him with that blasted spike, she had come within a half inch of ripping the man's eye out, instead laying open a long, bone-deep furrow from nose to jaw just below the ear, which bled profusely.

Thankfully they'd had the medical supplies Lucas had been hoarding at his first bug out location. The stash included some zip sutures. These had pulled the ragged edges of the wound closed, although Granger had some doubts about their holding power if this chase lasted much longer. He covered the entire mess with some antibiotic cream and a pad of gauze, but already he could see the tape around the edges coming loose and blood soaking through the white pad.

Damn Maggie Langton, Granger thought. Who'd have thought she was smart enough to pull off a stunt like that? And she'd led them on an insane chase for a mile or more across the Arizona grasslands, then down this arroyo into some God-forsaken canyon. And shot him! And damn it, his leg hurt, nearly as much, if not more, than when his cheek had been sliced open. He half wished he'd let Lucas shoot the woman when she first ran, instead of spoiling his aim.

Lucas had reached the bottom of the canyon and beckoned for Granger and Daniel to catch up.

"Come on. Langton's trapped. She can't go anywhere except lead us straight to her camp!" Lucas said, chuckling, and he struck off down the canyon, slowing as he approached a turn in the creek, then moving quickly around the bend, weapon held at the ready in case the woman was hiding there.

Granger knew Langton's handgun was out of ammunition, but there were other things down here that could be used as weapons if a person was creative. Just look at what the woman had done with that spike. She must have found it when they'd let her go to pee behind the trees, sawed through her rope, then kept it hidden until an opportunity offered itself.

He felt stupid. Lucas already made it clear he was holding Granger accountable for Langton finding the spike even though both of them had allowed her out of their collective sights. Granger was the one who said to let her go, however, and throughout the chase from the UTV to the canyon, Lucas had not let him forget it.

Granger and Daniel caught up with Lucas at the first jagged bend in the canyon. The footing was a mixture of sand, dirt and water-smoothed stones, all of which made Granger's leg ache even worse.

"Lucas, hold up," Granger said as he sat on a large rock that had a small sycamore tree growing out from under it.

"What?" Lucas said, turning to look at Granger with impatience.

"Like you said, she's not going anywhere. I'm bleeding. I need to check this leg." Granger unbuckled his belt, unbuttoned his jeans and pulled them down past the injury, wincing as the heavy, blood soaked denim scraped over the bullet wound. He hissed in pain.

The hole was roughly two inches above his knee in a meaty part of the thigh. It was still spilling blood, although not as much as when it was first struck, and the edges looked raw and torn. The back of his leg had an exit wound, much larger than the entrance. Fortunately for him, the bullet hadn't passed deeply through his leg, and the interior track was only two or three inches long. If the wound had been any shallower, it could have been considered a graze. Granger cursed his luck, although he had to admit it could have been a lot worse. The ricochet had lost a lot of its momentum when it hit the wall of the ravine, leaving it just enough energy to penetrate the denim and his own flesh. At least it had gone all the way through. If the bullet had been left inside he would have had to fish it out. He cringed at the thought.

He studied the wound, picked out a few strings of denim that had been pushed in by the projectile and palpated it gently. The pain was increasing, although the bleeding had slowed. Slowed bleeding or not, however, there was still a bullet wound in his leg, which would almost certainly get an infection if it wasn't treated. Even then, there was a chance the wound would go septic. He'd seen it several times since he and Lucas had been roaming northwest Arizona. Band members who'd received some form of deep wound got sick and died because there were no medical services out here and no antibiotics. A few times they'd had some medication they'd looted from a house or ranch—either pills or ointment—but with a wound like this . . .

He forced his mind away from the very possible outcome of this injury and back to the hunt for Maggie Langton and her camp. If he were lucky, they'd have some form of potent antibiotic there. For now, he just needed to stop the bleeding.

"Get me my pack, Daniel," he said to the boy who was viewing the injury to Granger's leg with horror. The boy had seen what happened to people whose injuries had become infected. He probably also realized that if anything happened to Granger, he would be left at Lucas's mercy.

Daniel brought him the gray nylon daypack Granger had been carrying. Ethan had put a small first aid kit in the bag before they left the UTV, not knowing when they'd return for the rest of the supplies. He'd thought it likely he'd need them for Lucas if his cheek kept bleeding. Digging through the contents, he found a pad of gauze, a tiny foil pack of triple antibiotic cream and a roll of medical tape. Gingerly he applied the ointment, squirting it deep into the wound, although it went against the instructions for puncture wounds on the packet. He opened another and emptied into the hole on the back of his leg. The bullet's pathway may not have been long, but he didn't know if the antibiotic would reach all of the torn tissue. Still, it made him feel like he was doing something.

By the time he'd applied the pad and the tape, pulled up his jeans and re-buckled his belt, Lucas was vibrating with impatience, eager to get on with the hunt.

Langton hadn't left many tracks in the mixture of rock and gravel. However, as Lucas had said, there wasn't anywhere else to go. No trails led out of the canyon, up to the rim above. No caves dotted the sides of the canyon in this area, although Granger was aware that this part of Arizona did boast a number of caves and cavern systems. There was an overhang in the limestone midway up the canyon wall, and Granger could see some ancient cliff dwellings tucked into that niche. However, there was no sign of a ladder or any other way to access those ruins.

The small stream ran along the surface of the canyon floor, gradually growing larger as several other springs fed the water flow. Occasionally the men saw a footprint in the wet sand and dirt, or several, the toe dug in deeper than the heel, indicating the person who left them was running. However, the placement, and the marks occasionally left by a dragging toe, showed the individual was either exhausted or injured. Granger knew that if multiple people were living in a camp nearby, then it was highly possible the tracks could have been left by anyone in the group, but he knew in his gut it was Maggie Langton.

Granger, Lucas and Daniel continued to follow the canyon as it started to widen out, leaving more room for brush, willow saplings and a few cottonwood trees on the banks of the creek. Sticks, dead grass and other debris caught in the trees' branches made it clear that some time in the recent past, the canyon had flooded, and Granger shot a look toward the sky.

Clear. At least the narrow strip he could see above him was the deep blue of early evening, so there was little chance of a flash flood carrying them away. Something was going right.

His leg was throbbing, and he feared it would give out, leaving him spinning in a circle on the ground like a fly with one wing.

They had covered close to two miles, maybe two and a half by Granger's calculation, although his leg made it feel like ten, when the canyon widened out again and a second ravine branched off, leading back up toward the north. Granger didn't think it went too far, considering they hadn't run into its upper end while chasing Langton through the grasslands above. Of more interest was a narrow trail switchbacking up the rocky side of the gorge to the rim.

Granger looked at the path, and his heart sank. His leg was getting worse, he was hungry and thirsty and he was starting to feel dizzy and nauseous. As his eyes traced the small cattle trail zigzagging across the face of the canyon wall, he knew there was no way he could climb that track. Lucas had gone a short distance up the path, then turned and picked his way back down through the rocks and cacti to where Granger and Daniel were waiting.

"There are horse tracks but no human footprints," Lucas said, keeping his voice low but not whispering. The blond man turned and walked off down the canyon, scanning the ground. He saw something that interested him, crouched, and examined a path of compacted dirt that paralleled the creek. He nodded in apparent satisfaction, stood and beckoned for Granger and Daniel.

Granger took a deep breath and took a step, staggering a little.

"Do you need help?" Daniel asked and reached out, putting his arm under Granger's elbow. Worry shone in his dark eyes.

"No," Granger said, keeping his voice soft. "Don't show Lucas any weakness." He gave the boy a meaningful look.

Daniel nodded, and the two of them walked slowly over to where Lucas was standing.

"She came this way," Lucas said, gesturing toward the track. Although this trail was hard packed dirt or smooth stone, in a couple of places a footprint was still visible.

"It's not far now," Lucas said. "There's a difference to the light up there." He gestured down the canyon. Granger couldn't see any change and didn't know whether Lucas actually did or whether he was just saying that to forestall any argument.

"Any lookouts?" Granger asked. If Langton had made it back to the camp before them, would the residents seriously not have any sentries posted? Were he and Lucas in the crosshairs as they stood here debating their next move?

"I don't see any. Might be when we get closer." Lucas didn't seem very worried about the possibility.

While there was more vegetation along the creek in this area, Granger felt as though he, Lucas and Daniel were largely exposed. Several hundred yards farther on, the canyon took a sharp turn to the left, then another to the right about seventy-five yards after that. This time even Granger could see the difference in the light.

Lucas was in the lead, Granger limping along behind him, and Daniel was bringing up the rear. All three hung to the right side of the canyon in case lookouts were posted around the corner.

A fine group we are, Granger thought, looking at Lucas's back. The man was practically thrumming with excitement. *One woman manages to nearly rip Lucas's face off and shoots me in the leg.* He glanced back at Daniel. The boy was dragging along behind. He hadn't spoken twenty words since finding out that his brother was dead. Granger would like to take Lucas's head off for the way he told Daniel about Andy's death. He wondered whether, if it came down to it, Daniel would be of any help in taking the camp or whether he was so utterly destroyed inside that he would be a hindrance instead.

Ahead of him, Lucas moved in close to the canyon wall, sliding in behind some desert willow, and started to ease around the corner. Granger followed closely, trying not to drag his injured leg. He felt Daniel trailing him and hoped the boy was up to the coming attack.

In front of them, Lucas sidled forward and peered around an outcropping of rock. Granger leaned back against the canyon wall, taking his weight off his leg as he watched Lucas and awaited a signal.

Then, to Granger's surprise, Lucas took a quick step backward, slung his rifle back over his shoulder, then dove out past the outcropping. Granger pushed himself away from the wall as he felt the ant-foot prickle of adrenaline course through his body. He heard a dog bark, a scream, a cry, and then a high-pitched yelp. He rushed for the outcropping, the agony of his leg temporarily forgotten.

Granger jolted to a stop at an open gate on the edge of a wide open grassy meadow. Several cows and horses were grazing mid-way down the length of the pasture, and at the far end, he saw a windmill and an old, wooden barn. The scene that shocked him the most, however, was Lucas gripping a fourteen- or fifteen-year-old girl by the hair. A strawberry blonde toddler was clutched in her arms, crying, and four feet away, a dog was struggling to rise.

"Lookee what I found, Granger," Lucas laughed as the girl struggled to free herself from his hand. He tightened his fist in her dark hair, and the girl froze, head tilted back, throat exposed. Granger looked at Daniel and saw the boy staring at Lucas, horror on his face. Granger turned his gaze back to the blond man, and it dawned on him why the boy was so affected. This girl could have been his sister, with her high cheekbones, dark hair and eyes, and darkly tanned honey skin.

The group that Granger and Lucas had originally put together had no children other than the brothers. Not that some of the members hadn't been parents at some point. The influenza virus had no discrimination, striking anyone, especially within populations exposed frequently due to need, such as healthcare workers, or those who initially denied the severity, or even the existence of the pandemic itself. It wasn't often multiple members of a family survived unscathed, such as in the case of Daniel and Andy Espitia.

"I bet that the Langton woman went down to the barn. This one here . . .," Lucas shook the girl's head by her hair, causing her to utter a small cry of pain ". . . is going to take us there."

The blond man let go of the girl's hair with a shove toward the far end of the pasture. He lifted the rifle and jabbed it into her back, propelling her several steps forward.

"Go," he snapped to the girl. "Let's go find mommy."

The small group headed across the pasture, Lucas pushing the girl in the lead. Granger looked over his shoulder. What was the girl coming down to this end of the meadow for, especially if Maggie Langton had made it back to the camp? He scanned the sides of the canyon and the loose scree that lined the edge. Several large trees were rooted along the base of the rock walls. No trails led to the rim. Granger frowned in concentration. It didn't make sense.

Then he saw it. Behind a large juniper tree was the dark opening of a cave. He'd seen other caves in the area, such as the Cathedral Cave Preserve south of Seligman and the Grand Canyon Caverns up toward Peach Springs. It appeared that this canyon had some of the same rock formations. Just like the mines, some of these cave systems would make good bunkers, and he thought Langton's people must have realized the same thing. He wondered if any of the group were in the caves already or if Maggie Langton's arrival at camp was what alerted them to the danger. Maybe this girl was the first one racing for cover due to her desire to protect the toddler.

Granger stared back down at the gray barn, and squinted in an effort to see who was waiting there. Lucas was making a straight-on approach, walking close behind the girl. Granger swallowed hard and followed Lucas in single file, with Daniel bringing up the rear. Granger realized the girl and the toddler would provide the three men both a hostage and a shield, should Langton's people try to take a shot anyway, but there'd been no indication anyone at that end of the field even knew they were there. A young girl and a toddler. Langton said the camp housed only her and six children—and he'd called her a liar—but now the first, in fact, the only, people they'd found were a teenage girl and a toddler who was obviously not the girl's child.

Granger was near enough he could now see the Langton woman with more children to the left of the barn, over by the stream. As Granger's small group drew closer to the gate that led from the pasture, he could tell the woman was slumped in exhaustion. Another girl about the same age as the one Lucas had captured was standing next to her and behind appeared three young boys, bare chested and bare legged. No guns were in sight, although another dog topped the bank.

The girl looked out toward the pasture, then turned quickly and said something to Langton, who looked toward the pasture and froze for a moment. She whipped back around and said something to the boys, who started to scatter. The dog, another Australian Shepherd from what he could see, apparently picked up that there were strangers in the field and began to bark.

Lucas pointed the rifle into the air and released one shot. It was as if everyone was playing a deadly serious game of red light, green light, and Lucas was the caller. No one moved. Even the dog was momentarily shocked into silence.

In that moment of stillness, Granger looked around the camp. It was remote and wouldn't be easily found by Enforcers since no road went right to it. From what he could see at the south end, there were the remains of a two-track, but it was overgrown, and there were no vehicles to be seen. *Langton and her people must be using horses for transportation, just as if they were freaking cowboys or something*, he thought.

Granger had never been on a horse, although his daughters had begged for ponies when they were younger and had gotten riding lessons at a local stable. Horses were damned expensive, though, especially after the geniuses in the state government limited water to agriculture, at the same time allowing unfettered use for people who wanted green lawns in the desert, swimming pools and waterfalls. It made the city dwellers happy until they had to start paying higher grocery bills due to the number of farms going out of business. Just like the government, make the donors and the high-density voter populations happy in the short term and hope that when the crap hits the fan down the road, someone else was in charge and could be blamed. He frowned at the thought. He really wished he could have gotten his daughters a pony.

Granger's gaze took in the old, gray barn, a windmill creaking softly as the blades rotated in the light breeze and a huge garden with lush, growing vegetation. Granger thought about the garden his group had created up on the mountaintop and realized why Langton had been so dismissive of their efforts. He looked for a house or cabin. Nothing. They must be living in the barn. Not ideal, but he'd slept in worse.

Granger looked back toward the Langton woman and her children.

Guess she wasn't lying, after all, he thought.

35

Maggie's heart crashed, and her mind whirled as she watched Alysa, Lindy and the men approaching. The grin on Lucas's face chilled her, the early evening air suddenly feeling more like January than late September or early October. She realized she had no real idea what day of the week it was, let alone the month. She hadn't gotten the children to the caves in time, and now they were at the mercy of Lucas. Granger made it clear yesterday that he wouldn't do anything to protect her if it came down to a choice between them.

How did they get here so fast? Maggie wondered. She hadn't been able to run the whole distance from the spring to the camp. But they were injured—or at least Granger and Lucas were. That damned Lucas was always one step ahead. She thought about him telling Granger that the exorcism team was surrounding the camp before a shot was even fired. Something else about that situation tickled her mind, but she didn't have time to focus on it.

The men were coming through the gate next to the barn. Alysa stumbled when Lucas jabbed the rifle into her back, nearly dropping Lindy. Dried blood still streaked his blond beard and crusted his face around the stained bandage. Maggie felt a quick lightning bolt of satisfaction, knowing she had outsmarted the man once and told herself she could do it again. Granger was limping badly, and Maggie could see the red-brown crust staining the leg of his jeans. She was disturbed at how much pleasure she got from hurting them both and cautioned herself not to embrace the desire for retribution too much. She'd seen too many people who had started to live for vengeance, even in minor situations, and it never ended well. The old saying "to a hammer, everything looks like a nail" floated through her mind. Those people who always expected to be wronged found those wrongs everywhere they looked, whether they actually existed or not.

"Honey, we're home!" called Lucas in a sing-song voice before laughing again. He reached out and grabbed Alysa's hair and shook her like a dog worrying a chew toy. The girl grimaced but didn't cry out, which seemed to make Lucas angry, and he pulled her back, eliciting a small whimper.

"Kyle, let her go," Granger snapped. "Langton can't do anything and she knows it. Look at her." Granger had limped up beside Lucas and now gestured toward Maggie and the other children. "All she's got is a bunch of kids. What do you expect her to do?"

Lucas looked over at Granger, a smirk on his face. "I expect her to do whatever I say for her to do. You get me, Granger?"

From the look on his face, Granger absolutely "got" Lucas but wasn't about to let the comment go.

"We still have a deal, Kyle. Don't forget it," Granger said, his voice so low Maggie had trouble hearing him. The look in his eyes made it clear what he meant, however.

The expression on Lucas's face said being reminded of this "deal" was having less and less of an impact on his behavior.

Where is O'Reilly? Maggie wondered. *I just need to keep us safe until O'Reilly gets here and rescues us.*

O'Reilly had been a day and a half behind her when she'd seen him come out of the trees at Lucas's hideout. If it took him a day and a half to get back to Hideaway, she just had to keep the kids and herself safe for thirty-six hours. Surely she could manage that, she thought, mentally steeling herself for the upcoming challenge.

Maggie stole a glance at Daniel. Mark was close to the age of his dead brother, even if they looked nothing alike, and she hoped he would have sympathetic feelings toward the boy. Nick and Ryan were quite a bit younger than Andy had been, but maybe those warm feelings would extend to them as well. From what she'd seen at Granger's camp and what little Andy had told her, Daniel Espitia had diligently cared for his brother since the pandemic.

Daniel was watching Maggie and the boys but stood well behind the men and too far away for Maggie to read the emotions on his face.

Only thirty-six hours. She took a deep breath.

"Hey Ms. Langton, why don't you come over here and introduce us to your lovely family," Lucas called, still using the mocking, treacly sweet voice he'd used when he'd repeated that old TV sitcom line. She saw Granger shoot him an annoyed look. Lucas ignored him and shook Alysa by the hair once more.

"I'm not going to ask nicely again, and shut that damned dog up," Lucas said, his voice transforming from mocking to hard in a heartbeat, and Maggie knew she couldn't put it off any longer.

She pushed her sweaty, tangled hair out of her face and straightened. She glanced back at Mark, "Hold on to Jack and don't let him bark." Then she stepped forward. She gestured to Christina and the boys to follow her as she whispered to them not to react to Lucas or Granger and not to say anything about O'Reilly. She slowly walked over to where Lucas, Granger and Daniel stood with Alysa and Lindy and stopped a few feet away.

Lucas pushed Alysa and Lindy over to Maggie, who gave the older girl a quick hug and took Lindy in her arms. The little girl tucked her tear-stained face into Maggie's neck.

Maggie stood staring at Lucas, unsure what to do. What was the proper etiquette when your home was invaded by a sociopath with an assault rifle and a grudge? Did Emily Post cover dealing with insane potential rapists and murderers taking you hostage?

With a sudden movement, Lucas raised the rifle and pointed it straight at Maggie and Lindy, the muzzle only three or four feet from the little girl's back. Maggie's eyes flew open, and she staggered backward, bumping into Christina. She whirled around, shoved Lindy into Christina's arms and turned back to Lucas, who was glaring at her from behind the gun's sights.

"I should blow your chest out your back, right here and right now for what you did to my face," he growled at her, his teeth bared in a grimace.

The thought went through Maggie's mind that if he shot her at this range, the bullets would rip right through her and into the children standing behind. She only had to hold things together for thirty-six hours and she couldn't even manage fifteen minutes.

"Lucas, stop it," Granger snapped. He grabbed the barrel of the gun and pulled it down. Lucas jerked it away and up toward his left shoulder.

"Get over it, Granger. I'm not going to do anything . . ." Lucas looked at Maggie and the children with a leer, ". . . yet. It doesn't hurt for her to remember I can. I do owe Langton for this." He patted the blood-stained bandage on his cheek. "Right now, though, I'm hungry."

Lucas focused his attention back on Maggie, "How about it, woman? Got something to feed some poor wanderers?"

The man's mocking tone made Maggie grind her teeth, but she knew she had no choice.

"Yeah, fine," she said, reminding herself to keep her voice calm. "The cow needs to be milked and someone needs to gather the eggs, though."

Granger gave Maggie an impressed look, and she thought back to his band of ghosts and their compound. Maggie and a group of children having what appeared to be a bountiful supply of fresh food must have been bittersweet. He looked toward Lucas, who nodded.

"Okay, the kids can do the chores. Daniel, you'll go with them, understood?" Lucas said, motioning toward the children with his rifle. "Make sure they don't take off." Lucas made a face and continued, "and lock that dog in the barn. I don't want to hear it."

Maggie heard a low growl from Jack and hoped Mark had a good grip on his collar. She looked toward the pasture, wondering about Gypsy, and her heart ached. The female Australian Shepherd had designated itself as Lindy's guardian since the little girl first arrived at the camp. The dog had been with Alysa and Lindy when they'd run for the caves. Maggie hadn't heard a shot, so she hoped wherever the dog was, it wasn't badly injured.

The light was going fast, and a lowing from the pasture let the group know Lizzie thought it was well past time for milking. Maggie told Mark to collect eggs. She knew most of the hens would be starting to roost for the night, but he shouldn't disturb them too much. She asked Alysa to milk the cow. One look at Lucas made it clear that trying to send all the children out to do the chores while she alone took the men to the house was a non-starter.

She turned on her heel and started for the western side of the canyon.

"Wait, where are you going?" Granger asked. He hurried up to her side, his leg clearly causing him pain, reached out and grabbed her arm.

"The house," Maggie said in clipped tones, "since you seem to be determined to move in."

"You don't live in the barn?" Granger asked, eyeing the large, gray building. He looked around the area. Maggie felt a smug surge of satisfaction at his confusion.

"We're not animals. We live in the house," she answered with a haughty edge to her voice. One of the boys giggled nervously, and she turned and shot them all a glare. There had been a few times, such as when the snake made an appearance from the hole in the floor or some scorpions held a convention in the pantry, when Maggie had declared the barn more suitable for living than the little stone house. She wasn't going to let the men know that, however, especially remembering their conglomeration of RVs at the mountaintop camp.

Maggie gestured for Christina and her brothers to come with her and walked off through the grass, deliberately heading toward the barn. She refused to look back to see if Granger and Lucas were following her. At the last moment, she turned left and skirted the edge of the old wooden building then came to a stop in the dirt yard next to the hitching rail, facing the cliff's edge around two hundred feet away, deep in the shadow of the coming night.

"Well, I'll be damned," Lucas said, and Maggie felt that momentary frisson of satisfaction once again, knowing that none of the three men had noticed the house, even with the skeleton of the addition out to the front. The gray, weathered barn board the addition was built of had blended into the shadows too well, and the house was built of the same rock as the canyon walls.

Maggie continued walking, keeping an eye out for Houdini, who tended to stalk the barnyard and the area between the chicken coop and the house. It would be just too much if he chose this moment to stage an attack, and she found herself retreating in an undignified scramble.

She didn't have to worry. Houdini and the rest of the chickens had retired to their roosts for the night. Mark ran over and shut the coop door, then went about his assigned chore of collecting the eggs, Daniel following close behind, clearly curious about the process.

The men looked around the front room of the little house built back under the cliff overhang, noting the table and chairs, the wood stove with the chimney leading out of the front wall of the structure, the counter, the sink that had no running water and the four closed doors at the back of the room. In spite of the warmth of the day, the house was cool. The small windows provided little light to the interior of the house, even with the addition of the open door, and Maggie lit a small oil lamp that sat on the old, oak kitchen table. The yellow glow filled the room, chasing the shadows out of the corners and banishing them from the home.

Lucas, rifle held at the ready, strode over to the far left door at the back of the room—Maggie's bedroom—threw it open and looked inside. Granger followed him and peered over the blond man's shoulder. She knew what they saw. Her bedroom contained just some shelves, an old, dilapidated twin bed, and a makeshift cot for Lindy. Lucas threw himself on the bed with a *thump* and a *thwang* of the rusty metal springs.

Oh, ugh! Maggie thought. *I'm going to have to burn everything.* The bed was old, and the mattress was lumpy and uncomfortable, and she'd complained about it on a daily basis. Now, however, it felt like a priceless piece of furniture that had been desecrated by Lucas, and she swore she'd never sleep on it again. She must have made a face because she caught Granger's eye and could see he was trying not to laugh.

Lucas rolled out of the bed, then poked through the grayed wooden shelves, throwing Maggie and Lindy's clothes on the floor in his search for what? Weapons? Regardless, she would have to make O'Reilly scavenge the area ranches for clothing or get her some deerskins or something because she was damned if she'd wear clothing that Lucas had pawed through.

Finding nothing more of interest, Lucas stepped back into the kitchen and moved on to the girls' chamber. He spent only a short amount of time in there, rifling through Alysa's and Christina's few possessions. Glancing at Christina, Maggie could tell she was as disgusted by the man's attention to her belongings as Maggie had been. Once again, no weapons or anything else of interest was found, and he walked to the boys' room.

He stepped through the door, and Maggie held her breath. Would he realize that an adult man had been sleeping in that room with the kids, or would he do a casual search and move on.

A few moments later, Lucas emerged from the darkened chamber, looking bored. Maggie blew out her breath and looked quickly around the front room to see if Granger had noticed. His eyes were fixed on Lucas. For a moment, she wondered if she could take him by surprise and grab the rifle, but then discarded the idea. Even if she could wrest the firearm from his grasp, she could see the handgun at his hip. If he or Lucas opened fire in the confined area of the house, she or the kids would surely be injured or killed.

Just thirty-six hours, she told herself. *O'Reilly will be here in thirty-six hours.*

Even with the light from the lantern, the front room of the home was getting darker, which turned the bedrooms from dim to nearly lightless. Maggie had several additional oil lamps, but she wasn't about to volunteer their existence to the invaders. The sleeping chambers of the house, tucked back into the cave-like overhang of the canyon wall, had no windows, so any light that reached them had to come from the front of the house or lanterns and Maggie didn't want to make raiding the camp any easier for them than necessary.

Lucas opened the door to the fourth room and whooped in excitement.

"Look what we got here, Granger! We won't be going hungry this winter, that's for sure." Lucas came out carrying a jar of beans and a package of venison jerky. "They've got tons of food put up, and with the eggs and milk, we're going to be living high on the hog!"

Maggie thought back to O'Reilly warning her just a week ago that they still needed more food put up for the coming winter, and she wondered whether O'Reilly was being overly careful or whether Lucas was delusional.

Yeah, Lucas was delusional, Maggie decided. She had always thought O'Reilly was a bit of a slave driver when it came to preparing food for the winter, but when she thought about the ghost's camp and the pitiful garden they had put in, she figured she'd put her faith in O'Reilly every time.

The door behind her opened, and when she turned, she saw Mark carrying a plastic bucket full of multi-colored eggs. Alysa was behind with the milk, and Daniel was bringing up the rear. Lucas looked at what they were carrying, sat at the kitchen table, leaned back and put his feet up on the wooden surface.

"Guess you're cooking, Ms. Langton," he said. "I like my eggs sunny side over."

36

Daylight was quickly disappearing as O'Reilly and his companions made their way down the narrow trail that switchbacked into Adobe Canyon, the horses trailing after their riders. O'Reilly had questioned the wisdom of taking the geldings into the canyon instead of leaving them tied on the rim or turned loose to fend for themselves. Eventually, however, he decided that abandoning their best means of rapid transportation would be a mistake.

O'Reilly was convinced that Lucas and Granger were at Hideaway. He had heard only one shot since the original bursts of gunfire earlier that afternoon. This time the sound seemed to come from ahead and to the right, just where the camp would be located in the canyon. Not knowing the target of that one shot was chewing at his gut, but when they came to the top of the trail, he hesitated. If the men had posted a lookout, a rider coming down the trail on horseback would be a large target, but if they were in the camp, it wouldn't matter. Still, it wouldn't hurt to make the bull's-eye on their chests a little smaller.

Dammit, he thought, clenching his hand around the horse's reins as they made their way down the trail. The horse behind him ducked its head and carefully placed its feet, occasionally kicking up a rock that rattled off down the steep side. O'Reilly scanned the canyon in front of him. He scrutinized the shadows, looking for something in the darkness that didn't belong.

He hated the not knowing. They were so close, and yet he felt farther away somehow than he had when chasing tracks in the dust toward Seligman. He didn't know if Maggie or the kids were safe in the caves. He didn't know if any of them had been shot. He didn't know where the men were holed up. All he had to go on was the knowledge of what he would do if he were in the same situation. Unfortunately, if Andy were to be believed, at least one of the three men they were chasing was a bat crap crazy lunatic, and O'Reilly didn't possess the mental agility to think like that kind of sociopath.

The three made it to the bottom of the canyon without becoming the recipients of bullets from unseen assailants, and O'Reilly breathed a sigh of relief when he reached the rock-strewn canyon floor. He glanced at the sky. Not long until dark.

Rickards led Jimmy up beside him and nodded toward the south, in the direction of the camp.

"What's the plan, O'Reilly?"

"We're going to leave the horses here. There's a good spot to tie them back that way, up a little fork in the canyon. Andy, you're going to stay with them."

"No, I'm not!" the boy blurted, to O'Reilly's surprise. Throughout the entire day, Andy had done everything O'Reilly said without much complaint, and it annoyed him that now they were this close to their quarry, Andy was balking.

"Danny's there. He doesn't know I'm alive. He'd of never left if he knew I was alive, so he can't know," Andy said, his heated tones changing to ones of urgent persuasion.

"If Danny sees me, and knows I'm with you, he won't attack. That's one less you have to worry about. Granger, he's always been a good guy. He's protected us from Lucas, so Granger won't shoot at me either. I know it." Andy sounded so positive O'Reilly was almost convinced.

"How will they know you're not a hostage?" Rickards asked, his voice low and neutral. "I agree they may try to avoid injuring you, but if they think O'Reilly and I are holding you in order to force their cooperation, it could actually put us in greater danger."

"Easy." Andy's voice was so scornful it made O'Reilly smile, even though Rickards had a point. "I got a gun. There's no way you'd let someone you had as a hostage carry a gun, so of course I can't be a hostage."

O'Reilly felt foolish. Yes, Andy had a gun, and if he was right, he was safe from Daniel and Granger, and the boy's presence might mean O'Reilly and Rickards were safe from them as well, but what about Lucas?

Andy must have read O'Reilly's mind because he went on to say, "Lucas is as crazy as a bug sprayed cockroach. He sees enemies and conspiracies everywhere. Some of the others even believed him, but not me and Danny, and not Granger. Still, I don't think Lucas would hesitate to take out anyone 'cept maybe Granger. No one's safe 'round him."

O'Reilly looked at Rickards in the rapidly waning light. Rickards looked back at him and shrugged.

"You're the leader of the posse, O'Reilly. What you say goes," Rickards said. His voice was noncommittal, giving O'Reilly no idea what the man actually thought.

After a moment, O'Reilly nodded.

"All right, Andy, you're with us, but you are to do exactly what I say when I say it, understand? I don't want you getting shot because you run out and get between me and this Lucas guy just because you see your brother." O'Reilly gave Andy a stern look, and the boy nodded his head so vigorously that O'Reilly worried his neck would snap.

"The horses stay here, though, hidden in the branch canyon. We'll leave them tied and saddled in case the men make a run for it and we need to go after them." He felt a moment's hesitation, knowing both geldings were pretty much worn out, but he didn't have a choice. There was no knowing if the other geldings were still in the pasture, or whether they could reach them without being caught.

Fifteen minutes later, the group reached the last bend in the canyon before entering the home pasture. Although the light was fleeing rapidly, he had been able to pick up footprints in several sandier locations, especially when the trail had crossed or moved closer to the stream. The majority were larger sizes. Men's boots, he thought. He picked up a drag mark several times, which seemed to indicate that at least one of the men was injured. He saw no sign of Maggie's smaller footprints, but they may have been obliterated by her followers.

O'Reilly crept around the outcropping of rock, rifle ready. If the men were down by the barn, they wouldn't be able to see him at this distance and in the dim light. However, if they were at the caves, they might be close. O'Reilly scanned the pasture to his right. The gate was open, but he didn't see any other signs of intrusion. There was nothing, other than one of the cows—it looked like Emily—dozing and chewing her cud. Her calf was butting at her udder and making soft slurping sounds. Neither seemed agitated. Several other cows stood nearby. Two of them lifted their heads and eyed O'Reilly as if assessing the threat level.

The men must not be close, O'Reilly thought. These cows were fairly gentle and used to humans, but even they would be snorty if strangers who were shooting guns were in close vicinity. Just to be safe, he examined the scree that led to the entry to the caves. No sign of intruders.

He stepped back around the outcropping and turned to Rickards.

"This end's clear. If we skirt the east side of the pasture, there's more brush for cover."

"Was there any movement at the south end?" Rickards asked. He didn't whisper, but his voice was low.

"None that I could see," O'Reilly answered. "It's not dark enough yet to determine if there's light in the house, and I'm not sure I could tell from this angle anyway."

"Your call, O'Reilly."

O'Reilly nodded, then led Rickards and Andy out around the rock outcropping. The gate to the pasture was laying on the ground, which made sense, he thought. When the castle is stormed by the ravening hoards, they usually don't close the front door after them. This time he let it stay down. If the cows and horses got out, he'd just have to hunt them down later. He didn't want Lucas or Granger to see the gate closed when they'd left it open, and realize that someone else must be in the camp.

He scanned the dark canyon floor again. The cows had become indistinct lumps, although he could still hear them as they ripped tufts of grass from the ground or chewed rhythmically. And he could smell them, a strong, musky, grassy odor that spoke to him of his childhood and now his life in the camp. It was soothing, and he took strength in it.

He nodded to Rickards and Andy and chinned toward the meadow. O'Reilly started into the pasture, then stopped with a jerk. Something was laying in the grass not far away. He gestured for the man and the boy following him to wait and jogged over to the white patch on the ground. His heart sank as he saw Gypsy laying on her side, a trickle of blood staining the fur of her face. He thought for an instant she was dead, then saw her blue and brown eye roll toward him, and she started to pant. She struggled to rise but couldn't, and he worried that her neck or back had been broken. He didn't want her to suffer, but he also couldn't risk a shot alerting the people in the house.

O'Reilly felt for his hunting knife. It might be the best way. He ran his hand over the dog's face and under her head. Then he stopped, and relief flooded his body. Maggie had never removed the collars from the dogs when she rescued them from an empty neighbor's house before leaving for the camp. The canyon floor in this meadow was mostly grass, but there were areas where large, flat rocks remained visible. It appeared that Gypsy had been struck and injured, and when she fell, it was near one of these flat stone plates. The tags on her collar had become wedged into a crack which was wide at the edge of the rock, but narrowed several inches toward the middle. He'd heard of dogs getting tags caught into floor heater vents, but never something like this. He took the knife and sliced through the collar. Gypsy struggled to her feet and stood unsteadily on three legs.

O'Reilly walked back to where Rickards and Andy were watching him. Gypsy followed behind haltingly as she avoided putting her left front paw to the ground.

"You picked up some reinforcements?" Rickards asked in wry tones, gesturing toward the injured dog while Andy seemed entranced.

"Yeah," O'Reilly said, but nothing more. He didn't mention that Gypsy would never leave Lindy willingly. If the dog was out here in the middle of the pasture, it meant Lindy had been nearby, probably being taken to the caves. It also meant whoever was carrying the little girl had almost certainly been captured. There was no way Gypsy would have been so far away from her idol that she could have been struck and injured while the person with Lindy made it to the caves safely.

Was that person Maggie? Why weren't Lindy and the rest of the children already safely in the hidden cave? O'Reilly started to readjust his estimate of timing and wondered with a tremor of dread what else he would be wrong about before the night was over.

O'Reilly moved stealthily along the bank of the creek and through the shrubs and grass that grew there. Rickards wasn't as silent, and O'Reilly cringed several times as the man tripped over an unseen boulder. Andy, who was bringing up the rear with Gypsy, made O'Reilly grateful for the running water and the cows in the meadow because maybe, just maybe, if the men had posted a sentry, they would mistake the noise for one of the nearby bovines. Or an elephant that had gotten lost from a zoo.

Fortunately, it appeared Lucas and Granger felt secure in their escape from the exorcism team and hadn't posted a lookout. It didn't take long for the three to skirt the home pasture and reach a spot just above what the boys called the swimming hole. The barn was blocking him from seeing the house, but it was also blocking anyone in the house from seeing *him*. He left the cover of the brush that had grown up along the banks of the stream and ran to the barn. Moving slowly, he walked along the wall and peered around the corner.

No one was in sight. A soft, yellow glow in the tiny windows of the stone house let him know someone was inside, and he prayed those someones included Maggie and the children. O'Reilly turned back and signaled for Rickards and Andy to come. It was nearly dark, but Rickards saw his motion and ran across the open land, followed closely by Andy and the injured dog. A bark from inside the barn told O'Reilly that Jack was probably locked in the tack room or a stall.

"Update?" Rickards asked.

"They're in the house," O'Reilly answered. "At least I hope they're all in there. I haven't been eyes on yet."

"Next steps?" Rickards asked again. O'Reilly couldn't help but smile. He had to appreciate Rickards' brevity. Over the past few months working with Maggie Langton, he'd had to explain everything and had all of his actions and decisions questioned to exhaustion.

"We need to get a look inside," O'Reilly answered. "I'm going to try to get near the windows and check the front room. It's dark enough now that as long as I stay out of the direct light from the window they shouldn't see me. You and Andy stay here."

Rickards nodded and turned to let Andy know what O'Reilly was going to do.

O'Reilly ran on an oblique line to the house, reaching the cliff wall just to the left of the stone structure. He studied the front of the rock house. Two dull yellow shafts of light spilled from the windows, and he could hear muffled voices from inside the thick walls. By his count, there would be ten people inside, and he wondered how they all fit in the tiny room without stacking them in the corner like firewood.

He took several steps back from the cliff and moved toward the window until he could catch a glimpse of the front room of the home. He could only see the large wooden table and the right side of the room from this vantage point, but it was enough to show him the two men who had kidnapped Maggie—Granger and Lucas, according to Andy, although he didn't know which was which. They were sitting at the table, eating. One man, a blond with an unkempt beard and wild hair, had a thick, bloodstained bandage on his cheek. O'Reilly remembered the blood on the spike and wondered if this was the man Maggie had injured. From the looks of him, if it was, Maggie was lucky she was still alive.

He could just see Christina and her brothers crowded back against the wall. He could also see the hands of another person who appeared to be sitting at the other side of the table and thought it likely it was Andy's brother Daniel.

O'Reilly also saw guns. The blond man had a rifle next to him on the table—an assault-style rifle from what he could see, although the angle made it difficult to tell. The other man was armed as well, with a handgun sitting on the table and a rifle next to him.

The sight confirmed O'Reilly's gut feeling that if he and Rickards tried to attack the men now, in that narrow, confined space, even if they rushed the front door to take the men by surprise, the chances of Maggie and the children surviving were next to nothing.

As he watched and debated the best move, the blond man with the bandaged face rose, picked up his rifle, and headed for the front door. O'Reilly stepped back into the deep shadows and forced himself to breathe slowly and calmly. He heard the man say something, then the door opened, and Lucas, if this *was* Lucas, stepped out. He paused for a second, examining the darkened barnyard, and O'Reilly looked toward the ground so that no light would glint off his eyes, and counted on the gloom to hide him. Apparently satisfied, the man walked over to the corner of the new addition to the house. O'Reilly heard the unmistakable sound of a zipper being pulled down and then water splashing onto the wood structure and hard packed earth below.

Maggie is going to make me burn the addition and start over if she finds out, he thought. The man's actions gave him an idea, however. If he waited near the outhouse, maybe he could get word to Maggie that he was there and to be ready if something happened.

As quickly as the idea came, he discarded it. There was no way these men would allow Maggie or the older girls to go to the outhouse unguarded. No, when he and Rickards made their attack, it would have to be out in the open, and he would have to count on Maggie thinking clearly and responding.

O'Reilly made his way back to the barn where Rickards and Andy were waiting.

"What do you think?" Rickards asked. O'Reilly had always admired the man's ability to remain calm under fire, and today was no different. He was happy that this time Rickards' controlled and clear mind was on his side instead of focused on hunting O'Reilly down to take him back to the APZ.

"I couldn't see the whole room, but it looks like they're all there," O'Reilly said. He looked down at Andy, who was cradling his rifle in his arms and nearly bouncing on the balls of his feet. "Could you see the man who came out to take a leak?"

"Yeah, that looked like Lucas. He's got that light colored hair and crazy mountain man beard," Andy said.

"He's the one you said was crazy?" O'Reilly asked, trying to get the men straight in his mind. If Andy were to be believed, Lucas was the one they had to worry about, and Granger might be open to negotiation.

"Yeah, Lucas is nuttier than a squirrel turd."

O'Reilly choked and nearly started coughing at the boy's use of the unfamiliar but entirely appropriate description. Where the heck did this kid get these sayings that seemed so totally out of place in his twelve-year-old lexicon? He prayed no one came out to use the outhouse at that moment.

"You okay?" Rickards hissed, grabbing O'Reilly's shoulder. He could see the captain studying the front of the house. The captain clearly felt the same concern that one of the kidnappers would come out at that moment and hear the noise.

"Yeah," O'Reilly said, his voice even hoarser and more gravelly than usual. He cleared his throat and went on. "Okay, both men are sitting in there at the table with their weapons close at hand. I don't see any option but to wait until morning when everyone comes out for the day and attack then."

"Because that worked so well for me the last couple of times I've tried it?" Rickards said. O'Reilly didn't know the man's voice could get any dryer. Then he remembered the last time the captain staged a surprise attack on this house. To say it didn't go as planned was an understatement with Houdini interrupting the stake out, causing one officer to shoot another.

A yip from his feet caused him to look down at the ghostly shape of Gypsy. She was focused on the front door of the house. As O'Reilly watched, the door opened, and a figure appeared, outlined by the yellow glow from the room behind. Enough of the light fell on the individual's face before he stepped up to fill the doorway so that O'Reilly could see the features of a young man with longer dark hair. The door closed, and the figure passed in front of the window to the right of the door as the boy started for the outhouse.

Andy let out a gasp, then took off at a run before O'Reilly could grab him. Rickards made a grab for the dog's ruff as she moved to go after the boy.

"Aw, sh . . ., "O'Reilly began as the young boy threw himself at his brother, tackling him in a huge hug. O'Reilly started to go after them, knowing if Daniel made a sound and Andy was found, the discovery of O'Reilly and Rickards wasn't far behind. Lucas might be nuttier than a squirrel turd, as Andy said, but he'd never believe the boy had been able to follow them this far and this fast without help.

"Wait!" Rickards hissed.

Daniel yelped in surprise, then realized who it was, bent and hugged the younger boy in return. Just as he stood up, the front door of the house was yanked open, and Lucas appeared, long wild hair silhouetted in the light from the lamp.

"What's going on?" the man snapped, starting out onto the packed dirt area Maggie called the patio.

Daniel apparently recognized the danger of letting Lucas and Granger know of Andy's existence called out, "I tripped on a rock and fell. Sorry!"

Lucas, apparently satisfied with Daniel's answer, turned back into the house, grumbling something O'Reilly couldn't understand, and closed the door.

Andy grabbed Daniel's hand and dragged the older boy across the barnyard toward O'Reilly and Rickards. O'Reilly's heart sank. What if Daniel was totally on Team Granger? He couldn't let him go back in if he was going to tell the men that O'Reilly and Rickards were waiting out here for them. But if the boy didn't return within a reasonable amount of time, they would come out looking for him. They might think he took off. But why now, when they were safe in the camp instead of any other time during their escape from the mountain?

O'Reilly's thoughts were cut off as Andy came around the corner with Daniel, who stopped in surprise.

"Danny, these are the men who saved me," Andy said in an excited whisper, and O'Reilly was grateful the boy remembered to keep his voice low. "This place is O'Reilly's camp. That's him." Andy chinned toward O'Reilly in the dim light.

There was nothing for it, and O'Reilly put out his hand to take Daniel's surprised palm and give it a quick shake. *I was right before. This whole evening . . . hell, the whole last two days has become a farce. I feel like I'm going to wake up any moment and find out last night's* chile rellenos *have affected my dreams.*

"I'm Jim O'Reilly, and this here is Captain Seth Rickards," O'Reilly whispered. "We're not here to hurt you. Maggie Langton is my . . ." he stumbled to a stop again, not sure what to say. Maggie wasn't his wife, or his girlfriend, even, although he was hoping something was developing, but she wasn't just a roommate either. What the hell was she? ". . . my friend and I take care of her and the children." God, Maggie would kill him if she heard him say that! She was not one of those women who needed a man to take care of her. *Hopefully, she'll never find out,* he thought. He looked around the corner of the barn toward the house. Time was running out.

"These are good guys, Danny. Way better than Lucas. Maybe even some better than Granger."

O'Reilly felt a little thrill of pride at being labeled "some better than Granger."

"Is everyone safe inside?" Rickards asked, getting straight to the point. They needed to wait until morning, when everyone came outside, to have a chance of keeping Maggie and the others alive, but if they were in danger now, he and O'Reilly might have to take the chance and break in immediately.

"Yeah. They're safe. Granger, he won't let Lucas hurt any of them." The eerie glow from the three-quarter moon made the boy's features almost indistinguishable, but his voice sounded shocked. Then he cleared his voice and continued. "Granger says he has a deal with Lucas where Lucas can't rape any women or hurt any children. Lucas sticks to it even though he's . . ." The boy hesitated.

"Nuttier than a squirrel turd?" O'Reilly filled in, enjoying the newly learned phrase.

White teeth flashed in the faint light. "Yeah. That." He turned and looked back at Andy. "I never would have left you if I'd known, Andy. You've got to know that."

"I know," Andy said happily. "I told them that. I told them Lucas must of told you I was dead."

"Yeah, he did."

Now O'Reilly could hear the cold anger in the older boy's voice, and he put out a hand and placed it on Daniel's shoulder.

"We need you to go back in and act like nothing has happened. Can you do that?" O'Reilly asked. He hoped that the urgency in his voice got through to the boy.

"Yes, sir. But . . ."

"When the men come out in the morning, we'll have a better chance of getting them without anyone else getting hurt. If you can encourage Maggie to bring the kids out early to do chores? Maybe say you'll watch them? Just something that gets them separated a bit from Lucas and Granger would help us out a lot," O'Reilly explained. He hoped the boy was up to the task.

"But, Granger, he was good to us. Without him we never would have gotten out of Phoenix," Daniel said, uneasiness and doubt clear in his voice.

"We'll do our best not to involve Granger," said Rickards, although O'Reilly knew the odds were not in the man's favor. He had, after all, participated in the abduction of Maggie.

"Okay," Daniel looked around the corner toward the door, obviously thinking he'd been out too long.

"Go on then, we . . ." O'Reilly started when he heard the creak of the front door opening. He gave Daniel a shove, and with one look back, the boy jogged across the open area between the barn and the house.

"Where have you been," said the figure in sharp tones. O'Reilly thought it was Granger, but he wasn't sure. He couldn't tell if the figure had a beard or wild hair, but the voice didn't sound like the one he'd heard earlier. It wasn't angry. More like the man was worried instead of annoyed.

"I thought I heard something over by the barn so I went to check, Ethan," said Daniel. O'Reilly's heart sank. Great! All they needed was for the man to come over and investigate some suspicious noise.

"Did you find anything?" the man asked, now simply curious. O'Reilly had to remind himself that Granger and Lucas had no idea O'Reilly even existed and no reason to suspect they were being chased, let alone that someone was waiting for them in the darkness.

"Nah," said Daniel, "It was just the dog, I think."

At that moment, Gypsy let out a frustrated bark which bolstered the boy's statement.

"Doesn't like being locked in the barn." Daniel pushed past the figure in the door and reentered the house. The man closed the door, appearing satisfied with the boy's explanation.

37

Granger looked at the plate Maggie Langton slapped down in front of him, chunks of yellow scrambled egg bouncing off and falling on the table. She chunked another plate down in front of Lucas and glared at the two men as if daring them to complain.

Granger examined the meal, took a deep breath and relaxed in pleasure. He'd been eating canned, dehydrated and freeze dried food for so long he'd forgotten what truly fresh food smelled and tasted like. Sure, they'd had fresh meat, but nothing except meat got pretty old after a while.

Langton had made a large batch of scrambled eggs with fresh vegetables and small chunks of venison jerky. He couldn't remember the last time he'd had fresh eggs. As his band had wandered northwestern Arizona, scavenging the homesteads and ranches, they'd found the remainders of many chicken flocks. Unfortunately, most had either died, locked into coops without food or water, or been decimated by wildlife.

On rare occasions, they found a few hens that had avoided the raccoons, skunks, coyotes, lions and other creatures that saw loose chickens as a welcome addition to the menu. These hens had been feral, wily . . . and delicious.

The two older girls had helped Langton with the cooking and had made sure the younger children were fed. Granger watched the strawberry blonde child follow the woman around. She reminded him of his older daughter when she was a baby. Once, when the toddler moved near him, he held out his hands to her, but she shied away. Langton noticed, scowled at him, picked up the child and carried her over to the oldest of the boys.

Granger felt embarrassed but tried to hide it from the woman and the girls. This was his and Lucas's camp now. Langton would just have to get used to it.

"I want a drink," Lucas said. He eyed the girls. "Don't tell me that you have nothing in your pantry that's worth drinking. You've got everything else." Lucas started to push himself up from his chair and walk over to the pantry.

"You won't find anything," Maggie Langton said, biting off her words.

As Granger expected, Lucas didn't listen and went to the storeroom regardless of what the Langton woman said. She watched him for a moment, then returned to picking up the dirty dishes.

"Christina, would you and Alysa go get water for washing?" she said, and the two older girls started to head for the door.

"Wait," Granger snapped. He looked at the dark night past the windows. "Where are they going?"

"There's a storage tank at the windmill. They'll get water from there." Langton sounded annoyed, and Granger supposed she had a right to be, but there was something in her voice, too. Something that didn't make him trust her.

He got up and limped over to the counter where she had stacked the dishes she'd been using to prepare the meal. At the end toward the front wall of the house was an old enameled cast iron sink, its drainage pipe leading into a five-gallon bucket. Next to it sat another pail. When he looked inside, he found it full of clear water. He looked back at Maggie Langton, and she met his eyes. Challenging.

"I think we'll let the dishes go for the night," Granger said, his voice mild. Langton hesitated, then nodded and turned toward the children.

"Okay, guys, let's . . ." she started.

A crash emerged from the pantry, followed by a string of curses.

"You haven't got a damned thing to drink in here," Lucas said, emerging from the small door. The two girls, Christina and Alysa, Langton called them, retreated to the wall next to the boys. The two who were clearly twins leaned into the brown haired girl, and she put her arms around their shoulders.

Lucas returned to his seat at the table, setting his rifle beside him on its wooden surface. Granger returned to his seat as well, and an uncomfortable silence fell on the room. Finally, Lucas pushed himself back to his feet, picked up the rifle and headed for the front door.

"Where's the outhouse?"

"Over to the left of the addition," Langton said. "Don't fall in," she added in mocking tones.

Lucas looked over his shoulder. "You know, you could be a lot nicer. You need a man here." He looked around the room, staring pointedly at the two adolescent girls. "You all need a man here."

"Lucas, drop it," Granger snapped.

Lucas didn't answer, just opened the front door and left.

Maggie Langton looked at Granger. "Why are you putting up with him. I know you said you owed him, but really, he's a loose cannon waiting to go off." She glanced at the girls and closed her mouth tight, her lips thinning as she bit down on her words.

Granger understood, and he sympathized. Daniel might be accustomed to Lucas and his ways, but these children were not, and Lucas's comments could be disturbing.

"I won't let him touch you or . . .," Granger started, but Langton brought her hand down in an abrupt chop, hitting the table with a bang, and he realized she didn't want to discuss Lucas's comments in front of the girls. He stopped, mouth hanging open. Daniel looked up at him with surprise, then looked over at Langton. Granger wasn't sure how much Daniel had been listening to what was being said, lost as he was in the grief of losing Andy, but the sudden end to the conversation had reached through the misery.

The door opened again, and Lucas reentered. This time instead of sitting back down, he walked around the room, pausing to look at the bookshelves. Then he walked over toward the two teenagers, where they stood with the younger children. For a moment he paused and examined them, looking up and down and nodding. Granger could see the brown-haired girl's expressions war between fear and anger. The other girl had more rigid control of her features, and it was hard for him to tell what she was thinking.

What Maggie Langton was thinking was clear, however. She stormed over to Lucas, and Granger thought she was going to attack him again. He rose quickly and stepped in front of her.

"Lucas! Leave the kids alone. Come on and sit down." Granger snapped.

Lucas looked Granger over and gestured toward his leg. "Looks like you need to sit down yourself, Granger. Before you fall down."

"Let me worry about my leg," Granger said, although he privately acknowledged that his thigh was stiffening and throbbing. He limped back to his chair and eased himself back into the seat. Lucas, having decided it was no longer worth irritating Langton or scaring the children, followed him, set his rifle on the table and dropped onto the chair. The old wood groaned at the sudden introduction of his weight.

Daniel, who had been watching the interaction with a frown on his face, pushed his chair back with a clatter.

"I need to go out," he said and grabbed his rifle. He stumbled for the door. Granger half raised himself from the chair again, but Daniel, standing in the open doorway turned toward him.

"I'll be right back," Daniel said, his voice strangled with emotion. Granger heard worlds below those simple words, but he allowed the boy to go.

One of the twins yawned—a giant, jaw breaking yawn— which triggered yawns from the rest of the children. Even Granger felt a yawn fighting his body, trying to break out, and eventually winning. In the end, he noticed that the only person in the room who hadn't caught the yawn was Lucas. He remembered seeing some article or tv news report that said those individuals who ranked high as psychopaths tended to be insusceptible to contagious yawns. He looked at Lucas from the corner of his eye. Maggie Langton had described Lucas as a sociopath. He wasn't sure if the terms were interchangeable. He didn't think so—quite. He'd tried to dismiss her comment, but after the last forty-eight hours, he was pretty sure she was right.

Lucas pushed himself back to his feet abruptly. *Why can't the man sit still for a moment? He should be just as tired as I am after the last twenty hours or so.* Granger thought back and realized Lucas had always been fidgety, but they were usually outside, with other people around, and there was plenty to do. Now, in this enclosed area, it became more obvious—and irritating. Or maybe they were just all exhausted.

Apparently, Lucas was thinking along the same lines as, without a word, he walked over to the first door on the left. The room that had appeared to be Langton's. Lucas looked over at the woman and gave her a sardonic smile. Then he looked back at Granger with the same smile, the white, blood-stained bandage on his cheek twisting his features.

"Put the woman and kids in the third room. It's got the most beds. Make sure you tie that door shut so they don't get out." He pulled the door shut behind him, and Granger could hear the bed creak as he lay down.

Granger looked at Langton and shrugged. "You heard the man. Everyone in the room."

"There are seven of us, and only four beds," she protested.

"You telling me you want to share with Lucas? I'm going to warn you, he snores," Granger said, knowing that her protests were shallow, more out of habit than anything. He was also sure that she knew there was no way Lucas, or Granger for that matter, would be willing to sleep uncomfortably out in the main room while all of the regular occupants of the house were comfortable in their own beds, and that there was no way they were going to be allowed to wander free during the night.

He fished a bucket out from under the sink and handed it to her. She snatched it from his hand, spun on her heel and herded the children into the third room. She turned and pulled the door shut. He limped over and shoved one of the straight, wood-backed chairs under the knob. He tested it. The legs of the chair caught and jammed on the uneven concrete and stone surface, keeping the door securely shut. Even if somehow she was able to break free, they would easily hear her in time, and the consequences would not be pleasant.

Granger took a deep breath and walked haltingly over to the door. Daniel had been outside a long time, and Granger was growing worried about the boy's mental state. He pulled the door open and peered out into the night. No sign of Daniel.

Granger had just decided he was going to have to go look for the boy, in spite of the pain in his leg, when Daniel came jogging over from across the barnyard, not from the direction of the outhouse.

"Where have you been," Granger asked, relieved to see Daniel unharmed but annoyed he'd taken so long and had nearly made Granger come looking for him.

"I thought I heard something over by the barn so I went to check, Ethan," Daniel said, gesturing with his arm back toward the looming dark shape of the old wooden building.

"Did you find anything?" Granger asked. Maybe one of the cows was out, or a mountain lion had come down to drink from the creek, or a raccoon was hunting for some eggs of its own.

"Nah," said Daniel, "It was just the dog, I think."

A bark sounded from the direction of the barn. Just a single sound of frustration. Granger thought briefly of the dog they'd left injured in the pasture and wondered if it was still alive. They'd never had dogs with the group. Lucas didn't seem to get along with them, or they him. Besides, with the struggle of feeding the people of the group, no one wanted to add any additional mouths to feed without reason.

"Doesn't like being locked in the barn," Daniel said and pushed inside the house. Granger stepped back and pulled the door shut. Maybe it would be good for Daniel to have a dog here, although it already belonged to Langton's kids. *Where did she get so many kids?* he wondered briefly, but another yawn banished the thought from his mind.

He looked at the door and saw no locks, then supposed it didn't matter. No reason out here to lock the house, and he turned back into the room.

"Looks like you and I are roommates, Daniel. We're in the second room there." Granger pointed at the one door still open. He picked up the oil lamp and followed the boy into the chamber.

38

Maggie lay on O'Reilly's bed, smelling him on the coarse cotton covering of the pillow. Lindy was cuddled close, and she prayed the little girl was far enough along in her potty training that she didn't pee, either on her or on O'Reilly's bed. That thought led to others of O'Reilly— wondering where he was, what he would do when he reached them. Maybe thirty hours left until he could have followed her back to camp. She just had to keep everyone safe for thirty more hours.

The sounds of soft, slow breathing told her the children were all asleep. There were only two bunk beds in the room, resulting in four beds total. Typically each male member of the household had a bed. O'Reilly's desire to discontinue sharing a bedroom with three young boys was only part of the reason why he was working on the addition to the house. Maggie knew his desire to possibly have a new roommate was the rest of the reason.

Tonight Nick, Ryan and Mark had tripled up in Nick's bed while Christina and Alysa each took a top bunk. Maggie had forbidden the boys from taking one of the upper beds amid many complaints since she figured one or more of them would fall out of the crowded bunk in the middle of the night. She did not want to deal with a broken arm or leg due to a fall on top of everything else.

Thirty hours, Maggie thought again, using it as a mantra, and she drifted off to sleep.

Houdini's crow filtered through Maggie's foggy mind. A crash and yelled curse, muffled by the thick stone walls, reached her ears, and she smiled. No light reached the depths of the room, and knowing the rooster, she was pretty sure the sun wasn't even near the horizon yet. Besides, even if she wanted to get up, there was nowhere to go since she was locked in. The door of the room where Granger and Daniel were sleeping crashed open, followed by the front door. She heard a squawk, and the front door slammed closed again. She hoped Houdini was okay. Another crow at a distance attested to the rooster's continued health. Maggie buried a smile in Lindy's hair. The house fell silent once again, and Maggie floated back down into her dreams.

Maggie jerked awake an unknown time later when Daniel pushed the door open. The faint light from the outer room told her morning had come. *Twenty-seven hours* she told herself as she untangled herself from the blanket, sat and picked up Lindy. The other children were shoving back their own covers and swinging legs out of bed. Bare feet smacked the floor.

Maggie hurt. She didn't know she could hurt so badly and still stand upright. Then she realized she was still sitting. Maybe she *couldn't* stand upright. Maggie groaned and pushed herself off the bed.

Yep, upright. Still hurts, but upright.

"Come on," Daniel said. His voice was low, but there was a strange degree of urgency in it and that confused her. At least he sounded as if he'd emerged from his crippling grief to some degree.

The boys pulled on their jeans, shirts and boots. The noise they were making seemed to make Daniel nervous, and he looked back out into the main room, then said, "Shhh! You need to be quiet. Granger and Lucas are still sleeping, and you don't want to wake up Lucas!"

The boys quieted a little bit, but they looked at Maggie with some confusion. Maggie was studying Daniel as well.

"I just thought we ought to go out and get the chores done. There are morning chores right?" Daniel said. He seemed wound tight this morning. Alysa climbed down from the bunk positioned above the bed the boys had vacated moments before. She'd slept in her clothes, as had Christina and Maggie, so didn't need time to get ready, and seemed eager to get out of the room.

"Yes, there are morning chores, but what's the rush?" Maggie asked.

"I've just never lived on a farm before. I want to learn the chores." Daniel kept looking over his shoulder, and Maggie tried to look around him to see if Granger had come out, or Lucas. Daniel had his rifle slung over his shoulder, which in itself was strange. The day before, all three of the men had kept their weapons in their hands and at the ready.

Maggie's confusion was growing, and that confusion made her nervous and a little irritable. There was no reason she could see, however, for not letting the kids go with Daniel. He'd seemed like a nice boy, and he'd taken good care of Andy. She was glad to see him looking happier, even though he'd been with Granger and Lucas when she was captured. He'd just never seemed like his heart was in her abduction.

"Go ahead. Get Lizzie milked. We were late collecting eggs yesterday, so there probably won't be anything, but you might as well check," Maggie said, marshaling the troops for the day's work. "Did you water the garden while w—ah, um I . . ." Maggie stopped herself and coughed to cover her mistake. "While I was gone?" she ended, hoping Daniel didn't pick up that she almost said "we." If Granger and Lucas found out about O'Reilly, they would be ready for him when he arrived. *Twenty-seven hours.*

"Yes," said Mark. "Christina and Alysa were real slave drivers."

Christina cuffed him on the shoulder while Nick and Ryan giggled.

Maggie smiled at the interaction and felt some of her tension melting away. She turned to lift Lindy, and a smell hit her. She frantically patted O'Reilly's bed where Lindy had been sleeping. Dry, thank goodness. Still, she needed to deal with the mess before she could go join in the morning's chores. She didn't like being alone in the house with Granger and Lucas, but she had no choice.

39

After meeting Daniel the night before, the men and Andy retreated to the barn. O'Reilly was only too familiar with Houdini's schedule, but he figured he and Rickards could get a little sleep before the rooster announced the start of a new day. Rickards took the first watch, with both men agreeing that O'Reilly, since he was more familiar with the ebb and flow of the camp's day, would be the best one to have watching in the morning when everything and everyone started moving.

Rickards had wakened when Houdini announced the coming dawn, even though it was still dark outside. He pulled himself over to the gap in the barn wall where O'Reilly was sitting, watching the front door of the stone house. O'Reilly side-eyed the man. He looked stiff and sore, and O'Reilly wondered if he would be able to fulfill his role today.

"Any movement other than that animated escapee from a stew pot?" Rickards yawned and scrubbed his darkly beard-stubbled face with his arm.

"Yeah, one of the men came out and threw a rock at him." O'Reilly shook his head, a twisted smile on his face. "That rooster has to have more lives than a cat."

"I sure haven't missed *him*," Rickards said. His voice made it clear he was again remembering that Houdini's crow had resulted in one of his officers shooting another member of his team not long ago.

"Well, he doesn't grow on you, that's for sure," O'Reilly answered, but he was distracted, staring so hard at the front of the house that he felt like his face would meld to the wood of the barn wall. There hadn't been a whisper of movement since the man had shut the front door after banishing Houdini from the windowsill. It would be about a half hour until dawn started to light the sky. Usually, there would be movement in the house by now, but these weren't normal circumstances, he thought. He settled in for the wait. Houdini crowed again.

O'Reilly looked up at the sound of the front door of the house opening. The three boys spilled out, followed by Christina and then Alysa. Daniel brought up the rear, rifle slung over his shoulder. O'Reilly could tell the boy was nervous. He looked quickly from one side to the other, a frown on his face. O'Reilly felt a surge of adrenaline. *Things are going to get western pretty quick now*, he thought.

"It's starting," O'Reilly hissed to Rickards, who was sitting next to him, dozing off and on. The morning light had increased to the point that O'Reilly could see the man's face. Even with the little bit of sleep they'd managed to catch last night, Rickards looked worn out, with dark circles under his eyes. With a start, O'Reilly realized he probably looked similar—dirty, unkempt, unshaven and exhausted.

When all this is over, I am going to take a bath, shave and sleep for a week or two, he told himself, *and not necessarily in that order. Although Maggie will probably wring my neck if I crawl into my bedroll wearing this much filth.*

He watched the children run across the open packed dirt of the barnyard, followed more slowly by the girls. *Where are Maggie and Lindy?* he thought with rising panic.

Rickards, watching through a neighboring crack in the wall, must have had the same thought.

"Where is Maggie?" he asked, and O'Reilly could hear a concern in the man's voice that matched his own.

"I don't know. Lindy isn't there either."

"Who's Lindy again?" Rickards asked.

"A toddler I found at a nearby ranch with her dying mother. She's only about two so she's almost always with either the girls or Maggie. I didn't see her with the other children when they came out. Did you?" O'Reilly asked.

Rickards grunted, but before he could answer, a flurry of movement at the barn's small single door drew O'Reilly's attention away from the crack. He turned, rose and took two steps before Nick and Ryan, seeing O'Reilly standing by the wall, rushed him, throwing their arms around his waist. Mark was slower but no less enthusiastic.

O'Reilly shushed the boys as they spoke, chattering over each other like water falling over the rocks in the creek. He hugged them in return, then looked over at the girls where they stood with Daniel. Andy, who woke when the noise started, had run over to stand with his brother, and was now watching Nick, Ryan and Mark's excited welcome of O'Reilly with interest.

O'Reilly pushed the boys back, then looked up at Christina and Alysa. He could see a mixture of gladness and fear on their faces. Christina took a hesitant step forward. She was chewing her lip, a frown on her face, but when O'Reilly's gaze met her eyes, her features brightened with a smile.

"Christina, where are Maggie and Lindy?" O'Reilly asked, his voice low.

"Lindy had an accident, and Maggie needed to clean her up, so she's still in the house," Christina answered and she glanced past O'Reilly as if she could see through the rough wooden wall and into the kitchen from her spot in the barn.

"She said she'd be out in a moment," said Alysa. She looked over her shoulder at Daniel and Andy, who were standing hip to hip, watching the reunion.

"O'Reilly, someone's coming out," Rickards said. His voice was intense.

O'Reilly whipped around and rushed over to the wall of the barn. He peered out the crack. The front door of the house had opened, and Maggie stepped out onto the packed dirt that she had designated the patio, Lindy in her arms. He felt a rush of relief.

"Here she is. She's coming now," O'Reilly started, then his heart sank. Immediately behind her was the blond man Andy had called Lucas, armed for bear.

O'Reilly looked at Rickards and said one word, his voice tense. "Go."

The captain nodded and went.

40

Maggie laid the little girl on the bed and unpinned the cloth diaper. *Geeze, I miss disposable diapers or at least plastic training pants,* she thought, pulling away the soggy cloth. When O'Reilly rescued Lindy from the S Lazy V Ranch headquarters, he had brought all the diapers he could find and then later brought back several pairs of plastic pants from his foraging mission to Wikieup. However, a toddler actively playing out in the dirt and grass tended to put holes in them quickly, and duct tape could only do so much. For the last month, they'd been doing things the old, old-fashioned way. She walked out into the kitchen, looking for the stack of clean cloths she'd been using as diapers and paused. It was strange standing in the quiet room, knowing Lucas and Granger were behind the closed doors along the back wall, and she was out here free. Why on earth had Daniel let them out of the room when the men were asleep? It made no sense. For all he knew, she would take off with the kids, and the chase would be on again.

Sure, Daniel had a rifle with him, but he just didn't seem like a killer to her. Maggie stopped mid-motion. Should she try and get the kids to the caves? Was it worth the risk that Daniel would shoot, or one of the men would come out of the house at an inopportune moment and open fire?

She was torn. There was slightly more than a day left before O'Reilly showed up. She was sure of it. If she took the kids now and made a run for it, and one of them got shot because of her action, she'd never forgive herself. Maggie hurried and pinned the clean diaper on the squirming little girl and hoisted the child to her hip.

Bang!

Lucas threw the door to his room open. Maggie spun around, and Lindy shrank back in her arms. The man strode out into the front room.

"What are you doing out here?" he snapped. He hadn't washed up since arriving yesterday, and the blood in his beard and on his shirt had dried to a dark, rusty brown, almost black, and was cracked and flaking.

Without waiting for Maggie to answer, Lucas walked to the empty room where she and the children had slept the night before. Seeing no one inside, he turned back to Maggie again. The cold blue fury in the man's pale eyes froze her, driving her breath from her body. She must have tightened her arms because Lindy whimpered and hid her face in Maggie's neck.

"Where are they?" Lucas exploded. "Where the hell have they gone?"

The door to Christina and Alysa's room flew open, and Granger rushed out into the kitchen, pulling on his shirt.

"What is going on, Lucas?" Granger asked. Confusion and annoyance fought for dominance over his features.

"Daniel's gone and he's taken all those other children with him. They left the woman and the little kid behind." Lucas turned back toward Maggie and Lindy. "Where are they, woman?" The fire in his eyes terrified Maggie, as did the fury she heard in his voice.

"Daniel said he wanted to learn how to do the chores. He came in fifteen or twenty minutes ago," Maggie said, trying to play innocent of any thoughts of escape. She turned toward Granger and said, "I thought he had your permission."

Granger frowned, looked at Lucas and then back at Maggie. "Why would you think he had permission when we wouldn't even leave the door to the room you were in unsecured last night?"

"I don't know," Maggie said. Annoyance was making an appearance in her voice, and she tried to squash it down. "Why else would he have come in? He had his rifle with him. What was I supposed to think?"

"If he said they were doing chores, then they should be out by the barn, right?" Granger asked. He seemed calm, especially in comparison to Lucas.

"Yes, I think so. The cow needs to be milked, and Jenny, the calf, has to be fed."

"Let's go see then," Lucas said, advancing on Maggie, making her step backward. She tripped on one of the rough stones in the floor and nearly fell. Lucas turned and glared at Granger. "That kid better have a good explanation."

Lucas gestured for Maggie to go ahead, and she walked over to the front door. It seemed like she could feel the man's stare on her back, and the hair on her neck tickled. Maggie wondered what would happen if they didn't find the children at the barn. She was a little worried for Daniel's continued health even if they did.

The children weren't in sight as Maggie stepped out onto the patio. She stopped and looked around. The chickens were still locked in the coop—all except Houdini, of course, who was scratching at some bunch grass near the aged, gray wood of the barn wall. He pecked at something, then raised his head and crowed, then ruffled his shining black and white hackle feathers. The rooster scratched a few more times before stalking off toward the coop where his hens were waiting. Lindy struggled to get down, but Maggie clutched the girl to her chest.

Lucas had come out behind her, followed closely by Granger. Both were armed, and Maggie felt as though a feather dropping could cause the barnyard to erupt into violence. Houdini crowed again, and from the corner of her eye, Maggie saw Lucas tense. The scowl deepened the lines carving the portion of his face that wasn't covered by beard or bandage.

I'd shut up if I were you, mate, she thought. She and Houdini had a long standing feud, but she really didn't want to see the rooster blown into a feather snowstorm.

"Daniel!" Granger called. There was no response. No sound of children playing. That was weird by itself, although the arrival of the men had put a damper on the kids' typical exuberance. She couldn't remember a time, though, when she couldn't find them by listening for their voices. The silence was ominous, and she could tell the men felt it too. She wondered if the children had run for the caves but then realized that explanation made no sense because Daniel wouldn't have let them go.

A bang sounded from somewhere near the garden, and everyone turned to look in that direction. Granger started to limp over toward the sound. It was clear his leg had stiffened even more during the night, and watching him was painful. He approached the edge of the old set of alleys the cowboys had used many years ago when one of them had been permanently assigned to the camp. Maggie had never used them, other than one time when she'd needed to try and deliver a calf. The cow ended up doing all the work, Maggie wound up with a much greater respect for large animal veterinarians, and the heavy wooden alleys proved they had been built to last.

Lucas had started to follow Granger when suddenly a man stepped out from around the end of the alley closest to the garden and took Granger by surprise. The man struck Granger hard on the head with his rifle butt, knocking him to the ground and kicked the gun from his hands. Maggie saw Lucas raise his own weapon, and she screamed a warning. The stranger hauled Granger to his feet and held the kidnapper in front of his body so Lucas couldn't shoot without hitting his own partner. Maggie didn't know if Lucas cared enough about Granger to hold his fire, but no shots rang out.

Maggie stared at the man now holding Granger hostage. It felt as though she'd been punched in the gut. Her mind blanked, and the world spun. She couldn't accept what her eyes told her was true. The man was Captain Seth Rickards of the Laughlin Enforcers—the man who had come not long ago with the intention of capturing or killing O'Reilly. There was no possible way Rickards could be there.

Lucas had spun and started to run back toward Maggie and Lindy. She tried to dodge, stumbled and ran out into the barnyard with Lucas close behind.

"Kyle Lucas, stop right there!"

Maggie heard the voice but couldn't grasp what it meant. Lindy was screaming, and Maggie whirled, trying to decide what to do. Where to run. She turned back toward the barn, and there was O'Reilly, rifle to his shoulder.

What the heck! He's more than twenty-four hours early, damned man, Maggie thought confusedly. She opened her mouth to scream at him to watch out for Lucas, but O'Reilly beat her to it.

"Maggie, get out of the way!" he yelled.

Instead of hitting the dirt or dodging to the side, Maggie spun around and saw Lucas approaching from behind her—crouched over, counting on O'Reilly not to risk a shot with the woman so close to the line of fire.

Maggie whipped around again and ran, making it two steps before Lucas grabbed her from behind, jerking her to an abrupt halt. Her arms flew up, and Lindy fell to the ground at her feet. The little girl's screams redoubled as Lucas pulled Maggie backward, left hand tightly fisted in her hair.

41

O'Reilly watched in horror as Maggie was pulled back into Lucas's grip. He'd seen enough insane people in the past to know Lucas was one of the most dangerous of the species. Up until this point, the plan he and Rickards had developed had worked well, minus a few minor hiccups. As soon as the kids arrived, the captain headed out through a side door and skirted the alley on the north end of the barn.

In their discussions the night before, O'Reilly and Rickards had determined the best way to handle things was to split Lucas and Granger up if at all possible. Maggie not coming with the children had thrown a wrench in the works, but O'Reilly had still been hopeful the plan would succeed.

And it had, at least until Maggie got in the way of his shot. Now O'Reilly had a hostage, and Lucas had a hostage. The score was even. He clenched his teeth.

Lindy was shrieking in fear at Maggie's feet, and O'Reilly crouched down, keeping an eye on Lucas. The man had his hand buried in Maggie's hair, and it was keeping him from bringing up his rifle and aiming accurately.

"Lindy, come to me now. Come on, baby," O'Reilly called, mentally urging the toddler to get up and come to him. Lindy continued to cry but pushed herself to her feet, unstable on her chubby legs.

For a moment she didn't move, but then one of the dogs barked from within the barn, and the toddler started for him in an uncoordinated run. When she reached O'Reilly, he scooped her up into his arms. He spun back toward the barn and saw Christina looking out the door.

"Here, take Lindy," he said, thrusting the toddler into the girl's grasp, "and get back in the barn, now!"

He turned back to the barnyard without waiting to see if Christina had followed his command.

42

Maggie stood frozen in place. It felt as though her scalp was going to be ripped from her head. Rolling her eyes to the left, she could see Rickards still holding Granger in front of him as a shield. O'Reilly stood next to the corner of the barn, rifle raised, ready to take any reasonable shot that didn't involve perforating Maggie in the process. They appeared to be at a stalemate.

At least this time Lucas was taken by surprise instead of knowing about the attack before it happened, Maggie thought with a faint thrill of satisfaction. *When you've got an insane sociopath trying to rip your hair off, you've got to take your wins where you can get them,* she thought grimly.

Before.

The word reverberated in her mind, and she remembered her thoughts and questions earlier in the day.

"How did you know the Juniper Mountain camp was going to be attacked that way before the first shot was ever fired?" Maggie blurted out. She didn't anticipate Lucas's violent reaction to her question.

"You shut your mouth!" Lucas snapped, jerked Maggie backward, and let go of her hair, but before she could move, he wrapped his left arm around her throat and tightened. Maggie struggled and rammed her elbows backward, aiming for his stomach. Her left elbow found its target, eliciting an exhalation of foul breath onto the side of her face. Her right elbow, however, missed and struck the rifle instead, hitting it hard enough to cause her arm from elbow to hand to burn and tingle. Her eyes watered. The blow jarred the rifle, twisting it from Lucas's hand, the trigger guard wrenching his fingers. A short burst of gunfire

325

kicked up dirt near the barn. He fumbled but couldn't regain his grip, and the gun hit the ground with a clatter. Growling in frustration, he pulled his hunting knife from a sheath at his waist and brandished it toward Granger and Rickards.

At the gunfire, O'Reilly had started forward again, then stopped when the rifle fell. Maggie saw movement from the corner of the barn and thought her heart would stop. Daniel stood behind O'Reilly, rifle braced against his shoulder but aimed at her and Lucas. Next to him was Andy.

Like a bolt of lightning, she remembered Lucas had told Daniel his younger brother had been shot and killed in the fighting—that his head had been blown off—yet Lucas had entered the barn before any shots had been fired. The entire story was a lie, and Andy was here now.

"You knew!" Maggie said louder. Lucas's arm across her throat tightened, choking her. Her arm was on fire from hitting the rifle. "You knew the exorcism team was there, and you didn't tell anyone. You lied." She could hear hysteria in her voice and tried to control it. "And you lied when you said Andy was dead."

Maggie's statement, made in a raised, raspy voice, reached Granger's ears, and she could see him freeze for a moment, then start to struggle in Rickards' grasp. He looked in the direction of Maggie's stare and saw the boys. Granger slumped briefly, then straightened. Fury infused his face, and for a moment she wondered if he would have a stroke right there in the barnyard and solve one of their problems.

"She's right," Granger yelled from across the packed dirt yard. "You came to get her and me at least five minutes before the first shot was fired. You knew the Enforcers were there, but you didn't warn anyone. You said you'd taken care of it, but you didn't. You left the camp to die. You told us Andy was dead, but you couldn't have known. You left him to die too!" Granger's final words were almost screamed, spit flying from his mouth. Rickards struggled to maintain a hold on the infuriated man. Lucas's arm tightened across Maggie's throat again, and she ripped at it with her hands.

"I saved you!" Lucas screamed back. "I saved you and that punk kid. You owe me. I saved your lives! Again!" Lucas wrapped his right arm across Maggie's middle, knife held to her side, drawing blood through her light shirt. He squeezed even tighter with his left arm and she struggled to draw a breath. Rolling her eyes back toward the barn, she saw O'Reilly, pale, rifle raised. He took several more steps forward as if trying to decide whether he could hit Lucas without injuring Maggie.

To her surprise, the rest of the yard seemed surreally calm. The hens in the chicken coop scratched the dirt and crowded at the door, clucking and fussing as they waited to be let out. Houdini was strutting outside, eyeing Maggie with his typical animosity. He didn't seem bothered by the people yelling at all. Maggie was almost angrier with the rooster at that moment than she was at Lucas and Granger.

"You let our people die! You made me abandon Andy!" Granger screamed back. "I should shoot you myself. You had all those weapons hoarded in the cabin. Weapons we could have used. You had food and you didn't share it with us. Then you didn't even rouse the camp when you knew the Enforcers were in the woods. And you told us that Andy's head had been blown off when you hadn't even been outside during the fighting. How could I have missed it? How could I have been so stupid?" Granger struggled some more, nearly breaking from Rickards' grasp.

"You owe me!" Lucas seemed to have completely lost all grasp of sanity. He tightened his arm again, and Maggie fought, afraid her neck was going to be broken. She saw O'Reilly start forward, rifle sighted, a determined look on his face.

The next instant, the whole world seemed to explode in a cascade of black and white feathers, spurs and the harsh, infuriated screech of Houdini, who had apparently decided Maggie had been in the vicinity of the chicken coop much longer than he liked. His wings beat against her legs, and he ripped at her with his spurs, falling back and flying at her again and again.

Surprised by the attack from such an unexpected quarter, Lucas stumbled backward and loosened his grip on Maggie. Thrown off balance, she fell to the ground, landing on the rifle as Houdini continued to beat on her shoulders and back, spurs and claws raking her hair and skin.

Without conscious thought, Maggie grabbed the weapon, turned, pointed it at Lucas and pulled the trigger. This time the safety wasn't on. The bullets, fired from only a few feet away, hit the blond man in the chest and blew him backward.

Maggie screeched and spun on her knees, eyes wild, and only a fast, undignified retreat kept Houdini from following Lucas to the afterlife.

O'Reilly rushed up to Maggie, and fell to his knees in front of her. He reached out and gently took the rifle from her hands and set it on the ground behind him. Maggie looked at him, feeling as if none of what had happened was real.

Then she focused on O'Reilly's worried face.

"I hate that rooster," Maggie said, then burst into tears and threw herself into his arms.

43

"Do you want me to shoot him?" O'Reilly asked. He stood in the cool, dim front room of the little stone house, watching Maggie, who sat at the table, head resting in her hands. Granger was sitting at the other end of the table with Rickards standing over him.

O'Reilly felt a bone deep fatigue. As he looked at Maggie, he thought her level of exhaustion went even deeper, and he worried that it would be a long time, if ever, before she recovered. O'Reilly looked around the room aware of a strange, disconnected feeling. He knew he'd left only three days before, but it seemed as if he had been gone for months.

Through the open door, O'Reilly could hear Lindy out in the barnyard, laughing and talking to Gypsy and the chickens. A crow joined in with the toddler's voice, letting the world know Houdini was still in command of Hideaway Camp.

Maggie lifted her head at the sound of the crow. "Shoot who? Houdini? You're asking me if I want you to shoot Houdini? If anyone's shooting that rooster it's going to be me."

"No," O'Reilly said, choking down a laugh that he thought might turn her ire on him. He slightly revised his estimation of her recovery time. It was if she had totally forgotten that a body was laying out in the barnyard covered by a brown canvas tarp from the barn. A body that had once been a man who had abducted, bruised, and beaten her, and threatened her family. A man whom she had deprived of life. "I mean him. Granger." O'Reilly nodded toward the topic of the question.

"I . . . yes . . . I mean no," Maggie shook her head as if trying to clear the fog, and she looked over at Granger and Rickards, then back to O'Reilly.

O'Reilly noticed that Granger's face had paled at the question, and he started to rise, but Rickards pushed him back into his chair. O'Reilly looked at the man, weighing the options going forward. His eyes met Rickards'. The captain shrugged, and O'Reilly knew it was up to him and Maggie to decide the fate of her only remaining abductor.

O'Reilly walked to the door and looked out. He could see the mounded tarp, but he could also see Christina, Alysa and Lindy playing with the chickens. Lindy, the rooster whisperer, was petting Houdini and squealing with laughter. O'Reilly had been worried the trauma of the showdown with Lucas would cause the little girl to retreat back into the muteness she'd experienced after being trapped with her dying mother, but it appeared that, for now, she had rebounded well.

The boys had gone to get the horses, and they hadn't returned yet. O'Reilly thought about the moment when the children had come pouring out of the barn following Lucas's shooting. Wide-eyed, they skirted the body, some averting their eyes and others staring at what was left of the man. Christina, in particular, was pale and tried to stay as far away as possible from the remains, and O'Reilly remembered that her father had been shot by Enforcers in front of her and the boys. *Bad dreams are coming for some of them*, he thought. He wished he could find a random child therapist wandering the ranch land somewhere. They were going to need one.

Moments after the shooting, when Andy raced toward Granger and Rickards, followed closely by his brother, Granger had torn away from the captain and ran forward. He scooped the younger boy into his arms and hugged him, and O'Reilly saw tears streaming down his face. He remembered that for the past day, Granger had thought the boy was dead. The emotion Granger displayed, and the affection the boys showed toward him, created a dilemma.

O'Reilly walked back to the table, sat and studied Granger. The man's sandy hair was uncombed. The stubble that peppered his face didn't hide the livid scar that ran across his left cheek. Granger's dark blue eyes met O'Reilly's brown eyes forthrightly.

"Mr. Granger," O'Reilly said, his gravelly voice soft. "We've got to make a decision, and I don't know what to do." He frowned and looked down, picking his words.

"We can let you go," O'Reilly started. "But how would we know you're not going to form a whole new band of ghosts and go back to kidnapping and killing people . . ."

"And hitting supply trucks to the APZ," Rickards snapped with the first emotion he'd shown since capturing Granger. "Two men died in that last poorly planned debacle."

Granger bristled at Rickards' designation of his attack on the supply trucks as "poorly planned," but wisely kept his mouth shut.

"*And* hitting the supply trucks," O'Reilly added. "Also, if we were to let you go and you were caught by the Enforcers, how would we know you wouldn't tell them all about the canyon and Maggie and I and the children in an attempt to cut a deal."

Granger nodded. Those were all valid points, and it was obvious he knew it. He had led a band of ghosts who had stolen and killed in order to further their own well-being. As far as giving up the location for the canyon went, O'Reilly knew most Enforcers would be in the shoot first, ask questions later camp, thinking Granger was just a run-of-the-mill ghost who needed to be exterminated. There was a slight chance, however, that he would be captured alive and questioned.

"Or," O'Reilly went on, "we could dispose of you." He fought to make sure no emotion showed in his voice. It was a legitimate option, although one that twisted a knot in O'Reilly's chest. The man had already created one band of ghosts who had, if Andy were to be believed, traveled around northern Arizona, stealing from others, killing when they thought it was necessary. Even if Lucas had set them on that path initially, Granger had cooperated, only drawing the line at hurting children and raping women.

Still, O'Reilly thought, was he or Rickards any better? Both had participated as Enforcers and as exorcism team members in killing anyone who was not willing to come into the APZs—and that *included* women and children. And this would be a killing in cold blood. He knew he couldn't do it.

"Let him go," Maggie spoke up unexpectedly.

Granger's gaze switched to Maggie's face, and O'Reilly could see relief cross his features.

"Yes, he helped to abduct me," Maggie continued, "But he did keep me safe from Lucas, and Daniel and Andy care for him. That should count for something."

"Thank you," Granger said to her, his low voice quiet. He started to say something else, then stopped.

"Okay," O'Reilly said. He looked at Rickards, and the captain nodded in agreement. O'Reilly thought he could see some relief on Rickards' face as well. O'Reilly looked back at Granger. "You're not staying here, though. As soon as your leg is healed enough, you'll leave."

"I understand," Granger said. "My leg is stiff, but it doesn't seem infected yet. What about Daniel and Andy, though?" Granger's voice took on a tinge of anxiety which overlaid the relief he expressed upon realizing he would be allowed to live. "They've been like my sons. When I thought Andy was dead, I . . ." His voice broke, and O'Reilly felt for the man. He also didn't know if the boys would be willing to let Granger go without them. It was clear from the scene following Lucas's death that they cared as much for him as he did them.

"If they want to go with you, where will you go?" Maggie asked, looking at him curiously. "They can certainly stay with us, but I think they care a great deal about you."

Granger cleared his throat and sat straighter in the chair. "When the boys first found our campfire down toward Phoenix, Daniel said they were trying to get to relatives who might still be alive in the four corners area. If the boys come with me, we'll start with that."

A clamor of excited voices sounded outside, and O'Reilly rose to his feet and strode to the door, Maggie following closely behind.

The boys were back with the horses, Andy running ahead toward the house as O'Reilly stepped outside.

"O'Reilly," he called, excitement in his voice as if nothing from the last two days had happened. "We got to the horses, and guess what! Thelma was there with them!"

"Thelma?" Maggie asked, giving O'Reilly a "do tell" look that said he better come up with a darned good explanation and make it quick. She'd had enough surprises recently.

"I didn't get a chance to tell you, Maggie, but there's a new female in my life," O'Reilly started, but he was interrupted by a low moo, and Thelma emerged from behind the horses and wandered into the barnyard where she stopped and looked around.

"What the . . ." Maggie said, then looked at O'Reilly, then back at Rickards and Granger. "Did you know about this?" she asked Rickards.

Rickards looked at Maggie with a slight smile on his face. "It was an interesting ride from Seligman," he said. "We thought we lost her in the mountains. I'm glad to see she found her way."

"Where did you pick up your new girlfriend, O'Reilly?" Maggie asked. She looked at him with teasing laughter in her voice.

O'Reilly was happy to see the haunted expression had left Maggie's eyes for the moment. He knew there would be periods in the future when the fact that she'd taken another's life, no matter how loathsome that life was, would torment her, but for now, she seemed at peace.

"I picked her up at a house on the road to Seligman. She'd been left in a small pasture. There was water, but she would have starved if she hadn't broken into the hay barn. The hay was getting pretty low, though." O'Reilly looked at the cow who was shaking her head at the Australian Shepherd, Jack, who wanted to check out the new resident of the camp. Gypsy, still limping and showing the effects of her encounter with Lucas, seemed happy to lay in the shade, watching Lindy.

"Didn't Lucas say there was a cow at the house where we stopped to sleep after our escape?" Granger asked Maggie, surprise in his voice. Maggie turned to Granger as if having forgotten he was there and didn't want to be reminded.

"Yeah," she answered in guarded tones, then relaxed as if forcing herself to remember the man was no longer the enemy. "He did say there'd been a cow there and he was wondering how she got out." Maggie examined the cow critically, and O'Reilly hid an inner smile. Maggie had never gotten closer to a live cow than the meat section at the local grocery store before having to make a run for Hideaway. Yet here she was, studying the little Jersey cow like a professional cattleman. Maggie looked back at O'Reilly, "I take it this is a two-for-one deal?"

"Yeah, she's bred. Probably due soon from the looks of her. She'll be able to cover the milk needs while Lizzie is dried up waiting for her next calf," O'Reilly answered.

O'Reilly surreptitiously studied Maggie's face as she watched Thelma. She was bruised, scratched, dirty, tear-stained . . . and beautiful, he thought.

O'Reilly hoisted Lucas's tarp-wrapped body onto Joker, one of the geldings he'd brought with him to Hideaway a few months earlier. He would have preferred to use Jimmy since the bay roan had been used to pack deer that O'Reilly had shot back to camp, and was used to the smell of blood. Joker wasn't as sanguine about the situation as Jimmy would have been, and pinned his ears, sidestepped, backed and tried to jerk away from Rickards, who was holding his lead rope. As O'Reilly shoved the awkward bundle over the seat of the saddle, the horn caught the edge of the tarp, pulling it back. A small pouch slipped out of the tarp and fell under the horse. Before O'Reilly could say anything, Granger stooped, picked it up and tucked it into his pocket.

Probably some money or something, O'Reilly thought. It didn't really sound like money, of course, more of a clicking sound than a clinking sound but decided it wasn't worth asking about. He didn't want anything of Lucas's left at Hideaway, including money.

When the bundle was finally in place across the saddle, O'Reilly threw a rope to Granger on the far side, and they secured it to the cinch. Joker stood tense, with his head cranked back and eyes wide, his tail swishing in an agitated manner. O'Reilly stood, catching his breath, and looked at Rickards and Granger.

"Need any help?" Granger asked.

O'Reilly looked at the man, eyes narrowed. "Too soon, Granger."

The man nodded, but there was a slight smile on his face.

It had been decided the men would take Lucas's body down the canyon several miles before burying it. Maggie was adamant that the grave be far enough away and deep enough in the ground that neither she nor the kids would come across it by accident. O'Reilly personally thought they would do better leaving the body exposed in a remote pasture for the wild animals and birds, but he agreed to do as Maggie asked.

The men found a loose bank several miles down the creek and dug a shallow hole. Just before O'Reilly started to shovel dirt back on top, Granger stepped up and threw the small, lumpy canvas bag he'd picked up into the grave next to the body.

"What was that?" Rickards asked.

"Something Lucas valued more than people," Granger answered flatly, and turned away. He started collecting large rocks to build a cairn so that the animals couldn't get in.

Early the next morning, Rickards, Granger, Daniel and Andy saddled four horses and rode up to the ridge where the UTV had been left waiting. As O'Reilly had predicted, the boys had refused to leave Granger. There had been a brief moment of panic when it looked like Alysa would ask to go with them after she heard where they were headed. Fortunately, Granger told the girl it would be best if just he and the boys went at first, and if they were able to find her people, they would get word to her.

The whole discussion brought home a worry that had occasionally tickled at the back of O'Reilly's mind. What would happen when the children were grown? They weren't going to be content to just stay at Hideaway. He'd seen Daniel looking at both Christina and Alysa and saw them look at him as well a few times, and he knew that he and Maggie didn't have much longer before some hard decisions would have to be made.

Once the group reached the UTV and loaded the food and supplies into its bed, O'Reilly faced Granger and Rickards.

"Ethan, I can't say it's been a pleasure, but I hope you find the boys' family and a place to live in peace." O'Reilly put out his hand and shook Granger's.

He started to walk away, then stopped suddenly and turned back, a question on his face.

"How do you think Lucas knew about the attack before it happened?" O'Reilly asked. "I guess it doesn't really matter. I'm just curious."

"I don't know. I wish I did," said Granger. "Lucas had become paranoid. Insane really. Maybe he heard someone move in the forest. I don't know. You're right, though, it doesn't matter at this point."

O'Reilly nodded.

Then he turned, shook Daniel's hand and gave Andy a quick hug.

Finally, he was faced with Rickards. The plan was for the men to take the UTV east, toward Highway 89, then up toward Ash Fork. Once there, Granger would drop off Rickards and head east for the four corners area, staying on the remote forest roads.

Rickards, on the other hand, would head west toward Seligman on Interstate 40. He would be on foot with a pack and two days' supply of water, but he hoped searchers from the exorcism team would find him well before the water was used up.

"Seth, I don't know how to thank you," O'Reilly said, looking at the man. He felt awkward and unsure. Two months ago, Rickards was his enemy, and now . . . Now he wasn't sure what he was, or what he could be, considering the circumstances.

"No problem. Glad it worked out," Rickards said, putting out his hand. O'Reilly took it.

Rickards turned and walked toward the UTV.

"Seth, wait," O'Reilly said.

The man turned back to look at O'Reilly, a question in his eyes. It was silent for a moment, the breeze creating a gentle susurration in the surrounding junipers and tall, yellow grasses.

"What are you going to do about the pioneers? The ones who want to leave?"

Rickards looked at O'Reilly, then up at the blue sky showing between the branches of the trees, then back at O'Reilly.

"I don't know," he answered and shrugged.

"You know, it seems like for decades now people keep wanting to make decisions for other people and get insulted when those people don't like it," O'Reilly said. "Like saying everyone needs to be where there is food and medical supplies."

He thought for a moment and went on. "It hasn't been just one sided, that's for sure. Every side cries about the other guy trying to take away their rights and wants laws to protect those rights. Then, as soon as the other side says they want laws to protect something they want, the first side complains that government is getting too controlling and shouldn't be used that way."

Rickards nodded, encouraging O'Reilly to go on.

"I think that's where the *Phase One* comes in," O'Reilly said. He saw Rickards' eyes sharpen at the mention of the memo. *Phase One—Reduction in Population.*

"I think it's one side or another deciding that they know what's best for everyone, just like they've been doing—trying to control everything instead of everyone being responsible for themselves." O'Reilly shrugged and frowned. "I guess I just think we need to get back to treating everyone with respect and stop trying to control what the other guy is doing as long as it doesn't hurt us."

Rickards nodded again. "Thanks Jim," he said. "You've given me a lot to think about on my trip home."

He turned and walked to the UTV, climbed into the driver's seat next to Granger and started the vehicle. The boys turned and waved as the engine roared to life, causing the horses in the string to spook and jerk back. By the time O'Reilly had them under control and turned back around, the UTV was out of sight.

He slumped in weariness, the night's sleep having done little to erase the exhaustion from the last few days. Then he went to collect the weapons, ammunition and supplies from Lucas's stash that he and Rickards had hidden in the brush a day and a half ago and load them on the horses.

Time to go home, he thought, then smiled, knowing Maggie and the children were there, waiting for him.

44

Rickards walked into his office the next morning, feeling bone tired but at peace with the decision he'd made during his long, lonely hike between Ash Fork and Seligman. He had to admit O'Reilly's final words resonated with him.

And he still knew Central Control would have his ass if he acted on them.

He wasn't sure that the *Phase One* memo was as innocent as O'Reilly made it out to be, then realized that the man hadn't made it into something simple or innocent—he had just made a statement toward its motivation. It was still a mystery about the actual action, whether the pandemic had been man-made or natural, although he was starting to lean toward the man-made answer. He knew he'd need to continue to dig into that situation.

Rickards had heard the high-pitched whine of the seekers, those orbicular silver drones the Enforcers used for surveillance, in what he estimated was the early afternoon. He stood in the middle of the empty, potholed pavement of Interstate 40, waving his arms to make sure they saw him and also to make sure they knew he *wanted* them to see him. A half hour later, Dan Clements arrived in the jeep he'd been driving three days before.

The exorcism team captain seemed to accept Rickards' explanation, especially since he was suitably bruised and scratched, and moved as though every muscle in his body ached—although that was thanks to the horse and not to being captured by a ghost who had escaped the net, and having to fight to regain his freedom.

Walking into the Enforcers' office of operations in Laughlin the next morning, he was greeted with cheers by most of the deputies, although he noticed Travis Harlan standing off to the side. The man looked a bit smug, which was strange in this situation. Maybe it was time to transfer him out to another APZ. He'd heard Miami was looking.

Rickards walked to the window and looked out on the buildings, trying to sort out in his mind how to put the plan he'd come up with into action. He wasn't sure how long he'd been standing there when a knock sounded at the door.

He turned and was about to call out for the person to enter when the door was thrown open, and four uniformed men walked in.

"Captain Seth Rickards?" the lead man snapped. He stood over six feet tall, with dark, close-cropped hair and an ice cold expression.

"Yes, and you are?" Rickards growled. Something was going on, and it irritated him.

"I'm SA Dean Sargent from Central Control. You are under arrest for suspicion of treason and insubordination in relation to a failed mission in northern Arizona two months ago. There are also questions regarding your interactions with subversive individuals at the APZ."

"I . . ." Rickards started, but before he could question the man, he was roughly jerked around, his arms pinned behind his back and handcuffed.

He looked up as Sargent grabbed his upper arm and pushed him toward the door. Travis Harlan stood there watching him, the smirk having grown to a malicious smile.

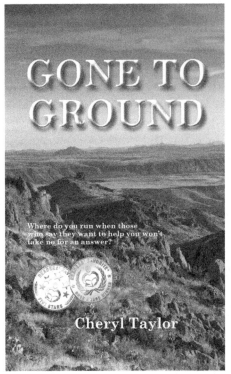

Following a deadly outbreak of influenza which decimates the population of the planet, the government issues orders that all remaining citizens are to report to designated Authorized Population Zones so that resources may be fairly distributed.

Journalist Maggie Langton, determined not to let her son, Mark, grow up in the dangerous environment of the APZ, decides to run for the empty ranch land of northwestern Arizona. When she runs into O'Reilly, a fugitive ex-Enforcer, she grudgingly admits she needs help developing those skills needed to live on a small ranch camp. What she doesn't expect, however, is that with knowledge of how to live rough, O'Reilly also possesses a darker knowledge: knowledge much more dangerous, and knowledge which the government will do anything to suppress.

Maggie and O'Reilly find themselves in a fight to keep their newly formed family safe and secure, and out from under the rule of the controlling new government. At the same time they discover a conspiracy much deeper than anyone had believed possible.

A phone call can change your life forever . . .

Abigail Williams gets that phone call. Gordon Dorsey, Abby's uncle and last living relative has drowned in the lake on his property, and Abby is his sole heir.

There are a few complications, however.

Abby's inheritance is a trout farm in Michigan, but she's a city girl from Phoenix, Arizona.

In addition, Abby doesn't believe the official story of her uncle's death.

And the biggest complication . . . the four-legged furry owner of the farm who seems to have her own ideas about how things should be run.

Culture shock is the least of her worries.

This is book 1 in the Up North Michigan Cozy Mystery series

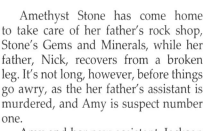

Stone's Gems and Murder

Cheryl Taylor

A Rock Shop Mystery

Amethyst Stone has come home to take care of her father's rock shop, Stone's Gems and Minerals, while her father, Nick, recovers from a broken leg. It's not long, however, before things go awry, as the her father's assistant is murdered, and Amy is suspect number one.

Amy and her new assistant, Jackson Wolf, have to unravel the tangled clues to find out who killed Carl, and why, as well as protect the shop itself from the Copper Springs town council which would like to see it condemned.

As Amy and Jackson dig deeper, they realize that there is a lot more going on than it appears on the surface, and multiple people have a reason to want Carl out of the way. They just have to figure out who actually did it before they become the killer's next victims.

Rock Shop Mystery Book 1

Murder on the Wind

Cheryl F Taylor

A Rock Shop Mystery

Amy Stone has recently returned to Copper Springs, a small town on Historic Route 66 in Arizona, in order to run her family's rock shop, Stone's Gems and Minerals. In a horrific welcome home, however, she was faced with the murder of the shop's employee, and forced to defend herself against the actual murder, with the help of the shop's new assistant, Jackson Wolf.

Now that things have settled into a more peaceful way of life, Amy and Jackson are looking forward to things returning to normal.

Unfortunately, a fun field trip to a local mine, organized by the local rock club and the Copper Springs Historical Society, throws their new found peace into turmoil as one member of the field trip is assaulted and the body of a miner who disappeared over thirty years ago is discovered.

Amy and Jackson are determined to clear their friend Pete Martin's name. That proves to be a difficult task, as Pete has been witnessed arguing violently with the assault victim not long before he was pushed into a mine shaft and left to die. Along the way, the duo find themselves faced with the older mystery... why was the miner killed, and who will he kill next?

Made in the USA
Monee, IL
12 September 2023

42574608R00195